S. S. BAZINET

MICHAEL'S BLOOD

BOOK ONE

The Vampire
Reclamation Project

Renata Press
Albuquerque, New Mexico

Published by Renata Press
Albuquerque, New Mexico

ISBN: 978-1-937279-10-3

Author's website: SSBazinet.com

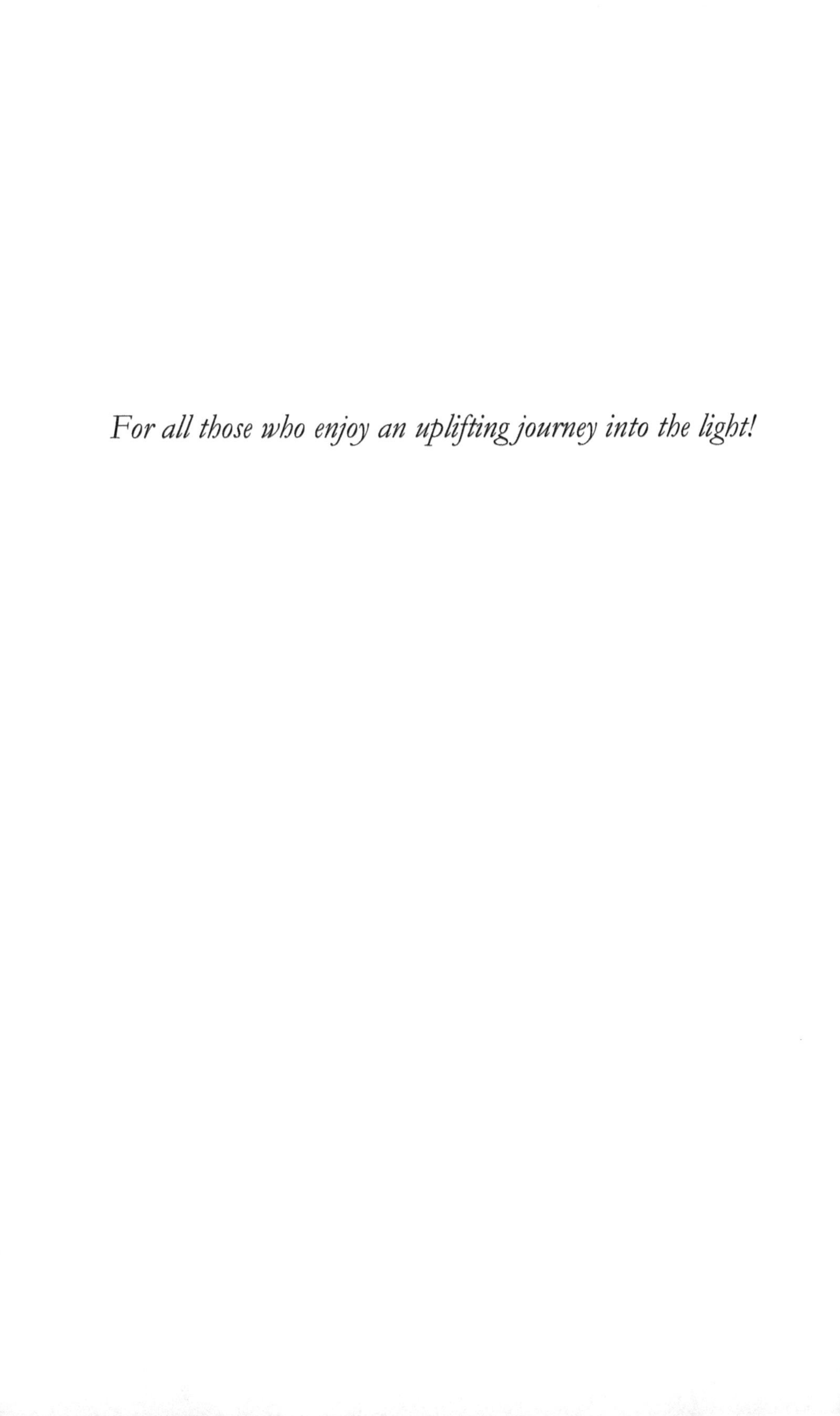

For all those who enjoy an uplifting journey into the light!

Acknowledgments

My profound thanks go to Laura Christine, my editing genius, and to my extraordinary copy editors, Anna Marie and Julia Ann. A big thank you goes to Gabriel for his wise and insightful editing contributions and for all the times he refused to give up on me. A big thank you goes to George for all his care and concern. My grateful heart goes out to Ricky Brian for always cheering me on and for his wisdom, and to Gene for his wonderful and loving dedication to helping me whenever the need arose. I am grateful to my two sisters, Beverly and Cynthia, for always nurturing my dreams. Also, many thanks go out to all my family and all my friends for their encouragement and support. I am incredibly blessed to have all of them in my life!

One

WITH CHICAGO'S HARD winter officially over, Michael sat in the living room of Arel's house and listened to a spring rain. It came down in driving sheets. As wave after wave pelted the windows, it reminded him of the night, many years before, when he'd taken on human form. For an angel, becoming physical was an extreme measure for an extreme circumstance. But Michael had always been Arel's guardian. When Arel hit a new low that bordered on complete despair, Michael had to act quickly. He decided to take on the body of a man himself.

Michael didn't orchestrate the conditions that accompanied his entrance into the world. It was a stormy night, with pouring down, near freezing rain. Experiencing the weather was a novel sensation as he stood on Arel's porch. His body shook with chills as he rang the doorbell repeatedly and pounded his fists on the heavy, wooden door.

When no one answered, Michael understood why. Arel was secreted away in the downstairs apartment of the sprawling ranch house. Michael could sense how infuriated the man was. Someone dared to have the audacity to disturb him. But more than anything, Arel was fearful. Why was someone trying to lure him out of his safe confines? The man's world was very small. It was also carefully arranged to meet his needs. When Arel came to the United States from England, he brought what he knew with him. Imported mahogany paneled his walls. Period furniture and artwork filled his rooms. To leave his beautiful, secure space, to go upstairs, was asking too much.

As the temperature dropped and the wind gusted harder, Michael kept pounding and ringing. He knew Arel's weakness. Arel hated noise, especially the kind made by someone battering down the door to his safe haven. Eventually, he'd have to respond and drag his near invalid status body from its bed. He'd been on one of his "I'll starve myself to death" campaigns, and he could barely walk. Still, Michael could feel the shift in Arel's attitude when it came. When he couldn't take another moment of Michael's insistent assault on his nerves and his house, he had to act.

A seething and resentful wrath bolstered the man's failing body. It gave him enough energy to leave his bed. Throwing back his comforter, he stood up and almost fell over, but his fiery anger kept him moving. He managed to drag his body slowly forward, holding on to his antique paneling, making his way to his handcrafted, inner door and the ornate stairs beyond. Gasping for breath and rallying enough strength to climb them, he clung to the railing. Slowly, he clawed his way upwards, cursing as he went, livid with outrage when he finally reached the foyer.

The first words that Michael heard with his corporeal ears were simple ones.

"Go away!" Arel's order was a hoarse, weak bark. For all his fury, he was still cautious in his helpless state, careful with his expressions.

Michael's answer was simple too. "Please, grant me a few minutes of your time." After his long wait out in the elements with only a thin jacket to shield him, his body was almost frozen. "I need to talk to you."

Arel was easily pushed to his limits. "Dammit, how dare you harass me!"

Michael had to be convincing, calming, and diplomatic, as if he were dealing with a frightened animal. "Just a few minutes, that's all that I ask. Please, sir, it's very cold out here."

It wasn't that Arel was heartless. He was truly afraid of the world and every person in it. But Michael's tone was working, soothing Arel's fears just a little, just enough.

Arel's voice was more confident when he spoke again. "One minute to state your business!" With shaky hands he drew back the dead bolt and disengaged a second lock on the door. The door creaked with disuse when he opened it a few inches. A blast of wind did the rest. A thirty mile an hour gust wrenched the door from his grasp. Skeleton thin and unprepared for the brutal weather, Arel was literally blown over by the unseasonably late, arctic blast. Michael rushed forward to help.

He'd been helping ever since that night. In the years that followed, he became Arel's caretaker when necessary, his confidante and teacher.

Have I helped him too much?

Michael paused to glance across the room. It opened into the foyer. The stairs that Arel climbed that first night hugged the far wall.

Can he handle what I've given him?

Michael thought about his decision to do something that had never been done before. He'd granted Arel's wish. He'd given the man his angelic blood. It was a bold and untested move on Michael's part. It also seemed to be a necessary one. Recently, in spite of all that Michael did to help him think otherwise, Arel was back where they started. He was giving up again.

Arel believed he'd been cursed when he was betrayed by his best friend, William. He believed he'd been made a vampire. His reasoning seemed to be backed up by a number of facts about his body. He had hardly aged in his many years. The sun was his enemy, and he craved blood. That last point drove him to do something horrendous. Since he had a strict moral code and would never harm a human to get what he needed, his sustenance came in the form of rat blood.

Off and on for years, horrified by his fate, Arel tried to starve himself to death. Recently, his goal was going to be accomplished. That's when Michael finally convinced him to give life one last chance, even if it meant hunting out a rat. Shortly after that, they found themselves in a dark alley late at night. When Arel discovered a rodent, he forced himself to kill it. However, that was as far as he could go. He refused to drink its blood.

"Michael, I can't do it," he said. "I can't do any of this anymore." With that, he dropped the rat and walked past Michael. He moved unsteadily towards the street. "To hell with you and all of it," he called out as he stumbled forward.

Michael replied immediately. "Arel, please, take care of yourself. You need your strength."

Arel paused and turned around. He targeted Michael with golden eyes that had lost all their light. His hollowed out cheeks and deathly pallor were those of a dying man. When he spoke, his voice was broken and hoarse. "I believed in you, Michael. For years, I believed in what you've been telling me. I dreamed that someday you'd share your blood with me. It gave me hope that I could find a way out of this hellish curse. Now I know it was all lies. There's no love in this world or in you. There's no redemption."

Michael walked over to where Arel stood. "We've talked about this before. I have a responsibility to you. So you know the dangers you'd be facing if I did what you want."

Michael's words seemed to give Arel a glimmer of hope. For an instant, his eyes came alive. In a burst of passion, he began to beg. "I'll try my best, I promise you." His voice rose in a ragged, breathless plea. "Please, Michael, have faith in me. You want me to have faith in what you believe. Now you have to take a chance on me."

When Michael didn't answer, Arel pressed on, grabbing Michael's hand and placing it on his chest. "You and I both know a vampire isn't dead, at least not this one. No, that would be easy, wouldn't it? To have no breath, no heartbeat and no life in me would be wonderful. There'd be no pain. But my heart feels everything more acutely than any normal, human heart. I can't stand the torment any longer. Help me!"

It was a defining moment on both their parts. Arel didn't think he could die. He believed his curse would keep him alive and in misery forever. Michael knew it wasn't true. When his pale, blue eyes traveled slowly over Arel's wasted form, he knew the end was near, and he made a decision. But before he acted, he had to take care of something. "Wait here," he told Arel.

Arel looked confused and hurt by the request, but he didn't seem to have the energy to argue. When Michael returned, Arel realized why he'd gone back into the shadows. He'd tended to the dead rat, thanked her for her sacrifice as he always did.

"I'm sorry that I killed her for nothing."

"It's okay," Michael said, smiling at him.

When there was a glimpse of movement in the alley, Arel smiled too. Michael had reversed the hold of death. He'd given back what Arel had taken.

Stumbling forward, Arel grabbed Michael's shirt, clinging to it with trembling fingers. "Help me like you helped that animal. Restore what's been taken from me! My body lives on and on, but there's nothing here for me but days of emptiness and tormented nights. Help me find some measure of peace."

Michael's face turned somber and exacting. "There are no guarantees with what I can give you."

Michael's words, and the warning behind them, filled the damp, night air. Promise and peril hung suspended as Arel closed his eyes. "I'll do anything to rid myself of this curse."

Michael countered Arel's argument. "I'm sorry, Arel, but that's not good enough."

"It's good enough for me. It's my life. I want it back."

"Dear friend, what if I help you, and you're not able to handle what will be loosed in you?"

"It's your blood, yet you talk about it as if it's something demonic."

"It's not demonic, but my blood does have purpose." Michael paused and studied Arel's eyes. "If I give you what you want, it will be a triggering agent—"

"Yes, you've told me all that before!" Arel cried out.

"But I don't think you fully understand what I'm saying. Everything you've ever hidden away will be under siege. Not just the curse, but all the darkness you haven't wanted to face will surface."

"I don't care what I have to face!" Arel pleaded. "Anything is better than what I've endured. Please, help me, Michael."

After that, Michael said three words. "So be it." When his gaze returned to Arel, he opened his arms wide, fully offering himself.

Arel nearly tripped again as he stepped backwards in a daze. "Really? After all this time, you'll, you'll do this for me?"

Michael saw Arel's shock. The man's eyes were wide with surprise. "Take what you need," he said quietly.

Arel hesitated and shrugged. "How do I proceed?"

Michael pulled back his collar. "Let nature guide your actions."

Finally, Arel stepped forward and put his mouth close to Michael's neck. "Michael, I've never done anything like this before. I don't want to hurt you."

Michael sighed. "It'll be fine."

Arel heaved out a breath and closed his eyes. In the next moment, with Michael's guidance, he was drinking Michael's blood.

Remembering that moment, Michael got up and went to the living room window. Angels didn't worry, but he was concerned about Arel's progress. It had been two weeks since he granted Arel's wish. He had tried to explain the hazards of his gift, but his cautions had been ignored. That fact had changed. Arel was quickly beginning to understand what he'd taken on.

Michael's blood was dangerous, not because it was the wrong blood type. It was more basic than that. His blood was too pure, too potent, too demanding. Most importantly, it was endowed with the purpose Michael had tried to impress on Arel. It was there to drive out the blight that held Arel captive for so long.

But that was only part of the campaign. All the traumatic and painful events in Arel's life, those that were buried deep in his subconscious, were also being targeted. They were coming to the surface. If Arel could face those hidden parts of his life, he'd experience a sense of freedom and even joy. But the process was moving more quickly than Michael had anticipated.

I warned you, dear friend, a battle is being waged, and you have to be strong, so very strong.

His thought was interrupted by a muffled shriek. Another followed that was even louder. The cries came from the lower level. Michael reacted at once and ran for the stairs.

Two

AREL COWERED IN a corner as the cane came down repeatedly on his back. Each blow sent spasms of excruciating pain throughout his body.

It's a dream! You're dreaming!

He tried repeatedly to wake up from the nightmare. Yet, everything seemed so real. As the blows kept coming, they were suddenly interrupted. Strong hands pulled him from the corner where he was hiding and gently shook him.

"Arel, open your eyes!"

He tried to obey the order, and yet he recoiled in terror when he saw the face of the drunken man who had hold of him. "Please, father, let me go!" he begged as his legs buckled under him.

"I'm not your father. It's Michael."

Arel held on to the voice, the kind voice that he recognized. Cautiously, he looked up. He sucked in a breath of relief when he saw Michael's bright countenance. "Thank goodness, it's you."

"Yes, you're safe."

Arel's eyes flitted about the room, blinking, trying to focus. Was he really back in his own world? He used familiar details to steady his thoughts, zeroing in on some of his favorite objects. He stared for long moments at a painting of a sailing ship. His gaze wandered over to a book laying on a nearby table. He'd always admired the craftsmanship of the gilt-edged, leather bound first edition. But as he tried to maintain his focus, his father's raging, bloodshot eyes flashed in and out. Reality was a mixture of past and present.

Michael put his hand on Arel's forehead. "You're burning up again. Let's get you back to bed."

"No!" Arel cringed at the thought. "Just help me over to the sofa," he ordered as he reached out for Michael's steadying hand.

"You need to rest. I can sit with you. I can help—"

"How? Are you going to give me more of your blood?"

Michael didn't reply. He held on to Arel's arm and guided him over to the couch. "Sit down and get your bearings."

Arel groaned. "What bearings? I'm going crazy." He knew it was true. It wasn't hard to diagnose his condition. He couldn't keep things straight anymore. Time and space shifted. Sometimes, the past and present all blurred together.

Michael stepped back. "Your mind is a little confused."

Even though Arel was still trembling, he let out a wild snort of laughter. "A little confused? That's like saying the Titanic hit a tiny piece of ice!" He laughed again, this time with more rancour and indignation. "Look at me. I'm turning into a delusional maniac. I'm seeing things. Just a few minutes ago, I thought you were my father."

"The subconscious is a funny thing. It—"

"Funny? How dare you use that word!"

Michael put up a hand and paused. "You know I didn't mean it that way."

Arel leaned back, clenching and unclenching his fists. He had to get a grip. Michael was only there to help him. "Sorry, I'm just a little sensitive."

Michael smiled. "That's like saying the Titanic hit a tiny piece of ice."

Arel saw the mirth in Michael's eyes and smiled too. "But I am going crazy, believe me."

Michael sat down across from him. "You're facing a lot all at once. Are you still having the nightmare about your mother?"

"The one where she's pregnant with me, and she already hates my guts? Not as often as before. Now it's more about my father, beating the hell out of me."

"You stuffed away so much. That's why you felt so stuck before. But that changed a couple of weeks ago."

Arel glanced at his watch. "Actually, it's been fifteen days, thirteen hours, twelve minutes and twenty seconds since the big event."

Michael stared back in surprise. "You're keeping track of every second?"

"No, I checked the time just now."

"Arel, you were never able to calculate time like that before."

"I think my IQ is going up. In another couple of weeks, I'll be the smartest and no doubt, the craziest lunatic in the psychiatric ward."

"Please don't project such a negative scenario."

"I don't think I'm projecting. Aside from being able to tell time a little faster, everything else is getting worse. My body is a wreck, and my mind is assaulted by one nightmare memory after another. Every recall is so vivid. Hell, I can tell you the eye color of the nanny who gave me my first bath." He let out a gasp and began to shake. "In fact, I remember my first bath. The room was so cold. That woman's hands were chap and rough—"

Michael snapped his fingers. "Arel! You can't let yourself go there like that."

"Am I doing it again?" Arel blinked back several times. "I slip into the past so easily! Make it stop, Michael!"

"Listen to me carefully. Your cellular structure holds all of your unresolved issues. The process is releasing them in detail. Your job is to witness the events and let them go. Otherwise, they'll keep repeating."

"But it's all coming up at once. I'm looking at a lifetime of crap! And you're telling me that your blood is the reason, that it's some angelic drain cleaner flushing out everything at the same time."

Michael looked down, letting out a sigh. "Sorry, but it's more than a lifetime's worth. There's also the carryover from other lifetimes."

"Other lifetimes? I'm supposed to deal with what happened in other lifetimes too? Well, that's it. I'm done. Put me in a straitjacket."

Michael stood up and walked over to Arel. "I wouldn't have given you my blood if I thought that it was hopeless. I believe in you. I know you can get through this."

"That makes one of us," Arel hissed back. Getting heavily to his feet, he pushed Michael out of his way and started to pace. He made his way from one piece of furniture to another, using them to lean on, to help with the constant weakness in his legs. "So how many others have tried this thing and survived? How many others made it through this angelic purification without losing their minds?"

"There are no others."

"What? I'm the first?" Arel stopped and gripped a side table with both hands. "You gave me your blood when its effects haven't been tested before?"

"We tried everything else. It was your decision."

"Great, blame the person who's doomed!"

"I promised to help you through this. We'll find a way—"

"What way?" Arel's hands clamped down tighter on the table. "My lord, how much of the damnable stuff did I drink that night?"

Michael shrugged.

"How much of your blood did I drink, Michael? A pint? A quart? A gallon?"

"Maybe a few ounces."

"That's all? It seemed like a lot more."

"It only seemed that way."

"A few ounces did this to me?"

"Don't forget that you weren't in good shape to begin with."

Arel's eyes went dark as he let go of the table and staggered back over to where Michael was standing. "You should have a skull and crossbones tattooed on your neck just in case you decide to try this on another victim."

"Is that what you think you are, a victim?"

Arel's jaw tightened. He knew he should take more responsibility, especially now, but he couldn't get past his anger. He turned and gave Michael a scathing look. "It's just that I had the stupid idea that I was dealing with an angel. And I asked myself, 'How bad could a messenger from God screw me?' Well, now I know."

Michael stiffened. "How do you expect me to help you if you feel like that?"

"At this point, I don't have a clue!" Arel hesitated next to a bronze warrior on horseback and put his hand over the cold metal, letting it draw off some of the fever in his body.

After a few minutes of silence, Michael cleared his throat. "Earlier, I was thinking about that night I arrived. It was so cold. I didn't think you'd ever open that door."

"That seems like so long ago," Arel whispered. "I wanted to hate you, but damn, you were very persuasive. I'm lying there on the foyer floor, mad as hell, but you were so kind. I was cussing you out, and you were trying your best to help me." He paused and fingered the metal horse's rearing hooves. "I never knew anyone could care about me like that, except for—"

"You're thinking about William?"

"Yes, William was almost a brother." Arel averted his eyes, but he couldn't avoid remembering a time when he and William were university students. In those days of heavy drinking, it wasn't unusual for Arel to end up in a drunken stupor, sprawled out on a London street. William would come to the rescue. He'd stare down at Arel with eyes that were almost as blue as Michael's. He'd extend a hand to Arel. "Get up, you idiot. Let's get you back to your room." His tone was firm, but playful. There was also kindness in his manner, a kindness that he didn't share with anyone else. But they'd become unlikely friends. At times, when William had partied too freely, it was Arel who was extending the hand of friendship.

Arel sighed with disgust. "He was almost a brother until he cursed me. So much for brotherhood." He made his way back to the sofa and sat down. He gave Michael a cursory glance and laughed. "It was bizarre to find out what you are, Michael, but I'll take an angel over a brother any day."

"Even if my blood is the equivalent of drain cleaner?"

Arel noted Michael's compassionate smile. "I do have a clue, Michael. You've been my only, true friend."

"Remember, that will never change."

Arel shut his eyes. His weariness was bone deep. "Maybe you're right. Maybe I'll go back to bed for awhile."

Three

AREL SLEPT FOR hours. When he woke up, he felt stronger and more rested. He didn't know how he'd accomplished a serene, dreamless sleep. Perhaps, for one miracle moment, he'd been able to bridge the gap between his own frantic struggle to survive and Michael's unwavering calm. Perhaps he was so exhausted that some childlike part had surfaced and let Michael in. It wasn't the terrorized child, but the one who had held on to dreams and a happy future.

It had been a long time since Arel thought about the hopeful boy he'd once been. Yet, once the door to his past was opened, a bright and curious child came walking in. He was small for his age, with a tangle of black, unruly curls and awkward mannerisms.

That child had an older brother, Aldwin, a brother who demonstrated the ease of growing up and becoming a man. That child believed he could achieve a similar goal with his brother's guidance. But his reveries of a flourishing future were lost the day that Aldwin was killed in a riding accident. It was the kind of accident that tears lives apart and leaves mutilated bodies in its wake.

With Aldwin dead, Arel was alone in the world. Instead of knowing the joy of brotherly support, he was gobbled up by the ravings of a father who had lost his oldest son, his beloved, golden boy. That kind of father does the worst of things while he's railing against God and the injustice that was thrust on him.

Arel remembered those horrible times with his father. He remembered crashing into furniture and clawing at the floorboards when the beatings wouldn't stop. Michael spoke about holding on to the calm of a dreamless sleep, but "calm" wasn't a practiced virtue. The effects of his father's hatred and bitterness were so much easier to slip into. With memories of the past flooding his mind with hopeless, emotional storms, he was overwhelmed very quickly. A thought about hiding in a closet and dreading the sound of heavy footsteps on the stairs was such a familiar groove for his mind to follow. If he was ever going to stop the cycle, he had to get a grip.

Michael's right. I have to take charge of what's happening.

Arel's first task was to fend off the fear long enough to entertain other, more positive thoughts. Michael said that even a daily routine could help. Most of his current day was gone, but he could salvage some of his evening. That meant getting out of bed, going to the closet, and getting dressed. He'd been raised as an upper class gentleman. Proper attire was as natural to him as brushing his teeth. When he slid open the closet doors, a familiar and comforting world greeted him.

So what should I wear tonight?

Zegna, Finamore, Gucci and other expensive, designer garments were carefully lined up on wooden hangers. Arel didn't leave his home very often, but that didn't mean he couldn't look his best. He ran his hand over a handsome, hand-tailored jacket and managed a smile. After years of bulking at Michael's suggestions to modernize, to join the rest of the world, he'd given in on a number of counts. He'd bought a computer and learned how to use it. Perhaps he'd been too enthusiastic about shopping on the Internet.

Michael's been right about bringing myself up to date.

It was a consoling thought that bolstered his mood as he grabbed a pair of charcoal trousers and a pale grey, Armani button-down. He hadn't bothered to look at himself for the past couple of weeks. He'd been too upset to do more than quickly run a brush through his hair, hardly glancing at his reflection. After he dressed, he pulled back his shoulders and approached the mirror with a little more enthusiasm.

Wouldn't it be amazing if I started to look like Michael?

He didn't expect to see himself glowing, but a more muscular, healthy body would be a sign that he was changing. All the pain he'd been going through would serve a purpose. One glance at himself was enough to crush his lofty aspirations.

I'm pathetic!

His face actually frightened him. It was so thin and his eyes were so lifeless that his breath was cut short. Compared to Michael's robust frame, Arel's body looked ready for a mortuary pick-up.

But one person I knew always looked his best.

His mind shifted, but not to his nightmares. He reflected on William again, a young, perfectly dressed William, a man who was ready to take on the world. Tall, formidable and handing out occasional, cavalier smiles like precious gifts, his air of superiority was like a great force that drew in the fashionable crowds wherever he went. Even before he became a vampire, he sucked people in with his charm, wit and sheer arrogance.

William was the one who first came forward and introduced himself to Arel. Over time they became drinking partners, arguing constantly. They were opposites. William was the extrovert while Arel was shy and reclusive. Even as a young man, he avoided people. He knew what they were capable of. How easy it had been for his mother and her fancy friends to ridicule him, to embarrass him repeatedly. Arel would have boycotted the social scene, but William dragged him to parties.

Arel recalled William's protective energy and huffed out a reluctant sigh of credit. When Arel was afraid in the world, William's presence could act as a shield.

No one laughed at me when I was with William.

William might have been the elegant, young lord who attracted a flock of women, but under his fancy clothes, he maintained a ruthless attitude when it came to most of humanity. People seemed to sense that part of him, to respect it. No one messed with William, and they extended that courtesy to his friend, Arel.

You made me think that I could trust you. But it was all a ruse, Will, a gross lie that sucked me in too!

As soon as Arel had the thought, the warm memory of William's friendship turned icy and sharp. Arel hadn't seen the man in a very long time, but the pain of William's treachery was still fresh and punishing.

But hopefully I'll be free soon.

He started out of the room determined to put that part of his past behind him, like the nightmares. He needed something to focus on, to bring him into the moment. He glanced around the room in a sudden panic. What if he couldn't do what Michael suggested? Earlier that day, he'd told the angel he was going insane. Was it true? Would he live in his nightmares forever? The idea was so terrifying that he balled his fists with determination. He hadn't given in to the curse. He wouldn't give into madness!

Stay focused on what's real . . . don't let your mind wander. Find something that's pleasing.

One of his paintings caught his attention, and he quickly walked over to where it hung. He grabbed hold of the heavy, gilded frame, making himself notice how solid and tangible it felt.

Michael insists that the here and now is an opportunity. Use it!

Arel's eyes moved over the canvas, slowly taking in details. He noticed the palette of color and the way the paint was layered. He even reached out and fingered the tiny ridges left by the artist's brush. That's when he looked at what lay beneath his touch.

For years, the painting hung in his bedroom, but he'd ignored it completely. The overall composition was lush and inviting with sensitive, Titian influences. Two lovers were featured in a garden. They gazed at each other with desire, caught up in all the sumptuous splendor of young love. The man was dark haired and slender of build. His mouth was slightly parted and full of want. His lips were poised above the woman's heaving breasts. She looked back at him with adoration and longing.

"She's so lovely."

Arel's words came out in a rush, filled with his own need, those fires of passion that lived in his loins. He'd resisted those urges for so long. Yet they stirred once again, testing the restrains, with fresh longing and appetite.

All my passion was put on hold . . . for all those years . . . and now—

Now, the fire was smoldering again, blazing up through his limbs as he reached out to the woman in the painting. But it wasn't just a painting if he let himself enter the garden too. With the slightest allowance on his part, he could become the lover, the man who would take the maiden from her post. He could be the one who laid her down on soft grasses. He could be the suitor who stripped off her clothes as she tore at his. He could be the devotee who brought her to a glorious state of ecstasy.

The scene played out before Arel knew what had happened. He was carried on a great wave of hunger that couldn't be stopped. He'd always prided himself on the principles of love, not lust. Even as a young man, he'd been able to control his needs. Yet, when the carnal flood of yearning seized hold of him now, it possessed a frightening power that he'd never known before. The fetters that held him bound were loosed in a heady moment of wildness and abandon.

After the wave crested and fell, and his senses were somewhat restored, he was left gasping. How could he lose himself so quickly to his cravings?

Michael's blood is doing more than resurrecting the pain. A lifetime of repressed sexual energy is coming up.

It wasn't part of the bargain. Michael hadn't talked about Arel's libido going into overdrive. He looked upwards, knowing Michael would feel his outrage. "Dammit! How could you leave out something like that?"

Four

AREL'S RUN-IN WITH his painting made him doubly intent on staying in control. He sat in his office and drummed his fingers on his desk. He had to choose his focus very carefully from now on. Even the idea of living in the moment had its dangers. After guarded reflection, he decided that going online would be his safest bet. There were so many choices that could keep him occupied. There was always shopping, but for what? His closet was full. He didn't need anything.

What about an old-time chat room? Get away from your own misery and spy on the world.

He had found a site, a room that he liked. There were discussions about current movies, pop songs, and bestsellers. He didn't engage in the conversations, but he sometimes found people's comments interesting. Logging in, he felt a wave of panic and pulled back. There was only one other person in the chat room. "Oh hell, this isn't good."

The other occupant noticed him before he had a chance to log off. "Hi, I'm Carol. It looks like we're by ourselves tonight. Everyone else must have a life but us."

He swallowed hard.

Don't be a jerk. At least acknowledge her and then log off.

"Hello, I'm—" He paused. He'd logged in as Mike, now he was stuck with the name. "I'm Michael, but you can call me Mike."

A moment later there was a response from Carol. "This is rather nice, isn't it? The chat room is quiet. I don't usually say very much when there are a lot of people around. I guess I'm a bit shy."

He took a deep breath.

She's shy. I'm petrified. Maybe we can find common ground for a few minutes.

***

When Arel logged out of the chat room two hours later, he remained at the computer, staring at the monitor.

What have I done? How did I get so carried away? Why didn't I bow out of the conversation with Carol sooner?

The answer was obvious. It was so easy to share with her. He paused as a distant remembrance made him pale. "It was like talking to—" He stopped himself immediately. "No, don't say her name," he whispered.

He sat up stiffly, trying to blank out the past. No matter what, there was one memory that he couldn't let surface. Instead, he forced himself to focus on his recent experience in the chat room. He quickly began to go over what had been discussed. There was nothing personal exchanged, but Carol definitely knew details about the art that he collected and his taste in music. And he'd learned a lot about her. He could tell that she was sensitive and caring. He sat back in surprise when he realized that he already liked her.

I'll tell Michael to tape my hands together. I won't connect with her anymore.

And yet, he'd agreed to meet her again, late on Friday night when the room would be quiet.

This isn't good. I'm in the middle of Michael's purge, and I'm talking to a stranger. So why don't I feel more upset?

He glanced at the monitor and remembered one of Carol's messages. "You're fun to talk to." Her simple statement made him feel almost normal.

Purge or not, she's a diversion. It's what I need.

He stood up and started back to his bedroom. Halfway there, as he filled his mind with more of Carol's messages, he almost smiled.

***

Carol lay in bed staring at the poster on the wall across from her. As a full time graphic artist, she played around with private projects when she had the time. The poster was one of her new designs. It would have made a nice, light hearted cover for a romance novel.

The Eiffel Tower stood in the background, and a man and a woman sat in a quaint café looking dreamily into each other's eyes.

"Am I becoming obsessed with love?" She clutched at Charlie, her aging, teddy bear. "After all these years of being single and enjoying it, I'm starting to want someone in my life again. And sure enough, I end up meeting a man, even if it is only in a chat room."

She paused, holding the bear out at arm's length. "He's a nice person, a regular guy. No, I take that back. He seems more refined than the average Joe."

When she logged out of the chat room, she felt a pang of regret that left her anxious for her next meeting with Mike. But the teddy bear's hard, black button eyes seemed to convey a different opinion. They stared back at her with a concern that she didn't appreciate.

"Don't worry, old friend. I'm thirty one years old, and I can take care of myself. Besides, I know all about stalkers looking for victims. He didn't ask about anything personal." She pulled the bear close again. "He asked me things that were very innocent. He wanted to know about my favorite books, my favorite flower."

She smiled as she went over their conversation, over the comment Mike made about her love of carnations.

"Ah, Jove's flower," he said.

"Who's Jove?" she asked.

"Roman myths cited Jove or Jupiter as king of the gods," he typed back. "They used the carnation as a tribute to him."

"I enjoy carnations because of their fragrance," she answered. "It's light and never pushy. Carnations are pure and gentle flowers."

His response was sweet. "I think that you have a unique appreciation of flowers and their true meaning. More people should be like you."

She let out a heavy sigh. "Charlie, you know most men aren't as quick to hand out compliments. He made me feel good about myself."

She'd had her questions too. Towards the end of their chat, she'd gotten bold. She asked for a general description of how Mike saw himself.

"My body looks young enough I suppose, but I'm afraid that I'm really ancient. And you?"

"I feel ancient too. Most women have a family at my age, but I've had other things to keep me busy."

"Are you happy? That's what's important. Hold on to anything that makes you smile."

"Yes, I'm happy." She'd told him the truth. She was content with her life, up until now.

She laid Charlie down on the pillow next to her and turned out the light. From the tone of their chat, she already sensed that Mike was a gentle soul. "I think that he's like a carnation, sweet without being pushy." She closed her eyes. "I can't help but like him."

Five

AREL LOST TRACK of time as the days and the weeks slipped by. He was still fighting to survive the unrelenting process that had taken over his life. Lying on the sofa with an ice pack on his head, he almost laughed at himself. If he had, it would have been a mocking, half crazed laugh.

I actually begged Michael for this!

He adjusted the icepack, trying to get a little relief from the constant pounding in his head. The pain resulted from another of his consuming nightmares. He was learning a little control. If he used all his strength and focus, he was able to find his way back to reality on his own, but the energy it took left him drained and hurting.

Michael says to remain a bystander, but he's never been a kid trying to live with parents who learned their child rearing skills from Attila the Hun. It's so easy to be pulled into the past again.

He looked at the clock. It was early morning. He had another day of battle ahead. His days weren't much better than his nights. Plagued with temptations of the flesh, he was easily lost in fantasies if he didn't stay guarded. He'd removed the painting from his bedroom and boxed up any sensual sculptures, but how did he remove the desire that kept surfacing? How did he box up his passions? Still, he refused to stoop to purely carnal needs.

Love is what counts. What is passion without love?

He pressed the icepack harder to his head. There was only one thing in his life that was working, only one thing that made getting out of bed worthwhile.

This evening I'll spend some time with Carol.

He smiled, thinking about the private chat room that he'd found, a tiny oasis in cyberspace where he and Carol could meet. Their nightly conversations were his comfort, a soft blanket for his tortured, frazzled soul. When he imagined Carol on the other end of their connection, his body felt calmer. His muscles relaxed. He was able to laugh when Carol told him a joke. He was transported to a place where he forgot about who he was. He became Mike, the easy going, nice guy who made Carol happy.

Of course there was a catch. He couldn't keep the truth from her forever. "And by the way, Carol, did I mention that I'm a vampire? And if that's not bad enough, I have angelic blood coursing through my body that's probably going to leave me totally insane."

He had to face facts. He'd never be normal. He'd never be able to have a real relationship.

But I can't stop thinking about her.

Carol was becoming more that a sweet source of comfort. It was so easy to imagine himself lying with his head in her lap. Instead of the icepack, her cool, delicate hand soothed his brow. He pictured his mouth on her lips. He thought about taking her to his bed.

Stop it! You haven't even met her. It's not right to think of her that way.

He wouldn't let Carol become an object of his lust. No matter how much need surged through his body, he wasn't like William. No, he wanted someone to cherish, someone who could love him.

You had that once. You don't deserve it again.

His fingers tightened on the icepack as he banished the image of the one woman in his past that he'd truly loved. It was the only memory that he absolutely refused to entertain. He couldn't. It would be the final straw that sent him over the edge. Still the feelings of remorse fired through his body. He threw the icepack across the room. It slammed against two, very old, very fragile, first editions. "I deserve to be damned!"

A voice immediately rejected his statement. "No, you don't deserve that."

Arel glanced over at the doorway and saw Michael coming in. A flush of embarrassment reddened his face. "How would you know? You don't have to carry around my guilt!"

"I know that your long standing self-judgment serves no purpose. You need to get on with your life."

"How can I? I'll never be like you. I thought that if I tried hard enough maybe I could, but I feel worse than ever about myself."

"Is that why you're talking to a woman online?"

There was an instant spike in Arel's blood pressure. The thought that Michael might interfere with his relationship with Carol, the only thing that belonged to him alone, made him go almost insane with anger. He went from a reclining position to jumping to his feet in a fast, jerky leap. His body wasn't prepared for the sudden move. Swaying unsteadily, he had to grab for the sofa arm to stabilize himself. "I'm warning you, I don't want to talk about her!"

Michael remained composed and unaffected by his outburst. "The point is that you're not taking care of your body. You need to use your energy to shore up your reserves, to get your strength back. It's a matter of priorities."

"Why? Who cares?"

"I do. I'm very concerned about you, dear friend."

Michael hit another button, another painful, oozing sore in Arel's psyche. "We're not friends! Friends don't try to destroy you. First there was William, now you!"

"William is a different matter."

Arel let go of the sofa and targeted Michael with a hard, glassy stare. "You're right. At least William gave me something that I could fight and keep at bay. But your blood is out to destroy me. And it's because I'm not perfect like you. When it finishes with me, there'll be nothing left."

Arel did look like he was slowly disappearing. Standing in front of Michael, barely maintaining his balance, his slender, five-foot-eleven body was hardly more than bones and skin.

"That's not what's wanted," Michael insisted more forcefully. "If you look in your heart, you'll know I'm telling you the truth."

Arel stumbled forward. "My heart? Do you know what's in my heart? It's the place where I keep that small part of myself that's endured, that's still alive after everything that's happened to me. But you're after that part too. I can feel it. I can feel your blood hating me, trying to get rid of the little piece of me that I've been able to hold on to. But I won't let you, even if it kills me, I'll hold on to it!" He screamed out the words, but his breath caught. He grabbed his chest. "Dammit."

Michael rushed over. "Stop it. Stop fighting or you will kill yourself."

Arel crumpled backwards and onto the sofa. He sat in a heap, taking gasping breaths and trying to deal with the pain that had hold of his chest. Half of the time he ranted and raved like a madman when Michael was around. As he calmed himself, he had a moment of clarity. "I'm so scared, Michael. I'm so afraid that you've deceived me too."

"Never, deep down you must know that I would never do that."

Arel shook his head. "After all these years, I must be a terrible disappointment."

"No, it's not true, and the blood isn't trying to destroy you. It's clearing away the lies, the things that have made you think there's something wrong with you."

"I've always felt like there's something dark and horrible inside of me. Why else would my parents hate me like they did?" Arel hesitated, but when he looked at Michael, his golden eyes were pleading, petitioning Michael for absolution. "I don't want to think about—" He tightened his jaw and forced himself to say the name that festered and burned in some deep, inner chamber. "I try, but I can't forget Justina and the mistake she made, loving me."

"That's all in the past."

"Am I totally wrong to want some small portion of happiness again?"

Michael clasped Arel's shoulder and shook it gently. "Love is what we all need."

"No, I'm not talking about love. If I could just connect to someone—"

"I know what you want. But this isn't a good time for that kind of connection. Give yourself a chance to stabilize first."

Arel's fists instantly closed on themselves. His need for forgiveness was replaced by a fresh storm of anger. "I need a break, Michael! Is that asking too much? All I'm talking about is a few minutes with someone so that I can forget this god-awful mess that I'm in."

"I understand, and I'm trying to help—"

"Forget it! I don't want your help! You've helped enough."

Six

ABRIGAIL STOOD IN the middle of the spring garden, smiling and feeling very proud of herself. As an angel, it was an accomplishment to take on a physical body. "Michael," she called out. "Look at me."

She directed her greeting to a tall, broad shouldered man a few feet away. When he turned, his blond hair framed his handsome face, but it was the light coming from his pale blue eyes that made her smile broaden into a delighted grin. "Michael, I did it!"

Michael put down his pruning shears and walked over to her. "Welcome."

Abrigail held her arms out from her sides and did a little pirouette, showing off her lithe, graceful body. Her silky, white dress flared out as she turned. "Is my form correct?"

"Yes, of course it is."

"I forgot how much energy it takes for one of us to create such a dense expression." Abrigail's gaze traveled over Michael's strong body. "How do you do it? How do you have the energy to sustain a human body over the years?"

Michael paused and scanned their surroundings. "It's easy when I spend time seeing to all the wondrous expressions of the Creator."

"The physical viewpoint is always a thrill for me." Abrigail reached down and cupped a daffodil, giving the delicate golden-yellow bloom her full attention. She let out a giggle of delight. "This little flower knows how beautiful it is. And everywhere I look, there are so many flowers blooming, so many other vibrant colors and shapes to admire." She put her hand over her heart and looked at Michael. "Seeing your garden like this almost takes the breath from my body."

Michael walked over to a nearby bench and sat down. "In spring, I also enjoy the newly leafed out trees. They exude a powerful desire, an eagerness after their long winter sleep."

Abrigail approached the bench and sat down too. "You've brought a touch of paradise to Arel's back yard. Your energy is part of every living thing in this garden."

"I'm hoping that Arel can enjoy it someday."

"I know he has an issue with the sun, but does he visit here in the evenings?"

A sigh of disappointment was Michael's answer. "I don't think he cares very much about what I do at this point."

"He's missing so much." Abrigail's focus went from a bed of tulips to another that was full of crocuses. In every bed, the flowers were crowded close to each other like showy sardines. "How did you manage to put so many into this space?"

Michael's eyes turned playful. "I might have been over zealous when I planted last fall."

"You're always a bit over zealous with everything that you care about."

Michael sat back with a sigh. "You're referring to Arel."

"Especially with Arel. He's so fortunate to have you."

"He wouldn't agree with you."

"Michael, you have to remember that he's a very challenging soul."

"This life's been extremely difficult for him. From the very beginning, he had to deal with his mother's resentment and neglect. As he got older, life became increasingly painful."

"And you were there, trying to help him. He would have never survived if you hadn't tempered the abuse with your support. But there's only so much you can do. A human's fear and anger create almost impossible barriers."

Michael laughed. "Arel is an expert at barriers. Of course, he's had a long time to perfect the walls he uses to keep out life."

"He's fighting everything, including you."

"He thinks that I don't understand what he's going through."

"How did humans get the idea that we're . . . that we're—"

"Stoic?" Michael paused, smiling again. "Arel equates feelings with emotional tirades. Maybe if I had a fit of anger, he'd think that I can relate to him."

"Perhaps if he knew the truth."

Michael looked away again, but he didn't comment.

Abrigail studied him carefully. "I know you've been living in the physical for quite a while. You're not getting caught up—"

"No, it's not that."

"Then what's wrong?"

"It was my decision to give him my blood."

She reached out and put her hand on his shoulder. "Your technique is original, very innovative. You've caused quite a stir among the angelic forces."

"I doubt that any would want to follow my example."

Abrigail sat up straighter, her eyes more direct. "Arel was losing all hope. You were trying to keep the vow you made to his soul."

"Only his soul is aware of that promise."

"Arel was deep in despair. You've tried to give him a chance to find his way back to himself, to that place where he can shine again."

"But there are big risks in this process. I don't know if he can survive all the pain that's coming up."

"There's a particularly difficult issue, isn't there?"

"Yes, as a young man, he found his one and only true love. Yet, their relationship ended tragically. He won't stop blaming himself."

"Was he responsible?"

"Not directly, but he loved Justina with all his heart. Shouldering the responsibility for what happened is his way of protecting her and himself from the truth. He's terrified of what really happened."

"You can explain—"

"He won't let me."

"Give him time. He's strong. You know that. How else would he be able to isolate himself for this long?"

Michael stood up, picked up a watering can and tended to a newly planted rose bush. "He's not completely isolated. There is someone."

Abrigail came to attention. "What? I didn't think he ever left the house."

Michael let out a hearty laugh as if the idea was absurd. "He doesn't. He's chatting with a woman online."

"Are you saying that Arel wants a relationship?"

"No, not a relationship. That would imply change. Arel has another approach. He's losing himself in a romantic, fantasy world."

"In other words, he's trying to control everything. But how is he going to maintain his fantasy if this woman wants more than Arel is prepared to give?"

Michael put the watering can down and returned to the bench. "If his fantasy backfires and he gets hurt, it could destroy any progress that he's making. He could end up in worse shape than when we started this process."

"So what can I do? Why did you want me involved?"

Michael sat down again. "Arel doesn't like discussing Carol with me, but he might consider confiding in you. I'd like you to be there if he needs to talk to someone."

Seven

THE MOOD IN the busy diner was cheerful. The jukebox played songs from the eighties, and people were enjoying their lunch. Carol barely noticed the music or her fellow patrons. She stared at her plate with its half-eaten veggie melt, twisting her napkin. Her friend, Peggy, was seated across from her, dreamily sucking up the last of her malt.

"I love these old tunes," Peggy said, coming back from her contented fog.

Carol gave Peggy the briefest glance and went back to staring at her sandwich. "Yes, I guess so."

"Are you alright?" Peggy's red, silky hair fell forward as she leaned in. "It doesn't look like you were very hungry."

Carol sat up a little straighter. "You're my best friend, Peggy, and I wanted . . . well I thought—"

"What is it? Is something wrong?"

Carol offered a quick smile. "No, that's just it. I'm happier than I've been in a long time."

"Well, that's good, but there's something you're not telling me, isn't there?"

"You're going to think that I'm crazy when you hear what I've been doing."

"Carol, really, you're one of the most level-headed people I know. Why do you think that I'd criticize you?"

"Because I know that if you told me something like this, I'd think that you were losing touch with reality."

Peggy's dark brown eyes flared as she leaned in further. "So tell me everything."

Carol sucked in a breath and met Peggy's eyes straight on. "I've heard that we need to visualize what we want in life. Every night before I go to sleep, I picture myself with the most wonderful man. He's handsome and charming. I see us having an amazing life together. Maybe we could even have a family someday."

Peggy sighed, clearly disappointed. "Is that all? You've been visualizing a guy? I think the old term for that type of thing is daydreaming."

"There's more."

"More?"

Carol blushed. "I think I've met the man of my dreams."

"What! You've met a guy?" Peggy's excited question came out in an overly loud voice. A number of other patrons gave her and Carol lengthy stares.

Carol's blush deepened. "Yes," she whispered back. "I met someone who's the nicest person, a really sweet man."

"Give me the details. What's he like? Is he tall, good looking?"

Carol grabbed her napkin again. "I don't know. I've only talked to him online."

"Online? Where online?"

"You know, in one of those chat rooms. For the past month, we've been talking for hours almost every night. His name is Mike, and I feel like I know him."

Peggy frowned. "So that's why you're not doing all the fun stuff we usually do. You've been telling me you're too busy with your workload, but that's been a lie."

"I'm sorry." Carol looked down at her napkin. She'd nearly destroyed it earlier. Now she started to pick at what was left. "I guess I got so involved."

"How involved?"

"I just mean that I love talking with this guy. I may not get to actually see him or hold his hand, but that doesn't mean he's not real." She paused. "I hope I'll get to meet him someday."

Peggy let out a gasp. "Hold on. You don't really know this guy. You've only communicated online. You can't just rush off to meet him."

"I guess."

"And let's back up for a moment. You're beautiful and smart and a total catch for any man, but you've always resisted dating until now. Why is that?"

Carol's green eyes lost some of their sparkle. "I never told anyone about some parts of my life. Please Peggy, if I tell you, this is our secret."

"Of course."

Carol pushed her plate aside and braced herself on the table, clasping her hands. "I was married when I was only seventeen. It was a terrible mistake for both of us, and it only lasted a few months. After that fiasco, I put my energy into my life, my work and my interests. I've kept men out of it."

"Then why did you start doing these, these . . . visualizations?"

"I don't know. I've been fine with being alone for a long time. But I've changed a lot in the past fourteen years. I'm successful, more self-confident now. I guess I want to give romance another go. Besides, when I visualize someone, he's great. What's wrong with a guy like that coming into my life?"

"Carol, think about it. You just told me that you have ignored the idea of relationships all this time. You can't just jump into a love affair now and think everything will be perfect. Besides, chatting with someone is one thing, but being with someone for real is another matter."

"But I've matured in the relationship area. At work, my graphic design team interacts with other departments all the time. I get along with all the guys I meet."

"Trust me, it's not the same thing."

Carol sat up and crossed her arms. "But what if Mike is someone who has everything I want? Isn't that possible? I know it sounds hard to believe, but maybe I just got lucky."

"It seems that you have your mind made up."

"I simply want to stay open, that's all."

Peggy reached out again. "Please be careful. I'm concerned about you. Promise me that you'll check with me before you seriously consider meeting this guy?"

Carol sighed. "I promise."

* * *

Carol stopped in front of her bedroom mirror, checked her makeup, and scowled.

I'm worrying about looking my best for an internet date. What would Peggy say about that?

She didn't care what Peggy thought. The time she spent online was important, and looking her best made the situation all the more real. Besides, she was lucky to have met someone as wonderful as Mike. As she made her way from the bedroom to her office, she couldn't stop thinking about all of his virtues. He was intelligent, funny, kind, insightful, and considerate. He was the most fascinating person Carol could imagine.

Peggy's wrong to be so suspicious.

She put an unruly strand of blond hair behind her ear, adjusted her posture, and quickly sat down at her computer.

Wouldn't it be something if Mike were the perfect guy for me?

It was a heady thought that sent waves of anticipation rippling through her body. When she realized the feeling of excitement was almost overwhelming, she pulled back and took a couple of deep breaths. Was she being too excited?

Of course not. Even Peggy admitted that I'm level-headed.

And she could certainly prove it to herself. She stared at the clock and waited. After two minutes passed the hour, she finally connected to the chat room. When she was satisfied that her body and mind were calm and collected, she logged in. Unfortunately, her excitement returned as soon as she saw that Mike was already waiting for her.

He must be as anxious as I am to talk.

Her stomach went queasy as she placed her hands on the keyboard again. She typed in her first message of the evening. "Hi Mike! How are you?"

* * *

Positioned in the corner of Carol's office, Michael stood next to Grace. Grace was Carol's angel. Both of them were observing the young woman as she sat at her computer.

"You seem particularly pleased," Michael said quietly.

Grace smiled. "Of course I am. It's been a long time since Carol has been this happy."

Clothed in their wispy, ethereal bodies, they remained invisible. But even in their non-physical forms, they were careful about their appearance. If someone had a psychic gift and happened to glimpse them, they'd appear to have human forms. As angels, they did all that they could to keep from frightening people. There was also the matter of wings. Some of their kind added that touch too, since many humans expected it.

Michael was visiting Grace in his casual attire, jeans and a sweat shirt. No wings. "Was Carol ever aware of you?" he asked.

Grace nodded. "When she was very young, Carol talked to me all the time. After she saw the movie about Cinderella, she thought I was her fairy godmother. But that was a long time ago. As she got older, she labeled me as her make-believe friend."

"You do look the part of a fairy godmother."

If seen by human eyes, Grace could have been described as a perfect example of the matronly, church social type. She had silver-white hair and wore a plain-cut, flowered dress. But Grace's grandmotherly look was simply window-dressing. Michael knew the truth about his formidable, fellow angel. She was very capable of carrying out her duties.

Grace gave him a playful wink. "The guardian angel business calls for a lot of compromises. Whatever makes Carol happy makes me happy. She is such a sweet soul."

Michael glanced over at Carol. The woman's blond hair hung loose on her shoulders, she had one foot tucked up under her. She was completely focused. Her delicate fingers moved rapidly over the keyboard, pausing occasionally. Each time she stopped to read the replies to her messages, her face lit up. Only Grace and Michael could appreciate Carol's energy field. Her blissful mood created lovely patterns of bright, pink sparkles that enveloped her in a cocoon of bliss.

Grace let out a heavy sigh. "I sometimes wish that she'd let me do more. If only we could chat again, I'd tell her how special she is."

"You're doing a fine job."

"I couldn't feel closer to her." As Grace spoke, her energy doubled, filling the room with a soft, but dazzling light. It was a perfect complement to Carol's dreams of love just a chat room away. The two energies, one human and one angelic, merged and made little rainbows of light dance in the air.

Michael's smile broadened. "I sense a bit of attachment."

Grace's reply was immediate. "Of course, we've been together in so many lifetimes. When the Forgetting happens, it's always rather difficult."

Michael paused, thinking about Arel. The man he was trying to help wasn't in a receptive mood. Arel was trying very hard to forget that Michael existed. "Sorry, Grace, but even if humans knew that we were around, they might not appreciate us."

Grace laughed. "You're right. At the moment, I'm sure that Carol would ignore me. The only thing that she thinks about is her computer friend. And that is how it should be. I've been hoping that she would find someone and fall in love." She glanced up at Michael. "And how about you? I've heard that you have a unique project that you're working on. Is it true that you're helping a very special soul?"

Michael nodded. When it came to information, the angelic grapevine could be better than a television or online news feed. Grace had obviously been tuned into that data source. Luckily, she seemed unaware of the details of his 'project.'

"Actually, that's why I'm here, Grace. I'd like to talk about Arel, or Mike, as Carol calls him."

Grace gasped. "You mean that your person is Carol's person?" Her delight made the room flash sunshine bright. "I'm sure he's a nice, young man. Carol thinks he's so wonderful."

Michael paused, keeping the scope of his news shielded. He had to tell Grace about Arel in a carefully planned, carefully worded way. She had a reputation for being a little temperamental. After working for ages with humans, even angels could be a little reactive. Grace was one of those angels. "Hmm. Nice is not quite the word to describe Arel. And he's not exactly a young man."

Grace went on instant alert. "What aren't you telling me?" she asked as her wings fanned out wider.

Michael understood her sudden concern. Distracted with how to impart his news, he'd sent out a disquieting signal that angels used when they needed to gather forces. "It's okay, Grace. Let me explain."

"Tell me everything, please," she insisted. "Who is this person, and why is he contacting my Carol?"

* * *

Michael's news did not sit well with Grace. After he filled her in on some details about who and what Arel was, her response was quite adamant.

"No, no, no, this will not do at all!" she cried out.

Even if human ears didn't notice her volume, Michael's angelic ones got the message. "I understand how you feel, but there's more involved here than I can explain."

Grace moved to where Carol was sitting and protectively placed her wings around her charge. "And of course I'm bound to honor that. But I also know that this situation is about more than a normal human being interacting with another human being. Carol's become emotionally attached to someone who could harm her."

Michael's eyes conveyed understanding, but also steadfastness. "We need to let events follow their course."

Grace's wings expanded in shield strength as she stared back at him. "But there has to be something we can do, some way we can help." She stiffened. "I refuse to let this . . . this thing, this vampire, come into my sweet Carol's life and play havoc with her innocent, unsuspecting heart. He could do horrible damage. And if there's any danger of her life being threatened, you know I can't stand idly by."

In an instant, she went from her sweet maternal self to an entirely different kind of angel. Human form was quickly forgotten. The gentle smile and soft body of a housemother was replaced by a fiery presence.

Grace's fierce, protective stance made Michael smile inwardly. Carol had a powerful ally on her side. Grace was one of the old ones who had championed celestial campaigns long before the conception of humankind. Diplomacy and reassurance were required.

"Actually, it's Arel that I'm more worried about."

Grace calmed herself, letting her blazing colors cool into soft pastels again. "Of course, you're right. I'm sorry if I acted inappropriately. Your wisdom is impeccable. But, if I may be so bold, I suggest that we should do something immediately. I can feel Carol's hopes and desires growing stronger every day. She's totally smitten with—"

Michael could tell that Grace was at a loss as to how to address Arel. He heard the word, parasite, flash through her mind before she continued.

"Carol is totally smitten with this Arel." As Grace spoke, her glow became noticeably dimmer. "And I know what happens when Carol gets carried away. She can make terrible choices."

Eight

CAROL'S FINGERS WERE at the keyboard, quickly typing out questions, needing more information. "So tell me all about being a suicide hotline volunteer. I'm really curious." She wasn't just curious, she was hungry. She wanted to know everything about Mike. Her crush was growing into something unexpected.

Could I really fall in love with a guy I haven't met?

The question frightened her, but her desires were getting stronger than her common sense.

On his end of the connection, Arel didn't feel either fear or desire. He was busy swallowing a hard lump in his throat, trying to remember all the lies that he'd told Carol. As the weeks slipped by, he'd become so relaxed, he'd boasted excessively.

Stupid idiot! Why did you do that? You're getting yourself into deep water here. What if you can't keep it all straight? What if she finds out you're a fraud?

He took a deep breath and typed in a reply. "It's scary being a volunteer. I just hope and pray every time I pick up the phone that I'll be able to say the right things."

Carol's face brightened as her heart did a small flip.

What a sweetheart Mike is! So concerned that he prays.

What would she do in his gallant shoes? Questions leapt about in her mind as she tried to understand the way Mike handled life. She typed out her next query. "What do you say to someone who wants to kill himself?"

Arel paused and blinked at the monitor.

Oh hell! Good question. What would I say?

He pushed a hand through his thick, wavy hair. Still trying to come up with an answer, he laughed, but it was curt and derisive. He knew what he'd say to a potential suicide. "Get out while you can! Bon voyage, you lucky bastard!"

Death, glorious death! With his mind and body shot to hell, he longed to rest in peace. If he could simply go out and face the sun, it would all be over in short order. But the thought of burning to death was too horrific. His hands went to the keyboard. "I tell people that they matter, even if they don't feel that way. I try to explain that beyond the feelings, there is a deeper truth to each of us."

As he typed out Michael's words, he knew he didn't believe them. But Carol needed lies, didn't she? She wanted to think everything was rosy and simple. If only she knew the truth about him, it certainly would change that perception.

Carol's reply came quickly. "That's beautiful. You must help a lot of people."

He laughed again.

Oh yeah! I'm the male version of Mother Teresa. Just ask my friends. Oh, I forgot. Except for you, I don't have any friends. Damn! Damn! Damn!

"I try my best," he typed back.

Carol felt her chest go tight.

I know you do your best, my sweet, dedicated man.

A daydream flashed through her mind. She stood on the rooftop of a tall building, ready to end it all. She'd been alone for so long. Why should she go on? The answer appeared out of the darkness. A gorgeous guy walked toward her. He was tall and handsome, but he was also so good, so caring, so kind. He was begging her not to jump, pleading with her to let him mend her heart. She ran toward him breathlessly.

As Carol started gasping for real, she typed in her feelings. "You're a real, live hero."

Arel immediately felt a pang of guilt. He was using Michael's words shamelessly and thought he'd better start mending fences.

At least tell her the truth about the advice, you cad!

"I think I'm misleading you. I can't take credit for my guidance. A friend taught me what to say. By myself, I'm often clueless."

Carol shook her head and sighed. She couldn't believe how honest Mike insisted on being. How many guys would fess up like him? Her reply needed to convey her new level of appreciation for him. "I don't think it matters where inspiration comes from. The point is that you use that advice to help others. Most people, the majority, never use the wisdom that comes their way."

Arel mopped his forehead with a monogrammed, linen kerchief.

Listen, sister, you have no idea about wisdom. It's not all it's cracked up to be. I'm a bloody wreck over here after giving in to Michael's wisdom.

He needed to change the subject. He was getting sick of the direction the conversation was taking. "Enough about me. You never told me what you did today."

"Oh, I had lunch with my friend, Peggy. Remember, she's the gal that I've talked about before. Anyway, she thinks I'm crazy."

Arel saw a red flag go up, a large, chilling, scarlet flag. Why would someone think that Carol was crazy? Was she crazy? Was he talking to someone with a mental problem? His fingers attacked the keyboard. "Why would she think something like that?"

"Because of you, Mike. I told her about you a few days ago, and now you're the topic of conversation at every lunch. She thinks that you're too good to be true, but I know better. I told her so."

Arel cringed.

Me? She's telling people about me?

His heart sped up, but he tried to remain as calm as possible. Still his fingers started shaking. "Thanks for sticking up for me."

Carol's nurturing hormones came alive. Her mind was flooded with a need to care for and protect the gentle soul on the other end of the chat.

Of course I stuck up for you. You're noble and chivalrous! There aren't many like you around anymore.

She smiled as she typed. "I wish we could really meet, and I could introduce you to Peggy. She'd see what you're really like. Do you think that would be possible some day?"

If Arel weren't already as pale as a sheet, he was bleached alabaster now. His fingers slipped from the keyboard.

Oh, my holy Creator! She wants to meet me! My worst scenario is happening!

He'd had a perfect woman once. The experience left him with enough guilt and heartbreak to last for an eternity. He'd never allow that again. He'd never get involved with another real relationship.

He pushed his chair back, stood up, and swayed with fear and anxiety. Grabbing the desk, he held on. "Never, never again!" he shouted. His heart leapt about so hard, he was sure it was going to end his existence by crashing through his chest wall.

You're going to spoil everything, Carol! I can't meet you! Ever!

A second scenario presented itself, and his heart stilled a little.

Even if I wanted a simple friendship, it wouldn't work, Carol. I'm a liar and worse.

As he went through his hopeless options, a message popped up on the monitor.

"Are you still there, Mike? Did I say the wrong thing?"

His mouth felt so dry he didn't think he'd ever swallow again. Then his vision went double.

Calm yourself, man! Stay calm! You have to tell her something!

He fell back into his chair, squinted a couple of times, and found the keyboard. "You could never say the wrong thing. I just spilled my coffee and was mopping up."

Carol's reply was quick. "Are you a coffee addict too?"

Arel's brow narrowed.

Coffee? Hell, no! Creatures like me don't drink coffee! I need blood! Nice, red, tasty blood!

"Coffee addict? You bet," he replied, wiping his forehead again. "Hold on, I'm getting a phone call. Oh heck, I think it's the hotline. They probably want me to come in early. Sorry, but I have to sign off."

Carol read Mike's reply and slumped back with disappointment. She couldn't believe he had to log off so soon. Still, she had to try to be at least half as noble as Mike. "Of course, I understand. Sharing you with people who desperately need your help is the least that I can do. Good night Mike."

Arel had never been so relieved to sign off. Afterwards, he let out a moan. After his conversation with Carol, he needed a suicide hotline himself. When he stood up this time, he staggered away from the computer as quickly as possible. His legs were ready to give out.

Just go to bed and try to forget it.

He was so exhausted. He had to get some sleep. Even a nightmare would be better than staying awake thinking that he'd have to meet Carol. He stumbled heavily toward his bedroom, lamenting as he went. When he climbed into bed, he remembered how Michael tried to warn him about getting involved with someone. Did he listen? No, of course he didn't. Instead, he encouraged Carol, night after night, with his deceits and fabrications.

But how long would she think I was a hero if she met me in an alley and watched me hunting rats? Would she think I was too good to be true if she saw me drinking blood?

The thought turned over and over in his mind as he tried to go to sleep. He kept imagining all the blood he'd ingested over so many years.

I'm a monster, Carol! A blood sucking monster!

It was the last thought he had before he finally drifted off.

Nine

AREL PAUSED AND glanced around the room, noting how different it was from his own bedroom. The white-on-white motif wasn't unpleasant, but he preferred a richer design. His choices leaned towards dark woods like mahogany or cherry, and he liked more color in his bedding. The quiet was a plus. There was something to be said for the lack of sound when a person needed to relax. Even his heartbeat was returning to normal. It was slowing down, finding its perfect rhythm as he let out a sigh of contentment.

Finally, I don't have to worry anymore.

Carol lay motionless beneath him. All his fears and anxiety about meeting her had been for naught. When they came together, he'd taken care of everything. He didn't deny his lies. He told Carol the truth. At first, she'd been surprised, but she'd also been curious. It wasn't long before her curiosity turned to touch. She was immediately drawn to the mystery of what he was, responding to his strength, his animal nature, that pure creature who coveted her.

He'd never expected things to move so quickly. As Carol made her neediness known, he realized how easy it would be to satisfy her. But there was more to celebrate. Carol understood him. She accepted him totally. It was such a liberating part of being with her. He had loved Justina with all his heart, but he'd never been able to share what he was with her. There was always a barrier of guilt and deceit between them. Carol was different. There was nothing to hide when she looked at him. She was so anxious, so filled with longing.

When he allowed his dark nature to take over, she didn't fight him. She gave herself completely. As he sunk his teeth into her flesh, she cried out with pleasure. Her enjoyment, her cries, added a sweet ecstasy to the moment. He drank from the fount of a woman who had never known a creature like him. She became an offering, a sacrifice to carnality, to nature's most detestable, yet enticing, creation. Her hot, sweet blood filled his mouth, and he swallowed it in great, gluttonous gulps.

When it was over, Carol lay quiet and lifeless. In their exchange, she had given her life for his. Yet, he felt no remorse, no shame. It was an unholy union, but one that was necessary. Justina had brought him grief and torment. Carol had given him freedom.

For the first time, he accepted who and what he was. In the past, he'd tried to deny his animal nature. He'd tried to rise above all that was base and ugly, but he'd always failed. Now, he was done with stinking alleys and rats. He was done with Michael and the hope that he could be different.

After he got up and dressed, he looked back at the bed. Animal or not, he'd been careful, and it showed. The linens were still pearly white except for a few red droplets where he had fed. But he did have a few duties to perform before he said a last goodbye. After living so long with certain routines, he still enjoyed order and neatness. When he left Carol's house, he'd make sure that everything was tidy.

He had just finished straightening a picture that hung a bit crooked on the wall when he noticed how cold he felt. That was strange. He was usually warm after he fed, but he wasn't concerned. Instead, he continued with his chores. He picked up a stuffed toy that Carol loved, that she'd described as her security bear. He looked at its fuzzy, worn face and let out a satisfied sigh. "You're off duty now, Charlie. You're off duty forever."

As he patted the bear, his stomach made an odd, gurgling noise and went queasy. That was also strange. He never got sick.

He was putting the final touches on the room when he had to stop. Dropping Carol's lacy nightgown to the floor, he grabbed his gut in pain. He had to sit down on the bed and try to breathe.

Dammit! What's going on?

After he felt a little better, he got to his feet again. Shaking off his bodily woes, he turned to the bed and the woman who still required a bit of his attention.

Arrange Carol's body respectfully, and you're done.

A few minutes later, he smiled again. The room was back to normal, and Carol looked peaceful under the white coverlet. He'd done a very nice job all around. He bent over to kiss her cheek. "Thank you, dear lady. I'm forever in your debt."

He was about to stand up when the nausea hit even harder. The pressing discomfort turned into a horrible urge to vomit. His lips barely left Carol's cheek when the queasiness struck so compellingly that he had no time to move. The vomiting started, not meekly, but with an explosive force. A massive quantity of blood spewed out of him, splattering everything in its path. Carol's body, the bedclothes, and the walls became a gruesome canvas of gore. Serene and pure became alarming and putrid. But he couldn't stop heaving. The heavy, dark wine of death kept coming. Deeply spoiled, it sprung from some inner source of grisly darkness, propelled by a force that he couldn't control.

Wave after wave poured out of him. Blood soaked his clothes and drooled from his mouth. Choking on his vomit, he couldn't breathe. He gasped and sputtered. The room started spinning. As he tried to steady himself, he felt Carol move beneath him. He tried to jerk back, to escape her grasping hand, but she was too quick. She had hold of his shirt and held him fast. When she opened her mouth, her teeth were razor sharp, ready for revenge, ready for his blood now. He struggled helplessly, suddenly weak and incapable, loathing what Carol had become. His spawn, his demonic issue stared back at him with lifeless, greedy eyes. He'd created a new monster who would soon feed on others, but first on him.

* * *

Arel woke up gagging and struggling for air.

Just a nightmare! I was dreaming!

The bed clothes had a suffocating effect, trapping him beneath their bunched-up layers. He tried to throw them off with hands that were shaking so badly they seemed incapable of functioning. When he finally managed to free himself, he sat up so fast that he almost fell off the side of the bed. He caught himself and clung to the silky comforter for support.

Breathe, calm yourself and breathe.

Saliva dripped down his chin. He tried to swallow and thought about the blood, the horrid taste of it when he was vomiting it out. There was bile rising in his throat now. Was the dream telling him that he could actually kill someone? Would he ever want to hurt the real Carol?

He clasped a trembling hand to his chest. His heart was pounding. Michael had often discussed the function of the heart. The vessel was a repository for the truth. If Arel listened to what it said, it wouldn't lie to him.

He sighed with relief. "If I did make love to you, Carol, I would never hurt you."

He thought about the part of the dream that he liked. In it, he was strong again, in his young man prime. He didn't look like some frightening ogre. He was handsome, with a body that a woman like Carol could covet. If he ever achieved such a physical state again and he met Carol, he'd be gentle and appreciative.

His voice became a whisper. "I'd love you in the same way that I loved Justina."

As soon as the words were out, he regretted them. If he was ever given the opportunity to love again, he would never allow that love to end like it did with Justina.

Justina, my beloved, I still miss you so much. If I could touch you one more time—

He reached out, wanting to caress the only woman he'd ever been with. His hand was shaking harder than before. Putting it to his head, he realized that the fever was back. He was on fire again.

He let his hand drop to the bed. He wasn't young. He wasn't strong. He was hardly a man anymore.

If Carol saw me, she'd laugh at what a pitiful thing I am.

He stood up and seized the heavy, carved bedpost for support. Hugging the massive piece of wood, he felt even weaker and more inadequate.

Face facts, no one will ever want you again.

The thought was too much to bear alone. Pushing his failing body off the post, he stumbled over to his dresser and turned on a lamp. Its glow was timid, barely spotlighting the area and leaving the rest of the room in relative darkness. But his hand knew the way to an alabaster box on the dresser. It held a small, gold key. Once he retrieved it, he had to steady his fingers in order to unlock the center drawer of the dresser. Feeling his way through its contents, he found what he was looking for, a miniature, framed picture of a woman.

How foolish I am to keep it locked away. Who would take it?

But he had to safeguard the photo, no matter how irrational. He fingered the glass that separated him from the image of Justina. "My dearest, look at what I've become." His chest caved as he remembered her, how much she loved him. "Would you still want me now?"

"I think that she would."

A voice answered out of the darkness, making him startle and jerk around. Who had dared to breach his privacy? Clutching the picture, he held it tight against his chest. When he scanned the deep shadows of the room, he saw a woman sitting on his bed. "Who are you?" His tone was raspy and demanding, but his initial panic was gone. His senses were acute in times of danger. They told him that the person in his room posed no threat.

"My name is Abrigail. I'm a friend of Michael's."

Michael! What's he up to now?

He paused for only a moment before he had a second panic attack.

Why isn't Michael here? What if Michael left me?

Abrigail immediately spoke up. "Michael hasn't gone anywhere, but he said you might enjoy some company other than his own."

"I don't want any company, period." His hold on the photo relaxed a little as he stepped forward, getting a feel for his guest's energy. After all his years around Michael, he was quite capable of knowing when an angel was near. But he'd never been exposed to one that had a feminine quality. As he tuned in a little more, he felt that this angel was milder, more yielding than Michael.

Abrigail seemed to understand what he was doing and laughed softly. "If you want, I could help you search much deeper. With a little assistance, you could learn a lot more about the angelic realm."

He gritted his teeth. "I know enough already, too much."

Abrigail laughed again and stood up. As she emerged from the shadows, she was still smiling. Her slender figure was clothed in a pale blue dress. "I understand how you feel," she said.

Arel glared back at her. "I'm sure you think that you do, but your kind has no idea about what a human experiences."

Abrigail ignored his statement and put out her hand. "May I see the picture that you're holding?"

He pulled back. "No!" His voice was sharp, protective.

She belongs to me!

Abrigail held her ground. "Please."

His grip tightened. Maybe he was wrong. This angel was more assertive than she looked. "Justina is none of your business."

"She loved you with all her heart, didn't she?"

His eyes flickered anxiously. Abrigail did seem to understand some things. The last time that he had been with Justina, she had worshiped him. She'd loved him too much. That was the reason for their quarrel, for the violence that followed. He'd kept the details of that event hidden for so many years, yet Abrigail's question had resurrected them.

He felt sick again. "If only things hadn't escalated so fast that last night, if only it hadn't ended like it did, with her dead in my arms."

As he spoke, his body began to lose what little strength it had. His arms fell to his sides. The photo slipped out of his hand. What good would it do him now? Falling back against the dresser, he couldn't focus. Everything was going black. He was passing out.

Ten

AREL SHOULD HAVE been thankful to Abrigail. She had been very kind in assisting him recover after he fainted. Now, he sat on the living area sofa, hugging the corner of the couch. Instead of offering her his gratitude, he frowned at her resentfully. He didn't need another angel in his life, especially one who insisted on talking about Justina. "You can go now, Michael's friend. And thanks for helping me to understand your kind a little better. Michael isn't a fluke. You're all bent on finding ways to make me more miserable."

Abrigail sat on the other end of the sofa. Her face was full of wonder and surprise. "Why would either of us want to do that?"

Arel rubbed at his temples. "I don't know. I'm too exhausted to think about why." He wasn't dizzy now, but he was still hot. He clasped at his hands, trying to still their movement. At first, he'd noticed an ordinary trembling that was normal to bodies that were afraid or weak. As the weeks passed, the condition had escalated into a rough shakiness that hit him whenever he was stressed. He was shaky most of the time.

"I was a wreck before this started. Now look at me." He held out a hand that seemed intent on tapping out some kind of frantic Morse code. "What chance do I have of surviving? A million Michael cells are attacking every part of me. When it's over, there'll be nothing left."

"What will be left is the real you, the person who's buried beneath the pain that you're feeling."

"And I'm supposed to be happy about that? People hide behind the pain for a reason. It's there so they can live with themselves." He glanced at the photo of Justina on the coffee table. "When I think about my life, I see my mistakes, horrible mistakes."

Abrigail glanced at the photo and back at him. "Tell me about her? Tell me how you met."

"Why?"

"You've already told me the worst. I'd like to know about the parts that were good."

"The good parts?" He leaned back into the deep plush of the sofa, surprised by Abrigail's inquiry. He didn't usually think about the joys of being with Justina. "The relationship wasn't something that I expected." He paused. "How could I have known that I was going to find the woman I'd always dreamed of? I wish I could have fallen in love before I became a, you know, what I am. Maybe I could have married and had a family like a normal person. But for me, love came after my life changed course."

He remembered the night when he'd first seen Justina, first glimpsed the woman who'd open doors that should have remained closed. Still, there was a slight stir of movement in his chest as a bit of the pain shifted, allowing the tiniest glimmer of joy. It encouraged him to go on.

"I was at the theatre. It was one of the few places that could distract me from the hell I was in. As usual, after the performance, I was in a rush to get back to my room. I didn't feel comfortable around people. I was hurrying through the door and didn't see Justina. She had dropped her program, and I bumped into her. I was so embarrassed. I almost knocked her over, but I was quick. I caught her as she fell, pulled her back. And then she was in my arms."

He'd been young and strong in those days. When he grabbed Justina, she felt light and delicate. Like a rare flower, it was natural to draw her close. Instinctively, he inhaled the scent of jasmine in her hair, on her neck. The moment was brief, but long enough for him to know that he already wanted her. When she looked up at him and their eyes met, he knew that his feelings were mutual.

"Justina was the first woman I held like that. Before I met her, I couldn't approach women. I was too shy. I wasn't like William."

Abrigail stirred slightly, looking curious again. "How was William different?"

He frowned and let out a snort of disgust. "I never wanted to know about William's exploits with women. Even before he became a monster, there was something about his eyes, a lack of anything caring in them. Women were just playthings that he enjoyed for an evening. For me, women were beautiful, mystifying beings."

"And Justina, was she what you thought a woman should be?"

"She was more than that." He shut his eyes and held the memories close, just as he'd held Justina's photo close. "When we were together, we couldn't get enough of each other. Everything felt right and good."

Justina was as ravenous a creature as he was. She'd responded to him from the moment he'd first brushed her cheek with a kiss. Still, he tried to go slowly, but she was impulsive and rash.

She was so young, you fool. Not even twenty. You were the first man in her life. All she knew was to give you her heart and her body. She had no concept of waiting or games.

"I can't deny that when I kissed her that first time, I was so eager." He looked away with a flush of embarrassment. "Sorry, I know that isn't part of your world."

"Love and the physical are meant to go hand and hand," Abrigail said with a smile. "It's very natural."

"I wanted Justina completely, but I was used to control after dealing with the curse. I knew how to be patient. Justina didn't seem to worry about anything. She was so alive, so playful, so ready to embrace life and me. I tried very hard to honor her, to protect her."

And you did. That part was good. You can be proud of that part.

He smiled as he remembered himself as that young man. "I guess I did okay. She was happy when I was with her. We both lost touch with everything when we were together. It's like our love built a wall around us, shielding us from the outside, from the real world."

Abrigail reached for the photo that lay on the coffee table, interrupting his musings. "She was lovely."

He watched as Abrigail carefully ran her slender fingers over the tiny, gold rosettes that framed the photo. It was easy to see that having a body, sensing things in a tactile way, was new to her.

"You don't know much about desire, do you?" he asked, feeling the distance between their worlds begin to widen.

Abrigail gave him a quick glance. "Desire isn't something that only humans feel." Her tone was forceful and conveyed her own passion. "It's part of all of us. Love is a state, yes, but when it becomes active, it becomes desire. The Creator desired both me and you."

"Desired me? Why? Did he need a whipping boy?" He lifted his chin defiantly and looked down at her. "Did he want me living in a family where I had a mother hating me and a father who beat the hell out of me?"

Abrigail shook her head as she looked at the photo again. "No, that's the world of human failings. Divine love is present in the heart. It was in Justina's heart. She wanted a life with you."

The remark was like a hard slap to his face. It brought him back from his self-pity, back to Justina. "You're right. She wanted walks in the park on a sunny day, a church wedding. What could I say to that?"

Abrigail leaned over and put her hand on one of the cushions that separated them. "But more than any of those things, she wanted you."

He cringed as if Abrigail had struck him again. "Justina didn't know what I was, what I'd become!"

Abrigail leaned in closer. "You said that you had that part under control. Perhaps, if you had told her the truth, she would have been happy to simply have what you could give her, the real you that existed in spite of the rest."

He looked away, trying to remember if he did have something of worth to offer Justina. After a moment, he swallowed the bitter truth. "Once the bloom of first love withered, once she saw what was underneath the sweetness and the charm, she wouldn't have wanted me."

"Would you have stopped loving her?"

"Never!" How could he have stopped loving Justina? She was his world. His face flushed a deeper red as his heart raced. "But she would have tired of me. I guess William was right. I was and am a walking misery."

"But you said Justina and the love that you shared was a gift. Why didn't you trust that it could sustain itself, that the love between you could grow and lift you out of that misery?"

"Love is the biggest lie of all. In the end, it's what destroyed both of us."

"How?"

"It was Justina being in love that made her want things. She begged me to marry her. She said that if I loved her, that I would."

Flashes of the fight they'd had on the night that Justina died wanted to surface. He stiffened in protest.

I'll be damned if I let myself go there.

He glared back at Abrigail, but he managed to keep his tone even and steady. "I tried to reason with her. I truly did care. I truly did adore her, but she turned it around. When I told her that I'd ruin her life, she thought that I wanted to get rid of her." His shoulders sagged with resignation. "Strange, isn't it? Loving Justina meant that I had to let her go. I didn't want to hurt her. I couldn't let her marry a blood lusting fiend or a hopeless, despairing loser. But she took everything I said as evidence that I'd never cared about her, that I'd lied when I told her how beautiful she was, how she deserved someone so much better.

"The more we argued, the worse it got. Justina became inconsolable. She begged me not to leave, to prove that I loved her." He clenched his fists, not wanting to go on. But he couldn't forget Justina's face. It was livid with rage as she screamed at him, demanding that he give her more than he had to give. "If only she would have let me go. Why couldn't she let me go? After that, I don't know . . . I can't remember what happened next."

A void, a black lapse of memory had always haunted him. It was followed by the worst nightmare imaginable. The next thing that he remembered was holding Justina. She was limp and covered with blood. He kept shaking her, refusing to believe that she was dead, but it was no use.

"I must have gone insane. I must have killed her." As he let the words come out in a whisper, he found himself once again in the past. Justina lay in his arms. How desperately he'd tried to breathe life back into her body, pressing his mouth against hers over and over. He'd begged God for mercy. "Oh please, please don't let her be dead. Kill me! Cut me into a thousand pieces, but don't let it end like this." But nothing could bring her back. His frantic kisses and tears anointed bloodless cheeks that grew cold as the hours slipped by. Still, he couldn't stop rocking her. He couldn't stop holding her to his breast, trying to numb the pain that tore open his heart. Everything in his life that was beautiful had died with Justina. Eventually, a terrible sorrow stripped him bare, leaving him adrift in hopelessness and despair. His words became a mantra of grief. "Oh, my sweet darling, what have I done, what have I done?"

The words were on his lips again when he opened his eyes and looked at Abrigail. But he felt too hot and flush to speak.

Abrigail got up and sat down beside him. "It's going to be okay, I promise you. But you have to let me help you."

He laid his head back. There was no fight left in him. After reliving Justina's death, nothing mattered.

"You matter," Abrigail said. She put her hand on his brow.

"No, I was foolish to believe Michael. I was foolish to think I should have another chance at life."

"Your guilt over Justina's death isn't right. Let me help you remember what really happened."

He sat up and pushed her hand away. "No."

"But why, Arel? Why are you doing this to yourself?"

"I can't explain it. I only know that what I'm doing is right. I won't let you convince me otherwise. Is that clear?"

Abrigail nodded. "Then let's move on. If you can't address Justina's death, let's try to understand why you're still here. Perhaps you're not getting the whole picture. If you didn't matter in the grand scheme of things, you wouldn't still be on this earth."

"I never thought in those terms."

"All life is precious. Your life is precious. Michael wouldn't be trying to help you if what I'm saying wasn't true."

He stopped and stared at her. For a long moment neither one of them spoke, but Abrigail's eyes were soothing blue pools of light. As they drew him in, he felt a little of the burning heat in his body begin to retreat.

Abrigail gave him an encouraging smile. "I know you feel that Michael's blood has been very difficult, but you're not seeing its benefits."

He wanted to protest, but his mind was like his body, completely useless. He sat mutely, slowly rubbing his hand over the sofa fabric.

"It's true. Michael's blood is helping you," Abrigail insisted.

He managed a weak laugh. "It's destroying me."

Abrigail was unmoved, her steady presence not giving an inch. "It's changing you, maybe slowly, but it is working." She smiled again as her tone became animated. "How long has it been since you've had blood?"

He took another deep breath as his brain flickered on and off like a faulty bulb. "I don't know. I told you before, I'm too tired to think." Yet a small part of him was inquisitive. "Why?" he asked in a dry, mocking voice. "Are you planning a little banquet for me, sending out for a rat?"

Abrigail giggled. "Michael said that you can be funny."

He moaned. "The funny guy needs a padded cell."

Abrigail crouched down in front of him. Using her eyes again, she locked on to his, urging him on. "Please, think about when you fed last."

"I don't no. I guess I haven't had anything since that night in the alley."

"Really? That must be almost two months ago."

He blinked back, trying to validate her statement. "But I haven't thought about . . . I haven't needed—"

Abrigail nodded. "Keep going with that thought."

As he absorbed the idea that his blood lust was coming to an end, he brightened. "I can't believe it. Something good is happening."

"Yes, it is."

His relief, a tiny burst of euphoria, only lasted a brief moment before he felt a new burden replacing the old. "Wait a minute. Wait a minute!"

"What's the matter?"

"After Justina, I didn't let myself even think about love."

"I see."

"No, you don't. For all those years, I was able to forget about the whole subject. Now I hunger for love. That means that I've exchanged one misery for another."

"Wanting love isn't supposed to be a misery. It's—"

"That's why I had to go online, why I was so desperate. But what if it keeps getting worse? What if I can't stop thinking about Carol?"

"Arel, please, you told Michael that Carol is just a friend."

He couldn't pay attention to what she was saying. "This could end so badly."

Abrigail reached up and put her hands on either side of his face. "Look at me. You don't have to project that."

He was forced to bring his eyes in line with hers. His were golden, liquid fear. Hers were crystal blue expressions of comfort and reassurance. His projection of doom began to dissolve under her gaze. "Do you really think it's going to be okay?"

"Yes, I do."

"Because I don't want to hurt anyone or be hurt again."

"I know."

"And what about what's happening to me? Do you really think that I'll survive?"

"Yes, but you have to believe in Michael and how much he cares about you. Let him protect you. Stop shutting him out."

"Look at me, Abrigail. There's not much left to protect. Soon I'll be an immortal invalid."

Abrigail stood up. "If you can start to believe in yourself, the blood will nurture you. The whole process will turn around."

"You're very convincing," he said, still sounding a bit cynical, but he almost smiled.

"I'm simply telling you the truth."

He stared back at her and noticed something strange. "I know you're in human form, but I think I got a glimpse of your wings."

"Really?"

This time he did smile. "I never saw wings before. Maybe something is turning around. And hell, if this process doesn't work out, if I did become an immortal invalid, it might not be so bad. You and Michael would have to take care of me forever, right? Your side would owe me that much."

Abrigail's smile widened. "I promise that I'll always be there if you need anything. And I know Michael feels the same way. Just call on either one of us." She offered her hand to him. "Now get up. Go back to bed and rest. Give the love that's in that blood a chance."

Eleven

AFTER ABRIGAIL LEFT, Arel knew she was right about his need to rest. Once he'd retreated to his bedroom, he lay under the soft bed covers feeling exhausted. Still, a glimmer of Abrigail's lighthearted message of hope buoyed him up and offered him a brief respite from the heavy gloom that he usually carried around.

And if she's wrong about things working out?

He even felt better about that scenario. He'd coined the phrase, immortal invalid. Now, it danced around in his mind, not as something morbid, but as a sort of 'get out of jail free' card. Would it be so bad if he was forced to stay in his bed forever? Would he care if his mind was stripped of everything, free from all worldly concerns with beautiful Abrigail smiling at him, holding his hand. And Michael? Plagued with guilt, he'd be Arel's slave forever, reading to him, bringing him roses from the garden.

"Not such a bad existence after the hell that I've endured."

His mind went to the one glitch that remained in his world. He'd have to find a way to keep Carol where he needed her to be, in the chat room, not in his life. But he could feel her desire wanting to thwart that plan.

I'm not the only one who's desperate. She likes me too much, like Justina.

But how could he turn things around without hurting her? Abrigail had told him that love and pain didn't have to mix. That was encouraging. Thinking about the angel made him remember how he'd seen her wings. He might have even heard her thoughts at one point. Plus, he didn't have to drink blood anymore.

My god, I am changing!

It was a heady thought, one that brought up more questions. Did he have other powers that he wasn't aware of? Was Michael's blood giving him other capabilities?

I wish I had some power that could help me with Carol.

An amazing idea popped in.

OBEs. I've read about out-of-body experiences. People can have them, even without angel blood.

What if he could visit Carol in his astral body while she slept? He could reason with her subconscious and give her a few suggestions while she was sleeping. He could tell her to forget about him. It seemed like a perfect solution. He started to make plans when he thought about his recent nightmare and scowled. Was he absolutely sure he'd never do anything to put Carol in harm's way?

Of course, I wouldn't.

He could understand why he'd had the nightmare now. Carol had frightened him, and the dream was his way of dealing with his fears. But he'd vomited out the blood in the dream. He'd punished himself. That showed his real character, didn't it? Besides, both Michael and Abrigail told him to trust himself.

By visiting Carol while she's asleep, I'm actually doing what's best for her. Even if I am trustworthy, I'm not dating material.

He glanced at the clock. Three thirty in the morning. After his online chats, he knew they had to be in the same time zone. It could be the perfect time to visit her. There was just one problem, finding her.

He smiled. Michael had talked about people having energy signatures. With his new powers, perhaps he could locate Carol by telling himself to seek out that signature.

Once I find her, I'll set some boundaries. I'll make sure she knows that we can never meet. I'll tell her that she needs to move on.

He shut his eyes, feeling rather contented with himself. It was a great plan. Unfortunately, he fell asleep before he had a chance to try it out.

* * *

When Arel opened his eyes and realized that he'd dozed off, he thought about Carol and looked at the clock. Was it too late to try his OBE idea? He'd only been asleep for an hour. He knew enough about Carol's schedule to think he still had time to do what needed to be done. Besides, he didn't want to wait. He'd lied his way into his situation over time. But maybe he could "suggest" his way out of it very quickly.

After Abrigail's pep talk, he felt surprisingly confident about accomplishing his goal. He had Michael's blood. He also remembered a past experience. When he was physically failing and at his worst, he'd naturally left his body. The experience was very brief. He'd quickly slipped back into his physical form just as naturally. Now, he'd take a purposeful journey. He shut his eyes and took several slow breaths to prepare himself. His body responded. As it began to calm down, he hesitated.

Maybe I'm being too hasty.

Was he crazy to try something as weird as astral travel? Except on rare occasions, he never ventured out of the house. Now he was trying to leave his body and go off into the ethers. What if his silver cord snapped? He'd read that it tethered him to the physical part of himself. If something happened to that cord, he'd be dead. It was a disturbing thought for about two seconds. Then he had one of the best thoughts he'd ever had. It was based on something Michael told him. The angel had been very insistent that Arel had done his best and would surely end up at the Pearly Gates when he died.

Oh my god, if that cord snapped, I'd be free. It'd be my ticket off this planet. And if it didn't snap, I could fix a potential catastrophe. Either way I can't lose.

He focused again. "Where are you, Carol? I need to find you." He continued with the process for several minutes and almost gave up when he heard a crack. He was sure it meant that his spirit was rocketing out of his body. A moment of panic was followed by more determination.

Crack away, my spirit! Because my next stop is either Carol's house or I'll have my wings!

After the cracking sound, things shifted quickly. A sense of rapid movement disoriented him. For a moment, he couldn't make his mind work. Rational thought stalled. On the positive side, he couldn't manage worry or fear. There was an automatic quality to the experience. All that he felt was exhilaration and freedom.

It was disappointing when things slowed. His mind came back online, like a machine that had been on hold. He felt his edgy self again. He also realized that he had a body of sorts. When he glanced around, his surroundings were bathed in shadow, but a night light provided some illumination. As he adjusted to the space and the light, he noted that he was in a bedroom. He was sure that it belonged to Carol. His confusion turned to smiles.

I am a talented bastard after all! From now on, I can travel anywhere without ever leaving home!

Unlike the room in his nightmare, this bedroom didn't have a white-on-white motif. Carol's tastes, like her cheerful, online attitude, were very feminine. She'd chosen a homespun, French country look, with a little garage sale thrown in. A distressed dresser. Yellow and blue, floral bed linens. Rustic rattan accents. Not very elegant, but cute, sweet and typical of Carol from what Arel knew about her.

Curiosity prompted him to approach Carol's bed. He'd imagined what she looked like. Now was his chance to find out if she was as pretty as he thought. He leaned in, but he couldn't get a good look at her face. She was snuggled down under the covers. But she had to be petite. She was lost under the flowery quilt.

She looks like she's sleeping soundly. That's perfect for what I have in mind.

He'd been thinking about the suggestions that he'd give her. Basically, he wanted her to forget any romantic ideas. He also wanted her to be less inquisitive. He'd decided they could still be friends, but he wanted to keep their communication on a very superficial level. As he decided on how to deliver his suggestions, he detected a slight movement. His astral body responded with a chill.

What's going on?

He wasn't alone with Carol. Someone or something else was also in the room. Before he understood who or what it was, he felt it. He was hit by an overpowering wave of energy. It slammed into his gut, making him instantly queasy.

Great, even in my astral body, I can get sick!

His next move was instinctive. He swung around fast and readied himself for what was stirring just out of his range of vision. When he got a full-on view, his breath caught. "Holy hell!" he yelled, jumping backwards. "What are you?"

He'd never seen anything like the creature that stood in front of him. It was big, taller than a man. And it was terrifying. Green scales covered its body. Its small, leathery wings were slightly flared in his direction. It appeared solid and hard muscled, with no indication of being part of an illusion.

He backed up, throwing his arms out protectively, putting himself between Carol and the creature. In spite of his legs wanting to buckle, he had to act as her shield.

The beast took a step forward.

Calm down! You're in an astral body! You can't die.

It would have been a great argument if he was sitting around the kitchen table, discussing the astral state with Michael. However, his heart was pounding out an SOS. Obviously, his astral body had properties that matched its physical counterpart. It was telling him that the dragon-like reptile was dangerous. Its small, yellow-rimmed, green eyes were trained on him. It studied him with a ruthless glint of disgust. As it probed his mind, he could feel the powerful energy that fueled the beast. He could feel its assessment. It despised him.

His own assessment was equally quick. A killing machine stood in front of him, and it was only a few feet away. He didn't know if he was breathing or not, but there was no doubt about what his nerves were doing. He felt like he'd swallowed a bottle of amphetamines.

His terror escalated when he heard a low, ominous sound. It came from the depths of the predator's belly. It lit up his brain, activating primal memory. Vicious animals had roamed the earth when man was in his infancy, animals who hunted humans. This thing was a throwback to those times.

Or maybe worse. This isn't a 'Prehistoric Park' monster! It's a lot worse than that. This thing has an intelligence that's at least as expansive as mine.

The intelligence that Arel sensed wasn't the compromising kind. The creature wanted to destroy him with brute force. He knew it was true when the beast lowered its head, exposing its murderous fangs, showing him their true size and lethal capabilities.

He dared to glance back at Carol, but she was still asleep, totally unaware of what he was battling. He was grateful for that. Then the unexpected happened. He heard the beast's words, a telepathic warning that filled his mind.

Get away from her!

His response was immediate. Scared or not, he wasn't going to abandon Carol to the monster. "You're not going to hurt her!" he shouted back with as much courage as he could muster.

I'm not planning on hurting her.

Its reply was sincere, so sincere that Arel realized what was really happening. It all clicked.

Oh holy hell! This thing belongs to Carol.

He was in the middle of a nature film. The scaly monster was protecting its own, protecting Carol. It saw him as a threat.

"I don't mean her any harm," he gasped with equal sincerity. He hoped his declaration was enough to make the damnable thing back off. It had the opposite effect. The creature began to advance again, to close the distance between them. He could feel its breath, hot and dry on his face.

You've watched enough stuff about nature. Hold your ground, but soothe the beast.

"I simply wanted to talk to her," he whispered, quieting his tone.

The reptile-like predator responded by spreading out its wings in an intimidating gesture.

No! This can't be happening.

The creature was going into attack mode. It wanted to rid the world of a menace, him. The thought pushed him over the edge of reason. He hoped he still had his own monster within, some of the vampire that he'd been. He'd never really explored that part, never allowed it to show itself, but he had to try something. What followed was more like trying to act the part of an animal, but he gave it his best. He snarled back, bared his teeth, and did everything he could think of to show his attacker that he was tough too.

His act didn't work. The beast stopped and stared at him, tilting its head with a narrowed gaze that clearly showed no fear. After a moment of observation, its conclusion was certain. It loathed what it saw. It moved even closer, breathing deeply and rhythmically. It sent fiery tendrils of smoke into the air as it exhaled.

Arel had his second realization. He was no match for Carol's pet. And somehow, astral body or not, he could die if it used its fire on him. The thoughts rendered both his mind and his posturing body practically immobile.

I'm going to be burned to death! God, no!

He held up his hands in surrender, trying to retreat, trying to escape the dread that was taking over.

Wake yourself up. Get your astral ass out of here. Now!

The creature seemed to be encouraged by his submissive gesture, not to leave him alone, but to glory in its ability to intimidate him. As he stumbled backward, it moved ever closer. The smoke coming from its nostrils was getting thicker. Small flames began to escape from its cavernous jaws.

Seeing the fire paralyzed Arel's body completely, but heightened all of his senses. They came alive, not in the moment, but in some distant past. He remembered the smell of burning flesh. Screams of agony and shrieks of torment filled his ears. He could feel his skin blistering.

The bedroom faded away. A new and sinister scene took its place. He was the main act. He was the object of torture and persecution. He was helpless, trying to scream out in agony, but he couldn't catch his breath. He couldn't move or save himself. The vision was so real, so completely vivid, that he found himself in the midst of a firestorm.

Twelve

MICHAEL STOOD AT the bottom of Arel's king size bed. Abrigail sat on its plush covers, holding an icy compress to Arel's brow. She glanced up with questioning eyes.

"Michael, I know this isn't helping much, and I know his situation has nothing to do with the physical, but what else can I do? He's burning up."

Michael observed the crimson color of Arel's normally pale skin. "I've tried to reach him, but I can't. He's barricaded himself into a place so deep inside, it's impossible to breach."

Abrigail's gaze swept over Arel's immobile frame as he lay on the gold sheets. "I've never seen such powerful shields around a human before. I know that Grace never meant to harm him, that she was only protecting Carol, but she must have been very frightening to cause this kind of reaction."

"Arel's enhanced abilities are surfacing. When he saw Grace's projection as a sort of dragon, his fear response must have escalated exponentially. It altered his perception. He viewed Grace's presence as a lethal threat, and a fiery one at that. His fear of being burned triggered parts of a past life memory."

"You're not talking about—"

"Yes, I was able to get a glimpse of what's going through his mind. He's terrified of what happened to him."

"He wasn't supposed to access that memory. He's not ready. We both know that."

Michael moved to the side of the bed. He placed his hand on Arel's heart, evaluating the vessel's performance. It was beating too fast, much too fast. And it was weakening. "It was the one recall that I thought was buried deep enough not to be exposed for quite some time."

Abrigail gave him an imploring look. "You've done all you can for the physical part of him. And I know that you've tried repeatedly to reach him on other planes, but you have to try again, Michael. You have to get through the barrier. He's not going to last much longer."

* * *

When Arel opened his eyes, he wasn't in Carol's bedroom any longer, but he knew he was far from safety. Fire, bright and alive, was everywhere, surrounding him with its hiss and crackle, reaching out with fiery hands. There was no escape. The intensity of the heat was so extreme, he was sure he'd soon explode into flame himself, dry kindling on a bonfire.

In panic and desperation, he held on to a heavy tarp that he'd discovered. After he covered himself, he lay on the hot, barren earth. He curled up, making himself as small as possible, hoping that the end was quick. In a daze of near hysteria, his mind blazed in and out of consciousness, losing all sense of time or place.

"Arel, answer me! Arel, where are you?"

A voice called to him from far away. It was so muffled that he didn't recognize it, couldn't hold on to it. He kept falling back into a void, a black place under the tarp that was suffocating. But at least he couldn't see the fire as long as he stayed hidden. After a while he didn't hear the voice anymore. Holding himself tight, he knew he'd imagined it.

* * *

This was Michael's last chance to reach Arel. The man's life force was failing. His powerful mind was creating a scenario that was scaring him to death. Michael had to find a way through the walls of fear that surrounded him. Without Michael's quick intervention, Arel wouldn't survive.

"Arel, answer me!"

Michael used their close, if not always cordial, bond as a compass. When he discovered a fragile trail of energy that still existed between them, he knew he'd had his first break. He was drawn to another plane of consciousness and quickly found himself in the middle of a firestorm. He continued to call out as he made his way through the dense smoke and flames. The inferno spread out as far as he could see. He was amazed at Arel's ability to manifest so compelling a depiction of his fears. Arel was also shielding himself at the same time. It was an unfortunate situation. All of Arel's reserves of strength were waning as he literally battled against himself.

Abrigail is right about you being very strong in some ways, my friend, too strong for your own good.

Michael began to cautiously draw on his own powerful energies to counteract the fires, knowing that he had to be careful. If Arel decided that Michael's power was alien or hostile, he would dig in even deeper, deeming Michael as his enemy too.

"Arel, let me in, it's Michael!"

He used the sound of his voice as an indicator that a friend was near. As he called out, he kept going forward. He also sent great waves of blue radiance to his surroundings. It illuminated his path and the area with a cooling energy. He became a calming shower of light as he forged through the inferno. Fortunately, as he advanced, there wasn't any opposition. His authority began to quell the flames as he passed.

"Michael?" Finally, a weak, failing voice answered back.

"Yes, I'm here."

A moment later, Michael felt the barriers go down. Acting at once, he transported to the spot where he'd heard the voice. It was stifling hot, but in the middle of a ring of blazing fires, there was a form on the ground with a covering draped over it.

"Arel?"

Michael knelt down and lifted an edge of the tarp. He sighed with relief as soon as he saw what lay beneath. There, cringing in fear, barely able to breathe, Arel looked up at him with bloodshot eyes.

"My poor child, there you are!"

Arel slowly lifted a hand in his direction. "I thought I'd lost you forever."

* * *

As soon as the tarp was lifted, Arel's first thought was that Michael brought a cool breeze with him, driving out some of the oppressive heat and bringing a bit of oxygen. He was able to breathe a little easier. Greedily, he tried to take in a great lungful of the stuff and coughed.

"Take it slow," Michael advised. "You're safe now."

Arel nodded, slowing his intake, grabbing onto Michael's sleeve like a safety line. "Where were you?" he wheezed.

Michael flung back the tarp completely and stared at him with a deep frown. "I was trying to find you, but you hid yourself so well."

Arel had never seen Michael look so distressed. "I had to hide to escape the flames." He looked around and saw that fires were still blazing in isolated areas around him. "Where am I?"

"I'll explain it later. It's time to go home now."

Arel tried to move, to get up from where he lay, but he had no strength. Michael helped to get him to his feet just as a fire flared up out of the ground. It was only a few feet away. He clung to Michael, but he couldn't take his eyes off of the flame. The longer he stared at it the hotter it got. He tried to scream as it flared out at him, but there was too much smoke.

Michael reacted at once. He pulled Arel closer and shielded his eyes. "Don't look at it! You're safe now."

Arel hid himself, trying to draw on Michael's strength. "Don't let them destroy me."

"Who? Who wants to destroy you?"

"People, the people who live in this ghastly world."

"Those are thoughts, feelings inside of you. I'll protect you until you understand the truth, unless you shut me out."

Arel opened his eyes and searched Michael's face. "Is that what I do?"

"Lower your shields when you need me."

Michael whispered the words in his ear, but Arel felt like they were going much deeper. In a flash, he saw himself barricaded behind thick walls.

"Oh yes. I see it now. I do shut you out, but I don't know any other way. I'm so scared."

"I know a way," Michael said quietly. "When you're feeling better, we'll talk about it."

* * *

After getting Arel back from his fiery dreamscape, Michael sat in the frail human's bedroom. Arel's troubles weren't over yet. He was still unconscious. He lay on the bed with Michael on one side and Abrigail on the other. His body was still and wasted, looking like he'd been beaten by his father again.

"At least his fever is down," Abrigail said as she removed a wet compress. "But he's so weak."

"We'll be able to help with that part," Michael said as he ran his hand over Arel's brow, cooling it as he always did when allowed.

"What about Grace and the memory that she rekindled?"

"I'll try to cover up the entire episode with Carol and Grace. He's not ready to face any of it yet. If I can help to push it back into his subconscious, it'll give him time to recover."

"Will he let you?"

"I have a small window of opportunity. After saving him when he was so scared, Arel trusts me right now, but that probably won't last very long."

Abrigail smiled. "You did an amazing job finding him in spite of his shields."

Michael stood up and sighed. "But I don't know how to slow down what's happening to him. The process is moving so fast. He barely made it this time."

"His abilities are already surprisingly powerful."

"That's true, but he doesn't know how to use them properly. Unfortunately, they're reinforcing and intensifying his fears. His body can't handle that kind of emotional stress."

"Arel seems to know that," Abrigail said as she picked up Arel's bony hand. She held it close to her heart. "He said something about becoming an immortal invalid."

Michael shook his head. "He was wrong. His concept of immortality was flawed to begin with. Now, at this in-between stage, his life is more at risk than he could possibly imagine."

Thirteen

AREL OPENED HIS eyes and immediately closed them again. His entire body hurt. Every muscle and joint ached. He grabbed hold of his pounding temples. Had he been fighting alligators in his sleep?

What the hell happened? How did I end up like this?

Still holding his head, hoping it didn't fall off his shoulders, he climbed out of bed. He tried to remember if he'd had any dreams, but his mind drew a blank. He couldn't even remember going to sleep. When he tried to recall what he'd done the night before, his mind kept slipping, as if he was navigating on ice. But he didn't have the strength to worry about it. All he knew for sure was that he was still exhausted, consumed with body pain and his head was killing him.

It was an effort to drag himself to the bathroom. Once there, he had to support his weight by leaning on the vanity. With a heavy sigh, he lifted his eyes to the mirror and gasped.

Damn, I knew I looked bad, but this is ridiculous.

His eyes were sunken and blood red, and his skin was almost the same color.

This is a new twist. What will Michael say about this one?

He grabbed his brush and tried to run it through his thick, unruly hair. He was struggling with the tangles when he noticed that his hand was barely able to hold on to the brush. In fact, his whole body was now vibrating unsteadily. He threw the brush on the vanity and started out of the bathroom.

And I thought it was bad when my hand shook.

It didn't matter. Who cared if he shook? Who cared if he was too thin or too red? Michael claimed that he did, but Michael didn't count. The angel had to say things like that.

Once he was back in the bedroom, he glanced at the clock. He squinted to make sure he was seeing the time correctly. He couldn't believe that he'd slept all day. How was it possible to get that much sleep and still feel so bad? But he had to keep moving. Carol would be waiting for him in the chat room in thirty minutes.

What did we talk about the last time?

He couldn't remember their conversation, but his stomach did a flip-flop. He suddenly felt nauseous.

He half staggered his way to his office and dropped heavily into his chair. As he reached for the keyboard, a horrible feeling of dread made his headache pound harder. He needed to go back to bed, but he wasn't one to bail out on a friend. He started to type, saw the gibberish coming up on the monitor and paused. His fingers were out of control and shakier than ever.

"Great, how am I supposed to type with these hands? And my stomach—"

He took a couple of deep breaths and got a flash of clarity.

It's Carol. Every time I think about her, I'm sick.

How could he have imagined that an online friendship was a good idea? When he thought about an evening conversing, he wanted to throw up. He'd have to make the chat session as short as possible. By tapping out a letter at a time, he managed to compose a message for Carol. He even had a few minutes to spare. He used them to do more breathing. Instead of feeling better, he kept swallowing back bile and the feeling that he was headed for disaster.

Finally.

He groaned out his gratitude when the monitor announced that Carol had logged in. As soon as he saw her name, he used an unsteady digit to hit the send button.

"Dear Carol, I'm sorry, but I'm too ill to talk tonight. Please forgive me. Until tomorrow, Mike."

He didn't wait for a reply. He logged off at once and put his hands on the desk to steady himself. Hopefully, with Carol out of the way, he'd calm down and his body would relax. He waited for relief, but the queasiness only got worse. His anxiety was building too. As the minutes passed, he became fixated on a vague but certain feeling that Carol would somehow be his ruin. She would search him out, find him and . . . .

That's as far as his mind would go, but his body seemed to know that whatever happened, it was going to be very bad.

Dammit. I bet this isn't about Carol at all. It's the damn, blood thing again.

"Michael!" He yelled out the name with as much volume as he could muster. "Michael, get down here, now!"

* * *

Michael walked into Arel's office and took a seat on the sofa. He had worked on Arel's wounded psyche while his friend was in a receptive, sleep state. Afterwards, he'd deliberately stayed away. He didn't want to set off any alarms again. Arel's paranoia was very close to the surface. Anything could trigger it. When he heard the tone of Arel's summons, he knew there was more work to be done. In spite of his physical infirmities, Arel did have the ability to sound like a drill sergeant ordering around a recruit. "You wanted to see me?" he asked quietly. "Did you sleep well?"

Arel glared back. "What do you think? Look at me." He held out his hands for inspection. "I can't stop shaking! And check out my skin! I'm like something out of a horror movie."

Michael eyed Arel silently, not offering any reason for Arel's tremors or the fact that he looked like he'd fallen asleep on a blazing hot beach in the middle of August.

Arel let out a huff of disgust. "What's going to happen next? Brain aneurysm?"

Michael exhaled a bit too loud. He didn't think Arel's brain should have any problems. It was Arel's heart that caused him concern. "If you could go back to bed for awhile, I think it might help."

"You need to come up with something better than bed rest. I want an explanation."

Michael hesitated. How could he tell Arel what the problem was? How could he explain that Arel's cellular makeup was still flushing out the powerful scenario where he'd been burned alive? Michael had done what he could to repair the damage that Arel had suffered, but a part of Arel was very busy trying to challenge his intervention. It was the part that didn't trust Michael, and it was active again. It was searching out Michael's angelic work, his attempt to repress the dream terrors and a past life recall. It was treating Michael's involvement as a foreign act of sabotage.

You're dismantling my work, Arel. You're looking for trouble, literally.

Arel sat up impatiently. "Don't just sit there and stare at me, tell me why I'm like this!"

"Perhaps you're worried about Carol."

"Carol?" Arel's red complexion edged towards a bright crimson as he gasped out the name. "It's weird, but I no longer think of her as sweet and innocent. Every time she comes to mind, I get the feeling that she's something rising from the depths of Hades."

Michael understood the connection, and the reason for Arel's body temperature soaring again. Carol's threat to seek him out and Grace's fire-breathing image had merged in Arel's subconscious, magnifying his fright.

But I can use your fear to help you this time.

The thought made Michael smile inwardly as he got up and went over to the desk. He stared at Arel with a calm determination. "Do you want Carol out of your life? Would that be helpful?"

For a moment, Arel sat immobile, blinking back with disbelief, as if Michael had offered him the moon. "I don't understand it, but maybe you've got a good idea, Michael. For some reason, things don't seem to be right when I think about Carol."

"Then let me help you."

Arel leaned forward cautiously, gripping the edge of the desk. "You'd help me sever our friendship?"

"You know I'm here to do whatever I can. If that means saying goodbye to Carol, let's get started."

Arel's posture stiffened with a new, attentive attitude replacing his earlier impatience. "Yes, perhaps . . . yes . . . I think that's exactly what I want."

"Good, then it's settled."

"You mean it could be that easy?" Arel's tone carried a tiny spark of optimism. "I guess, since this blood thing started, I've felt like I've been on my own."

It was a truthful statement. Arel had isolated himself. He'd been threatened by everything, including Michael's help.

Michael put his hands on the desk and leaned in too, closing the distance between them to a mere two feet. "I'll help you to put things right with her." He gave Arel a playful pat on the arm. "Come on, we can take care of this little matter, can't we?"

The gesture seemed to lighten Arel's mood. He rubbed the desk surface with care even though his hands were still shaky. "I guess you're right. It doesn't have to be a problem."

"Of course not. You've maintained all along that you're not interested in a relationship."

"That's right, I have, haven't I?" There was the hint of a smile about to happen, but Arel cut it short. "On the other hand, we can't lose track of the serious matter that we're dealing with." As he spoke, his voice took on the tone of the proper, English gentleman. "Carol has to be treated with respect." He drew himself up in his chair and cleared his throat. "I will insist on some ground rules. I'd like to be gentle in how we handle this."

Michael kept his smile masked too. Arel had to maintain his code of honor, but his energy was definitely getting lighter and more exuberant as he saw a way out of his dilemma. It was also having a very beneficial effect on his body. His tremors were beginning to ease and his skin was losing some of its deep color.

"I agree with you completely," Michael replied. He stood at attention and crossed his arms, mirroring Arel's stern posture. "However, just to be clear, my understanding is that you don't want to be involved anymore, right?"

His question made Arel's eyes flare with excitement for a brief moment before he reined in his outward display of delight. "Correct, I want a clean break, where neither party is injured."

"Of course, and the next time you're online with Carol, I'll help you."

"Good." Arel's face registered a moment of bliss. "I'll be counting on that."

Michael could feel Arel's guarded nature backing down. After a moment, he felt Arel lower his shields.

That's what I've been waiting for.

It was a perfect opportunity for Michael to step in as a heavenly magician. While Arel enjoyed his reprieve, Michael quickly accessed the psychic wound that Grace had inadvertently caused. This time he used a more powerful, energetic bandage on the injury. He put another one over the past life memory that had been so traumatic. He used an additional precaution, disguising his angelic patches with

Arel's own energy signature. When he was finished, he felt satisfied that this repair job would remain hidden.

Arel seemed to notice a pleasing difference immediately. "It feels cooler in here now, not so hot and stuffy."

"You're starting to look much better."

"I guess the craziness has passed. I don't know why I was so afraid."

"You know what they say, 'You can't keep a good man down.'"

"Are you talking about me?"

Michael gave Arel a satisfied smile. "The one and only. I'm proud of you. Be proud of yourself."

Arel's eyes softened. "Thank you, Michael. I'm happy that we can work as a team again."

Fourteen

CAROL FROWNED AT the monitor. It was Friday night, and Mike had bailed on her, not even giving her a chance to reply to his curt message. Was he really the man of her dreams?

Sick or not, that was rude.

Impatiently, she ran her hands through her hair, pulling it back into a pony tail and securing it with a hair tie. She'd been looking forward to her time with Mike from the moment she woke up. Now she felt cheated. Glancing over at the sewing table, she let out a moan. A pile of fabric was waiting to be transformed into new curtains for the bedroom. It was the only thing that she had going that weekend.

"My life has hit a new low," she grumbled as she stood up.

She was grateful to have a job that she liked and a good friend like Peggy, but she needed more. The decision hadn't been a conscious one. Meeting Mike had been an accident, but they hit it off. Afterwards, they chatted frequently, exchanging ideas and thoughts about everything. As time passed and they got to know each other, a part of Carol took the next step. She began to dream about Mike in a more personal, romantic way.

Is Peggy right? Am I being foolish?

She walked over to the sewing table, picked up some of the fabric and tossed it down again. Instead of sewing, she considered a long hot bath. A nice soak, with some music and candles, seemed like a better idea. On the way to the bathroom, the telephone rang. She recognized Peggy's ringtone.

Oh great.

Did Peggy have a sixth sense? Did she know Carol was ready to fill her glass with self-pity? She groaned as she went to answer the phone. Gathering up her shoulders, she readied herself for Peggy and the advice her friend handed out so generously. "Hi, Peggy, what's happening?"

She held the phone close, listening intently.

"No, I'm not busy. What? No . . . no, I can't. I'm not showered. No, I better not. What? Alright, if you insist. See you soon."

After Carol hung up the phone, she wanted to be irritated with Peggy's pushiness. Instead she smiled. Forget the bath, forget the candles, she was going out with friends. She'd already met Peggy's fiancé, Tim. Tonight, she was going to meet Peggy's brother, Kevin.

***

Kevin knuckled down on the steering wheel and shifted his gaze to the rear view mirror. He scowled at his backseat passengers. His sister, Peggy, and his best friend, Tim, were completely lost in each other's arms. He was happy for the engaged couple, but he wasn't happy about his destination. "This is a bad idea, Peg. I've told you over and over that I'm not ready for another relationship. And I don't see why you're trying to fix me up with your friend."

Peggy's reply was quick and insistent. "It's been three months since you broke up with Dahlia. It's time to get out and enjoy life a little. We'll pick up Carol and go to the movies. What's the big deal?"

Kevin let out a snort of hopelessness. Why couldn't he say "no" to his sister? He was a successful, senior systems analyst. He knew that he could manage people and situations. Yet he always gave in to Peggy. He was the big brother, but he didn't remember ever winning an argument. "I just hope that your friend is nicer than you."

"Carol is wonderful, and so am I," Peggy laughed. "Right, Tim?"

Kevin tightened his jaw. "Tim, don't answer that. Peg has you completely brain washed." He glanced in the mirror again to see if Tim agreed and was rewarded with a romantic scene. "Give me a break you two lovebirds. We're just about there. Peggy, take your lips off of Tim's face and look out your window. Is that Carol's apartment?"

Peggy let out a blissful sigh as she glanced up. "Yes, she lives on the ground level in 110B. And look, Kevin, she has her porch light on. That's a positive sign. Go get her while we wait here. And don't worry, she's expecting you."

Kevin narrowed his gaze into a frown. "Don't steam up the windows. I don't want to be embarrassed when I get back."

***

Carol hurried to the door. When the bell rang a second time, she was fresh out of a quick shower, newly dressed, and smoothing back her damp hair. "I'm coming as fast as I can," she protested quietly. She lowered her voice to a barely audible whisper. "Please, please, please let this be easy!"

Even if it was with Peggy's brother, Kevin, it was still a blind date.

No, that's not true. Peggy says he's just out of a painful relationship. He's not looking for anyone. I'm simply going out with some friends.

She fidgeted with the two locks on the door and managed to get them open before the bell rang again. She paused long enough to take a deep breath and noticed how fast her heart was beating.

I'm putting too much pressure on myself. I have to relax.

After one more swipe at her hair, she swung the door wide and looked up, way up. Her breath caught. The guy in front of her was tall, blond and handsome, with the darkest grey-blue eyes that she'd ever seen. It was a surprise. Brothers who were still unmarried when they were in their thirties were supposed to be deficient in some way.

She extended a hand in greeting. "Hi, I'm Carol."

With a hint of shyness, the man flashed back a smile as he shook her hand. "Nice to meet you. I'm Kevin."

"Come in for a moment, while I get my purse."

Kevin obeyed, moving into the small entrance area, filling it with his broad shoulders. He was at least six foot four. That meant that he was more than a foot taller than she was. But she liked his short, curly, fair hair, and the fact that he looked like someone who'd be at ease on the ski slopes.

"Sorry to keep you waiting. I wasn't expecting to go out tonight."

"I hope I didn't rush you. After being cooped up in the car with Peggy and her fiancé, Tim, I'm sure I'm more impatient than usual."

"I'm so thrilled for the two of them."

Kevin nodded. "Yeah, me too. They've known each other since childhood. It's time they tied the knot."

Carol gathered up her things, ready to leave when she noticed Kevin's smile slip away. "Is something wrong?"

"I'm guessing that Peggy has told you all about me. I hope that she didn't bully you into coming out with us tonight."

"Well, she told me a few things, nice things. She said that you're a great brother."

"That's a relief. I never know what to expect." He glanced down and studied the floor. "She's talked about you too."

Carol clutched at her purse. "Oh, I see."

Peggy has probably been telling him about how looney I am, how I went online and fell for somebody I never met. But, Mike and I are just friends.

As soon as she had the thought, she knew she wasn't being totally honest with herself.

Fess up, Carol! You've had more fantasies about Mike than you dare to admit.

Kevin gave her a sideways glance. "Peggy said that you were pretty, but she was wrong. You're beautiful."

Carol didn't know what to say. It had been a long time since a man paid her such a nice compliment.

Except for Mike, but that was different.

Kevin fidgeted uneasily. "Did I say something wrong? Am I being too forward?"

Carol smiled. "No, you're being very sweet."

Kevin stepped back and gestured to the door. "We better not keep Peggy and Tim waiting too long. Since they set the wedding date, they have this tendency to make out whenever they get a chance. We'll be lucky to get the windows cleared up." His face suddenly flushed red. "Sorry, there I go again, blurting things out. Peggy would kill me if she heard that."

"You're honest and straight forward. I like that," she said as she stepped out the door.

You're just like Mike!

* * *

From a lofty vantage point above Carol's apartment, Grace watched as Carol and Kevin walked out to a car in the parking lot. Her fellow angel, Fred, who was Kevin's guardian, was next to her. She smiled at him. "They seem to be off to a good start, don't you think?"

Fred's energy brightened. "Yes, and I'm very happy for Kevin. He's been through a few rough patches when it comes to women."

"I'm quite relieved for Carol too. She was involved with someone, well not really involved, but chatting with a person on the internet. I had an unfortunate incident with him."

"Oh, yes, I heard something about that."

"It was quite awful. Things got out of hand, and I really frightened the poor thing."

"A vampire, right?"

"Well, not quite. Still, he did some out-of-body trick and showed up in Carol's bedroom. I suppose I was overly protective."

"That's your job."

"I know, but if it hadn't been for Michael, I think we might have lost him."

"That is unfortunate."

"I tried to help afterwards, but Michael thought it best for me to—" She paused.

"Keep your distance?"

"Frederick, I do feel responsible! However, he was quite unpredictable. At one point, he acted like some kind of animal. I tried to read his energy, but he's very good at putting up barriers."

"That's interesting. We can usually see beyond the shields that humans erect."

"This man has Michael's blood."

"Really?" Fred's energy flashed even brighter. "I've heard that Michael took on a physical form, but I didn't know about the details. So you're saying that he gave this person his blood?"

Grace sighed as her thoughts turned to Arel. She sent out a mental apology to her unintended victim.

I'm sorry about what happened, Arel. I didn't mean to scare you.

Fred smiled. "You'll be happy to know that Kevin's heart is true and loving. He's a little impulsive, but he really tries his best."

"I'm glad. Carol needs someone whom she can rely on."

Giving her a quick glance, Fred had a playful glint in his eye. "Somebody who's not a former vampire?"

Grace didn't answer. She wasn't wholly convinced that Arel was totally beyond his previous needs.

Fifteen

AREL LEANED OVER his desk, watching the computer monitor. It was Saturday night, and he'd been waiting for Carol to sign into the chat room for the last half hour. Drumming his fingers with a growing sense of frustration, he glanced over at Michael. "Tell me what's going on? Last night I made a decision to put you in charge. Now, I've even approved of your suggestion that I come clean and tell Carol the truth. So where is she? She always shows up in the chat room on the agreed upon time."

Michael was trying to adjust his large frame in the uncompromising, wooden chair next to Arel's desk. Finally, he seemed to realize his efforts to get comfortable were getting him nowhere. "I thought that you'd be happy to have some time to reflect on the idea of being truthful with Carol."

Arel leaned back into his cushy, executive model chair. It contrasted sharply with the French antique that Michael had been forced to occupy. But Arel wasn't thinking about the angel's comfort. "I just want to get this mess over and done with," he protested. "You know that patience isn't one of my strong points."

"Right," Michael sighed as he pushed himself out of the close confines of his seat. He walked to the couch, sat down and stretched out with a look of relief. "Perhaps we can go over what you might say to Carol."

Arel placed his hands behind his head and rocked his chair back again. "I hope that you know that I'm counting on you to tell me how to explain things. Angels know how to put things eloquently. Hopefully, something that sounds like BS coming from me, will sound sincere when you put it into words."

Michael gave him a curious look. "Thanks for the compliment, I think, but I'm not here to transform lies. What I will do is help you tell the truth in a way that makes it easier for Carol to feel less violated. We don't want her to think that she can't trust life. She'll hopefully understand that you were very insecure, careless, and totally ignorant. But, that in spite of being all those things, you want to acknowledge that she's wonderful. She's been so wonderful that it's made you feel compelled to confess your wrongs and to apologize."

In one jerky movement, Arel released his chair from its tilted position and sat bolt upright. His eyes were wide with surprise and repugnance. "I guess I spoke too soon. Angels don't always have a silver tongue."

Michael blinked at him innocently. "By helping Carol to believe in herself, she'll be more likely to understand you and forgive your lies. It's in your best interest not to hold anything back."

"But does that mean I have to sound like the scum of the earth? I'll admit it. I was wrong when I told the lies, but did I really know any better? Wasn't I blinded by my need to be wanted? I did what I had to do to get her to care about me."

"That's not an excuse."

"Why?"

"Every sentient being has a guidance system inside. It's something that tells them if they are doing the right thing or the wrong thing."

"Oh hell, Michael, belief systems, mass hypnosis, all kinds of factors can come into play and muck up the 'guidance system.'"

Michael inhaled deeply but remained silent.

Arel could feel Michael digging in his heels. "So, let me get this straight. I'm supposed to get online with Carol and say what?" He paused, contemplating his confession. After a long moment, he cleared his throat. "How about this? 'Sorry Carol this is *not* Mike. This is a cad named Arel. I lied to you about my name and about everything else. And you, Carol, were too nice to even realize what a colossal fraud I am. You're the type of person who gives others a chance, who takes them at their word. And I'm the kind of person who takes advantage of sweet, caring people like you. I'm sorry if I hurt you, but please realize that because of who you are, you've helped me to understand that I need to stop the lies, to learn how to deal with the fact that I'm completely dishonest.'"

Michael nodded approvingly. "That's actually pretty good. Maybe you should write that down."

"Great! A lot of help you are. Don't I get to retain even a shred of decency in her eyes?"

"Being truthful might be the best way to impress her."

"Oh it'll impress her alright. She'll be so impressed that she'll never go online again, at least not to access a chat room with someone like me."

Michael shrugged. "We'll have to take that chance."

"We? Where is there a 'we' in all of this?"

"I'm here to help," Michael said, sounding sincere.

"I see. Do you know what this feels like to me? I'm like some private in the army during a war. He gets his orders. 'Take this message across enemy lines. Give the message to our guys.' So the private takes the message and delivers it. He's running back to his unit. Unfortunately, he gets his head blown off before he can return to safety. Later, his Sergeant comes up to his carcass and announces, 'Congratulations, soldier, *we* got that message across.'"

Michael chuckled. "Like I told Abrigail, you have a very dry humor. Your subject matter is rather dark, but your delivery is perfect. You could have done well in comedy."

"Yes, I could have been a vampire on the comedy circuit. I can hear my intro. 'Let's hear it for Arel. He's a vampire with a very, dry sense of humor! But you can fix that for him, folks. After the show, step backstage and let him have a little 'feed' back.'"

Michael laughed again. "You're great."

"Thanks. I'm so glad that one of us is smiling."

Michael's eyes sparkled. "You have a very unique perspective. It's witty."

"Vampire humor, it's a real niche." Arel sulked, but his eyes flickered mischievously. "Maybe you'd like me to start a comic strip. I could call it, *'Doomsbury.'* Picture this, a vampire who's also a company boss. He's in a business suit. He's standing over his victim saying, 'Hate to eat and run, Bob, but I have to get back to the office.'"

As his mind conjured up ideas, Arel realized that it had been a long time since humor had been a part of his thought process except for his brief moments of laughter with Carol. He stared at Michael with wondering eyes. Had angelic blood given him a more amusing outlook? "I know this is a strange question because I haven't seen much evidence of it, but here goes. Do angels engage in humor?"

Michael laughed, filling the room with a deep resonant tone of delight. "Of course we do."

Arel frowned so deeply his brows became a straight line of annoyance. "So you've been holding out on me?"

"I didn't think you'd enjoy my sense of humor, since you take everything so seriously."

"I could have used a little cheering up. All these years and I'm thinking you're the serious one, St. Michael. Be reverent around the guy!"

"Arel, please, you haven't always been reverent."

"Whatever! Your vibes, and I hate to say this, but for an angel, they're heavy."

"Really? So you want me to bring in more humor?"

"Absolutely."

Sixteen

SUNDAY NIGHT WAS both wonderful and terrible for Carol. It was wonderful because she was spending another evening with Kevin. It was terrible because she was ignoring Mike. The evening before, she'd totally forgotten about him. She'd never once thought about their usual online meeting. Now, she sat at the computer, typing out lies. She couldn't bear to tell him the truth.

Sorry, Mike, I'm having too much fun with Kevin to think about you.

Mike wasn't making her situation any easier. As she tried to beg off another day of conversation, he seemed so intent on chatting with her. He was so intent that she'd blurted out an excuse that was absurd. She told him that her sister was having a baby, and she had to be there for her. The truth was that she didn't have a sister, much less a pregnant one. Signing off and quickly closing down the connection, she felt a lump in her throat, a big, horrible lump of deception.

I know it's wrong, Mike, but I just can't explain what's going on, not now. Kevin is waiting for me.

She walked into the living room carrying two bowls of popcorn and a heavy load of guilt. This kind of behavior wasn't like her. No matter what Peggy thought, she wasn't one to get carried away, to forget her responsibility to someone she cared about.

"Hey, what's wrong?" Kevin asked as soon as he saw her.

"I've let someone down." She put the bowls on the coffee table and took a seat next to him. "He's just a friend, but I've been neglecting him since I've met you."

Kevin's face brightened. "A friend?"

"Yes, we usually chat on the weekends, but I've been having such a nice time with—" She stopped herself, staring at Kevin with penitent eyes.

"So I'm the culprit?" Kevin smiled and put his arm around her shoulders. "I've been too demanding, taking up all your time. Is that it?"

She couldn't resist his smile, or the way he looked at her with a thoughtful, yet slightly devilish gaze. "Yes, I guess you have."

Kevin sat back. "I'm sorry. Is that a problem?"

Goodness no!

She wanted to shout out the words. Kevin wasn't a problem. He was great, what romantics call a dream come true. "I'll have to explain things to my friend tomorrow."

"I was hoping that you'd say that."

"Am I a horrible person?"

Kevin tilted her chin up, staring at her with eyes that had now been purged of the devil. They were bright, sincere. "No, you're not horrible. You're the nicest woman that I've ever met. I'm sorry for your friend, but I'm afraid I'm too selfish to regret a single moment that we've had together. And if it's okay with you, I'd like to have a lot more."

"I'd like that too."

She felt like she could see beyond Kevin's handsome face, beyond his strong, inviting body. She saw who he really was. It was easy. He didn't hide anything. Unlike her, he was totally honest about what he thought and felt. It was so easy to like him. If she let herself, she knew that it might be easy to love him when they got to know each other better.

That's a crazy idea. First you thought you might be in love with Mike, and now you're gaga over Kevin. After all these years of avoiding men, you're running romance central through your brain 24/7.

She snuggled closer to Kevin anyway. It felt so good to have his gorgeous flesh and blood body next to her. Peggy was right. It was different than chatting online. She couldn't forget about Mike or her guilt, but for the moment, she could put those subjects on hold.

* * *

With the movie credits rolling on the television and Carol cuddled close to him, Kevin was in heaven. It had only been a couple of days since they had met, but he was already asking himself an amazing question. Had he found the perfect woman at last? Maybe part of it was that Carol and Peggy had been close friends for a long time, and he'd heard a lot about Carol from his sister. From everything that he'd experienced, Carol was even more wonderful than Peggy had told him. When she stirred in his arms, he reluctantly let go of her.

"Can I help you?" he asked as he watched her stand up.

Carol began to gather up the snack dishes. "No, there isn't much here." She glanced over at him. "Did you like the film?"

"Maybe I shouldn't answer that. It was . . . interesting."

"Maybe I shouldn't have suggested *'Bridget Jones' Diary'*," she said with a blush of embarrassment. "Next time, we'll watch something a little more middle of the road."

"As long as we're watching it together, you can choose whatever you want."

Kevin hadn't cared one way or the other about the film. He'd hardly paid any attention. Carol had totally distracted him. He'd wanted to kiss her, to touch her smooth, silky skin with more passion. It was everything he could do to fight his urges. But he respected her. He didn't want to rush her or to frighten her away. "Please, let me help," he said quickly, standing up too and grabbing whatever dishes were left.

He noted as he always did, that he dwarfed Carol with his height and ex-football build.

She's so tiny, so fragile. Be careful with her, you big oaf.

She smiled up at him. "It's nice to see a guy who's interested in being thoughtful."

"I don't know if it's that. Growing up, Peggy was very insistent that we do our equal share of the chores. I suppose I'm a product of my upbringing."

Carol led the way to the kitchen. "Your sister is a jewel."

He let out a sort of half laugh. "I think of her more as a little gremlin. Do you know how many times she tried to beat me up when we were kids? I was always twice her size, but that didn't stop her. Plus she knew the rule about a boy not being allowed to hit a girl. Damn, I came close to breaking that rule many a time."

"I'm an only child, but I wish I could have had a brother."

He gave her a sidelong glance. His teasing grin was broad and unguarded. "So you could beat him up?"

"Of course not. If I had a brother, I think we would have had adventures together. He would have taken me fishing and maybe we could have built a tree house." She laughed. "I was a tomboy as a kid. I don't remember wanting to play with dolls as much as most of the girls I knew."

"Did your father take you fishing?"

"I wish."

Kevin wedged himself into the place where Carol was standing as she rinsed dishes and put them in the dishwasher. "Move," he ordered playfully. "I'll take care of these."

"Okay, if you insist." She let him have her spot at the sink and grabbed a towel to dry her hands. "My Dad was sweet like you, but he was a workaholic. He made sure that I knew he loved me, but he was very busy most of the time."

"What did he do?"

"He was a district attorney, and he eventually became a judge. But that was after he and my mother got divorced."

"Divorce? That must have been tough," Kevin said as he rinsed a dish. "Do you see your mom and dad very often?"

"Mom lives in California and Dad's retired on the east coast. I visit them occasionally, but we're not very close."

Kevin dried his hands too and turned to admire her. "You don't look like you were ever a tomboy. However, if you want to go fishing someday, I'm game." He stepped closer and reached out for her hand. "Do you think that you'd still like to try it?"

She let him pull her closer. "Maybe."

He took a deep breath, enjoying her perfume and her smile. "You know you're a very rare type of woman."

"Really?"

"I'm not an expert on dating, but I've done enough. Many of the women that I went out with had an edge to them. You're not like that."

"If I did have an edge, I think you're the kind of man that would make me want to put it aside. You're very nice."

"Ouch, I hope I'm more than that."

She laughed. "Why is 'nice' a bad thing? I like being with you because you are sweet and thoughtful."

"And maybe a little exciting?" he asked playfully. When she blushed and didn't say anything, he waited for an answer.

"Yes," she finally admitted. "I do find you exciting."

Carol's tone and the way that she hung on to the front of his shirt, made Kevin bold. He didn't like to force things after being burned a number of times, but now he had to let his desire have some leeway. He bent down and kissed her tenderly. When their lips parted, he knew he'd never felt so close to any of his former girlfriends. "I'd like to see you again, very soon."

* * *

Carol couldn't stop thinking about Kevin after he left. As she got ready for bed, she kept remembering how wonderful it felt to be in his arms.

Have I found a man who's everything I've always wanted? A good man . . . a considerate man . . . a gorgeous man.

She stopped herself. She'd had some of the same thoughts about Mike. In her daydreams, he was gorgeous and almost perfect too.

"Maybe I'm in love with love," she moaned. "I wish I could talk to somebody and get a fresh perspective."

Peggy came to mind, but she was Kevin's sister. It didn't feel right to talk to her. The next thought was inexcusable.

Oh my, no matter what Kevin says, you are a horrible person, Carol Ann.

She wanted to talk to Mike about Kevin, about the idea of a relationship. He'd be the perfect person to confide in. Besides, he was someone who helped people all the time.

If only Mike could help me sort out my emotions.

Was she falling for Kevin too fast? Was she being naïve to think that love could happen after only a few dates?

She paused.

I'm a user. That's what I am. I want to use my friend, my sweet, kind friend.

She paused again.

But that's just it, Mike and I are only friends. All the romantic stuff was in my head. I didn't lead him on, did I?

She did a quick file check on their conversations. No, they never discussed anything that went beyond the boundaries of friendship. So she didn't have to feel bad about Kevin being in her life, just about the fact that she'd lied to Mike. She'd also failed to show on Saturday. Big apology for that too.

She climbed into bed, pulled the cover close, and reached out for Charlie Bear. Since childhood, the stuffed animal had been a steady presence who listened attentively. "Charlie, what's it all mean? First there's Mike, and now Kevin. All this time without a relationship, and now I have two, really great guys come into my life. I thought I liked Mike, but—"

After a moment, with Charlie staring back with little to say, Carol's eyes strayed. They followed patterns on the wall as the moonlight and wind played with the tree outside her window. Its shadowy limbs became dark performers, leaping about, dancing with life. She smiled as they prompted answers that brightened her mood.

Perhaps Mike was a warm up for the real thing, just a shadow of what I want. But Kevin is real, tangible. When he touches me—

She didn't want to hurt Mike's feelings, but their relationship wasn't what she needed. They could talk forever, but it wasn't the same as someone being there in the flesh. Just the thought of Kevin made little chills race through her body. When he held her close and kissed her the first time, she felt like the princess in Sleeping Beauty.

"He woke me up, Charlie. Now I want to stay awake. I want Kevin to be my prince. That's not wrong, is it?"

She put the bear back in his spot on the adjoining pillow and turned out the light. "When I talk to Mike tomorrow, I'll straighten everything out."

Seventeen

AREL'S OFFICE WAS quiet, even peaceful. His voice was a whisper, but it was a determined whisper. "I can do this." As his jerky fingers tapped keys on the keyboard, as he connected to the chat room, he had to be brave. He was preparing for his showdown with Carol.

But his destination wasn't just a chat room. In the past, it had been the castle where he met with the fair damsel, Carol. It was the place where, in Carol's eyes, he performed valiant deeds. Maybe that's how the idea of acting like a suicide hotline volunteer got started. If Carol thought that he saved lives, she might be more inclined to see him in a favorable light. Who didn't love a champion?

But there'd be no wonderful roles for him to play this time. As he watched the monitor screen and noted that he was logged in, the castle was replaced by a dark room, brightened in the center with one harsh, glaring light. The light was aimed at him, demanding that he expose his lies, his shortcomings. When he did, he'd no longer be Mike the wonder boy. He'd be Arel the scoundrel.

Arel had asked Michael not to attend the chat session. He had to have the courage to face Carol alone, especially after hearing Michael's suggestions. Still, he pulled back sharply when he saw two letters appear on his screen. They were an 'H' and an 'i', letters in a friendly greeting. But in reality, he knew what they were really telling him. "Confess, you bastard!"

Gritting his teeth, preparing himself for the worst, he forced himself to do his duty. "Hi, Carol, before we talk, I have to tell you something," he typed back. For a moment his fingers stilled. He was intent on proceeding, but he needed to take a deep breath first. He didn't get the chance. There was an immediate response from Carol.

"Before you do, I have something I have to say! I lied to you, Mike."

He stared at the screen and the words Carol had written, but he couldn't make any sense of what they meant. The idea of Carol being deceitful was so unexpected that he was stopped in his confessional tracks.

What? You lied? You've always been so sweet.

"What do you mean?" he typed back.

"Mike, I'm sorry. It was only the one time. I told you that I was with my sister who was having a baby. But the truth is that I don't have a sister. I lied to you because I didn't know how to explain the truth."

He frowned as he saw himself stepping out of the glaring light and putting Carol in his place.

"You only lied once?" he typed, slowing his breath. "What couldn't you tell me?"

Carol continued. "Before I explain, would you please try to forgive me for the lie and for not showing up on Saturday? I value our friendship. The time we've had online has been great."

He blinked at her message.

Yes, it has been great, but why does that sound so lame to me?

His fingers pressed on. "I feel the same way. And 'yes' the answer is 'yes.' I can forgive you. One tiny lie? That's not so serious."

He was lying again. Forgiving Carol was tough. If he had to forgive her, it meant that there was a blemish on her halo. He didn't want that. He wanted her to be that beautiful woman, that perfect person he could look up to in the castle window.

"Thank you, Mike. Your understanding means the world to me."

He managed a smile as he replied. "Good. Now tell me what this is all about." He tried to pretend for her sake, to assume the role of a gallant counselor. "What's going on?"

"Mike, I met someone. His name is Kevin."

He felt the impact of her message hit him with a brutal force. It came out of nowhere, crushing his chest. He couldn't breathe.

You idiot! You wouldn't admit it, but you've been pretending that Carol was another Justina.

He knew it now, but it had been an unconscious act up until a second ago.

And I pretended that Carol cared about me, that she wanted me. Oh, how utterly stupid I am.

Carol's next message came up on the screen. "Mike, I didn't plan it. It just happened, out of the blue, isn't that weird?"

He still couldn't breathe.

Don't talk to me, Carol! We have nothing to say to each other!

Grabbing the computer mouse, he positioned it over the log off button. For a moment, he was a stationary object, rooted to the ground of his own folly. Then the pain flooded in. It was a kind of pain that he'd felt once before, long ago, when he was stabbed by a sailor over a game of cards. But that knife had entered his shoulder. Carol's knife penetrated his heart.

Another message appeared on the monitor. "Mike, did you mean it? Am I forgiven?"

He sucked in his breath, his mind spinning, unable to get a grip on anything. He went into an auto-response mode. His hand eased off of the mouse. He typed a reply.

"Sure."

He could practically feel Carol's relief when he read her next message.

"You're the best."

"Right."

Carol typed on. "Now tell me your news."

A few minutes earlier, his news made him queasy. It made him feel small and guilty. Now, all that changed. His feelings were in transition. They were in a temporary limbo. He felt quite stoic about confessing his wrong doing. What did he care what Carol thought of him? He already knew that he didn't matter. There was someone else in her life. As his mind turned over the concept of the person she called Kevin, the stoicism was replaced by anger, the deep smoldering kind that came from his gut.

So I never meant a damned thing. I was just some loser you used when you were lonely. Thanks a helluva lot, Carol.

Suddenly the anger exploded. It went from smoldering to flaming resentment. His hands clawed at the keyboard. His words were fast and cutting. He wanted to hurt Carol like she'd hurt him. He wanted to retaliate.

"How can you be so uncaring? I actually thought you liked me. But you're like the rest. This whole damn world is pitiless." Before he sent the message, his hand stalled for a moment. In that brief space of time, he glimpsed a bit of gold sticking out from under some papers on his desk. He swallowed hard as his hands left the keyboard. He knew what had caught his eye. Reaching out, he retrieved the gilded frame that housed the picture of Justina.

Oh my darling! I miss you so much. You were the only one I could ever count on.

He fingered her face slowly, forgetting about keyboards and confessions and Carol. Justina began filling up his mind, mixing with the pain in his heart, turning back time. He could see her so clearly. She was standing in his arms, laughing with him, loving him. She was telling him something.

As he listened to her whispering in his ear, he began deleting the message on the monitor. He watched as all of his hateful words disappeared. Long ago, he'd hurt the one person he loved. Now he was trying to hurt this woman named Carol.

Why? Because she told a lie? Because she found someone to love? What right do I have to chastise her for that?

Instead, he knew that he'd tell her the truth about himself, except of course for one important fact. He'd leave out the part about being a vampire for so many years.

As he began typing again, his expressions of anger were replaced by a simple message. "I've lied to you too, Carol, even about my name. I'm not Mike. My name is Arel."

* * *

Carol didn't interrupt the message that came across her screen, a paragraph at a time. She was too stunned, too angry.

"So, dear Carol, now you know who I really am," Arel concluded. "I'm a fraud and a liar, but most of all, I guess that I'm a coward. I don't expect forgiveness. I do expect that we'll part ways now. I'm sorry. I wish you the best."

Carol's eyes narrowed as she read his closing statement. "Wait a minute!" she typed back. "I'm not letting you off the hook that easy, AREL!" She was shouting the words in her mind each time she sent her replies.

Arel's response was slow in coming. "What do you mean? What more can I say?"

Carol never thought of herself as a fighter. In fact, she hated conflict. But her hackles were up, and she was furious. She had lied once. The man she thought of as honorable had been lying all along, playing her like some patsy.

"Listen to me. I think you owe me a few more minutes. Sure you can disconnect right now and run away from facing this situation, but I don't think that you should."

The answer was very slow in coming this time.

"Why not?"

She scowled at the screen, trying to remember that only a few minutes ago, she was talking to a friend, a friend who had cheered her up on countless occasions, a friend who advised her about how to feel better about herself. She couldn't simply forget all that. Mike or Arel, whatever his name, was more than his lies. He was a person who had to be hurting to resort to such devious ways of communicating.

"I just thought of something," she typed. "A couple of days ago you told me that you needed to have this conversation. Why did you want to blow your cover? Did you want to get rid of me? End our friendship?"

His answer was almost immediate. "No!"

"Then why?" she asked, still angry.

"I couldn't lie anymore. Because I really like you, Carol. I haven't had anyone, not in a long, long time. You were my friend. When I really believed that, I wanted to tell you the truth."

She blinked and took a deep breath. She could feel her resolve to stay angry melting. It wasn't in her nature to hold a grudge.

"What are we going to do with you, Arel?" she typed.

Again, there was a long pause. "Do with me? What do you mean?"

She smiled sympathetically. After so many hours of talking with Arel, she could feel his alarm.

"I've been thinking. You and I have something in common. We've both hidden ourselves from the real world of relationship. But now that I've met someone, I realize how silly I've been. I should have broken out of my shell years ago. And that's what you need to do."

This time she waited, but he didn't reply.

"Arel? Mike? What would you like me to call you?"

After a moment she got an answer.

"Arel."

She said the name aloud.

"That's a beautiful name. It fits you when I think about the bottom line."

"What bottom line?"

"I forgive you. You're still my friend if that's what you want."

Again, no reply. She realized that he hadn't expected her to forgive him.

"Would you like to stay friends?" she typed back.

"I guess so."

"And one more thing," she added.

"What's that?"

"I have to know where you live. Not your address, just the city you live in. Please."

A very long pause. Finally, a one word response. "Why?"

"Just tell me, silly! It's no big deal."

Again, no reply.

"My goodness, I think you're more introverted than I am. But you can tell me the city, right?"

"Chicago."

"Really? I live in Chicago too," she replied. "Arel, I'm getting a very strong hunch. We definitely need to meet and have a cup of coffee together."

"No. I don't drink coffee. I forgot to include that in my list of lies. I'm sorry."

"Tea? Soda?"

"I've got to go."

"Wait a second, please. Meet me at the Salt and Pepper Diner, on Clark Street, on Thursday night. Eight o'clock. I won't take no for an answer. Bye."

She sent the last message and logged off before he could refuse. Afterwards, she sat staring at the monitor. She often had a sense about people that she attributed to womanly intuition.

"Peggy was so wrong about you, Arel. You're not dangerous. You're a very frightened soul. I'm sure of it."

Eighteen

MICHAEL STOOD NEXT to Abrigail as they both observed Arel from the bottom of his grand, king-sized bed. Arel had taken refuge there ever since his interaction with Carol. He stared at Michael with glowering eyes, eyes that were almost the same color as the fancy linens. Like a shrinking, young prince holding court, Arel lay propped up on a half dozen, silky, cognac-gold pillows. The matching, di Firenze, luxury bedspread had been kicked aside, but now he was clutching at it as he covered himself again. Michael came forward beseechingly, preparing himself for a conversation.

Arel returned a wrathful look. "Whatever you've come here to say, I don't want to hear it."

Michael sighed. "I know, but we need to talk."

Abrigail leaned in on the bottom bed rail and smiled. "Dearest, it's not good for you or your body to stay in bed."

Arel's unhappy scowl deepened. "From now on I'll decide what's good for me. And as for being in this bed, I'm never leaving it again. I don't care how long it takes. I'm staying here until I die."

Michael glanced at Abrigail and then back at Arel. They had both been monitoring Arel's energy. It was plummeting under another assault of self-pity.

"We're here because we care," Abrigail said.

Michael came around to the side of the bed. "I can't stand by and let you waste away like this," he said softly. "You asked me to help you, and I promised that I would."

Arel stiffened. "What's that supposed to mean?"

Michael reached out and took hold of the coverlet. He began to pull it back.

Arel's scowl turned into a glare of outrage as his bony fingers held tight to the bedding. "What the hell do you think you're doing?"

Michael's eyes were kind but resolute. "You're going to get up and exercise, even if it's just a few turns around the room."

"Get away!"

"No, I'm sorry," Michael said as he continued to tug at the cover. His strength far exceeded Arel's pitiful efforts, and he was successful in not only pulling the blanket towards him, he was moving Arel's clinging body to the edge of the bed.

At the last moment, before he was thrown off entirely, Arel let go. "Damn you! You can't do this!"

Throwing the cover aside, Michael reached out for Arel this time. "Just get up and move around a little, please."

Like a wild, terrified animal, Arel jerked back, but Michael was quicker and snagged his arm. The battle that ensued was a fierce one, with Arel kicking and yelling obscenities as Michael forced him from his bed. It wasn't a long battle. After a minute, Arel seemed to know he was doomed and quit struggling as quickly as he'd started. This time, he went limp, trying to collapse to the floor. Again, Michael wouldn't let him have his way. Supporting Arel under his arms, he held on to him. "You have to walk, even if it's only a few feet."

"I won't! I won't do anything ever again."

"Dearest, please, your wellbeing is at stake," Abrigail said as she joined them. She held out her arms in a welcoming gesture as Michael handed over Arel's sagging body. Arel collapsed against her, a burden being shifted from one angel to another. Abrigail held him tight and rocked him gently. "We couldn't possibly stand by and let you die like this."

Arel came to life just enough to hang on to her, but he was in full scale victim mode. "No one would care if I died. I thought I had a friend, but Carol has thrown me aside like a piece of rubbish."

"That's not true," Michael insisted. "Now let's take a small stroll around the room. You need to keep your body going."

"I said no!" Arel cried out, grasping at Abrigail like he'd grasped at the blanket. Raising his head briefly, he looked at her with eyes that were better suited to the city pound and the poor animals waiting hopelessly in their pens. "Don't let him bully me, Abrigail!" He buried his head in her shoulder. "I don't want to go on trying in a world that's only waiting to punish me further."

Abrigail gave him a motherly hug. "Michael loves you. That's why he's doing this. I love you too."

"You say that, but what good is it?"

"We're here for you. Don't you feel that?"

Arel finally lifted his head again. "I don't understand why the world has to be so cruel." As he slumped with weariness, he began to disengage his tight grasp, allowing Abrigail to take one of his arms as Michael took the other.

Abrigail encouraged him to take a step. "I believe in so much more than cruelty, and I believe that you deserve so much more."

Arel took two steps and balked again. "You two can gang up on me and force me to leave my bed, but there is no way that I'm going to meet Carol. Is that understood?"

Michael turned him around and gave him a fatherly look. "Neither I nor Abrigail would ever force you to do something like that. We're simply trying to make your life easier. Lying in bed, waiting for death would not be enjoyable, believe me."

Arel stared back at him and let out a deep, wretched sigh. "She's horrible, Michael. Carol is a traitor."

"Is she? Or do you want to see her that way?"

"She lied!"

"So did you."

"She betrayed me!"

"How?"

Arel's body slumped again. "I thought she liked me."

"She did, and she still does. Why else would she want to meet you?"

"Who knows? She might be twisted. She might want to humiliate me for lying to her." He hesitated, but finally glanced up at Michael. "I can't believe I'm asking for your advice again, but do you think I'm right about her?"

"I don't think that at all, but I won't tell you that you should meet her either."

"Why? What do you know?"

"What I know is that you're free to make up your own mind about Carol."

"You're keeping something from me, aren't you?"

When he didn't get an answer, Arel turned and looked at Abrigail. Her eyes were full of compassion, but she shrugged.

Arel began to take a few steps on his own, paused and reached out for Michael and Abrigail's support. "That's just great. Two angels are here with me, and they don't know a damn thing. How is that possible?"

It was Michael's turn to shrug. How could he tell Arel the truth? Arel wouldn't believe it, but it was clear that Arel's own soul was keeping secrets from Arel's conscious mind and from them.

Nineteen

THE CAFÉ WAS one of Carol's favorite places to have lunch. Bright colors dominated the fifty's theme, along with chrome legged tables and chairs. A rocket ship flying across the wall announced the name of the diner. She sat in a booth across from Peggy, smiling. "Strange, I didn't grow up with this style, but I like the cozy feeling. I would have suggested meeting Mike here, I mean Arel, but it isn't open in the evening."

Peggy put her napkin down and reached in her purse for her lipstick. "I'm relieved that you asked me to be there when you meet him. He sounds like he's the shady type."

"I don't think so. I know that he's a liar, but I think it's because he's so insecure."

Peggy smoothed the lipstick over her lips and then put the lid back on with a snap. "This from the woman who recently described this creep as the man of her dreams."

"You're not helping. If you're going to be like that, I don't want you to come with me."

Peggy's furrowed brows remained fixed, but she sat back. "I'm sorry. I'm just looking out for your best interests."

"If you want what's best for me, please try to be more positive. I need support, not criticism. That's why I liked Arel. He was always nice. Whether he was talking about a book we both read, or he was giving me advice on how to be kind to myself, he was polite and sweet." She paused and lifted her chin. "So don't call him a creep. He was my friend, and he's still my friend."

Peggy's brown eyes widened in surprise. "Wow, you can really be very strong when you want to be."

"I've had to be. In fact, I know a little more about the darker side of life than you realize."

"Like what?"

"Remember how I told you that I was very young when I got married?"

"Yes."

"I ran away from home when I was almost seventeen. I lived on the streets for a few months before I met someone and got married. Believe me, I know all about the shadier side of life and having to protect myself."

Peggy didn't respond, but stared back with alert, questioning eyes.

Carol shifted nervously. "Are you alright? I didn't shock you, did I?"

"Sorry," Peggy said, getting her voice back. "It's just that you're so steady, so down home, so pure. I would never, in a million years, ever guess that you had that kind of background."

"Well, I was, you know, pure and innocent before I got the stupid idea to run away."

"Why did you?"

"I don't know. My parents loved me. I never wanted for anything. But they went through a very painful divorce. And I couldn't stand it. I adored them both. To watch them argue constantly, tearing apart all the things that I loved was too much. One day I just ran away from it all and started hitch hiking."

"Did they try to find you?"

"Of course, but I was smart about evading them. It took a year for them to track me down. And when they did, my running away added a huge burden to their guilt and pain, to what they'd already been going through with their divorce. It was a horrible mess all around."

"What about your marriage?"

Carol shrugged. "It was so short that the guy I married was gone before my parents found me."

"How did you get your life back on track?"

"It wasn't easy, but I went back to school and got my college degree. I pursued graphic arts. It was a good choice. I eventually got a job that I really liked. Step by step, I brought order back into my life."

"And I thought you were a naïve gal that somebody could take advantage of."

"Now you know the truth." She squared her shoulders. "So when you meet Arel, please leave out the hostility. He needs a chance to prove himself."

Peggy laughed. "I don't think I have any choice, Tiger Lady."

As they got up to leave, Peggy touched Carol's arm. "I almost forgot to ask about how you and Kevin are doing. I haven't seen him lately, but he's usually a clam when it comes to telling me anything. He says I'm too bossy with my advice."

"You? Bossy?" Carol gave Peggy a good-humored nudge. "Anyway, Kevin and I had a nice time."

"Did he call you after your double date on Friday?"

"Maybe."

"Tell me," Peggy demanded.

"I've told you enough. We'll talk later in the week."

"But I won't have time to talk until I see you on Thursday night. I've got all this wedding planning stuff going on."

"Then we'll talk on Thursday. Otherwise, you'll have to talk to your brother, the clam."

Twenty

AREL SAT BACK in his office chair and did a couple of stretches. Michael and Abrigail had been right. He did feel better now that he was up and about again. However, glancing at Michael, who sat on the couch, he didn't feel like he needed a babysitter.

"You've been there reading for hours. You don't have to stick around, you know. I wouldn't dare go back to bed."

Michael put his book aside. "I thought you might like some company. You spend too much time alone."

"I'm fine now. I have something to keep me occupied."

"Yes, how's the new website coming?"

Since his exposure to the world of computers, Arel found that technology could be a wonderful diversion. "It took a bit of study, but I think I'm well on my way to creating a site that will be interesting for people to visit."

"What's it about?"

"You said that I've got a unique viewpoint. Now let's see if the world is ready to learn about the reality of the vampire world."

Michael sat up straighter. "Really, you're going to give thousands of people, maybe millions of people a chance to know things about you?"

"Hey, I'm one of a kind. Everyone is concerned about endangered animals. What about vampires? You don't know any besides me, do you?"

Michael paused, looking upwards, as if he were saying a quick prayer of thanks. "Not off hand. But, I don't understand. You're a very private person."

Arel snorted. "I'm not sharing my personal hell, not totally. That would be a fun website, wouldn't it? I can see it now, a live online cam showing me crying myself to sleep."

"You'd be surprised at how many people might share your feelings."

"Forget it. Like I'm not depressed enough, all I need is a bunch of people contacting me, telling me about how they relate, telling me about their problems. No, all I'm doing here is expressing a few thoughts and observations."

"What kind of observations?"

He crossed his arms. "Oh, I could go on and on about angels, couldn't I?"

"I thought this site was about the plight of the vanishing vampire."

"Exactly. And when I vanish, I want people to know how it happened, that angels aren't all that they're cracked up to be."

Michael smiled. "There's your sense of humor again."

"Right. My Doomsbury comic will show all the gory details. Arel meets Michael. Arel bites Michael. Arel ends up in the alley where he used to hunt rats. Only now, the rats are feasting on his dead body."

Michael frowned playfully. "Too dark, people need something a little more uplifting."

"I tried uplifting and look where it got me."

"I really am sorry about Carol."

"Yes, Carol. Carol the flirt. Carol the backstabber."

"Arel—"

"Fine, but no matter how hard you try to convince me that she's nice, I'm not going there."

"I haven't tried that at all, have—"

"She's like a loose cannon on the battlefield. No way am I going to offer myself up for target practice."

"Have I once suggested that you should?"

He avoided Michael's gaze. "No, and at least I'm grateful for that. Now go back to your book and let me keep working."

Twenty-One

CAROL PAUSED OUTSIDE the apartment door, looking up at Kevin. "Dinner was wonderful," she said, drawing out the words more dreamily than she intended.

Control yourself, Carol. You're moving way too fast.

With her face going into a full blush of dismay, she turned to unlock the door.

Kevin reached out for her hand, foiling her attempt to put the key in the lock. "Come here."

Kevin's voice was soft, but there was a forceful undertone that couldn't be ignored. She turned around to look at him again. His eyes were bright and wanting, making her blush a deeper red. Did Kevin feel the same excitement that she was feeling? As if to answer her question, he bent down and kissed her. It was a gentle touch on the lips, followed by a second, much more passionate exchange. When he released her, he stepped back. His expression shifted. He suddenly looked like the kid who had taken a cookie out of turn. He cleared his throat.

"I'm sorry. Too soon?" he asked.

She didn't answer, but she knew that her smile told him what he needed to know.

Kevin reached out for her hands, staring at her with animated, probing eyes. "Where have you been all this time?"

She looked down at the way Kevin was holding her. Her hands were almost lost in his. His grasp was gentle, but she could tell he didn't want to let go of her. She squeezed back. "I didn't know that I could feel this way either."

"Maybe we're both finding what we've been looking for."

"I hear people talking about relationships, and they seem so complicated. Can it be this easy?"

Kevin shrugged. "I don't think I have any more answers now than when I was seven years old in Mrs. Burn's class and she asked some tough math questions. But I'd like to think that love is easy."

"Love?" She blinked back anxiously. "I don't think we can be in love, not yet."

"Did I say love? Sorry. You're right. That is crazy."

She bit her lip nervously and avoided his gaze. "It's getting late."

Kevin released her at once. "You're right. I better get going. We both have to work tomorrow."

"Yes, work," she mumbled. She turned back to the door, trying to fit the key in the lock. "I'll see you on Friday night." She tried to keep her voice steady. She was afraid to say more, but she was thinking it.

Oh, my goodness! We're both moving too fast! Love? At this stage?

Once she got the door open, she turned and waved a brief goodbye. Kevin seemed self-conscious too. He returned her wave, but he didn't linger. He quickly started walking down the sidewalk. As he disappeared into the shadows, she closed the door. She didn't want to think about anything yet. She threw her purse on the side table, went directly to her bedroom and started to undress. She was about to hang up her sweater when she paused and smiled. The sweater smelled like Kevin's cologne. She buried her face in the soft fibers and inhaled deeply, taking in the lingering hint of balsam mixed with spices. The scent was magical, transporting her to an earlier time in the evening. For a moment, she was in Kevin's arms again.

She glanced over at Charlie. The old bear was sitting on a nearby chair. "Could we be in love, Charlie? Do you think it's possible?"

When he stared back with hard, doubtful eyes, she returned a defiant look. "It could happen," she insisted as she placed the scented sweater on one of the bed pillows. "There are cases of people who knew right away that they were right for each other."

She put on her pajamas and went to the bathroom. She needed a good night's sleep if she was going to feel her best at work. She was about to grab her toothbrush when she caught a glimpse of herself in the vanity mirror. She hadn't thought much about her oversized, floral PJs before. They were a birthday present from an aunt, and her practical side simply accepted them as suitable. But what if Kevin saw her in them? What would he think?

Oh lord, I look like I'm dressed for an old age home.

It was time for a complete overhaul. That meant a trip to the mall. On dates, she normally wore slacks or jeans. Some pretty dresses would be a nice addition to her wardrobe. And why hadn't she thought about wearing some cute heels instead of flats? As for sleepwear, she needed some attractive lingerie.

The more she thought about changing her appearance, the more excited she felt. A whole new life might be in front of her, and she wanted to be ready for it.

Twenty-Two

IT WAS STILL early evening, and the dimly lit tavern wasn't busy yet. Kevin had elbow room at the bar as he put down his beer. He gave Tim a quick glance. At six foot three inches, Tim was an inch shorter in height than Kevin. They were only six months apart in age, but Kevin looked up to Tim as a kind of older brother. "So, are you nervous? The wedding is only six weeks off."

Tim shrugged his broad, muscular shoulders, but he smiled back confidently. "It's time to settle down."

"Settling down with my sister, that's scary."

"I can't believe we waited this long. I've known you and Peggy forever. Hell, we all grew up together."

Kevin turned his bottle slowly. "Yeah, the good old days. Now you two are taking the big plunge."

"We want to get a house after we're married."

"A house? Do you know how busy you're going to be? My sister will find so much crap for you to do. She loves projects."

Tim let the threat slide off with a chuckle. "I'm looking forward to owning a home. I want to mow my own grass. I miss a yard after living in an apartment for so long."

"Right. Consider how happy you were that summer when you were mowing lawns for extra money. I never heard so much complaining."

"I was a kid. That was different. Doing stuff with Peggy will be great."

"That's the 'love is blind' part of you talking. Do you remember what a pain she was when we were kids? How she was always hanging around and bugging us?"

"We were pretty bad ourselves. We sent her on wild goose chases and made her prove her allegiance by eating a worm."

"Yeah, I guess. But those were the fun times."

"I don't know if Peggy remembers them that way."

Kevin prodded Tim with his elbow. "You really do love her, don't you?"

"Yeah, I do."

Kevin laughed. "Tim is going to hitch his wagon to 'Peggy Leggy, Queen of the Beasts.'"

Tim was sipping his beer and choked. When he got his breath back, he frowned. "Geez, I forgot that we called her that. I remember the skinny legs part, but where did the Queen of Beasts idea come in?"

Kevin took a long drag on his beer. "That's the part I can't forget. What a nightmare, with Peggy hauling in two stray cats and begging Mom and Dad to keep them. 'Just for a little while,' she whined."

Tim nodded. "Oh yeah, didn't you guys have a lot of kittens for a while?"

"We had ten. Days after Peggy's rescue, both those felines had babies. Their kittens were all feral hellions. Every time one of them got out of Peggy's room, it turned into a Freddy Krueger. I don't think that a curtain or a piece of furniture in the house escaped their claws."

"Sounds like you had your own version of 'Nightmare on Elm Street.'"

"Yup, and when Dad said they were all going to the pound, Peggy was worse than the cats. She threw a fit. You never saw so much screaming and pleading. Damn, Mom and Dad ended up having to find homes for every one of those dang kittens."

"Hey, are you trying to scare me this close to the wedding?"

"Nope, you know Peggy almost as well as I do."

Tim gave Kevin a friendly slap on the back. "That's right, and I also know how you took care of your sister, how you protected her. You were always getting your face punched when she got herself in trouble."

Kevin let out a sigh of disgust. "She had a knack for pissing off every bully in the neighborhood."

"And you were always there, warding them off."

"I couldn't win an argument with her, but I was able to take on most of the bullies."

"You looked like hamburger a couple of times."

"What choice did I have? She's my sister." Kevin turned to Tim, raising his beer in a toast. "To Tim, Peggy's new champion. I'm turning the job over to you."

Tim returned the toast. "Thanks, but that's enough talk about my upcoming event. Tell me about Carol. Did you two hit it off?"

Kevin started turning his bottle again. After a moment, he gave Tim a sheepish look. "You have to promise that anything I say does *not* get back to Peggy. She was always on me when I was dating Dahlia. It was like getting advice from a pile driver."

"I know she can come on a little strong, but Peggy really cares about you."

"I know. Still, I don't want her in the middle this time, especially since Carol is her best friend. I want to have some space."

"Got it, anything that you tell me goes no further, I promise."

"Scout's honor?"

"Scout's honor," Tim pledged as he gave Kevin the once over. "But I don't think I'll need to say anything. I know that look that you have on your face. If Peggy sees it—"

Kevin turned back to his beer. "What 'look'?"

"You know," Tim laughed. "I remember when I first saw that 'I'm in love' look. We were in the eighth grade, and you had a big crush on Stephanie Baker."

Kevin's face turned a deep shade of red. "I guess I can't hide it. I really like Carol."

"It couldn't be because she's blond and very attractive."

Kevin's flush deepened. "It's more than that. She's great. I guess we just click."

"Good, but I better warn you right now. Unless you put a bag over your head, Peggy is going to know everything too."

"You're right. So it's up to you to keep her busy with those wedding plans instead of pestering me."

Tim finished his beer. "I'll do my best. But you know that you're damned lucky to have your sister, Kevin. That last girlfriend was a horror show. If it weren't for Peggy's so-called interference, you'd still be with her."

"Yeah, but with Carol, it's a whole, different story."

Twenty-Three

THE LIBRARY AREA of Arel's downstairs living room had a comforting feel to it. Over the years, he'd infused the space and his large collection of books with the fragrance of countless sticks of incense. Michael had suggested its use as a calming aid. The combination of reading and incense was perfect for relieving stress and escaping worries. Now, taking a deep, weary breath, he was too tired to read. It was five o'clock, Thursday morning. He'd worked at the computer all night. Finally, he'd had enough and withdrawn to the place he used as a sort of retreat from everything. But he couldn't retreat from his thoughts about Carol. That evening she'd be sitting alone in some diner, waiting for him. But if he never showed up, it would be her just dessert for tossing him aside for someone named Kevin. At least that's what he kept telling himself.

He closed his eyes and slowly rubbed his hand over the padded arm of the chair. Sometimes, the simple movement was a distraction. If he really focused on the feel of the smooth fabric, he could forget whatever was bothering him. Unfortunately, this wasn't one of those times. Carol refused to be repressed by a simple hand gesture.

When they chatted, she was consistently sweet and agreeable. Had she suddenly changed? Did she really want to meet him just to punish him? His persistent excuse for feeling the way he did was brought up for inspection and shot down.

He'd only had two women in his life that meant something, Justina and now Carol. But he hadn't really had Carol in his life, had he? Did online friendships count?

For me it did. And it did for Carol too. She wanted to meet me. I was the one who refused the invitation.

So he couldn't even hold her at fault for getting involved with someone else. And he couldn't hold himself at fault for refusing to meet her early on.

I couldn't . . . I can't.

He'd read about people like himself who had paralyzing phobias. His were getting worse instead of better.

How long has it been since I lived a normal life.

He couldn't remember. Any semblance of a normal life had ended with the curse. After that, he'd retreated further and further from everything. Then there was the Michael thing. That wasn't something a normal person tried.

And it's all come to this.

He did a quick survey of his physical woes. At the moment, his nerves were as taut as strings on a steel guitar and there was a double bass drum pounding in his head. All in all, par for the course.

But lots of people are physically stressed. Think about all the drugs they're taking.

Maybe, he wasn't as bad off as he imagined. Plus Michael said he had to have a more positive outlook.

Stop being such an alarmist with this Carol business. She invited you to a diner named after condiments. How bad could that be?

He gave himself an order. He needed to go to bed, get some sleep, and stop being a self-absorbed idiot.

* * *

Hours later, Arel woke up with a message. The words were streaming through his head, ticker tape fashion, over and over again.

You don't have to be stuck forever. Go meet Carol.

As evening drew near, as the bell tolled, he couldn't resist the mental memo. A surge of courage fired through his body, and he decided to take the challenge. After his shower, he slid open the doors to his closet and stared at the garments. When was the last time that he dressed to go out to meet someone? His mind drew a blank.

As he went over his choices, his hand moved to a Zegna sports jacket. It would go well with a button-down shirt and dark slacks. Impulsively, he reached for a tie and stopped, reminding himself that he was expected at a café.

Try to fit in, dammit.

After he finished dressing, he took a last look at himself and scoffed. But he wouldn't let his physical failings stop him at this point. He'd made his decision and would stick to it. He did push his shoulders back a little. He also tried to maintain a more erect posture as he started for the living area. Michael and Abrigail were waiting for him there. A little earlier, he had given them the news about going to meet Carol. Now, they were like parents preparing to send their kid off to his first prom. Of course he'd never gone to a prom, but he still felt a little like their kid on parade when he stood in front of them.

"Do I look alright?" he asked.

Sitting on the sofa next to Michael, Abrigail smiled as soon as she saw him. "You're very handsome."

"Are you sure?" He didn't know why he was asking an angel for an opinion? What did Abrigail know about such things?

"Abrigail is right," Michael chimed in. "You look great."

Arel took a deep breath. "I know that I said I wouldn't meet Carol, but I've reconsidered. I know how her mind works. She'll be fretting like some misguided mother hen if I don't show up. So I'll meet with her, let her know that I'm perfectly fine, and then I'll never see her again. She'll have closure."

Abrigail nodded. "That's true."

He glanced at his watch. "It's getting late. I better be going."

* * *

After Arel left, Abrigail turned to Michael. "He looks different."

"It's his hair." Michael smiled when he thought about Arel's dark locks. They were still damp when Arel left the house. They were also combed straight back from his forehead, giving him the more classic vampire appearance that one saw in the movies. "When he was talking to Carol and told her about his hair being unruly, she suggested using gel. I think he used a little too much."

Abrigail's eyes brightened with mirth. "You're right, I'm used to seeing him look like a truant schoolboy."

"Yes, and our truant schoolboy is on a mission."

"He was so sure about staying home. Tell me how you managed to get him to even consider going out tonight?"

"Surprisingly, he kept his shields down while he was napping. I had the opportunity to slip in a few ideas while he slept. He seems very taken with the thought of closure, but I think his curiosity is helping to motivate him. He wants to see what Carol looks like."

"So you think this meeting is a good idea?"

"Arel's at a crossroads. If he doesn't go, he's going to feel even worse about himself. He may retreat back to his bed for good this time."

"But Michael, I'm getting a very unsettled feeling about it all."

"I know, and your feelings are well founded. I was given a glimpse of what might be coming. Key events could be set in motion with this meeting. If that happens, the only thing we can do is be there for him. We'll have to help him stay afloat when the storm hits."

Twenty-Four

THE BOOTH CAROL and Peggy had chosen was across from the diner's entrance. Carol had an excellent view of everyone entering and exiting the establishment. She kept alternately glancing at the door and checking her watch. Arel was late. Would he show up? She bit her lip and gave Peggy a look of concern. "I hope that Arel's okay. He was always on time when we met online."

Peggy looked very elfin in a size four, apple green top. But when she shook back her red hair, there was a scowl on her face. "I'm sorry, and I don't want to be negative, but maybe he's a jerk after all."

"Don't start, please."

"I just want you to know that I'm here to support you. That's all."

Carol let out a sigh. Maybe Peggy was right. But when she checked the door again, her breath caught. She gestured towards the entrance. "Oh my goodness, it's him. I'm sure of it."

Peggy turned around, her dark eyes flashing in the direction that Carol indicated. "That guy?" She squinted, scanning the man from head to toe. "Very well dressed. But why do you think it's him?"

Carol hesitated. In her daydreams, she'd imagined Arel as strong and well-built. But deep down, she'd felt a different, more sensitive type of person on the other end of their conversations. The man at the door to the diner fit that description. "You get a feel for a person after you interact with them for awhile."

"Wow, he's kind of cute, what there is of him."

Carol held up her hand and waved. "Arel? Over here," she called out, trusting that she was right.

Her summons seemed to work. The hauntingly, slender man stopped instantly in his tracks. For a long moment, he didn't seem able to move. He stared back with wide, blinky eyes. When Carol smiled and waved again, it helped to get him moving. He nodded and started walking in her direction. His eyes darted back and forth nervously, and he nearly tripped over another patron's foot that was partially stretched out in the aisle.

Carol and Peggy both had a knee-jerk moment of motherly concern.

"I think that I owe you an apology," Peggy said. "I don't want to sound demeaning, but when I look at your guy, I get the feeling a tenth grader could take him out."

Carol bit her lip again. "I know, maybe that's why I thought we should meet. He probably needs a friend."

* * *

Arel continued towards a table on the far wall of the diner. He knew his face was turning a bright red. Thankfully, he recovered his bearings after tripping. When he'd arrived at the diner, he'd tried to tell himself that he was very capable of exchanging a few words with the person he'd gotten to know online. Unfortunately, his body wasn't cooperating. As soon as he saw Carol, it went into a "duck and cover" mode. While he was checking out everything to his left and right, he tripped over a foot stuck out in front of him.

Hell and damnation! I'm off to a good start.

A part of the problem was seeing that Carol hadn't come alone. She had a friend. He was sure it was a woman named Peggy. She fit the description Carol had given. The small and cute parts were fine. But Carol also talked about how judgmental Peggy could be. It's just what he needed, a disapproving busy-body.

You only have to stay long enough to meet Carol and then you can leave. But you are not going to turn and run.

The stern order that he gave himself had to be repeated as he continued towards the booth. The short distance seemed almost impossible to navigate. He was battling two stiff legs and a body that had lost all fluid motion.

You look like an idiot. At least try to smile.

He managed to make his mouth comply with a modest expression of pleasure as he walked the last ten feet to the booth. He was greeted as soon as he reached his destination.

"Hi, I'm Carol," one of the women offered cheerfully. "I'm so glad that you could make it."

Carol's smile made ten of his. He quickly worked his jaw, loosening it enough to speak. "Yes . . . I'm . . . I'm Arel. It's very nice to meet you," he said glancing around. He normally lived in a quiet, fixed setting. As soon as he'd left his familiar sanctuary, his senses had become acute. Standing in the middle of a well-lit, noisy diner, the feedback was overwhelming. People laughed too loud, a waitress moved past him too quickly, and Carol was eyeing him like he was a newly discovered species from the ocean depths. He forced himself to ignore it all long enough to stand in place and greet her. She was even prettier than he'd expected, with blond hair and an open, caring face.

"And this is my friend, Peggy," Carol said.

His attention shifted to Carol's companion and stalled. As soon as their eyes connected, he felt his body stiffen even more if that was possible. His eyes wouldn't disengage. "I know you." The words slipped out of his mouth without his permission. They were accusing words that matched the painful distrust that had hold of his gut.

The petite redhead reacted too. At first, her face went blank, then questioning, and finally angry. "How do you know me?" she demanded.

He stepped back as she studied him. "Lovely red hair, delicate, pretty. Carol's talked about you many times," he explained. Again the words rolled off his tongue just as mysteriously as when he'd said that he knew her.

Peggy remained unappeased. In the brief silence that followed, her disapproval dominated the small space they occupied. It was enough time for Arel to understand her better. In a flash of clarity, he took in her personality. Peggy was the pushy type. She was the kind of woman who goaded a person when they needed to be left alone. If there was a scary basement, where all the ghosts and spooks were kept, Peggy would be the type who pushed a person towards the stairs and beyond. There was one word to describe her. She was dangerous.

His instinct was to distance himself, to flee from the table and from the diner. But he had to ignore that instinct. A policy of etiquette demanded that he be polite, even if it meant sacrificing his own comfort and safety. That kind of proper conduct had been drummed into his brain from the moment he was old enough to sit at the family's formal dinner table where every piece of silverware was carefully positioned, where he was taught to sit straight and never utter a complaint. "I'm sorry, did I offend you?" he asked. "I didn't mean to say things that were inappropriate."

Peggy reined in her gaze. "Never mind," she said in a huff. Her eyes shifted from his face to her drink. She reached for it with a shaky hand, as if the sweet contents in her glass could return her to a more soothing reality.

Carol eyed Peggy with concern. "Are you okay?"

"I'm fine," Peggy insisted. She even tried to laugh as she peeked at Arel again. "You're really just a lamb, aren't you? One that got lost along the way."

Carol leaned in towards Peggy. "What are you talking about?"

Peggy shrugged. "I don't know . . . nothing," she whispered as she sucked up her coke. The first mouthful caused her to choke and then spray the table with a small shower of soda.

Carol immediately came to her aid, reaching for napkins. She gave Peggy several and then began to mop up the table.

Arel stood watching, feeling like he should help too, but he couldn't. His body was consumed by a crazy feeling that they were all doomed.

What is my problem? Her drink went down the wrong way? What's the big deal? Sit down, you lunatic.

He glanced at the booth. It looked tight, claustrophobic, but he forced himself to try out its lack of space. He let his body slide down the slick upholstery, still watching Peggy recover. He finally came to an uneasy 'butt meets vinyl' seating arrangement. But as soon as Peggy looked back at him, his eyes dropped to the table.

"Sorry about that," Peggy said.

He kept his eyes averted. "I just wanted to stop in long enough to apologize to Carol again, but I better get going."

He tried to take a deep breath, but his lungs wouldn't expand. What the hell was he doing? How did he talk himself into coming? He had to get away so he could breathe again. He wasn't being a coward. He simply had to get some oxygen.

"No, please, don't go yet," Carol moaned. "I've looked forward to meeting you for a long time."

"I'm sorry," he apologized. "I feel awkward about all this. Maybe we can do it again another time."

He had to take charge of the situation. He'd tried his best, but the close proximity of the two, strange women was too much. With relief, his body was in motion again, sliding out of the booth. "Carol, thanks for your kindness. I'm so glad that you've met this fellow, Kevin, right?"

Peggy came alive as soon as he was on his feet, staring up at him with the most animated eyes he'd ever seen.

"Don't be silly!" she said as she reached out and clasped his hand, pinning it to the table.

The gesture was paralyzing.

No! Don't!

A nightmare flash blotted out the diner. He was standing in darkness, bound tight, helpless to stop what was about to happen to him. He knew he'd never escape the horrors that were waiting for him. The petrifying moment lasted almost forever before a waitress rescued him. After she came over to the table, her presence was enough to make Peggy pull back, releasing him from her grasp and the nightmare. He stood shaking, almost whimpering, and clutching at his hand. It was hot and painful, like Peggy had branded him with her touch.

"Are you alright, sir?" the waitress asked, shielding him from Peggy, giving him the full focus of her blue eyes. They were so reassuring. He felt immediate relief.

Abrigail? Is it you?

His query was soundless, but the waitress smiled an acknowledgement.

Don't worry. Michael and I are here for you.

She was right. He thought he caught a glimpse of Michael sitting a couple of booths away. He tried to connect with the angel.

It's not Carol and Peggy doing this to me, is it? This is the blood again.

When Michael looked away without answering, Arel was left with the feeling of how ridiculous he'd been behaving with the two women. Now Abrigail ignored him too as she played out the part of the dutiful employee.

"How are you ladies doing?" she asked with pen poised over a paper pad. "Jeanie had to take a call. I'm taking over for her for a few minutes. Can I get something else for you?"

"Nothing more for me," Peggy said as she busied herself with her straw.

"I'm fine, thank you," Carol said.

Abrigail looked at him again. "Can I get you something, sir?"

"No, thank you." He was going to add, "I'm leaving," but the dismal look on Carol's face stopped him. She'd been so happy when he arrived. Now she was confused and miserable, something that he'd never intended. Peggy was equally, if not more, dejected. She sat staring at the table with a blush of red on her cheeks. His reaction had obviously made her sorry that she was there.

"Carol, Peggy, could we start over? I feel like a complete fool," he said as he slowly sat down again. He did remain perched very close to the edge of his seat, just in case.

Both women glanced up at him at the same time. Both of them looked relieved.

"Are you sure you don't want something to eat or drink?" Carol asked. "Their pie is delicious."

He shook his head, "No, nothing for me. I just had a big dinner. I couldn't eat another thing." Trying to smile again, trying to start over, he ran his hands through his combed back hair, disrupting its smooth style, allowing it to break free of form. As his hands came away, his thick wavy, dark locks fell forward into their normal pattern, gracing his forehead as they usually did.

"I'm sorry . . . if I've made you uncomfortable," Peggy said quietly, looking at her soda as she spoke.

Her voice was so genuine, so contrite that he nervously put his hands on the table, as if to show her that he knew he'd misjudged her. "You're very kind to say that."

Peggy's face finally eased into a weak smile. "I like your English accent."

"I was born in England, but that was a long time ago. I didn't think I spoke with a discernable accent anymore."

Carol laughed. "I'm sorry to have to tell you this, but you sound like you just arrived."

Peggy carefully pushed her glass to the side. "I always loved guys from abroad. They have that fascinating Euro feel."

"Sorry, no Euro feel here," he announced apprehensively, not wanting to feel different. "I'm all American."

"Of course," Peggy said.

For a moment, all three went quiet.

"This is yummy," Carol exclaimed as she sipped the remains of her shake enthusiastically.

He could tell that she was simply making conversation. Inwardly, he smiled.

That's the Carol I know.

When they had chatted online, if there was an awkward pause between messages, he could always count on her to salvage the moment. Now he knew why he'd come to meet her. He wanted to experience her first hand. Yet, he'd hardly let himself look at her, except for that initial glance.

Hell, just what I was afraid of. She's so lovely. And that smile. I already know it. I could feel it in her messages.

He turned his attention to Carol's gestures, to the way she tossed her hair to the side when she spoke to Peggy. She wasn't just pretty, she was beautiful, just as Justina had been beautiful.

She reminds me of Justina.

His body froze at the possibility.

No! Tell me it's not my Justina!

He knew that it could be true. Justina could have reincarnated. She could have come back and be sitting across from him at this very moment.

Is that why I've been so insanely nervous since I got here?

On some soul level did he know that Carol was his former, one true love? He glanced in the direction of the booth where he thought he saw Michael sitting, but there was no one there.

"You look a little pale, Arel. Are you feeling okay?" Carol asked, leaning in towards him.

Shaken by his latest thoughts about who Carol might be, he was sure that he was wearing a zombie face. His eyes were stuck in a frozen glare, and his mouth was probably hanging open. He swallowed hard and tried to pull himself together. "No, I've had a flu bug. I thought that I was over it, but I guess I'm not. I have to go."

He reached for his wallet, grabbing at some bills and throwing them on the table. "So sorry about this," he groaned as he pushed out from the booth.

Carol seemed to understand his distress. "Please Arel, leave your phone number or email address. We'll do this another time."

"Email?" He blurted his address out without much thought. He was already in motion, making his legs hold him upright, making them find a path out of the damnable place that was supposed to be a simple diner. He could feel Carol and Peggy's eyes on him as he rushed to the door. His floundering limbs battled to open it. Once he managed the almost impossible feat, he fled into the open air. Gasping, he looked around, not knowing what he was looking for. He remembered his car. Where was it parked? Before he got the answer, he remembered Carol's face. Or was it Justina's face? He stumbled over to a street lamp and grabbed hold to steady himself.

Arel, it's alright. Carol has no connection to Justina.

He heard Michael's voice in his head. It had been in the background, trying to get through. Now he was able to listen to what he was being told.

Are you positive, Michael?

It was just your fears, nothing more.

Thank goodness!

Relief swept over him, leaving him in a state that teetered between euphoria and collapse. His instincts were quick to remind him that he was in a public area. He forced himself to stand up again and keep moving towards his car.

Dear god, Michael, I've been a twitching bundle of nerves and craziness tonight. I've been shy, even awkward before, but this evening I was some kind of first class clown. You were there, I know it. I could feel your presence.

Yes, I was there.

Arel let out a scoffing laugh.

You saw me. I was paranoia unleashed, hardly able to sit for two minutes in that booth. I know I stared at that Peggy woman like she was the devil incarnate. I don't know what she and Carol think about me, but if they look back on this night as a low point in social graces, it'll be a valid judgment.

Michael laughed too, but it was an understanding laugh.

You haven't been out in the world for a while.

It's more than that.

Arel went over his performance again. If he could have felt sorry for himself, it would have been comforting. Instead, shame and humiliation made him cringe. In earlier periods of his life, when he fought the vampire curse, he could feel good about never giving in to its desires. He'd had a sense of pride and honor in his strength. Now, no matter how hard he tried, his fears always got the upper hand.

He retreated from his conversation with Michael and started talking to himself.

Forget it, just go home.

When he reached the car, he got in and started the engine.

But what am I going back to, a house full of stuff that I've collected? A closet full of expensive clothes?

He'd surrounded himself with material possessions, like a ghost trying to hold on to the physical world. But he didn't belong in the physical world.

I am a ghost. I have no power over anything, especially my life. There's nothing here for me, nothing to hold on to.

It was a strangely freeing thought and different from the idea of giving up. In the past, he'd held himself up to some kind of standard, some kind of measure of what a man should be. When he failed those standards, he felt hopeless. But that wasn't the case for a ghost. A ghost was beyond the world and its standards.

He began to mumble aloud. "I guess you're right, Michael. Fighting is getting me nowhere. I need to simply accept what I am, a walking phantom, and that's okay."

If he simply let go and embraced the nothingness in him, he'd have no obligations anymore. He'd be that lost spirit that finally lets the light take him back, like in the movies.

His breath caught when the solution presented itself. The sun was that light. All these years it had been there for him, waiting to take him out of the world. He was so afraid of what that meant. Now, the fear was replaced by a sense of liberation.

Michael's voice broke through his musings.

Surrendering to despair isn't what I was recommending.

Arel smiled. "It doesn't feel like despair. I feel calm about it all." He put the car in gear and eased off of the brake. As the car pulled away from the parking space, he had a new goal. He wasn't going home. He was headed for the freeway.

Michael was still trying to get through.

What are you going to do?

"If I start now, I can drive far enough away to find a place that's deserted, a place out in the open where I won't be able to change my mind. At least I still have the sun on my side. It'll solve everything."

That's not the answer. Besides, you don't want to burn yourself out of existence, do you?

Arel's hands tightened on the steering wheel. For a moment, he couldn't swallow the lump in his throat. The thought of fire almost made him turn around. It was followed by an even more needy thought. Once and for all, he had to stop caving in to what scared him. He had to be free. "I'm not afraid anymore, Michael. Be happy for me."

Michael's tone was stern.

You're making a mistake.

He laughed. "It's what I do, and now I'm okay with that."

Twenty-Five

PEGGY SAT STARING at the diner's exit door. She couldn't figure out what just happened. How did she go from feeling like a friend helping out a friend, to feeling like a horrible person? No matter how she tried to excuse her actions, she'd done something to make Carol's friend, Arel, look like a frightened rabbit facing its doom. She knew she had a reputation for being forthright, even outspoken. But no one had ever looked at her like she was going to have them for dinner. She felt even worse when the waitress came over to the booth and gave her a look of concern.

"Is your friend okay?" the heavy-boned woman asked. "He left in a hurry."

Peggy frowned at her. The stocky woman had been their original waitress. The slim, gorgeous one who had helped out earlier had disappeared. "I don't know exactly why he left."

"He wasn't feeling well," Carol offered.

The waitress glanced at the table and noticed the money sitting there. Two crisp, hundred dollar bills were waiting for her. She glanced at the door again, then back at the money.

"He's a big tipper. Hope he comes back."

"I wouldn't count on it," Peggy said.

The waitress swiped up the money and tucked it into her apron. "Well, you two gals have a nice evening," she said as she moved away.

Carol sighed. "Arel just got here, and now he's gone. I'm more worried about him than I was before, but I guess that's me being silly, isn't it?"

When Peggy didn't answer, Carol ignored her silence. "Are you ready to go?"

Peggy shook her head. "You're not being silly. I've never seen a human being that looked as wretched as your Arel. When I grabbed his hand, did you notice how his body went all weird? I thought he was going to pass out."

Carol put her napkin on the table and unfolded its bent edges. "Maybe you're reading things into his reaction. It wasn't your fault that he was jumpy."

"I guess so, but he was so thin and . . . sad. You never told me how sad he was."

"He didn't seem that way when we chatted. He was always being funny or telling me stories about his hotline heroics."

"Are you kidding? That guy couldn't rescue a bird that fell out of its nest. When he was leaving, I didn't think he'd get the door open."

Carol let out a short burst of laughter. "I'm sorry. I'm not laughing at Arel. I'm laughing at myself. If I don't laugh, I think I'll cry." She bit down on her lip. "I can't believe that I could be so wrong about everything."

Peggy rallied. She had to stop thinking about herself and make sure Carol was okay. "Don't blame yourself. Sad or not, he lied to you."

"Yes, but now I know why. He must not have any friends, anyone to turn to."

Peggy sat back, remembering Arel's face, but not the frightened one. She pushed that image aside, sat up straighter, and tried to find something positive to say. "He does have potential, if he could get a grip."

"Yes, I agree," Carol said with a sniffle. She snatched the napkin from the table and rubbed at her nose. "I guess I have to think of him as being okay."

"That's right," Peggy insisted. Carol was a softy. She needed a friend who was strong, not someone to make her feel worse. "I was wrong. We're both being silly. He'll be fine."

Carol brightened. "You think so?"

"Sure," Peggy said with a smile. She almost had herself convinced until she remembered something disturbing again. "But there is something about his eyes."

"I thought they were very nice."

"They were, but they were so intense." Peggy had a twinge of queasiness as soon as she acknowledged Arel's consuming gaze. It was her body's instinctive reaction when something was wrong. It acted as a warning.

Forget his eyes! Go home and forget Arel.

"Intense? In a bad way?" Carol asked.

Peggy shrugged and tried to laugh off her sudden nausea. "No, I just think his eyes are different, like they have x-ray vision."

It was true. Even if Arel's body looked gaunt and frail, his eyes were penetrating, golden lasers. They seemed to breach her outer persona effortlessly. They had the capacity to go deeper, stirring up memories she couldn't quite bring to mind, memories she knew she didn't want to examine. She nudged Carol. "We should get going."

Carol retrieved her purse. "Who knows, maybe Arel is special after all."

Peggy began to gather up her things. She didn't want to think about Arel anymore. She paused and gave Carol an inquiring look. "Special or not, you're dating Kevin now. How is that going?"

Carol blushed. "It's good."

Peggy smiled again. Her brother needed someone who was sweet and nurturing like Carol. "I'm really happy to hear that."

"You were right when you told me about an actual relationship being very different than chatting."

"Relationship?"

Carol smiled too. "Stop it, you know what I mean. I enjoy going out with him."

"Good, I was hoping you'd like the big dope."

"Peggy, Kevin's not a dope."

"I'm kidding. I know he's a great guy, but don't forget that he's my brother. I tend to still see him as a big kid." She rubbed her upset stomach and sighed. "The bottom line is that I want Kevin to be happy. I'm thrilled that you two hit it off."

"Me too."

Peggy glanced at her watch. "It's getting late, and Tim and I have a few things to go over this evening. He's been a peach with all the wedding details."

"From what you've said, he's supportive and dependable."

"One hundred percent dependable. Ever since we were kids, Tim has always been the one with the level head and a heart of gold."

"You're a lucky woman."

"Yes, I know." Peggy slid out of the booth. Standing up, she took a deep breath. It made her stomach churn again. She tried to pass it off as something she'd eaten that didn't sit well. The idea that it was a bad omen wasn't a welcome one. She didn't like her premonitions. The first one occurred right before her dad received news of her grandma's passing. Another time, Kevin fell from a tree and broke his leg.

Carol let herself out of the booth too. "What's that look?"

Peggy grabbed her stomach again. "Arel said he had a bug. You don't think he could have given it to me this fast, do you?"

Carol took hold of Peggy's arm and led her forward. "Do you know what I think? I think that you're very sensitive, that you sometimes act like you're tougher than you are."

Peggy shrugged. "Maybe you're right. Do any of us really know ourselves?"

Twenty-Six

AFTER PEGGY DROPPED Carol off at her apartment, she pulled out of the complex and got on the road as quickly as possible. Her stomach was still acting up, and she was happy to be going home. Tim would be waiting for her. He'd serve her a cup of chamomile tea and help her to relax.

Once she was out on a main street and stopped at a light, she fidgeted with the car radio. She needed to put the whole diner disaster behind her. Some upbeat tunes always put her in a better mood. Unfortunately, all her favorite stations were on commercial breaks. She switched off the radio with a sigh. Why was she so nervous? Why did she keep thinking about Arel?

When the light turned green, she pressed down hard on the gas pedal. Her intention to forget about the man she'd only met briefly wasn't working.

And it's my own fault! I'm the one that had to go and grab him.

Touching Arel's hand had been a big mistake. Not only did Arel go bonkers, she'd had her own reaction. She'd felt a connection, like she knew him from somewhere. But it wasn't like remembering an old friend. It was like remembering a bad dream. Just thinking about it again made her stomach do a couple of flips.

Her nausea was getting worse. It was turning into a gripping pain in her gut. Half keeping an eye on the road, she flipped open the glove compartment. She felt around, hopeful that she'd find some antacid tablets that Tim had thrown in.

"This has to be a flu bug," she moaned as she sat up empty handed. As soon as she said it, her mouth went dry. She knew that she was lying to herself. Her body was trying to tell her something. Could she be having another premonition? Was one of her loved ones in danger?

Tim is safe at home. And I'm sure that Kevin is watching the game on TV. When she thought about her parents in Florida, no red flags came up.

Come on, Peggy, get it together.

Carol was right about her. She did put on a tough act, but at times she didn't feel tough at all, especially if she was anxious about her family and friends.

Stop stressing. Think about something that makes you happy.

She was going to be Mrs. Timothy Werner soon. It was a dream come true, something she'd fantasized about since she was ten years old. Now, Tim was her rock, the person who was always there for her.

I'll be home in ten minutes. I'll be fine once I see Tim.

She smiled with anticipation and noticed a slight reprieve from her gut. The pain eased off a little as she was about to change lanes. Doing a quick check for traffic, she glanced at her rear view mirror.

"Oh my god!" She didn't see any cars. She saw Arel's golden eyes staring back at her, making her lose control, making her swerve into the other lane. A fast approaching car, coming up on her right side, gave her the horn.

Like the two events weren't enough to totally unnerve her, another pain shot through her lower tract, sending out signals that something terrible was about to happen.

No, its not. Arel did give me his flu bug. That's the connection, that's why I'm thinking about him and seeing things.

She had to keep her mind on her driving, on the red light ahead. She was coming up on it too quickly, but her mind and her body were out of sync. She hit the brakes too hard and too soon. There was a sudden jolt as the car behind her, a big SUV, slammed into her small compact. She let out a shriek as she was thrown forward and back in a violent, jerking motion. It was so fast, so unexpected. For an instant, she blacked out. She lost touch with time and with what was happening to her. Instead, she saw Arel staring at her again, but this time his face was so young and innocent.

I do know you. You're not a stranger!

Recognition was accompanied by dread. Her body shuddered as a grisly scene opened up and revealed more details. It was nighttime, and this younger Arel was bloodied and bruised. He was surrounded by men who were jeering and spitting on him as they pulled him forward along a narrow street. His hands were tied behind his back. His clothes were coarse garments that were torn and dirty and stained with blood. He was faltering, barely able to walk. When he glanced back at her again, his tormented eyes were lit up by the torches that people were carrying.

Oh god, what are they going to do to you?

Their minds connected the moment she asked the question. She knew what he was thinking. She could access his thoughts as though they were her own. He was apologizing to her.

"I'm so sorry that I couldn't protect you. I'm so sorry."

He wasn't afraid for himself, but for her. His helplessness, his failure to be there for her was a burden of sorrow that overshadowed his physical misery.

She answered him in a sobbing, miserable shriek.

But it's not your fault! I'm to blame for this!

She knew that she was the one who was responsible for what was going to happen to him. In that moment, she also knew that she was going to lose him, that he was being dragged to his death. The feeling was so all consuming that her heart shattered with grief. Everything that she loved was taken from her in that moment.

* * *

Peggy opened her eyes, trying to make sense of where she was. She remembered the accident and being hit from behind. She was still in her car, but every time she tried to move, a paralyzing pain kept her in her seat. There was also the pain of her recent vision, with all its horrible implications. She didn't realize that she was sobbing until she saw the kind face of an older woman who had opened her car door.

"Try not to cry, my dear," the lady said as she squeezed Peggy's hand. "Someone has already called 911. Help will be here soon."

Peggy wished that she could stop the tears. But there were too many. But it wasn't the first time in her life that she felt inconsolable.

* * *

When Peggy was four years old, she was playing with her dolls, mothering them, giving them their bottles, kissing them. She didn't pay attention to the movie that her father was watching on television in the next room. But suddenly her world of sweetness and make-believe was interrupted by a high-pitched scream. Peggy's four-year-old ears had never heard a sound like that. But it was a sound that every human being, no matter how young or small, recognizes. It was a sound of someone being hurt in the most horrible way. Peggy ran for safety, seeking out her father's arms. That's when she saw the television set. Her father was watching a movie about Joan of Arc. Peggy put her hands over her ears, trying to shut out the horror of a woman being burned alive. But it was too late. When she saw the woman engulfed in fire, Peggy began screaming too.

Her father scooped her up and tried to comfort her. He tried to stop her pitiful cries, but the harm was done. She'd learned something very important that day. She learned what could happen to a human being. Her mind had been branded with knowledge and a clear picture of the most horrible suffering.

Afterwards, little Peggy did everything in her power to protect herself. In many ways, she succeeded. As the years passed, she got stronger. The vision was buried, along with her interest in dolls. She wanted to be tough like the boys. Of course, her heart wasn't closed to those she loved, or to the less fortunate. She looked out for those beings, human or animal, that couldn't help themselves.

Now as the adult Peggy sat shaking in her car, waiting for the ambulance, she knew the scar from the past had been ripped open. She felt like the child again, unprotected, vulnerable. She also knew who was responsible for resurrecting her misery. As soon as Arel saw her in the diner, he acquainted her with the truth.

"I know you," he said. His tone had been soft, barely a whisper. But sometimes, softness can be deceptive. As soon as Arel voiced those words, she felt his pain. It was the pain of helpless creatures being abused, body pain. It was also the kind of pain that occurs when hearts lose everything that they love.

She added to that pain when she reached out and touched his hand. Later, in the car, he retaliated. He did to her what she had done to him. But he didn't grab her hand. When he gazed back at her in the rear view mirror, he took hold of her heart. He went straight to that place inside where she kept her deepest fears hidden. He ripped away everything that protected her from the truth.

Now, sitting in her car, she couldn't escape those fears. Putting her hand on her heart, fresh tears surfaced, and she began to sob again. She wept for the young man in the vision, and for the man with golden eyes in the diner. She kept seeing him run from the place, crippled with fear. She cried for herself and the part she'd played in the horror that she'd seen in some distant past.

"Try not to think about it too much," a voice whispered in her ear. It belonged to the woman who stayed with her as she waited for help. The lady squeezed her hand again as the sound of a siren got louder. "I know it's hard, but he's not alone and neither are you."

"What?" Peggy asked. Her eyes went bright with questions. She tried to turn her head to look at the woman and cried out in pain. The woman disappeared as others rushed to her aid.

* * *

The woman let go of Peggy's hand when the ambulance arrived. As the EMTs took over, she backed away and disappeared into the night. She literally disappeared because she wasn't a woman at all.

For a short time Peggy's angel, Glory, had assumed a human form, a friend-in-need form. She wanted to give her charge as much support as possible. The memory that Peggy was dealing with, was a core issue, one that had tainted many of her lives since its tragic origin.

You're not alone, my sweet child. I'm watching over you.

Glory issued the message as she resumed her normal, angelic state. Ascending heavenward, her luminous body expanded into glorious rays of light that rained down like starry moonbeams on the situation below. It washed over Peggy as she was being helped by human hands. It surrounded the ambulance and the accident scene like a silver-pink halo.

A few moments later, Abrigail appeared next to Glory and added her own loving concern and healing brilliance to what was happening.

"Thank you for coming," Glory said to her fellow angel.

"I understand how distraught Peggy is," Abrigail replied. Her gaze filled with compassion as she watched the people gathered around the young, injured woman.

Glory let out a sigh. "Humans seem so fragile at times."

"Yes, but they're also amazingly strong in some ways. For so many lifetimes, Peggy and Arel have soldiered on in spite of everything. They're two, very brave souls."

"They're souls that have been torn apart by the suffering that they endured in that pivotal lifetime that they shared."

"Yes, you're right."

"Oh dearest Abrigail, if only they could get beyond that terrible event."

"Michael is trying to help them to find some resolution, to release what happened to them."

"But pain has a way of distorting truth. I'm sure his job isn't an easy one."

Abrigail nodded in agreement. "No, it isn't. We'll all have to work together as pieces of the past come to the surface."

Twenty-Seven

THE DRIVER'S SIDE window was down all the way on the black Mustang as Arel traveled west, away from the city. He took deep breaths, inhaling the pure, sweet smells of farmland. He gloried in the wind on his face as it ushered in a sense of freedom from the fearful, closed life he'd known. He was leaving all his worries behind, putting distance between himself and Carol, Peggy and the idea of angels. For a few hours, he could enjoy the wholesome fragrance of the earth and the starry heavens above.

He felt more at ease with each mile that slipped by. He didn't have to hide in his house anymore. He didn't have to double check the locks on the doors so that he could feel safe. Speeding along in the car, he could totally enjoy his last hours. Soon he'd be gone from the world.

A thought interrupted his reverie. "I hope the movies are right about what happens when a vampire meets the sun." He recalled films that showed them burnt to a crisp. "I don't want to traumatize some farmer if my body isn't completely incinerated."

Another rather terrible thought followed. What if the sun didn't kill him, but only burned him and left him alive? What if Michael's blood affected him in some crazy, unexpected way?

He lifted his chin higher and refused to think about it. He had to concentrate on what he was doing. He was on a happy flight to oblivion. Knowing that he could finally end it all was the most exquisite gift he could give himself. He wouldn't spoil that gift with projections about Michael and his blood. Instead, he would appreciate the moment and the driving conditions. There was hardly anyone on the road. It's what he'd dreamed about. He had a bit of the earth, or at least a bit of the highway, to himself. And it all felt new. He couldn't remember the last time he'd ventured so far from home.

Home is a beautiful word, but have I ever truly felt at home anywhere? Hell, I've always been a misfit, the one who didn't belong.

But that didn't matter now. He belonged to the night and to the welcoming feeling of something uninhibited. He put a foot to the brake and pulled off the road. He needed to put the top down on the car.

Why did I buy a convertible, or a sporty car for that matter, if I wasn't going to enjoy it?

He knew the answer. Michael had practically dared him to do something different, to prove that he was sincere in his desire to change his life. He had complied hesitantly and bought the vehicle.

But Michael was right. I love the car.

As he undid the latches for the convertible top, he realized he was humming. It was a surprise. He didn't know he could make such agreeable tones. It happened so naturally. He liked the idea that his body could do something pleasing for a change. He swung open the car door and stepped out with ease. Another surprise. His muscles were relaxed and able again.

The area was so quiet, such a contrast to the diner. He looked up and smiled. A black velvet void was overhead, dotted with countless, twinkling lights. Every star in the heavens seemed to be giving him its blessing. "I should have made this trip years ago."

He pulled back the convertible top, secured it and got back in the car. He turned the key in the ignition and paused to enjoy the sound of the Mustang's four hundred plus horsepower engine. In the past, he'd grown to like the car, but he'd never bonded with it. Now he had a chance to play, to be that driver who took control and put a car through its paces. "Show me what you can do," he said as he boldly stepped on the gas.

* * *

An hour later, the Mustang sped effortlessly along the two lane highway. Arel had never felt so in touch with everything. His face was buffeted by the wind. His lungs enjoyed the sweet, damp air. Any residue from bad nerves was disappearing, being soothed away by the relative darkness all around him. As fertile fields rushed by on either side, his chest expanded with a newfound joy.

"Damn, I think I'm bonding with the dirt! And I'll be part of it soon, ash that blows over the land. I'll be scattered from here to Missouri."

The center lines of the highway were guiding him to his goal. The pavement became his road to OZ. When he arrived at his destination, the wizard would be a bright, fiery ball called the sun. Long ago, as a boy, he loved the dawn. He stared at the purple and grey skies with a sense of expectancy. Sunrise meant that there was still hope in the world and warmth. Now sunrise would mean even more. It would bring release from pain, from guilt, from failure.

The night I became a vampire, I lost that orb of light forever. Now it will shine bright on me one last time.

Death would be fast, over in a few seconds. What were a few seconds after all he'd been through?

At least I hope it'll be quick.

His moment of doubt made his heart beat faster.

No, don't go there.

When he reflected on the past, it was all a farce. All those painful hours, days and years of being alive had been worthless. He was always battling depression and loneliness, always wishing for some respite and getting nothing but more misery. Now, he had an opportunity to experience a little happiness. He wouldn't pollute his precious moments with old programs of panic. He wanted to enjoy the glorious comfort of the night, and the wonder of the machine that responded to his every whim. All he had to do was press the accelerator and the Mustang, like its namesake, flew across the flatlands. It was a thing of grace and speed that let him put miles between the living torment he'd endured and his new objective.

Dying will be the ultimate triumph.

A Zen-like smile began to slip into place, making his face as pure as it had ever been. An unspoiled, genteel smoothness replaced the frown lines. His smile remained unchanged when he thought of Carol's eyes and her kindness. She became part of the night and the stars.

"Beautiful," he said as he accelerated. "It's all perfect when you're free of the pain."

With death only hours away, all his cares had vanished. Yet, he still had a few questions before he died, like why had he even been born? He pondered the idea for only a moment, then laughed.

"It doesn't matter." He shouted the words, let them fly off into the night. He loved the feeling that everything that frustrated him could be released at long last. One with the car, he asked it for more speed. It had no problem granting his request. Ninety-five miles per hour, one hundred? The Mustang responded without protest. "Yes, sir!"

The road was treacherous in spots. Navigating around the potholes at high speeds could be challenging. Even that seemed appropriate.

"Maybe I won't need the sun. If I crash this car and it explodes, that will take care of my problems too."

His eyes brightened with expectation when he thought about how he might be dead in a moment. But the miles rolled past him uneventfully. He was in his element. He'd always thought of his body as lacking, but his reflexes were excellent behind the wheel. For a guy who couldn't stumble his way across the floor of an eatery, he was capable of fast braking and holding the road around turns. It was as if he'd been transformed. Freedom from a miserable life became a life-changing miracle drug for body and soul.

If only it could be bottled and sold at every local pharmacy, the whole world could find some peace.

A voice shattered his hopeful musings.

"This isn't right, Arel!"

He glanced over at the passenger seat and nearly lost control of the car. Abrigail sat a couple of feet away. Her unexpected intrusion into his euphoric world made him swerve and hit the rutted shoulder. His body went into immediate survival mode, overriding his death wish. As his hands clutched the wheel and managed to get the car back onto the highway, an explosive anger was building in his gut.

"You're not supposed to be here!" he yelled, giving the angel another fleeting glance. His entire body joined him in a rigid spasm of resentment. "How dare you interfere with my decision? Leave, now!"

"I can't! I've come for your help," Abrigail insisted.

His resentment turned into a rising, outburst of temper. He pushed the car harder. The readings on the speedometer climbed obediently. At least his vehicle responded to his wants.

Abrigail continued. "That woman that you met, Peggy, has had an accident. She's in the hospital. She's asking for you. Arel, you have to turn back."

"I don't care! This is my life, and I'm ending it today!"

He kept his eyes forward, focused on his task. He was a seeker of freedom, a person who'd been tested to his limits and found a way to have peace at long last. No angel was going to take that away from him.

Abrigail responded with a short statement. "The sun isn't going to kill you, Arel!"

At first, he couldn't decipher what Abrigail was telling him. "What?" he screamed back.

"It's true. The sun won't harm you."

"What?" This time his one-word question was barely whispered. Like someone believing the world was flat and seeing a picture of the Earth from space, he was left breathless. Ability was replaced by a numbing failure to think clearly. In the span of a few moments, he went from skilled driver to incompetent dunce. The distance between his belief and Abrigail's factual statement was too great. His only option was to ease his foot off the gas petal and steer the car to the side of the road.

Abrigail kept trying to explain. "It's good news, dearest!"

He didn't want to listen to her. As the car slowed down, his hands were white-knuckled on the steering wheel. "Good news? I'm totally screwed!"

If Abrigail was telling the truth, and of course angels didn't lie, Michael's blood was working, working to keep him earthbound, working to keep him a prisoner forever.

Abrigail reached out to him. "It's what you've wanted all along. You're not cursed anymore. You don't need blood. You can go to the beach if you want."

He paused. Abrigail had a point. He had wanted to rid himself of the curse. So why wasn't he happy that he'd gotten his wish? Why did he feel cheated by what Abrigail was telling him?

"But I'm still not normal. I know it! Maybe I'm not a vampire like I was, but I can't function properly. Everything is out of control.

I feel like something is driving me just like I'm driving this car. It's always pushing me, and I can't put on the brakes. I'm crashing constantly."

"I know that change can feel scary. Try to have faith in what's happening to you."

He glared back. "If I'm not a vampire and I'm not normal anymore, what am I?"

Abrigail hesitated. "You're in an iffy stage."

"That's not an answer! Tell me what I am?"

"I can't. I'm sorry, but Michael doesn't know what form this process will take, what will happen exactly." She paused and smiled at him. "He's kind of winging it."

Her sweet tone was a sharp stick on his fragile nerves. As soon as the angel showed up, his body became its edgy, anxious self again. "What do you mean he's winging it? And why are you smiling at a time like this?"

"Notice the phrase 'winging it'? Michael said you'd like us to use more humor."

His mouth gaped. "If that's angel humor, heaven help all of you."

"Sorry. I guess I don't have the hang of what makes humans laugh."

"Laugh? Now? The one night that I get the courage to finish it, you come and tell me that I'm what, an experiment gone wrong? A hybrid? Like one of Michael's roses?"

He'd been clutching the steering wheel. As he talked to Abrigail, his fingers closed tighter. When he tried to let go, something gave way inside of him. He felt like he was letting go of his last shred of hope. "Lord give me strength," he moaned.

"The Lord is giving you strength, Arel. Haven't you noticed that you're stronger now? When you really decide to do something, look at how it changes you. And I'm here, aren't I? I'll help you."

Abrigail's sweet offer, meant to be caring, forced him from his seat. He might not be able to transport himself to freedom, but he didn't have to listen to more angelic ideas about how fortunate he was. He exited the Mustang, slammed the door, and started walking.

He'd been wrong to ask for strength. Strength meant that he'd suffer longer. As for angel humor, both Abrigail and Michael were hopeless when it came to understanding the human condition and how to comment on it. All that they could do was smile and tell him that everything was going to be okay. It was complete nonsense.

He'd been a wreck forever, and his ship was finally going down for the last time. Maybe he wouldn't die, but at this point, he welcomed insanity. To be divorced from reality, weaving baskets in a quiet, padded cell might have been scary when he first started the purge. Now it drew him in with its simplicity. And it was certainly better than knowing that he'd tried his best and couldn't manage five minutes in a diner. No, his mind was not his friend. Perhaps he could request a lobotomy.

As he made his way along a field, he heard Abrigail calling out to him. When he didn't answer her, he heard her calling out for assistance, for Michael.

He stopped and braced himself against his knees. He'd been letting himself vent, but the truth was that he wasn't going to walk his way to freedom. He was already getting tired after five minutes. The only sane thing to do was turn around.

Twenty-Eight

IT WAS STILL dark outside, and the white center line on the highway was a steady marker as the Mustang made its way back to Chicago. Arel was driving, but he had the top back up on the convertible. With the thrill of freedom dashed, he had the cruise control set to the speed limit. His face adopted a stony expression as Michael continued to reason with him from the passenger seat.

"Let's look at the bright side again," Michael said. "As Abrigail reminded you earlier, tonight should be a wonderful sign that you are capable of feeling happiness. And your body responded, didn't it? You even felt strong again."

Arel could feel Michael's bright, blue eyes bearing down on him, trying to shift him out of his gloomy mood. Instead, he kept his narrowed gaze on the road. He'd be the model driver. He'd maintain perfect posture, with two hands on the wheel, and use his mirrors to check on traffic, but he wouldn't be pulled back into Michael's world again.

Michael countered Arel's silence with a deep sigh. "Okay, do you want me to agree with you?" he asked solemnly. "Do you want me to say that you're right about it all, that I should join you in defeat? I didn't think that I'd ever stoop to being negative, dear friend, but maybe that's what you want."

Michael's depressed tone and his threat were unexpected and unwelcome. Arel might be ready for basket weaving, but there was no way, he'd allow Michael to follow in his footsteps. He scowled back. "Go negative? You? Oh no you won't!" he shouted. "And do you know why you won't?"

Michael shrugged. "Why?"

"Because I'll be the one that gets blamed for it. I can hear your cronies now. 'Michael got bit by a vampire, and now he's going to hell in a handcart! Gone all negative. Arel wrecked a big shot angel.'"

Michael stared back at him, first with raised brows, followed by a large grin, followed by a loud outburst of laughter.

"Oh stop it! It wasn't that funny."

"I can't help it," Michael insisted. His usually calm eyes were glassy with mirth. "This is why I could never give up on you."

"What do you mean?"

"You're sitting there feeling very down and disappointed, but you wouldn't tolerate my giving up for an instant, would you?"

Arel looked at Michael again. The angel's face was bright and encouraging, like always. "No, of course not, because I know you've tried too, Michael. You've done your best to help me."

"We've both done our best. It wasn't easy for you to go to that diner. It took a lot of courage, more courage than you realize."

"I don't know. It was a diner."

Michael patted Arel's shoulder. "You cared about Carol sitting there and worrying, admit it. You wanted to put her mind at ease because you're a good man, Arel, even if you don't think so."

Michael's reassuring touch and comforting words reminded Arel of their bond, their friendship. "We make a good pair, don't we? An angel who won't give up, and a guy who's scared of just about everything."

"A guy who was determined to rid himself of a curse no matter what hell it meant he'd have to face."

Arel laughed. "I was sick of rats, that's all."

"No more rats, and now you can check out the garden."

"Before we talk about that, Abrigail said something about Carol's friend."

"Peggy," Michael offered. "She was in an accident. She's in the hospital."

"How bad was she hurt?"

"All that I can tell you is that she wants to see you."

"Well, forget that. She's dangerous." He thought about his hand. Even if the sun couldn't harm him, Peggy could.

"She affected you that way because of your fear. But she needs your help to get over her own. She's in pain, and you can help if you'll go and visit her."

"And you can guarantee that I'll be safe around her."

"You have to believe in yourself, Arel, like you did tonight. You went past your fears."

"I guess, but even if I did go to see this woman, how would I say that I got the news?"

"Carol sent you an e-mail."

"And of course you read it?"

Michael smiled. "I don't have to read your e-mail to know things."

He glanced at Michael again. "Knowing things seems to be an off and on thing with you. Are you sure about the sun not frying me to a crisp? It would be ironic if I agreed not to kill myself, and then I became a piece of burnt toast the first time I stepped out for a peek of sunshine."

Michael gave Arel's shoulder another sound shaking. "I'll prove it to you."

Twenty-Nine

DID AREL REALLY trust Michael's theory that the sun wouldn't harm him? His answer was standard issue. "Hell no!"

But Michael's enthusiasm was at a peak. Arel had never seen the angel show such an outward display of happiness. Michael had always been kind and caring, but he maintained a rather serene, easy-does-it attitude. That suddenly changed when they were in the car, coming back to Chicago. Michael had actually laughed, out loud! Later, when they talked, Michael smiled broadly, and he made it clear that he was very proud of Arel. It was such a fatherly gesture, such a pure and genuine tribute that Arel felt compelled to let the angel have his due. Michael wanted to prove that Arel was free to live in the sun again. And Arel had finally agreed. He'd visit Michael's garden.

Still, when Arel was getting ready for the big event, he knew there was one issue that Michael hadn't addressed. Michael had no idea about what Arel was becoming. Arel wasn't nearly as confused. His place in the grand scheme of things was perfectly clear. When he looked in the mirror and a pathetic, wasted face looked back, he labeled himself in scientific terms. Two words clearly described his state. He was a lab rat. If he wanted to glorify his position and put Michael's angelic blood into the mix, he could add a word. He was the Creator's lab rat. And now that rat was being placed in a very dangerous situation.

Arel's only choice had been to take measures into his own hands. He would test the sun, but he'd experience its rays with prudence. He put on numerous, thick layers of protective clothing and a winter jacket. He'd even found a pith helmet to wear, scrounged from his African collection. Opaque sun glasses added a final touch. As he trudged towards the back door, he felt like a 'great white hunter' who was joining a polar exploration. But he didn't care how ridiculous he looked, at least he'd have some measure of safety when he was blasted by solar rays.

* * *

Arel stood in the kitchen, looking out the back door. There wasn't a cloud in the sky. The sun was at its zenith. Its fiery light was there for every flower and blade of grass. The setting was exactly what he'd prayed for when he wanted to die. Now he was holding on to life again, hoping he was over the worst of the purge, wondering if another surprise was waiting for him.

His body agreed with his mental reservations. It wouldn't move. When he tried to take a step forward, his feet felt leaden and weighted. He glanced at Abrigail. "I think my body knows I shouldn't do this."

"I believe your body needs your encouragement," Abrigail coaxed. "It needs its captain to tell it that all is going to be fine."

"Captain?" Arel's mind scrambled to understand her point. He'd never thought of himself as a man in charge of a sea vessel, but his feet did feel like a couple of ship anchors.

Abrigail continued to explain. "You have to have a positive attitude so that your body feels safe."

"How can I have a positive attitude? Neither you nor Michael know anything for sure. This could be a big mistake."

Michael came forward. "I do know some things, and I know you'll be fine."

Before Arel could reply, he saw Michael give Abrigail a signal. "What are you doing?"

Instead of answering him, each angel took hold of an arm. They began to edge him, inch by inch, out the back door.

Arel instantly braced booted feet out in front of him. "Are you crazy?" he yelled. He suddenly trusted his body more than the angels. He resisted their efforts with every ounce of strength he had. But he didn't have a chance of holding back. Angels, even slim ones like Abrigail seemed capable of incredible brawn. Of course he was in pathetic shape. At this point, he probably couldn't resist an eighty year old granny.

As soon as he was outside and the first ray of sun hit him, Arel knew he was lost. He heard himself let out a scream of panic. His banshee shriek was followed by a loud assessment of his condition. "I'm burning up! Too hot! You bastard, Michael, I'm going to die!"

Abrigail seemed to find his protests amusing. He could see that she was restraining her urge to smile. "You'll be sorry that you laughed when I'm dead!"

"You're okay," Michael said in a soothing voice. "You're wearing too many layers of clothing for such a warm, pleasant day. You're overheating."

Arel was desperate to make himself heard. "You know nothing, nothing!"

Abrigail clung to Arel's arm as he struggled against her efforts to propel him forward. "You've already been out here for a few seconds, dearest. And look, you're not being harmed at all."

"The sun hasn't touched my skin! That's why I'm fine," he cried.

Abrigail frowned back. "But Arel—"

"Face it, you two don't know anything about vampires, do you?"

"I've been observing one up close for quite a while," Michael said. "Besides, this is what you were going to do anyway, out in the Illinois cornfields."

"That was different. Now it's all iffy."

Michael frowned. "I think we need to get through this a little more quickly. Your body temperature is beginning to soar from all your fear and the clothes."

Arel saw the look in Michael's eyes, that 'let's take it to the next level' look. "Please! I can't do it!" he screamed again.

"Start by taking off a glove," Abrigail said.

Arel gasped. "No! I need my hands. I can't type without my hands."

Michael paused and stared at him. It was time enough to allow Arel to think there was hope after all, that the angel had changed his mind. He started to turn around when the unthinkable happened. Michael reached over and removed the heavy helmet from his head, plucked it away with a swift hand, exposing his dark, sweaty hair and pale, white face.

"No!" Arel only had time to scream out the one word. As soon as the helmet was off, the sun hit him with its powerful, high noon rays. The blazing flash of light short circuited his brain. Everything began to spin. The spinning rapidly turned into total blackness. As his legs lost all strength, he pitched forward in a heated faint.

***

Arel opened his eyes and saw heaven. There were angels around him. They didn't have wings, but they were glowing, just like the beautiful trees in the background. The music of heaven consisted of birdsong. There was also a fiery orb. Heaven even had a sun shining down on him.

"Oh well," he said dreamily. "I forgive Michael. Burnt toast or not, I made it to the Garden of Eden."

"You're burning up," the lady angel said. She looked a lot like Abrigail.

"Yes," he muttered back as he squinted at her. "Heaven is a little warm. But it's still pretty."

He continued to enjoy the blue skies and the lovely flowers blooming in profusion all around him. As he gazed blissfully at his new surroundings, heaven turned into a flood. Water poured down on him in a deluge as the male angel emptied a bucket over his head.

"Sorry, Arel, you were overheating," the male angel said. "I had to cool you off quickly."

Arel sputtered and tried to breathe, but he was so relieved to be dead. Perhaps, the water dousing was a heavenly baptism. "Very refreshing," he coughed as he was pulled to his feet. Heavenly conduct was unusual, but he supposed that was because it was heaven. He smiled broadly. "I can't believe it. I finally made it. Do I have wings?" The two angels who had helped him up were dragging him towards a familiar looking structure. "Gee, heaven has a house for me, just like the one I had on earth."

A moment later, as he was led inside the structure, he couldn't see anything. He was in total darkness. He was also suddenly aware of how hot he was. Perhaps he'd been too optimistic. Perhaps he was being taken to hell. "No! I won't go! Take me back to the light!"

He heard the lady angel talking to someone. "I'm concerned. He seems so disoriented."

The male angel answered her. "Sunstroke could be his next trick."

"He'll do anything to escape, won't he?"

"Sunstroke? In heaven?" Arel asked with a rising panic.

"I think it's time to bend a few rules," the male angel said.

* * *

When Arel woke up a second time, he wasn't in heaven anymore. He was in his bed, under a lightweight sheet. "That was quite a dream I had." He remembered flashes of brilliant light, glowing flowers and trees, and a couple of angels. There was also a part where he was thrown into darkness. He'd never felt so hot. Thankfully, he didn't remember anything after that. In contrast, he felt quite comfortable now. In fact, he felt better than he had in a long time. No headache or shakes. The room was dimly lit and quiet. He was just thinking about going back to sleep when he saw a stranger sitting on a chair in the corner. Grasping at the sheet, he pulled it close. "Who are you, and how did you get in here?"

The woman got up and came over to the bed. "Hello, my name is Glory."

He moaned when he got a good look at his visitor. "Oh great, you're another of Michael's friends, aren't you?"

The woman smiled. "Yes, I am."

Arel was accustomed to being around angels. Michael and Abrigail appeared solid and as physical as any normal person. But the woman in front of him was the real thing, an angel who looked like an angel. She glowed brightly around the edges, and her form shimmered in and out. Tall and beautiful, with sparkling, spun gold hair, she was outfitted in a warrior's garment, complete with gleaning breast plate and a golden sword by her side.

After he studied her for a long moment, he decided that he approved of her appearance. As a child, he loved books and stories about knights, noble ideals and chivalry. This angel would fit into that world very nicely if she stabilized her form a bit. What he didn't appreciate was another angel invading his space uninvited.

The angel seemed to understand his feelings. "I'm sorry if I surprised you."

"What do you want?"

"Peggy could use your help. I was hoping that you could visit her as soon as possible."

"Why? I don't even know the woman."

"I can't explain the situation. You'll have to talk to her. My purpose is to make sure that you know how important this matter is. I'm looking forward to seeing you at the hospital."

He rubbed his brow. "Oh yes, the hospital. I forgot."

"She'll be so relieved to see you."

He was about to protest, but the regal angel was already fading from sight.

Abrigail walked into the room a moment later. "Feeling better?"

He answered with a scowl. "I had a visitor."

"Yes, Peggy's angel." Abrigail came up to his bedside and took his hand. "Dearest, I know this is a lot to ask, but Peggy is really having a terrible time. It would mean the world to her if you'd visit."

The serious nature of the request was obvious, but Arel hated the idea of seeing Carol's friend again. "I don't know—"

"Glory wouldn't ask if it wasn't urgent."

He wanted to protest, but then he remembered how many times, he'd been helped recently. He thought about his decision to go to bed forever, and how Abrigail treated him like the loving mother he'd never had. It seemed that it was payback time. "Fine, I suppose I could look in on her."

"Wonderful," Abrigail said with a smile.

He remembered something that brought a smile to his face too. "I had the strangest dream. I went to heaven." He glanced up at Abrigail. "Did you know that they baptize you as soon as you arrive?"

"I'm sorry, Arel, but that wasn't heaven," Michael said as he came in and joined Abrigail by the bedside.

Arel greeted him with a deeper scowl than the one he gave Abrigail. "It was my dream, Michael. I think I can remember my own dream."

"And it wasn't a baptism," Michael continued. "But that's not important now. I'm afraid the hospital visit is a priority."

"Fine, when are evening visiting hours?" Arel glanced over at his bedside clock. "Eight? Eight thirty?"

"You can go right now," Abrigail offered.

He snorted at her. "I think you're forgetting something. It's two in the afternoon." He stared at them expectantly. "The vampire thing . . . I can't leave the house until dark."

Abrigail glanced at Michael and pulled him aside. "Oh my, I think Arel's in denial about what he experienced today. That doesn't mean we have to do it all over again, do we?"

Michael shrugged. "Do you have a better idea?"

As Arel listened to their conversation, his mind dredged up some very strange images. A bizarre looking human, bundled and wrapped like a Pillsbury dough boy gone safari. Michael throwing a bucket of water on the guy. The guy screaming his head off as he sat in the dark, feeling hotter than Hades.

The images all began to gel into a continuous pattern of events. The events became a picture of what he'd gone through earlier. How could he have forgotten such a horrid experience? "Dammit," he yelled. "I'm the guy you tried to kill with the sun, Michael. When that didn't finish me off, you tried to drown me! What kind of angel are you?"

Michael returned a rare frown. "Our intentions were similar. You've often said that you wanted your life back. This was an opportunity. I wanted you to know how well you're doing, to prove that you're moving in the right direction. But things escalated very quickly when your fears took over."

"So it's my fault that I'm a little concerned after all these years of knowing the sun could kill me?" Arel turned to Abrigail. "And you were laughing at me!"

Abrigail stepped back. "You looked so adorable with the helmet and those sunglasses. I'm sorry."

Michael put a hand on the bed and offered one of his most winning smiles. "On the bright side, or should I say the sunny side of things, you're now free to enjoy my garden anytime you wish."

"Did you say sunny side?" Arel glared back. "I have an announcement, Michael. You may be the Creator's right hand man, you may be wise and caring, but as far as humor goes, you better go back to being serious."

Michael retrieved his hand. "Right. I'm glad you said that. There are more important things to attend to than visiting my garden. It's time for you to get dressed for your hospital visit."

Thirty

AREL HAD SEEN hospitals on TV. That was one type of experience, sort of like seeing a war zone on the news. But to be placed in the middle of a battle, or in his case, a hospital, was appalling. As he walked down the wide, cavernous hallways, his first reaction was to gag.

His scented handkerchief offered a small comfort. He held it close to his nose, trying to avoid breathing in the disinfectants and other strange, medicinal odors. Still, he couldn't escape the large, florescent lit corridors. His eyes flitted over the sterile space, looking for a bit of softness or beauty. He was rewarded with pasty green walls and a slumped over wheelchair patient hooked up to an IV.

"Couldn't I have just called Peggy?" he whispered to Michael. The angel was walking slightly behind him.

Before Michael could answer, a small group of people suddenly came out of a room they were passing. Arel nearly collided with a middle-aged lady and jumped aside. "Sorry," he said as he backed away. The woman was dabbing at her eyes when their gaze connected. The woman's eyes offered him a deep down bleakness he'd known on the dreariest, grey days of winter. It seemed to be connected to someone she loved. As she moved on, he glanced in the room she'd just exited. A man lay in the bed surrounded by medical equipment. He was deathly pale and unmoving.

"Oh hell, that guy isn't going to make it much longer, is he?"

Abrigail was walking next to him. She took his hand. "Come along, dearest."

Arel obeyed, but his gut was doing some kind of belly dance of woe. Sickness and misery hung in the air. It seemed to saturate the walls themselves.

"Now might be a good time to put those shields in place," Michael suggested.

"Tell me again, what am I doing in this horrid place? Never mind, I know the answer. Where else would a lab rat be?"

"You're only feeling the negative," Abrigail said softly. "If you let yourself feel the healing parts of—"

Michael cut in. "Actually, it's best if Arel just focuses on not feeling right now."

Arel ignored both of them. He had no patience for advice. "Let's just get it over with."

"It's better if you go in alone," Michael said quietly. "Peggy wants to see you, not two strangers."

Arel gave Michael a petitioning look for mercy. "What? Go in by myself?"

"You don't have to stay very long."

"I hate this!"

Michael gave him an understanding nod. "I know."

"Like hell you do!" Arel's voice was a sharp whisper as he took a final, deep breath of air through his handkerchief. With a shaky hand, he removed it from his face and peeked into the room.

Oh, thank goodness!

Glory, Peggy's angel, smiled back at him from her bedside post. Still dressed in dazzling, etheric armor, she projected so much strength and compassion that he found himself completely taken with the sight of her. With a face that shone brighter than her golden breast plate, she was a wondrous vision who personified the term 'guardian' angel.

Finally, there's something of beauty to see in this place.

It helped him to forge ahead, to walk over to the hospital bed. Of course, he had his orders to ignore Glory since Peggy couldn't see her. But he wished he could simply look at the angel instead of the person he'd come to see. His earlier experience with Peggy in the diner still made him shudder. Now he was on his own. Not even Carol was there to act as an intermediary.

Glory's gentle voice sounded in his mind.

Try to put your fears aside. You know how to be a friend! That's what she needs.

He couldn't believe how much she could affect him. Her words seemed to strengthen his whole body and help to clear his mind.

Maybe it was because she was a more angelic example of heavenly help. He'd begun to think of Michael as more earthly. It was probably a mistake on his part, but there wasn't anything to do about it now.

Glory smiled broadly again. He saw her energy expand like a big bubble of pink light that encapsulated him and helped him to approach the bed. With a quiet sigh, he looked down at the bed's occupant.

Bloody hell!

As soon as he saw Peggy, he forgot about himself and stared at the fragile, pale girl who lay on the bed. The pretty, perky looking woman from the night before was gone. The new version of Peggy looked awful. And she was in pain, lots of pain. It radiated out from her in waves that hit him in his gut. His solar plexus went from belly dancing over his hospital woes to a frantic pulse of alarm.

He instinctively knew he should heed his gut's warning. His hand went to his pocket, wanting desperately to use the handkerchief again, not for his nose, but to push back the sick feeling that took hold of him. As he paused, trying to collect himself, Peggy opened her eyes.

"Arel? Is it really you?" Her gaze immediately locked on his face with a pathetic fierceness, but her voice trembled when she spoke.

Be a friend like Glory said!

He had to give himself the silent order to keep from running from the room. He tried to smile, but he couldn't manage it. "I'm sorry about your accident."

"It was my fault, all my fault."

Peggy's admission of guilt made him forget her condition as the diner scene replayed itself in his mind.

Yes! You burned me!

He wanted to chastise her, to tell her that she had no right to touch him ever again, but when he came back to the moment, he couldn't. It would be like yelling at a frightened child.

"I didn't brake in time," she continued.

His mind calmed down enough to know what Peggy was really telling him.

She's not talking about hurting you, she's talking about the accident, you idiot.

Still, he couldn't escape Peggy's eyes. They were pools of regret.

Peggy stirred a little and winced. "I'm so glad that you could come. I was worried about you after our meeting."

He let out his breath cautiously. Could she really care about him? "No problem."

"Last night, I was too forward. It's the way I am sometimes. I want to say that I'm sorry. I hope you won't hold it against me."

He watched her hand move ever so slightly towards him and pull back.

He sighed. Some inner need to be gracious made him reply appropriately. "No, it wasn't you. I was a complete fool."

Peggy stared back, looking red-eyed and ready to cry, but she tightened her jaw instead. "I want you to know that if you need a friend, I'm here for you. Promise me that you'll remember that."

Peggy's voice was so genuine that he felt his face warm with shame. He'd made all kinds of judgments about her. He'd thought the worst, while she was all sweetness and concern. Reaching in his pocket, retrieving his spare handkerchief, he quickly handed it to her. "Please don't upset yourself." He didn't know why, but he wouldn't be able to stand it if she really started bawling. He needed to reverse time and have the spunky, brasher version of Peggy back. It would be so much easier to push her away if she wasn't so exposed and hurting. "Don't worry about me," he said, forcing a smile. "You need to take care of yourself."

Peggy frowned, squeezing her eyes shut.

He could feel her fighting her pain. "Should I call someone to help you?"

She relaxed a little and looked at him again. "Just give me a moment. I have a case of whiplash from last night's incident. Such a stupid thing. I wasn't paying attention."

"Sometimes things happen. You shouldn't keep blaming yourself."

"Please, if possible, could you come back to see me again?"

Peggy's request was delivered in a pleading tone. He tried to resist it, but it was like resisting a stormy wave, crashing into him. He was carried to a place where he had to try and relieve her suffering. He went into auto-mode, reaching out and putting his hand on hers. There was searing pain, but he was in a place far removed from the hospital room. In that place, if sacrifice was needed, he had to endure.

I'll do my best to help you.

He knew that he was making a silent vow to her. No, he was repeating a vow. It was an old, ancient promise, and its memory opened some portal between them. He felt himself drawing her torment into himself. A flash of grief, then shooting pain invaded his body. Absolute misery followed.

Glory stepped forward and broke the connection between them. *Stop taking on Peggy's pain! It's not what's wanted.*

Her order brought Arel back to his senses. He realized how close he'd come to some terrible fate. He nervously backed away from the bed. "I have to go," he muttered, moving hastily towards the door.

* * *

As soon as Arel left, Peggy felt the tears return. She'd been crying ever since the incident in the car. But she hadn't been sure if her feelings were real. Maybe they were based on some horrid nightmare that surfaced from seeing a movie at the age of four. That's why she needed to see Arel again. Was there a bond between them? Were her feelings based on fact or fantasy?

When Arel appeared at her bedside, she'd made herself control her inner grief. She was afraid she'd scare him away otherwise. While her present emotional chaos was something unusual, she was sure his phobic responses were a more permanent feature of his personality. He was definitely a wounded, scarred person.

What if she was to blame? What if she had somehow betrayed him ages ago, and he'd never recovered? Was it possible for that type of bond to persist for lifetimes?

What am I thinking? I don't even believe in other lifetimes!

Maybe not, maybe she would only live the one life, but when Arel stepped inside the hospital room and came up to her bedside, all reason and all doubt about what she'd seen vanished.

Oh my god, he is the same man that was in my vision.

It wasn't just that he had the same fine features, the same gentle mannerisms, the same slightly, sagging shoulders. It was something so much deeper. Could people's hearts communicate with one another? She didn't have rational answers when he stood by her bedside.

But I know this man.

She knew his eyes. She knew that they'd once looked at her with only love. A crazy, but absolute feeling of certainty and fact put her doubt to rest.

He was my brother once, my protector . . . until I betrayed him, and even then he didn't blame me.

She tried to sit up and the spasms in her neck and back went into a tortured frenzy. Perhaps she deserved it. Maybe it was a punishment for what she'd done to him. She wanted to start sobbing again, but she knew that wasn't the answer. She had to think about what was best for Arel.

You haven't changed, have you, brother?

When he visited her, he'd reached out to her, touched her so compassionately. He'd sacrificed himself for her again. She knew it. For a moment, he took away all her pain.

No! That's not what I want between us!

She hated the idea that misery still connected them. She wanted a bond of love. It already existed in her heart, but it was clear that Arel was afraid to link himself to her. And why shouldn't he be afraid after what he went through long ago and even now?

She clutched at his handkerchief, bringing it to her face to swipe at the steady stream that wet her cheeks. As she inhaled the cologne that scented the linen cloth, its wonderful woodsy spice fragrance interrupted her pain. Her mind quieted a little. In that still space, she got a brief glimpse into their shared past. In a time that seemed forever gone, she saw a handsome, young man, embracing life with open arms, dancing with her, cheering her up when she was sad, always so strong. That was Arel's true nature, and it was up to her to help him find it again.

Thirty-One

AREL PAID NO attention to Abrigail or Michael even though they were following him down the hospital hallway. He had lied to Peggy. He wasn't coming back.

Get out of this place. Drive back home, lock the doors, and never leave your safe haven again.

He did make one stop at the nurses' station, to report Peggy's condition to the nurse in charge.

She gave him a happy smile. "Are you Arel?"

"Yes," he frowned. "How did you know?"

"That young lady you asked about has refused pain medication all day. She insisted that she had to be clear headed if you came in. I'm so glad that you made it."

He gave her a weak nod. "Me too." Another lie.

Moving away from the station at a brisk pace, he headed for the elevators. Once he reached them, he didn't have to wait long for one of them to ding out its arrival. He retreated back when its doors opened. There was a hospital bed inside, with a young nurse standing close by.

"I can take the next one," he insisted nervously.

If you think I'm going to join you in that little cramped box, and be forced to look at another sick person, think again.

The old lady on the bed caught his eye. "Please come in. I need a little company," she said with a weak smile.

Damn! Damn! Damn! Be nice. She's old.

His head sagged to his chest as he walked into the elevator, moving to the back so that Abrigail and Michael had room too.

"You go ahead," Michael said. "We'll take the next one."

He tried to give them one of his most hateful looks, but the doors glided shut before he could put the full impact of his wrath into it.

The old woman on the stretcher gave him another caring smile that made him regret his display.

"I won't bite," she whispered as she watched him move more tightly into the corner. He was practically hugging the wall.

She put her hand out to him. It was withered, spotted and bent with age and arthritis. Her skin was translucent, allowing the veins beneath to stand out blue. She was deeply bruised from so many IVs.

"Come here, young man," she demanded sweetly.

His hackles went up. Someone else wanted to touch him. But the woman's voice and kindly face reminded him of the grandmother who had visited him on a couple of occasions when he was a young boy. She was one of the few, bright spots in his childhood. Being held in her arms after a nightmare was a rare comfort. He'd never forgotten her.

The memory and duty propelled him forward. His angst made him grit his teeth. If only he could let out the primal scream that lived in his gut. If only he could find a way to let everyone in the world know how hard it was to be alive. But instead of screaming, he put his hand out too, letting the old woman take it. Her grasp was fragile. She wasn't like Peggy. He felt safer in her hands.

"Oh my," she exclaimed. "You're so cold."

He tried to pull away, his face going red with embarrassment. Why wasn't Michael's blood warming him? Why was it making him cold like some hideous reptile? Then he remembered how hot he'd been earlier when he'd overdressed and the sun nearly roasted his brain. He couldn't win.

"It's okay," the woman said quietly, as if she understood his plight. "You just need some mothering, you poor thing."

He brightened at her words. He was a poor thing. Why didn't the angelic forces recognize that? Why didn't they protect him from sick people?

"You're very kind," he replied, praying that the elevator would reach his floor soon. The old woman was nice, but he needed to escape, to get away from neediness and the woes of ailing people.

The old woman stared at him with cloudy, blue eyes. They seemed to hold a lifetime of memories and wisdom behind their failing sight. But now she used them to probe Arel's own golden gaze.

"You have lovely eyes, young man." She hesitated, still probing. "Sad eyes."

He let out a soft protest.

Tell me something that I don't know.

She let go of him, pulling her weak arm back with difficulty as if it weighed far too much for her to maneuver.

He reached out to help, again without thinking. He lifted her hand and arm with careful touch and pressure. He didn't want to bruise her further as he placed her arm on the bed.

She gave him another smile. "Thank you, dear. I'm Mrs. Hayes. I'm on the cardiac floor. If you need someone to talk to, come see me."

As she spoke there was a stopping motion. The elevator doors began to function. When they opened, he felt like Peggy had looked when he visited her. He wanted to cry, but his would be sobs of relief.

"Goodbye," he said hastily, walking away as fast as social graces would permit. Once clear of the doors, he practically ran down the hall towards the exit and the parking garage.

Michael and Abrigail's elevator arrived soon after his. They did double time trying to catch up with him.

"We're coming, dearest!" Abrigail said as she ran.

He glanced back at them as they caught up, but he didn't slow his pace. "I feel like a damned candy striper. People are grabbing me from every direction. Everyone wants me to visit them. And you two are horrible. You're never there when I need you!"

He slammed open the doors to the garage and hurried into its darkness.

"Slow down," Abrigail called out. "This is a busy place."

Ignoring her, he sprinted for the Mustang. He was inhaling forcefully, trying to get the hospital smell out of his nasal passages. Car fumes were far superior to the clean stuff he'd just been subjected to.

Following him into the garage, Abrigail made a comment to Michael that he overheard. "Arel looks like he's feeling stronger."

Her words were like a match on dry tinder, making him come to a full stop in the middle of the lane. "Stronger? Is that what you call—?"

His question was cut short by a fast moving car swinging around the corner of the garage. Brakes squealed as the driver tried to avoid hitting him.

Bloody hell!

His legs were welded to the spot. Any ability to leap out of harm's way failed him. His traumatized mind overrode his reflexes. Still, the car stopped before it collided into him. It was a small miracle since it was going too fast to brake in time to avoid him.

"I'm sorry!" the woman shouted from inside the car.

Practically riding the hood of the vehicle and grabbing his heart, he saw his life flash in front of him. He despised every minute. What a pathetic recall. Something had to change.

Engaging the woman's eyes with his own, he held up a hand, trying to find his legs, trying to move out of the car's path. His face was still frozen, but he was livid with indignation, cursing silently with expletives that would have burned the driver's ears if he'd been able to give them voice.

Abrigail joined him, taking his arm as he staggered to safety. "Are you alright?"

"I'm done with you, with this Peggy person and all the rest," he replied. "Not heaven or hell is getting me out of my house again."

"Even if you don't think so, we're watching out for you," Michael said calmly.

Arel glanced at the angel and understood. Michael had stopped the car that almost hit him. Now Michael's kind eyes reminded Arel of those of the old lady in the elevator. The truth came through in a rush of clarity. Michael wasn't his enemy.

But I can't seem to stop putting him and everybody else in that role.

By the time that he got to the car, his anger was replaced by weariness. He leaned on the side of the Mustang for support. "I'm sorry for blaming you all the time. That car almost hit me because of my own stupidity."

"You've had a difficult day."

Arel shook his head. "I'm so tired of hearing myself complain, and I don't know why I keep reacting like I do." As he spoke, he put his hand to his heart again, trying to rub away the heaviness sitting on his chest. "Peggy was sweet, but to be around her . . . I can't." He looked up at Michael. "It's all too much. I don't understand any of it." He reached into his pocket and pulled out his car keys. "Here, you drive. I'm too tired."

* * *

Michael pulled into the garage and turned off the engine. It had been a quiet ride back from the hospital. Arel fell asleep shortly after they were on their way. He was still slumbering in the passenger seat, still clutching at his chest. His brows were drawn together as his breath rose and fell in a shallow, uneven rhythm.

"He does look like a poor thing," Abrigail whispered from the back seat.

Michael sighed, agreeing with her. Physically, Arel was worn down and exhausted. His battered heart was hanging in there, but the emotional trauma that it was being dealt was overwhelming it's already unstable function. Michael was reluctant to discuss the fact with Arel. The man already had too much on his mind.

Another serious concern was Arel's energy field. Ideally, it should have been an illumined, sparkling sphere of light. Instead, it was dense and heavy with large patches of muddied darkness. An aura of tragedy and persecution followed him from one lifetime to another. Now, everything he experienced was filtered through its veil of suffering. He'd become humanity's victim. Peggy wasn't someone who could be a source of love. She was a bundle of misery, a bundle of misery that wanted relief.

Abrigail's bright eyes were scanning Arel too. "He shields himself from us, yet he doesn't know how to protect himself from the negative energies of the people that he's around."

"Yes, I know."

"He's also becoming very powerful in some ways. He was only open to Peggy's pain for a moment, yet look how much of it he's absorbed."

"Arel has imagined himself as everyone's whipping boy for a long time. He plays that role very effectively."

"What's going to happen to him? I know that your blood is supposed to help him, but he doesn't know how to use it. Its power is amplifying his experiences."

169

"He'll learn, with our help. You saw how quickly he can recuperate when he's happy."

"You sound encouraged."

"I know him. I know what he's capable of."

Abrigail smiled. "He did look confidant when he was driving to his supposed doom. And he showed a lot of fervor when he thought he was in heaven. He has a way of always surprising me."

Michael smiled too. He wasn't surprised that Arel could show such resilience. He'd been waiting for it, knew it was there if only Arel could get past his self-imposed judgments and one of his biggest hurtles, his fear of betrayal.

He put his hand on Arel's heart, drawing off the new pain, Peggy's pain. As he cleansed the vessel of the newly acquired energies, Arel stirred slightly, letting out a soft groan in his sleep. After a few moments, his face relaxed a little, his brows slowly leveled out.

Michael also attempted to draw off the old, impacted energies in the surrounding areas, but as usual, the barriers that Arel had in place were too strong. Michael's golden light bounced off thick walls of resistance.

"Do you think that he's out of the woods, so to speak?" Abrigail asked.

"Not exactly."

"What does 'not exactly' mean?"

"It means that I think the worst is yet to come."

"I was afraid that you were going to say that, but I have a thought that might help a little. Arel definitely doesn't like our version of humor, but perhaps you can strengthen his own idea of playfulness while he's sleeping."

"I can try, but he might not let me."

Arel carried around his grim attitude like a badge. His laughter was rare, cynical. Still, he was funny. Michael almost laughed again when he thought about their return trip to Chicago and Arel's comebacks, how he refused to let Michael turn to a life of negativity because Michael's 'cronies' would end up blaming Arel.

Sorry, but I only said those things to shake you out of your mood. Just remember, I can never change who I am. And in truth, you can never change who you are. It's all about perception.

"Let's get him to bed so he can rest," Abrigail suggested.

"Yes, I agree." Michael turned to wake up his exhausted passenger, and paused. Arel's slightly grasping fist had fallen unto the center console. It was a skin and bones testament to Arel's staying power. He'd held on through a mother's bitterness, a father's hatred, and his best friend's curse. Now Michael knew that Arel was facing a final trial of fire. "Hold on a little longer. Hold on tight."

Thirty-Two

KEVIN FIDGETED RESTLESSLY in the cramped hospital chair, trying to make his two hundred pound plus, heavy boned frame fit a seat designed for someone much smaller. But hospital seating was the least of his concerns. A soft whimper coming from the bed a few feet away reminded him of why his body was tight with tension and worn from worry. His sister, Peggy, was in trouble, and he didn't know how to help.

What the hell is going on with her?

The question repeated over and over in his mind.

He got up, went to the bed, and grabbed hold of the steel bed rail. His grip tightened as he stared at his sister. He wanted to do what he always did, protect her. But from what? What made her eyes fill with tears when she was awake? Why didn't she talk to him and tell him what was wrong?

The doctors claimed that Peggy didn't appear to be seriously injured, but he knew better. When had his brassy, full-of-advice sister ever refused an opportunity to mouth off with him? When had she ever acted like some weak, pitiful child? She didn't talk or respond to Tim either. That was unusual.

My sister and I don't always communicate well, but Tim has always been able to connect with her.

There was only one person Peggy seemed interested in, some damnable guy named Arel. He already hated the name.

If this guy, Arel, did something to my sister—

He knew he might be wrong in jumping to conclusions, but who else could have made Peggy look like she visited hell and got stuck there? Clenching his jaw, he felt a bristling energy take hold. He needed to put things right, but for now, he had to wait.

He let go of the railing and went back to his seat. Trying to get comfortable again, he looked at his watch and then at the door. At least he wasn't alone in his miserable vigil. Tim had gone on a coffee run, but he'd be back soon. They'd been there for each other since they were kids. Now, Kevin was grateful that they were watching over Peggy together.

* * *

Tim walked quickly down the hospital corridor. He'd traveled the halls numerous times since Peggy's accident. Now as he headed back to her room again, he tried to steady his nerves. The doctors were keeping Peggy another day for some additional tests. In the meantime, he had to stay the course, to stay calm for her sake.

But his fiancé wasn't the only one he had to worry about. Kevin was barely holding it together. Tim recognized his best friend's mood from when they were boys, when Kevin used his fists to help his sister with bullies. Now, that brotherly and volatile part of Kevin's personality was active again. It didn't come out very often, but when it did, look out.

So it's up to me to be the mature one. Dammit!

He didn't feel like being mature. He was worried as hell too. What could have made Peggy go from being her confident self to being totally lost? She'd been in another accident several years before and handled that one like a champ. But this time, she acted like she'd suffered some kind of breakdown. "Just come back to me, sweetie," he whispered almost like a prayer.

When he got back to her room, he could be grateful for one thing. Peggy was sleeping. The meds that she'd finally agreed to take were working. On the other hand, Kevin looked edgy as hell. He sat in a chair by the window. His brows couldn't furrow any deeper, and his fists were clenched tight. Fortunately, he smiled when he saw Tim.

"Great, more coffee," Kevin said in a hushed tone. "Hope it's stronger than the last brew."

Tim walked over and handed him a cup. "I think we've had more of this stuff than we should, but we need something to stay awake."

Kevin started to remove the lid. "Dammit!" he yelped when he spilled some of the scalding liquid on his hand.

"Shh! You'll wake Peggy!" Tim whispered as he quickly retrieved some tissues and handed them to Kevin.

Kevin put the cup down and wiped his hand. "My nerves are shot."

"You have to hold it together. We both do, for Peggy's sake."

Kevin's red rimmed eyes filled with fresh anger. "We need to do more than that. We need to find that guy she was asking for. The damn bastard came and went in the ten minutes I left the room. Can you believe that?"

"Don't blame yourself. You—"

"I'm not! I'm blaming him. How could he be so inconsiderate? He should have stuck around."

Peggy stirred in her sleep, moaning out a protest.

"You have to keep it down," Tim insisted.

Kevin stood up and stared at the bed. "I'm trying, but I'm going nuts wondering what's going on."

"And you think that I'm not?" Tim's tone was curt. He could feel himself losing the maturity battle.

Kevin crossed his arms over his chest. "So what do we do now? I can't keep sitting here doing nothing."

Tim let out a snort of agreement. "We'll come up with something."

Thirty-Three

CAROL WALKED INTO Peggy's room and hesitated. She was reminded of one of those movies where soldiers were waiting to go into battle. Both Tim and Kevin were crouched over in their chairs, clenching their hands, rigid and ready for action. When they glanced up at her, their faces were masks, hard but alert. But this wasn't a scene from a war movie. It was supposed to be a hospital where her friend was recuperating after an accident.

I thought she was going to be fine . . . what's going on?

Carol held on to a large bouquet of flowers as she walked over to Peggy's bed. Her friend's usually bright face was pale and drawn. Even in her sleep, Peggy grimaced and let out little cries of pain. Carol's hand tightened on the flowers as she turned back to the men. "What's wrong with Peggy?"

Tim responded by jumping up, putting a finger to his lips. "Please, we don't want to wake her."

Carol moved away from the bed. As she did, Kevin was also getting to his feet, but this wasn't her Kevin. Like Peggy, he'd changed too. She'd always liked his broad shouldered presence. Now, as he came towards her, his bulk was intimidating.

"We need to talk," he growled as he took her flowers and tossed them on a side table. "Come with me." He grabbed her arm and half pulled her out of the room.

Carol instinctively tried to free herself. "What's going on?"

Kevin let her go when they were in the corridor. His grey eyes had always been warm. But they'd turned stormy and cold.

"That's what I want to know. Tell me what happened to my sister?" he demanded.

Before she could reply, Tim joined them. His eyes weren't as hostile, but it was obvious that he wanted answers too.

Carol backed up, putting some distance between herself and the men. "I thought that you said that Peggy wasn't in any danger."

"The doctor told us that she should be okay, but I'm not sure that's true," Tim said.

Kevin moved closer. "Yeah, we want to know what the hell this guy, Arel, did to her."

Carol couldn't believe that she was being grilled by two men who had always been so nice in the past. "Arel? What does this have to do with him?"

Tim remained stiff. "Kevin and I both feel that she's disturbed about something that happened before the accident. She's insisted on talking to this friend of yours, Arel."

"Yeah, and we want to know why." Kevin's eyes were getting even harder.

Carol shrugged. "I don't know why, but I'm sorry about not being able to take your call earlier. I was in a special workshop all day. I was the presenter. I didn't think this was an emergency."

"You thought wrong," Kevin barked back.

Tim put a hand on his shoulder. "Kevin, it's okay."

Kevin retreated, but he didn't take his eyes off of Carol. She felt like they were an extension of his hands, grabbing hold of her again.

"I don't know what to say. I did send Arel an email asking him to visit Peggy. Did he come by?"

"Yes, but we both missed him," Kevin said.

"It's a shame we couldn't talk to him," Tim added.

"How could Arel have anything to do with this? Peggy met him last night for a few minutes. That was the extent of their contact. When she dropped me off afterwards, she seemed a little bothered about Arel's shy attitude, but we both felt that way."

Tim and Kevin looked at each other, then at her.

"No, he's mixed up in this," Kevin insisted. "You didn't see how crazy Peggy was when we tried to get her mind off of him." He crossed his arms. "Why did you and Peggy go to meet this guy? Didn't you know that it could be dangerous?"

"I didn't think so, but Peggy told me the same thing. That's why she insisted that I take her. But I thought that it would be okay, and it was. Arel was nice."

"Nice?" Kevin exploded. "You saw Peggy. She's a wreck! He must have done something to her."

Kevin's harsh insinuations felt like blows to Carol's already delicate state. She'd come to the hospital trying to be a friend in need, but underneath she was worried about Peggy too. "I'm sorry. I don't have any answers. I thought everything was fine."

As she spoke, she knew that nothing was fine, that Peggy wasn't the only one who was hurting. She hoped she could hold it together, but her world was crumbling. The man she thought she could love had turned into an ogre. She looked up at him with a rising sense of outrage. "Why are you talking to me this way? Why are you acting like I did something wrong?"

Kevin continued to hold her in his sights. "Don't you know that you were both stupid?"

His words triggered a part of Carol that was used to blame. What had her father said to her after he found her on the streets? He'd asked her a question. "How could you do this to your mother and me? Your thoughtless actions nearly drove us insane with worry."

Carol swallowed the lump in her throat. "I love Peggy too. She's my best friend!"

Kevin's eyes narrowed. "If you're such a good friend, tell this Arel that we want to see him."

Carol tried to hold back her tears, but they came anyway. "Yes, I will." She felt small and foolish as she moved away from Kevin, trying to distance herself from his anger and blame. "I'm leaving now, but I'll talk to Arel, I promise."

As she walked down the hall, she heard the men's final remarks.

"We need answers. I hope that she can contact him again," Tim said.

Kevin replied in a loud, forceful tone. "She better. I'm going to get to the bottom of this."

By the time Carol got to the elevator, she was reeling from the guilt and rejection that Kevin had thrown at her. She was still shaking when she got to her car. But as she buckled up, she made herself calm down. She had to stay strong and clear-headed. It was a tactic that she'd learned to use after her running away fiasco, one that served her well in times of crises.

I will not be one of those women who let themselves become an emotional wreck over a guy. I'll get to the bottom of this whole thing like I promised.

As she wavered between anger and weeping, she realized she might be kidding herself about the emotional wreck part. At least she hoped that she could put that part on hold until the Arel situation was sorted out. When she got home, she wasted no time. Going directly to her computer, she accessed her email program. Her fingers were trembling, but she persevered.

"Dear Arel, I need to talk to you."

When she finished her message, she typed in his address and hit the send button.

Great, I did it!

There was an immediate sense of relief, followed by a vision of Kevin looming over her. What a fool she'd been to have trusted him so completely. Again, she pushed his image away. She got up and went to her bedroom. She knew she'd be more comfortable getting out of her work clothes, but she sat down on the bed frowning. She couldn't care about comfort. She couldn't care about anything. If she did, she'd start crying.

Then cry and get it over with. You're entitled.

She waited for the tears, but nothing happened. She sat dismally, then angrily, staring into space. What had she done wrong? What did Arel have to do with Peggy? None of it made any sense. Glancing at the clock, she wondered if she'd hear from Arel. She'd given him her phone number. She wasn't paranoid like Kevin. Arel could be trusted. She was sure of it, wasn't she?

Ironically, one week ago I met a wonderful man. Now he hates me. And then there's Arel, the liar, but he was kind and sweet when we met. But what if I am stupid? What if he is bad news?

She got up and snatched her bear from his observation post. "Oh Charlie, I hope Kevin's wrong. But if he's right, and I'm responsible for Peggy's condition, I'll never forgive myself."

Thirty-Four

AREL WOKE UP slowly, his nerves smooth and relaxed. It was a nice change. Normally he came awake like a soldier in a foxhole, ready to check on battle conditions. Stretching and enjoying the easiness in his body, he surprised himself with a smile. He couldn't know that while he slept, Michael had helped him again. The angel had succeeded in strengthening Arel's more lighthearted vibes. It was having a wonderful effect on Arel's mood.

I took care of my responsibilities to Peggy, and now I'm not only rested, I'm free!

As he pushed away the bed covers and stood up, he remembered waking up in the car and going directly to bed afterwards. He hadn't even bothered to change out of his clothes. He was still wearing the ones that he'd worn to the hospital. They were thoroughly wrinkled, but he didn't care. To wake up feeling decent was a triumph, and he wouldn't squander it on having to be neat. Instead, he strolled to his office. Once seated in his desk chair, he even did a couple of bounces, enjoying its cushiness just for fun.

"Let's see if my books have shipped." He went directly to his email account. He'd ordered a number of old editions from a favorite online bookstore two weeks before, but he hadn't received a confirmation on their shipping date. When his email came up, there was only one new message waiting for him. It was the second one of the day from Carol. He frowned, but he quickly realized that she probably wanted to thank him for visiting Peggy. He opened it with a fast click, anxious to clear his inbox.

"Dear Arel, I need to talk to you. Thanks, Carol."

She had also included her phone number.

Why does she have to thank me personally? An email would have been enough.

He felt his blood pressure rise a few points, but he took care of it with a couple of deep breaths. Snapping up the phone, his fingers tapped out her number effortlessly. His shakiness was gone, at least for the moment. He sat back, expecting to wait for Carol to pick up, but she answered after only half a ring.

* * *

Carol hadn't moved from her spot on her bed since she'd sent Arel the email. With her phone by her side, she held Charlie in a fierce bear hug as she waited. She wanted to let out all the hurt she felt about Kevin's harshness and accusations, but her emotions wouldn't cooperate. They remained bottled up, making her body miserable. Her stomach was in knots, and she had a tension headache, but nothing would distract her from her vigil. Time was lost as she stared into space.

The phone brought her out of her stoic daze, making her jump with anticipation and hope. That's when she understood what she hoped for. She needed redemption in that moment, someone to tell her that she hadn't screwed up again.

She read 'Unknown' on the caller ID. "Oh, please let it be Arel, and please let him be the wonderful person I think he is."

When she heard Arel's voice, it was soft and caring, just as she'd needed it to be. It was a key that unlocked all the pain that she was holding back. She started crying at once, sobbing almost hysterically, hoping that he'd understand how sorry she was for all the sorrow her life had caused. She became a teenager wanting forgiveness from her parents, a friend wanting forgiveness from Peggy.

* * *

Arel did his best to help Carol, but his best didn't seem to be enough. "Please don't cry. It's okay. Carol, now listen to me." He was using every word of advice, every angel trick that Michael often used on him. Of course, what did angels know? In his mind, he was also screaming out for help.

Michael, emergency, emergency! I need you.

Then it was back to Carol. "Please, I know it can't be that bad. Please calm down so we can talk about this."

His words prompted an eternity of Carol reciting her woes and weeping simultaneously. All the while he gripped the phone, trying not to hold it too close, trying not to take in too much of Carol's sad tale. Finally, two things happened. Carol's sobs started to trail off into sniffles, and Michael showed up in Arel's office. At first, he was so relieved to see Michael that he simply held out the phone. His eyes were pleading with the angel.

Take it, please!

Michael looked back with compassion, but he shrugged his shoulders.

You're her friend. She needs you.

Arel shook the phone at him.

I'm drowning here . . . in her tears.

"You're doing very well," Michael whispered as he sat down on the couch.

He shook his fist at Michael.

You're supposed to be here for me!

"Arel, are you still there?" Carol's voice called from the phone.

With a final 'dagger to the heart' look at Michael, he cleared his throat. "Yes, yes, I'm here. Do you feel any better?"

His words sent Carol into another loud round of inarticulate sobs. He put the phone on the desk for a moment, taking more deep breaths. He used the length of her crying spell as an oasis in time. It was a small space that he used to calm his nerves. When he put the phone back to his ear, he made a mental note not to ask distraught women any questions. Bad move.

* * *

After saying goodbye to Carol at least ten times and not succeeding in getting her to hang up, Arel finally put the phone back in its cradle.

"Holy mother of all that's merciful!" he cried as he got up. He dragged himself to the living area and barely made it to the center of the room. Carol's voice was still chattering away in his mind as he fell to his knees. For a moment, he wanted to lift his hands in prayer as if he'd finally found church sanctuary. But he didn't maintain his pious position for long. He crumpled to the rug in a heap and finally rolled over spread eagle.

Michael smiled down at him. "That's a new pose."

"Never ask a woman to share with you. Once Carol started, I couldn't stop her. I know the story of her life. I think she even slipped in her shoe size at some point."

"I think you handled the situation very well. I listened to what you said, and you were very caring."

"What else could I do? I was on my own."

"Carol needed you. You made her feel safe. She was able to express her feelings because she knows you and trusts you. She wouldn't have felt that way with me."

"Really? You're not just saying that?"

"Of course not."

Arel's eyes brightened. "I do feel rather proud of myself. And she thanked me numerous times. Carol is different than Peggy. Somehow she doesn't make me feel all weirded out."

"That's what I've been trying to tell you. You do have purpose. You're very helpful and very understanding."

Arel closed his eyes and sighed. "I guess after all that I've been through, I know how Carol feels. Poor woman, she's had quite a bad time of it."

"Is that why she called?"

"That's one reason, but she wanted something else too." Arel blinked back and moaned. "Oh god, I can't believe that I did what I did."

"What?"

Arel stared at Michael, suddenly white-faced, suddenly aware of the commitment he'd made. "I've agreed to meet Carol at the hospital tonight." When he'd said yes to Carol's teary request, he'd been under some kind of spell, her crying spell. Now, he was coming to his senses. His eyes blinked awake. He was in the foxhole. He began to mutter to himself as he slowly righted himself and stood up. He thought about what he had to do. "Bloody hell, I'm doomed, doomed."

"What do you mean?"

"I don't know, but I have this sinking feeling."

"Maybe you're projecting."

Arel started for his bedroom in weary resignation. "Who knows? After that conversation with Carol, I can't think straight." With the sound of Carol's sobs still fresh in his ears, he couldn't back out. He went to his closet and slid back the door with a forceful shove. "I can't believe that I'm returning to that horrid place." He looked at his wardrobe with resentful eyes. "Why me? I never get a break."

In a sudden need to express how trapped he felt, he attacked his clothes. Immaculate shirts that were carefully hung and evenly spaced, were yanked off their hangers and thrown on the floor. Within a few minutes, the rug was littered with garments that failed to make him feel better. As each item was added to the heap, he became more agitated.

Michael stood back, quietly observing his wild display. "I thought you liked to keep your clothes in order."

"Order!" The word filled the room with a seething vehemence as Arel felt something snap inside. The peaceful feeling he'd had when he woke up was long gone. "What order? I've given up on order!" he yelled as he practically ripped off the wrinkled shirt he was wearing. "My life is a roller coaster of chaos!"

"I see," Michael said as he walked over to the shirts and retrieved a pale green button-down from the pile. "Can I help in some way?"

Arel snatched the shirt from Michael and dusted off a piece of lint. "I'm beyond help. I've gone from being a hermit, to having people coming out of my ears." He paused, staring fearfully into space. "My god, in one day, I've become involved with Peggy, Mrs. Hayes from the elevator, Carol, Tim, and Kevin."

"Did you say Tim and Kevin?"

"Yes, I have to meet Peggy's fiancé and her brother, along with Carol at the hospital cafeteria in—" He looked at his watch. "In forty five minutes."

"Are you sure about this?"

"What am I supposed to do? Carol begged me."

"Remember, whether you feel it or not, I'll be there."

"That's not good enough. I need the proverbial band of angels! I have a very bad feeling about what's coming."

"What's coming?"

"I see blood, Michael. I'm serious. Check it out," Arel demanded as he opened his mind to Michael. "Tell me what you see?"

"You're right. I see blood, your blood." Michael put his hands on Arel's shoulders. "You don't have to go."

A glimpse of a brave knight flashed through Arel's mind. It was the knight from his daydreams. "Yes, I do. Carol gave me a chance even after I deceived her. Now, she's so desperate. I have to help her. It's only right."

"Carol wouldn't want you to get hurt."

Arel went back to the closet and took out a pair of Italian loafers. As he put them on, his jaw tightened. "I'm tired of being a coward. I have no choice if I want to retain any self-respect."

"Believe me, you're not a coward," Michael said with a calm steadiness to his voice.

Arel grabbed his car keys and started for the door. "I guess we'll find out if that's true tonight."

* * *

When Carol got off of the phone, she was cried out. She didn't know where the deluge of tears came from, but she was grateful for the person who helped her get through them. Arel may have lied about being a suicide hotline volunteer, but he had certainly been there for her when she needed a guiding hand.

"He's a good person, Charlie," she said as she put the bear back on her pillow. She glanced up and saw her sweater close by. She was sure that Kevin's scent still clung to its fibers. "Forget you, Kevin Bailey." She took the sweater to the closet and deposited it in the clothes hamper.

Arel helped her to see things clearly. Now, she realized how wrong it was of Peggy's brother to blame her so readily. She hadn't been negligent the night before. She met Arel in a public diner, and she didn't exchange any personal information with him. In fact, she noted that Arel tried to walk away from the diner with the intention of having no further contact with her or Peggy.

"Then he gets my email, saying he has to go to the hospital and see Peggy, who is almost a total stranger. Talk about an unreasonable request. Why should he have to go to see her?" She leveled her eyes on Charlie's black, plastic ones. "But now, he's agreed to meet with Kevin and Tim." She didn't feel so alone anymore. She had a champion.

Thirty-Five

AT NINE IN the evening, the Medical Center's cafeteria was almost deserted. Only a few visitors, nurses, and aids on break were scattered around the large dining expanse when Carol walked in. She did a quick head check and scowled. Tim and Kevin were sitting at one of the tables in a corner of the room. As she walked over to join them, both of the men stood up.

"Hi." Her tone was flat, but she knew it didn't hide her anger completely. Still, she disliked confrontation and would try to maintain a layer of civility.

Kevin eyed her with a drawn, apologetic stare as he pulled out a chair for her. "It wasn't right to put all of this on you. After you left, Peggy woke up and told us the same story that you did."

She avoided his eyes and ignored his offering, taking another seat instead. "Whatever, I shouldn't have dragged Peggy into my business. Anyway, I feel it's my duty to make sure that you know that Arel isn't the bad guy you think he is. That's why I've asked him here."

"Thanks for arranging the meeting," Tim replied quietly.

Kevin nodded. "We just want to ask him a few questions. Peggy still seems concerned and upset about him for some reason. Maybe he can tell us why."

Carol's glaring eyes finally met Kevin's, letting him know that his conciliatory tone didn't inspire any forgiveness in her bruised heart.

Kevin avoided her gaze, looking down at his hands. They were clasped tightly on the table. "Look Carol, Tim and I are so damned tired. The last twenty four hours have been a nightmare. Again, I apologize for any unreasonable behavior on my part."

She noticed that when he glanced up briefly, his grey blue eyes seemed to be searching for absolution. "I don't want to talk about it."

All three waited silently after that, but she kept glancing at the wide entrance to the room. Where was her friend, the man who'd been so sweet and kind on the phone? She needed his physical presence to assure her that she wasn't alone, that she was right about Kevin and what a jerk he was.

"Oh look, there's Arel now!" Her face broke into a wide smile when she saw a slender man enter the cafeteria. She waved at him as he walked towards their table.

* * *

Arel arrived at the hospital cafeteria, paused, and did a quick scan to locate his party. When he saw the threesome at a table, his breath stopped in mid inhalation. "You have got to be kidding," he gasped.

Carol was sitting across from guys who could have been linebackers for the Chicago Bears. Tall, broad and virile, with not an ounce of fat on them, they were excellent examples of what a man was supposed to be. While he, on the other hand, was an excellent example of the words 'slight of build.' Either of the men made two of him.

He knew he should think 'vampire strength,' use it to bolster his confidence, but he was pretty sure that whatever strength he'd once had was corrupted by the process Michael had started in him. He felt about as strong as Mrs. Hayes looked.

By the time he'd traveled half the distance across the dining area, his knees started to shake. It was a reaction that he couldn't control. His body seemed to understand the situation perfectly and knew it was no match for what he was up against. He was facing a lot of testosterone, and he didn't like the feel of it, never had.

Carol stood up and started walking over to him as he approached the table.

"Thank you for coming," she said in a happy, bubbly tone. "Kevin and Tim are eager to meet you."

"How nice." He hoped that he didn't sound as jumpy as he felt. Carol on the other hand was totally animated. She latched on to his arm as if he was a trophy she'd won and was anxious to show off.

Both men stood up when they arrived at the table, each ready to extend his hand in greeting.

Oh, hell, here we go.

Yielding to social etiquette and knowing that he was destined to be touched by everyone he met, Arel had no choice but to reach out to the men. He tried to meet each man's grip with as much brawn as possible, but he'd been told that his were the refined hands of a pianist. He knew it was true. His hand disappeared into Kevin's big mitt. The guy's grip was a bone crusher too, as was Tim's. They both seemed oblivious to the pain that they inflicted. Taking a seat, he tried to flex his hand back to normal, relieved that the male bonding ritual was over. After a moment, he glanced up at Kevin and Tim. Their eyes were riveted on him. It was obvious that they were waiting for him to speak.

"How can I help?" he asked, hoping to take care of business and leave. "Carol said that you think I have something to do with Peggy's condition."

Kevin was the first to speak. "We want to know why she asked for you. It's as simple as that."

Arel's brows narrowed as his brain did a quick query and came up empty. How in the world was he supposed to know the answer to that one? But he could hear the concern in Kevin's voice and shrugged. "I have no idea."

Tim was up next. "Well what did she say to you when you saw her this afternoon?"

Arel's tight brows became deep furrows. He didn't want to think about the visit or Peggy, but he didn't have a choice. Carol was counting on him. "She said something about wanting to be my friend. She seemed very tired and in pain."

"That's it?" Kevin glared at him with impatience. "That's all she said?"

"Yes, after I left the room, I stopped at the nurse's station and told them that she needed assistance."

Tim leaned across the table. At only two feet away, his expression was intense and probing. "And you have no idea about why she felt it was so important to see you?"

Arel felt Tim's anxiety from the moment he sat down. Now, the man's questions were reasonable on the one hand, but he didn't like being the object of Tim's interrogation. "Gentlemen, I can assure you that I don't have a clue." How could he tell them how he really felt?

Peggy scares the hell out of me! That's all I know.

He wished he could shout out the words, but he knew that the less he said the better.

Carol had been quiet, but now she spoke up. "I think I know one reason a person would like Arel to visit."

As if she'd offered them some secret bit of information, all three men shifted their gaze to her.

"Why?" Kevin queried.

"Arel is kind and caring and supportive. He's very special." Her tone was passionate and determined.

As soon as Arel heard her explanation, he shook his head.

Please Carol. Don't help me.

"I'm not special," he said quietly. "I'm just like everybody else."

Carol's eyes flared as she stared at Kevin. "No, Arel, you're not like everyone! Most people don't really care if they hurt you. That's what I've learned. They use excuses for being mean to you."

Kevin scowled back at her. "I said that I was sorry."

"And that's enough?" Carol asked. "Do you know how terrible I felt after you called me 'stupid' and insinuated that I was thoughtless, and that I had possibly endangered Peggy's life?"

"I say things without thinking them through," Kevin countered. "Plus I'm worried as hell about Peggy. Cut me some slack."

Tim held up his hands. "Calm down, guys, this isn't going to help anything."

Carol sat up straighter. "Yes, it is. It's going to help me. I'm tired of being hurt. I guess that's why I went online to meet someone. Complete strangers can be much nicer than the people that you know personally. And a shining example of niceness is sitting here at this table. Arel was a real gentleman when Peggy and I met him, a breath of fresh air. His words were carefully chosen. He didn't blurt out the first inane thing that came to mind."

Both men turned their attention to Arel. He felt them examining his expensive clothes, the way he'd been taught to hold himself like a gentleman. He'd been raised to inhabit an estate in the English countryside while Kevin and Tim were Sunday afternoon, football candidates. They were totally different, and he knew 'different' always seemed to bring out the worst in people.

On the other hand, Carol's eyes became soft pools of admiration as she continued to expound on his virtues. "Maybe when Peggy met Arel, she recognized something she didn't see very often. Maybe she saw that he wasn't like every Tom, Dick, and Kevin that you usually meet."

Kevin's jaw tightened as he looked at her and then back at Arel. "Are you saying that he's better than us?"

Arel's internal heating system flared, making small beads of sweat appear on his forehead. He tried to connect with Carol, begging with his eyes for her to stop, but she wasn't paying him any attention. Her glowering gaze was on Kevin.

Carol, please! For the love of god, don't get these guys worked up.

As he begged mentally, he knew the last thing that he needed was a couple of angry maniacs getting upset with him. He had to do something fast. He pushed his chair back and stood up. "Please, could you stop for a moment? I don't have any other information that I think would be useful. I believe it's time for me to leave."

All three stared at him as soon as he made the announcement.

Carol was the first to protest. "I was just trying to let you know that I appreciate you."

"Yes, thank you for that acknowledgement. I'm pleased that you feel that way," he said, trying to control the lump forming in his throat. "But I have to go."

Kevin stood up too, his face contorted with confusion and anger. "Just like that? My sister is up there in a hospital room moaning and crying and yelling out your name and you don't care?"

"Don't yell at him!" Carol shouted back.

"It's alright. I'm fine," Arel said, trying to reassure her. His eyes went to Kevin next. "I wish I could be more helpful."

"You can," Tim said, joining the conversation.

Arel stared at him and sighed. "How? What more can I do?"

"Let's all of us go upstairs right now to see Peggy. She was awake when we came down. We told her that we were going for coffee. Let's go back and see what she says when she sees you."

Arel hated conflicts. He hated hearing Kevin and Carol fight. He hated being in a hospital. But most of all, he hated the idea of seeing Peggy again. There was no way he could face her after all he'd been through that day. "Can't this wait?" he asked as a deep down exhaustion took hold.

Kevin looked at him and turned to Carol. "Oh, he's a charmer alright, a wonderful human being. He's so wonderful that he can't take the time to see Peggy for five minutes!"

"I didn't mean it that way," Arel protested.

"Then let's go," Kevin demanded.

"No!" Arel said in a firm voice. "I'm leaving." He'd been pushed too far. He'd had all that he could take.

I don't give a damn anymore! I'm getting the hell out of here. If you have a problem with that, fine. I was ready to die in an Illinois cornfield, and I'm ready to die here, you bastards.

He stared at the men defiantly, his golden eyes filled with bitterness as he backed away from the table. As he made an attempt to escape, Kevin's stare went wide. The big man tried to grab hold of Arel's arm. He didn't succeed, but his movement caused Arel to counter with equal swiftness, leaping backwards. What Arel didn't realize was that Kevin wasn't being hostile. He was trying to help. There was a chair pulled out from the table behind them. It was directly in Arel's path of backward retreat.

"Dammit!" Arel shrieked as he lost all control. Toppling over the chair, he caused it to flip. He hit the floor just before the back of the chair hit his face. The blow was enough to make him extend his list of obscenities as he fought the indignity and the pain at the same time.

Kevin, Tim, and Carol gathered around him at once, all trying to remove the chair and check for damages. But Arel was in full out fighting mode, trying to push them away.

"Leave me alone!" he gasped as he tried to touch his nose. Generous amounts of blood were pouring from the injured body part.

Despite Arel's protests, Kevin and Tim were determined to help. Each of them took an arm and lifted him to his feet as gingerly as they would lift a stricken puppy. Carol crooned out, "Poor baby!"

As Arel tilted his head back and searched his pocket for a handkerchief, he saw Michael, beautiful and bright in misty angel garb for a change, looking down at him from above. Michael was smiling and telling Arel something.

They're friends. Let yourself remember that you knew them long ago.

"Friends?" Staring at Michael's radiant eyes, something shifted in Arel's perception. The room faded. The world as he knew it slipped away.

* * *

The clouds lay low and heavy, like black, mourning clothes over the ancient battlefield that Arel saw around him. But he wasn't the Arel that he knew. He was a warrior and part of the disarray. When he tried to take a breath, the air was heavy with the smell of blood and sweat of those who had fought. As dusk claimed the distant hills, the injured and the dead alike lay scattered on the field. The groans of those who were still fighting for life filled the air like a dirge of misery.

Arel, as a seasoned soldier, knew his battle was over. Fresh blood flowed from his chest and his vision was failing. He did have the comfort of his friends to console him. One of them cradled his head, telling him to hold on. This man was young, blond and battled hardened, but his voice was weak with emotion. A second man pressed down on Arel's chest, trying to staunch the bleeding, but his cheerless, despairing eyes told the real story.

Arel reached out to them one last time, his comrades, his brothers, but their faces faded from his sight and his hand fell heavily to the ground.

The entire episode came and went very quickly. Arel was still being settled into a chair by Kevin and Tim when the battle scene took on the quality of a dream. But it left a profound feeling of longing in him. The bond of comradeship was paramount in the life he'd glimpsed. He missed it now as Kevin and Tim tried their best to help him. He only had a bloody nose, but they seemed to care that he was hurt. Their former mistrust was replaced by frowns of concern as they checked out his injuries. In turn, he surrendered to their ministrations, still caught up in the vision he'd had.

"Doesn't look too bad," Tim offered.

"No, I don't think it's broken," Kevin agreed as he gently took Arel's nose in hand and felt for problems. "Trust me, my nose has taken a beating so many times over the years, I'm kind of an expert."

Arel didn't know how to respond, so he simply sat in the chair, holding a silk handkerchief to his face. The cloth was quickly filled to capacity and blood dripped down, forming a large red spot on his crisp shirt. When the flow finally slowed down, he stood up. "I'm fine, and I know that I'm a mess, but if you want me to go up to see Peggy, let's go."

Tim shook his head and laughed. "I don't think so. Peggy would think we tried to kill you if she saw all that blood. Come back tomorrow."

Carol handed him napkins to take with him. "What about one o'clock?" she asked timidly.

When Arel nodded in agreement, Kevin reached out and took Arel's free hand and gave it another crushing shake. "Thanks for coming. Take care of yourself."

As Arel started on his way out of the cafeteria, he heard Tim's voice and his remark.

"Carol is right. He *is* a nice guy."

Thirty-Six

THE NIGHT WAS cool and clear, and a half moon hung in the dark skies. Arel lay back on a thick cushioned, lounge chair in the garden. He glanced over at Michael who sat in an identical lounger. "I sound funny when I talk," he said with a nasal twang.

"Yes, but hopefully the condition will be better soon. Besides, you have your English accent going for you. Peggy seems taken with it."

"I forgot that she said that. I don't think she's right, is she? I don't want to sound different."

"She thinks that it makes you sound very charming."

"I guess." Arel touched his nose, drawn to the prospect of exploring just how sore it was. "Wow, it really hurts."

"I think you should leave it alone. Your body doesn't need more pain."

"How do I look? Has the swelling gone down any?" The last time Arel had checked a mirror, he'd noted that he had two black eyes and a nose that was clearly too big for his face.

Michael crossed his arms, but seemed to be stifling a chuckle. "It's—" He looked upwards, as if the night sky held the description he was looking for and let him down. "It's still swollen."

Arel slumped down deeper into the lounger. "I hope it's better by tomorrow. I can't believe I'm going to the hospital again, but the memory of the battlefield has helped somehow. I hardly remember it now, but the feeling is still there, especially the part where I died. It was so easy." He glanced over at Michael. "Why didn't you tell me how easy it is to leave this world?"

"I'm trying to help you to live, not die."

"Yes, but it was such a peaceful feeling." Arel stared wistfully heavenward, at the vast, velvet darkness above. "In my vision, simply saying goodbye to life was so simple. Something inside of you slips away, simply leaves this life behind. The next thing you know, you're gone."

He shut his eyes and smiled, taking in the fresh air in gentle gasps. "Yes, it's so easy, nothing to it. I know how angels must feel ... to be above it all ... to be swept away." As he spoke he imagined himself slipping away now, rising upwards into the night sky. "That's what I want ... to be in the heavens ... to join the stars."

Arel's body seemed to be listening, seemed to know what he wanted. He felt his heart flutter erratically, like a frantic, caged sparrow wanting the skies again. "No more pain, no more worries or fear, that's what I want." As he contemplated his dream and intended a vacation from life, his vision blurred and a loud, cracking sound followed. Something inside of him did break loose, and he began to soar upwards.

* * *

Michael's eyes flew open when he felt the shift, when he felt Arel projecting his energy outward, expanding it into the ethers. "Arel, what are you doing?" Leaping out of his chair, rushing over to Arel's lounger, he put his hand on Arel's heart. "No, no," he repeated sternly. "It's not time for you to leave this world." He kept his hand in place, letting his energy rouse the languid vessel beneath, reminding it that it was forgetting about its duty. At the same time, he gazed upwards.

"You're just finding your friends," he said soothingly, directing his words to Arel's life force, coaxing it to come back into the body. It wasn't an easy sell. Calling back a runaway soul could be tricky. But this one hadn't gone too far ... yet.

"It won't make it any easier in the long run. You have to face yourself, dear friend. You'll have to come back again. Don't prolong the misery."

* * *

Diving. Diving. Diving. Crash! When Arel opened his eyes, he was grabbing for something, for anything. He thought he'd fallen off of the chair, but he was still lying in the lounger. Had he fallen asleep? He remembered holding his chest, feeling his heart doing funny things. Now, as he clasped it again, it seemed to be better.

Steady she goes, captain.

Why was he thinking about Star Trek and voyages into deep space? And why was Michael hovering over him. "What happened?"

Michael stepped back quickly, letting a smile slide into place. "I thought I better wake you up. It's getting a bit chilly out here. You might sleep better in your bed."

The tall, confidant angel was usually as calm as dry toast. Now, his manner was almost edgy.

"What's going on with you?" Arel asked. "Am I missing something? You look like you saw a ghost."

"I'm just happy that you're here, enjoying this wonderful world."

"Where else would I be?" Arel stretched out his body, thinking that Michael was right. His bed would be more comfortable. Finally, he stood up. "I must have been dreaming. I thought I could fly. It was nice. What do you think? Should God have given human beings wings?"

"I think you already have everything you need."

Arel paused and scanned Michael's face. "I still think you look kind of strange."

"I'm fine. Now go to bed and get some rest, please."

As he walked to the door, Arel paused and looked up. "I don't care what you say, someday I want to fly."

* * *

After Michael closed the door to his room, he let out a sigh of relief. Arel was safely tucked away in his bed downstairs. Still, Arel's idea about people having wings made Michael reflect on the evening's turn of events.

You don't need wings to fly away, Arel. You almost exited the world with your willpower alone.

After successfully coaxing Arel's soul back into his body, Michael had to use more of his energy to conceal Arel's newest trick from his conscious mind. He hoped it would be enough to keep Arel earthbound.

I don't know if I'll get you back if you try that escape route again.

A person only died when it was their time, when the soul decided it was right. However, in Arel's case, the rules were changing. His will and his soul were being very quirky, exploring options that were worrisome. If the man left his body for a bit too long, his heart wouldn't make it. Every time that he decided to explore the ethers in so daring a manner, he was putting himself at risk. And knowing Arel, he might use his new found power to leave for good if he knew he had that option.

Thirty-Seven

PEGGY STARED AT the two empty chairs across from her bed. She'd convinced Tim and Kevin to go home and get some sleep. Now, if she was going to be ready for Arel's return visit the next day, she needed to be rested too. She closed her eyes and tried to relax. She had to be careful not to make any quick movement that might set off the pain in her neck and back. The meds were helping, but she had to quiet her mind if she was going to sleep soundly.

Her thoughts drifted to the night before. She recalled the brief time she was sitting in her car, waiting for the ambulance. A sweet lady had stayed with her.

What did she say to me? Something about not being alone.

The woman's voice was so kind and reassuring. Just thinking about her soothing tone helped to put Peggy in a dreamy state. Glimpses of her childhood faded in and out, not the scary parts, but parts when she'd been a happy child. She loved summer and running around with the other kids in the neighborhood, hanging out with her brother and Tim. She loved sitting on the cool, green lawn under the big oak tree in the back yard. Sometimes she found a four leaf clover there, or she made daisy chains out of the clover flowers.

Those are such sweet memories.

They were so sweet that she slipped into a dream as she pondered them.

* * *

Peggy sat under her childhood maple tree, but she wasn't a child. She was her grown up self. Everything was just like she remembered, the house she grew up in, the flower beds along the fence, and the bare spots in the lawn where Kevin and his friends played ball.

There was one thing that was different. A tall, pretty lady was coming towards her, carrying a puppy.

"Hello," the woman said. "My name is Glory."

Peggy gave the lady a welcoming smile, but her real interest was in the dog that the woman was holding. She got up and approached her visitor. "Where'd you find him?"

"I'm afraid he was abandoned."

Peggy stared at the skinny puppy in Glory's arms. It was a white terrier with black spots around its eyes. When she reached out to pet the puppy, it pulled back. Its body shook with fear.

Glory held it gently but firmly. "You have to be patient. He's a very unhappy, little guy."

"I see, but he's such a sweet baby," Peggy said, hoping not to startle the timid animal again. "Do you think I could take him?"

"He needs a friend. That's why I thought of you when I found him."

Peggy reached out for the struggling pup. Once she had her hands around his thin, bony body, it wasn't easy to hold on to him. He was small, but he was determined to fight his captors, and anyone he didn't know, fit the description.

"Don't worry. I'll take care of you," she said quietly. "You've got a home with me now."

Glory smiled. "You have to take things slow. Please don't rush."

"Sure, I know." The puppy continued to fight Peggy's efforts, but she was determined to help it to know that she was its friend.

The feeling remained when she awoke from the dream. In fact, she smiled broadly for the first time since the accident. She had a plan.

Thirty-Eight

AREL LOOKED IN the mirror and grimaced. He was due at the hospital in an hour. He'd held on to a glimmer of hope that he'd heal up fast. When he was in his vampire prime, his body bounced back quickly. Now, he could thank Michael for another change for the worse. The bruising on his face was darker and more purple-black than the night before. The swelling had barely gone down at all. There was one consolation that Michael pointed out. Carol and her friends would expect him to look injured.

Maybe they'll take pity on me and leave me alone.

Partially appeased, he still scowled. He'd neglected his body in the past, but he'd never looked like he belonged in a circus. Brushing back his hair and smoothing out his shirt, he hoped to look presentable. Maybe something about his appearance could compensate for his face.

Who am I kidding? I'm a wreck.

He did come up with a partial solution. A pair of wrap around glasses hid most of the area around his eyes, but his nose was an affront to his dignity.

Oh well, do you really care what they think?

Sadly, he did, at least in a small way. When he remembered Kevin and Tim, they looked at him with genuine concern. They really seemed to care.

Oh hell, I bet they'll want to shake hands again.

He stood up straighter, searching for courage, working his hand, preparing for what was to come. At least he didn't have any more hunches about his blood being spilled. On his way out, he gave the mirror a final sneer. He was determined to put in a quick and final appearance at the hospital.

I'll show up, give my regards, and leave.

When he got upstairs, there was a pleasant surprise waiting for him. Abrigail and Michael stood in the foyer, smiling, offering him a gift.

"These are for Peggy," Abrigail said, handing him an exquisite bouquet from Michael's garden.

He smiled back. The bouquet was large, so large that it would surely give him some visual protection if he kept it out in front of him. The fragrant flowers would also help him ignore the hospital disinfectants. "Thank you, it's perfect."

Thirty-Nine

CAROL DELIBERATELY ARRIVED at Peggy's hospital room only minutes before Arel's scheduled visit. She wasn't going to get stuck having to make small talk with Kevin. His attempt at being apologetic the night before hadn't changed her opinion of him. Underneath his easy going exterior, he could be very judgmental and a real cad.

And a few nice words aren't going to change that fact.

After cursory greetings all around, she took a seat by the window. She'd barely settled in when Arel knocked on the door. The bouquet that he carried, a beautiful mass of long stemmed white roses, hid his face, but as usual his dress was impeccable and made a handsome backdrop to the flowers.

But it wasn't Arel's exterior graces that made Carol smile. His presence was comforting. He didn't have Kevin's impressive body, but what there was of him was kindhearted. Their phone conversation replayed over and over. He'd been so patient with all her crying and complaining. She'd never met someone who listened so compassionately, and with so much need to calm her shattered sense of self. When he showed up at the cafeteria, he was so modest and mild, even embarrassed when she bragged about him.

You are unlike anyone I've ever known, you sweet, gentle man.

Now, seeing Arel in the doorway, her heart did a little leap of joy again. She rushed over to him before he even got in the room. Her gallant knight had arrived. "Oh, how gorgeous," she said, admiring the bouquet that he held.

Peeking out from behind the flowers, Arel gave her a weak smile. "I hope Peggy likes them."

Carol gasped as soon as she saw his face. "Poor you! Are you in much pain?"

Arel shrugged, avoiding her eyes. "My ego is hurting, but my body will survive."

"That was quite a fall last night, but at least you're here now. I'm so thrilled to see you." She paused, reminding herself that he wasn't there for her. "Peggy will be happy that you were able to make it."

She forced herself to move aside and let him get on with the real reason for his visit.

Forty

AREL WAS GIVEN a warm welcome by Carol. She was turning into his official greeter, complete with a sunny smile and effervescent voice. But his gut wasn't fooled. There was emotional turmoil below the surface of her cheerful display. After they exchanged pleasantries, he found himself wondering about her welfare. As she moved aside so that he could visit with Peggy, he inquired about her feelings.

"Are you okay?" As soon as he asked the question, he clamped his mouth shut. Hadn't he promised himself not to ask her anything like that?

"I'm fine." Her tone was curt as she glanced back at Kevin. "Because you're here."

"That's good." Arel was doing his best to make a fresh start, to let down his guard a bit, to see the people waiting for him as something other than the 'enemy.' But it was clear that Carol had not moved on from yesterday's complaints.

Kevin and Tim made sure that he didn't have time to worry about Carol. Both men came over to greet him too. Carol backed away immediately. He was left alone with the two man as they crowded in on either side of him.

Oh hell, give me some space, guys!

His resolve to relax was gone in an instant. A memory about old friends was one thing. The idea of two hulking men towering over him was another. He tried to calm himself with some deep breathing, but his nose was almost swollen shut. He was forced to gulp at the air like a dying fish.

Kevin and Tim didn't seem to notice his problem. Both stared down at him openly. He never felt so small or frail. He was accustomed to his slender physique. And being around Michael didn't bring out the same feeling of inadequacy. But these guys were huge. He realized how far he fell short in comparison.

As he gauged his shortcomings, Carol intruded long enough to take away his one, small shield.

"Give your bouquet to me. I'll get a vase," she said. With Kevin nearby, she was suddenly all order and stiffness. She relieved him of the flowers with a quick, fluid motion.

As he watched her move away, he felt totally exposed.

Tim moved in even closer and extended a hand. "Thank you for coming."

Arel winced at the thought of Tim's offering. Raising his own hand reluctantly, there was no way to avoid the young man's tight grip and repeated pumping action. Kevin reached out too, but he went for Arel's face. Being somewhat careful, he took off Arel's dark glasses.

"Wow, those are some impressive shiners," he said as he leaned in and took a closer look. "That's some schnoz you have there too. Glad it's not me for a change."

As Arel was examined by the men, he did surprise himself. He wasn't comfortable, but it wasn't like the diner. Peggy's touch had practically sent him into paralysis.

Maybe these guys aren't so bad. I simply have to get used to them.

He'd barely had the thought when a voice shattered his shaky grasp on composure.

"Hey, you guys, Arel is here to see me," Peggy called out from the bed.

Peggy's tone had a shrill quality that made Arel's body stiffen. When he glanced over in her direction, she was raising the bed into a sitting position. As she came slowly into view, he cringed. She stared at him with eager eyes and a face that was bright with determination. She'd changed since the day before. The penitent waif was gone. She seemed much more like the dogged person he'd met in the diner, only more frightening.

"Well, look at that," Tim said with a broad grin. "My sweetie is coming back from the depths, even though she said she didn't feel well enough to sit up."

"I can't be a bad hostess," Peggy said as she cautiously steadied her head and neck. She shifted her gaze to Arel. "Hello again. I'm sorry about your accident, but I'm so happy you're here. Please, come over and let me see you."

How could a few words wreck a person's confidence so completely? Arel didn't know the answer, but he was instantly at Peggy's mercy.

* * *

Peggy welcomed Arel over, but when she got a good look at him, she couldn't believe how nervous he seemed. He reminded her of her dream and the puppy with the two, black eyes. She reminded herself to stay positive. She smiled. "Heavens, you do look a bit worse for wear, but I'm used to Kevin looking banged up. He was always getting hurt when he was younger."

As she made small talk, she noted that Arel's blackened eyes were furtive. He didn't want to be there. He wanted to leave, just like when they'd met in the diner. But she had a responsibility to him. She had to help him. She had to help herself too if either of them was going to put the past to rest. Her courage faltered when she turned her neck a little too far and a fresh spasm of pain punished her.

What am I doing? Arel and I shared a life that ended so badly. I don't want to go back to all that misery and my part in what happened.

Her entire childhood had been about learning to face bullies, those who hurt the helpless and the innocent. It was her inner strength that turned a skinny girl into a force that battled for what was true and good. Now she had to face something more frightening, her fear and guilt.

She gritted her teeth. In her recall of the past, Arel had tried to be there for her. Could she deny him the help he needed now? Again, she thought about her dream. She thought about how she reached out to the pup and held it when it struggled. It made the situation at hand seem less scary and brought her into the moment. She and Arel were in a hospital room with friends. There were no people around trying to hurt either of them. She made a decision. She had to take charge of the situation. "Arel, please, come closer," she said, patting the bed rail.

* * *

Arel felt like a helpless child again when he glanced at Peggy's insistent eyes. He began to raise his hand to the steel rail and pulled it back. Child or not, every time he got close to Peggy, some loud, warning alarm went off in his psyche.

"I'm not going to bite," she persisted.

His face reddened. Was he being paranoid? Were all his scary projections simply his fears going unchecked? He looked back at Carol to gauge his reaction. She smiled at him reassuringly, as if to say, "You're being so silly. The woman in the bed is my wonderful friend."

Maybe she's right, and I'm just crazy.

He gulped in more air and looked at Peggy again. "Sorry." He slowly raised his hand and rested it on the steel bar.

Peggy smiled broadly. "Good!"

As soon as he saw her eyes flash in triumph, he knew it wasn't paranoia. He could feel Peggy's energy expand, drawing him into her web of desire. He started to withdraw again, but he wasn't fast enough.

"Please, Arel, it's fine!" With a daring move, Peggy repeated her diner act, grabbing his hand again, making it clear that she was the one in control.

No! Stop!

The words couldn't be voiced because he was powerless again. How many times had his rights been violated? How many times had he felt like others could take what they wanted? In that instant, any sympathy that he felt for Peggy vanished. He hated that she thought she could have her way with him. He tried to retreat, but her grip was amazingly strong for such a small person.

"Just listen," she ordered. "I know you might think this is strange, but here goes. I want you to be part of our family."

Arel had been worried as hell about some dark covenant, some old bond that held them together. Now, Peggy switched gears and fooled him completely.

Family? I know what that means.

Family wasn't about an old bond. Family was fresh and raw in all the nightmares that he'd been having. Family was about his mother wishing he'd never been born. Family was his father's raging

206

dialogue, his words screamed out in a drunken rage, words that were crueler than his cane. "Why didn't God take you? Why have I been left with a worthless bastard for a son?"

Family meant hiding in his closet, trying to be so small that no one could find him. But his father always did. Now it was Peggy's turn. Her hand was holding him captive, but it was her offer that was a steel trap poised and ready to snap on him, to hold him forever in its steely jaws.

No, I'll never be part of a family again!

He tried to say the words, but his voice was useless. His protest was as mute now as it was when he was seven. How can you protest when the breath is being thrashed out of your lungs? As soon as he had the thought, he was a boy again. His father was shrieking out obscenities as he beat him like he beat a worthless hunting dog that went after the chickens.

But I'm not that child anymore.

He was losing track of reality and tried to pull himself back to the moment, but that meant facing Peggy.

Michael! Help me! Please!

As he mentally begged for help, he suddenly realized what reality really meant. In the end, no one was there in a way that really helped. That thought sparked a very dark memory that only surfaced for a split second. A part of him remembered crying out in pain many lifetimes before. The angels had no power to intervene, and he knew they didn't have any power now.

Do angels even exist?

His fears widened in scope, taking in more of his life and the way that he experienced it. Was he ever a vampire? Or did he fabricate that idea too, so he had an excuse for his failings? His eyes stared ahead blankly as he wondered about his sanity again. Maybe he'd created the vampire and angelic worlds as places to hide, just like the closet.

"Arel, do you hear me?" Peggy cut in, her tone unrelenting, dogging him with her desire, her need to drag him into her world.

But he was able to silence her demand for a moment of revelation. All these years, he had been tweaking reality to suit his needs. It was a trick of his demented mind. Angels, holy blood?

I'm insane! I've created a whole world of insanity!

He felt so old and tired. Even if his body looked young, he was failing. His hold on reality was being overrun by the stories in his feeble mind.

"Arel? What's going on?" Peggy demanded, squeezing his hand even tighter.

This time her voice found him, took hold of him, and spun him around so quickly that he was thrown into his past again.

Please, let go of me!

His father's hands were dragging him out to the center of the room, cursing him, wanting to beat him until he was dead. He was like a captured animal, one that knows when its life has been snatched away. It knows the feel of fate. It knows when it's having a last fleeting moment in the world. Yet even that last moment was filled with terror. Life and punishment merged with each other.

Michael, be real for me one last time.

It was his last plea. It was a last insane prayer as he felt a dark pit of despair swallowing him whole. His body couldn't maintain its balance. There was too much stress, too much fear for its breakable state. He began to fall.

***

Michael witnessed the hospital scene in his angelic form. He understood what was happening. Arel's fainting spells originated in childhood. His mind and body learned to retreat into unconsciousness when the outer world became unbearable. On the other hand, Michael had to stand by and watch Arel slip away from him, from his care. Arel was right. Michael was powerless to intervene even though he wanted to help.

I'm here, my dear friend! I would never desert you!

His words hit the hard, icy wall that stood between them. It was a barrier that came from a very deep fear in Arel's subconscious. It was there again in spite of all the years that Michael had been working to tear it down. It had taken so long for him to be allowed to touch Arel's hand in friendship, to convince Arel that in some small way that he was wanted in the world. It had taken so long to try to repair some of the deep wounds of ignorance, hatred, and betrayal that had accumulated from this life and others.

I haven't left you, and I promise that I never will!

But Arel had been trying to escape for so long. Now, he was pulling back once again, issuing orders. "Hands off!"

Arel was retreating from everything and everyone. Michael had to figure out how to convince him otherwise. But glancing ahead at events that had been set into motion, he didn't know how.

* * *

Tim and Kevin were watching Arel. They were keen observers of this stranger that had become so important to Peggy. If questioned, they'd have to admit that they too had begun to fall under his mysterious spell of fragility. Arel invited caretaking. As soon as the two of them rescued him from his ungracious fall the night before, they were both pulled into guardianship. Neither of them thought about his new role. It was simply something that had been activated in their brains, or maybe in their hearts.

"He's going to faint!" Kevin yelled when he saw Arel's body begin to sway. Moving with the speed of a football running back, he dashed around the hospital bed. This time he was successful in his effort to catch Arel. Tim was right behind him, helping to stabilize Arel's descent.

"Good golly," Kevin gasped. "This guy can't stay on his feet."

* * *

Peggy let out a cry of distress as she watched Arel break their connection by fainting. "I guess I sprang the family idea on him too soon," she moaned with regret and tears. "I was just trying to give him the support he needs."

"Of course you were," Carol said as she rushed over and took Peggy's hand.

Peggy started to sob. "What's wrong with me? I shouldn't have been so demanding!"

Carol squeezed her hand. "Don't blame yourself. I think you're very sweet, very caring. How were you supposed to know that Arel would react this way?"

"Still, this is terrible!" Peggy remembered the dream she'd had and the part that she'd forgotten. When she held the puppy too tight,

Glory took it back, telling her that she had to lighten her touch. If she wanted to assist him, she'd have to win over his confidence first. Perhaps Peggy hadn't wanted to remember that part. If there was one failing that she hadn't overcome, it was being impatient, especially when she was worried. She wanted to make things right, instantly. Now she'd made a major mistake. Before Arel passed out, he had stared at her with more fear and distrust than ever.

Forty-One

AREL OPENED HIS eyes and shut them again. He didn't know where he was, but a name escaped his lips. "Michael!" he whispered hoarsely.

"Who's Michael?" Carol asked as she abandoned Peggy and joined the men leaning over Arel.

Arel stared at her for a moment, and it all came back. His wonderful fog of forgetfulness cleared.

Michael's nobody. A figment of my imagination.

"A friend," he lied. It had become a habit. He always tried to make things sound better than they were. The truth was too painful. Now he realized how long he'd been lying to himself.

"Do you want me to call him for you?" Carol asked.

Arel's attention flickered from her to the men and then to Peggy, the horrid person who wouldn't let him go. "No, I'll be okay. It's hospitals, I don't do well in them."

"That's for sure," Tim said as he helped Arel up. "But maybe you should sit down for a few minutes."

The thought made Arel stiffen with resolve. There was no way he was going to stay in the room a minute longer. "No, I have to go."

"I can walk you to the elevator," Carol volunteered.

He took a couple of breaths and steadied himself. "I'm alright now. I just had a momentary, panic attack."

"Please be careful driving home," Peggy called from the bed. "You don't want to end up like me."

"I'll be careful," he answered.

I'll be careful to stay away from you from now on, no matter what.

He gave Carol and the men a short wave as he started out of the room. He walked to the elevator in a daze of depression. He should have felt some sort of victory. He'd escaped Peggy, but at what cost? He'd discovered how deluded he was.

I created the perfect illusion, an angel to watch over me. What a glorious ruse.

His grandmother had told him about guardian angels when she held him in her arms. She'd come to visit unexpectantly when he was eight. She'd been told that Arel was sick. Still, she insisted on seeing him. Even though she was an emotionally steady woman, she cried when she saw him. He was barely able to reach out for her with his small, battered limbs.

"Your guardian angel sent me here," she said. "Soon, I'll take you home with me." She made the promise as she cradled him against her. She tried to be careful, but every inch of Arel's body screamed out in misery as she rocked him. He could stand the pain. He was used to it. As long as he could cling to her, as long as he could hold on to the thought that she'd take him away with her, he was happy. Finally, someone would want him.

His grandmother never kept her promise. His father was a proud man. He forbade her in his house after she told him what she thought of him. She fought back, begged him to relent, but in the end, she lost. She died a couple of years later without Arel ever seeing her again.

Standing at the elevator, he thought about how courageous she'd been to stand up to his father. If only she hadn't been driven away, how different his life might have been.

I would have had a chance at happiness.

When the elevator doors opened, he remembered Mrs. Hayes. Her eyes were kind and understanding like his grandmother's. She had asked him to visit her.

Visit her? After what I just went through with Peggy?

But he found himself thinking about his grandmother's arms, how safe he felt in their embrace. He looked over at the directory posted next to the elevator, searching for the cardiac floor. Maybe Michael was a delusion, but Mrs. Hayes was real.

* * *

When Arel appeared in the doorway of Mrs. Hayes' room, the nurse who sat by her bed, looked up.

"I'm sorry, sir, but only family are allowed in here at this time."

Arel's anxious gaze swept over the room. Something was wrong. The nurse's voice had a nervous tremor, and Mrs. Hayes lay too still in the bed. The room itself was filled with a heavy, somber energy.

His body came to attention as his mind came up with immediate answers, a clear knowing that flooded in without any effort on his part. First of all, there was only one reason for the nurse to be sitting there. Mrs. Hayes was dying and there was no one else to witness the event. Secondly, the nurse was very young and afraid. She'd never been alone with a dying patient before.

He was sure he'd interpreted the situation correctly. But his sudden ability to 'know' things expanded. When he glanced at Mrs. Hayes again, his insights exploded into a visual feast of her life. From birth to death, her days on the earth revealed themselves to him. Her life became a flip book of images. He saw her as a curly haired girl in a yellow dress, as a young, pretty woman taking a handsome man's hand in marriage, as a mother who nursed skinned knees and a daughter's first steps into adulthood. He saw her growing old with an enduring dignity and grace. Her book of life was bound in strength and goodness. A feeling of gentle concern for others was a part of every page.

He came back to himself with a gasp.

What the hell is going on?

His sudden visions and insights scared him. How could he tap into facts about a woman who was a stranger? How could he know all that stuff? Again, there was a simple explanation.

I'm having more delusions of grandeur. If I can't have angels around, I'll make myself some psychic, super hero.

But one part was true. Mrs. Hayes was dying. He was sure of it.

"I'm her grandson." His lie was delivered in a firm, truthful tone as he let himself into the room and walked over to the bed. If delusions were all that he had left, he'd use them.

The young nurse stood up and smiled. "Oh, that's wonderful. I'm so glad you're here. I'll give you some privacy." She started to leave and paused next to him. "If you need anything just press the buzzer."

He nodded and watched her go. He could feel her fear dissolve at her good fortune. For a moment, he felt her burden shift to his own shoulders.

What am I doing? Why am I here? I have to leave this room too, before . . . before—

But he didn't leave. He loved the story he began to tell himself. He looked at Mrs. Hayes with relief.

You're my grandmother now. I waited for you to come back for me. Now I've come to you.

He lifted her hand and held it carefully, examining it, caressing its softness, wishing away the bruises with a kiss. There was no malice there to frighten him. Her frail hand held the capacity to stroke his face in kindness, not slap it in anger or abhorrence like his mother's hand, to soothe his fears, not add to them.

"Is that you, my dear?"

He almost jumped at the sound of Mrs. Hayes' voice. Her eyes were half open as she looked up at him. After a moment, he relaxed as he felt the concern in her gaze.

"Hello," he said with as much reverence as possible. He hadn't seen his grandmother in so long, but now he'd been given a second chance to be with her.

But it's not my grandmother, is it?

A cruel, unwanted part of him was trying to spoil everything, but he pushed it away, clinging to a part of his past that he needed desperately.

"My dear?" Mrs. Hayes' gaze widened as if she was trying to get her bearings too.

"Yes, I'm here."

She smiled. "I thought I saw my husband when he was a young man." Her breath was short and difficult. "But now I know you. I met you yesterday. Oh, your face . . . what happened?"

"I'm surprised that you can recognize me. I had an accident."

"Are you alright?"

He nodded and replaced her hand on the bed carefully, like he'd handled a sacred object.

Mrs. Hayes' eyes were watery blue orbs of mildness and equanimity as her confusion seemed to clear. "I'm so glad to see you again. I didn't think you'd remember me, that you'd bother with an old lady."

"Really? Why wouldn't I?"

She smiled shyly, a school girl in an aged body. "A young, handsome man like yourself? You must have more important things to do than spend time with an old lady."

He looked down. "You couldn't be more mistaken. I'm nothing."

"Nonsense, from the moment I saw you, I knew that you were very special." She tried to lift the hand he'd been admiring, but she couldn't manage it.

He picked it up again, eager to help. At once, she used his strength to press on, to reach out for his face. Her hand trembled with the effort, but she touched him with so much love and fondness. It was a grandmother's touch.

If only she didn't have to leave me with my parents? If only she could have taken me with her?

The boy in him hated his father for what he'd done to his grandmother, how he'd screamed at her, called her horrid names and banished her forever.

"I'm so sorry for everything," he said, wanting to forget his father and all his cruelty.

Mrs. Hayes let out a compassionate sigh. "My dear boy, we all have to die, but now I have you here with me, so I won't die alone." She followed her explanation with another smile, a smile that contained a lifetime of nurturing.

Her kindness filled him instantly, soothing the rawness in his heart like a balm. But the feeling was soon replaced by the sound of his father slamming the door, shutting out his grandmother forever.

"Don't leave me, please," he begged in a whisper. "I can't stand the thought of losing you."

Please, I don't have anyone else.

Mrs. Hayes' gaze filled with understanding as if she knew that she was playing a role for the man in front of her.

"Shh, that's enough of that," she whispered back. "We have this moment, and for me, it's perfect. How lucky I am. I have a nice, caring man here with me."

He started to answer, to explain that he was the lucky one when his vision blurred. A strange ability to see things in a new way made him gasp. Beyond the old woman's wrinkled skin and failing eyes, a halo of radiance surrounded her. It began to infuse her body with light and transform it.

Oh my god, how beautiful!

An eternal youthfulness replaced fragility and age. Not even Justina was as fair as the woman in front of him. His breath caught with a new joy, knowing he was privy to something extraordinary. He was able to observe the old woman's true self, her true essence. Perhaps he was witnessing her soul.

"If people could see you like I do, the whole world would be at this bedside. There wouldn't be any room for me."

Her hand caressed his cheek again. "Then I'm glad that it's the way it is. Because, dear one, at this moment, you are my world." She almost said more, but instead she let out a quiet exhalation. Her eyes went bright and held on to his face for a brief instant before they closed.

Arel's breath was suspended as the heart monitor by Mrs. Hayes' bed gave off a warning alarm. It became a loud siren of death. It broke the stillness of the moment that she'd just given him, a moment of complete absolution and adoration.

Arel's own shrieks of protest joined the sound of the machine. "No! Don't leave me! I'll stay with you! I'll take care of you!"

He clutched at her hand more fiercely, rubbing it to his cheek again, trying to give it his own life. "Please! Don't leave me!"

But she was gone.

His awareness was still wide open, but now it brought in waves of darkness and abandonment. Justina's face, lifeless in his arms, flashed through his mind and drove the dagger of loss deeper into his heart. Everything went cold around him except for the tears that filled his eyes. They were hot and harsh reminders that he was utterly alone.

Blinded by his grief, he didn't see the flurry of activity that began to fill up the room. He didn't know how to move. It was as if Mrs. Hayes took a part of him with her, the part that he needed to survive.

I'm lost, totally lost!

Finally, the feeling was so excruciating that he couldn't stand it. Something short circuited inside his mind, and a kind of dullness settled over his perception.

Forty-Two

ABRIGAIL ENTERED THE hospital room as quietly as possible. Michael was by her side. They grabbed Arel's arms and quickly led him into the hallway as people rushed to Mrs. Hayes' bedside. He didn't fight them. He seemed to be in a daze. Abrigail gave Michael a questioning glance. "He can't see us, even in physical form, can he?"

Michael shook his head. "The trauma he's experienced is too much. He's in a mental fog, similar to those times when he passes out physically. He can't find his way back to the here and now without bringing in all the pain, so he's blanked us out."

"What can we do?"

"We have to be prepared for what's next. When he comes back to us, he'll be in full battle mode, armed with the knowledge of all that's been taken from him."

Abrigail cringed at the thought. She kept going back to it as Michael drove them home from the hospital. There wasn't any more discussion about what was happening behind the scenes. In silence, she observed Arel's energy field as it intensified. He sat like a wooden soldier in the back seat next to her, but she could see what was behind his blank expression. Some inner, deeper part of him was pooling his anger, his outrage, and all the horror that accompanied his loss. It was gathering in his gut. Muddied, red pools of explosive rage waited for him to awake to his grief, to ignite them with his wrath.

* * *

Still in a stupor, Arel made his way through his quarters, contented with the idea that he'd go straight to bed. His mind was nearly void of thought, but sleep would be even better. As he passed through the living area, he noticed a small object on one of the shelves.

I forgot about you.

Going over to the bookcase, he picked up a small, glass angel, a gift from his grandmother. She'd left it behind in his keeping before she was sent away. Her voice was so sweet when she told him about her gift. "This angel's name is Michael, and he's a wonderful friend. When you look at him, remember that I love you, and that I'll see you again very soon."

His fist tightened as he studied the glass statue and remembered how her words used to repeat over and over in his eight-year-old mind. When his parents made his life hell, he'd lie in his bed holding the figurine up, letting the rays of sunshine refract through the glass. He'd imagine that the colors on his wall belonged to a beautiful angel.

It was all a lie. I started living a lie when I was an ignorant child, and I haven't stopped.

As a boy, he'd been naïve, always playing his games. He pretended that he'd be like the angel, Michael, someday. Only he'd be a knight with a sword. He'd use it to fight people like his father when they hurt others.

What a dreamer I was.

He began to laugh at himself as his gaze flickered over the large, glass collection that adorned every nook and cranny of several shelves.

I never became a knight. I just learned how to be more of an idiot child. My god, I'm a grown man collecting all these stupid baubles because I've refused to grow up.

He looked at the angel in his hand again. He'd studied it so many times as a child that eventually his grandmother's face appeared whenever he stared at it for very long. Now he saw her looking back at him once more. But this time, he despised what he saw.

You never came back like you promised. You died, just like that old lady in the hospital.

A surge of anger fired through his body. It blotted out his grandmother's face. It made him grit his teeth as the truth fueled his rage.

She was a powerless, old woman. She lied to a child who didn't know any better than to believe her!

His hand tightened on the glass angel as he remembered how many fantasies it had inspired. "But never again!" he screamed as he hurled the angel at the fireplace.

He started grabbing more of the glass objects off of the shelves. Each became a missile of his smoldering wrath. Lalique, lantern vases, symbols of harmony and balance, were rendered pointless as they met the walls and exploded into countless shards. Glorious, multi-faceted Swarovski lions, panthers, and eagles followed. Blown glass angels, dogs, and horses, met their doom in the same way.

When he'd exhausted the glass collection, he walked over to the library. He rummaged in the side-table drawer and found an antique letter opener. Testing the cold metal in his hand, his eyes narrowed even more as he walked over to his wall of paintings. "There's nothing beautiful in this world! It's all just make-believe, the folly of crazy artists who like to pretend like me."

He lifted his arm to drive the dagger into the billowing sails of a painted ship when someone grabbed his arms and held them motionless.

"This isn't going to bring her back."

If he didn't know the truth, he'd have thought it was Michael's voice.

"You're nothing to me," he hissed. He struggled to free himself, but he was too tired to go on. His whole body was shaking with weariness. He dropped the knife and tried to catch his breath. When he loosed himself from whatever had hold of him, he let out a final sigh, a final summing up of his life. "It's all worthless."

He needed to go to bed, but once he was there, he couldn't sleep. Like his glass collection, he was shattered, fractured and in pieces. Every thought was a cutting reminder that he was a fool. Everything he believed in met a wall of destruction and was rendered nil and void.

Forty-Three

THE UPSTAIRS OFFICE of the townhouse that Tim and Peggy shared was neat and orderly, but Tim paced its length nervously. He stopped in front of Kevin and frowned. "It's been a week since the accident, and Peggy's getting more upset every day. How is she going to get better if she can't relax?"

"Hold that thought," Kevin whispered as he crossed the room to the door. After he closed it, he turned back. "She's downstairs in the living room, and as you know, she's got great hearing."

"You're right. I'm so preoccupied with her situation I'm not thinking clearly."

"I know how that is." Kevin walked over to a chair and sat down. "But this is still about Arel. That's why she's worried. I can't believe that he's being so ignorant. Carol has sent him countless emails explaining the situation, and he's never replied."

Tim dropped into an adjoining chair and let his shoulders sag. "You saw the guy. He can hardly take care of himself."

"Yeah, but Peggy thinks that she's to blame for his reaction after she sprung the family idea on him."

Tim shrugged. "She also insists that he's in trouble. Her intentions are good. She doesn't even know him, but she's bent on helping anyway."

Kevin crossed his arms over his chest. "That's my sister. When she gets like this, god knows what she'll do."

"I tried to talk to her, to convince her that he's not her problem—"

Kevin interrupted with a loud laugh. "You can't talk Peggy out of something once she makes up her mind."

"That's not true. She can be very reasonable."

"Aw, come on. We both know better than that. No, if we want her to get better we have to do something. I've come up with some ideas about finding this guy."

"What ideas?"

"When I was in college, I worked in a parking garage like the one in the Med Center. There are always cameras in those places, images of the traffic in and out. Maybe we can track Arel down if we can get a license number."

"After all this time, would there still be a record? And how would we get access anyway?"

"I'll find a way. And if I can get a license number, I have a friend that works at license renewal."

"I'm impressed."

"I'm not going to let Peggy down."

Tim sat up straighter and leaned forward. "I'm with you. I'll do whatever."

For several minutes, both pondered Kevin's plan. Finally Tim broke the silence. "By the way, how's it going with Carol?"

Kevin snorted. "I tried to apologize a couple of more times, but she won't let it go. It's not right. Look at this mess her involvement with Arel has caused."

"I don't know, Kev, you might be off base with this one. I don't think you can blame her. Technically, she didn't do anything wrong."

"Yeah, I guess you're right. It just makes me mad. This whole thing is crazy. Besides, I never meant to hurt her."

"From what Peggy's told me, she's very sensitive."

Kevin's frown softened. "Yeah, and I've screwed up whatever chance we had."

"Maybe not. Things could still work out." Tim stood up and started for the door. "Come on, let's go down and cheer up Peggy. Maybe we can go out for lunch. Get her mind off of Arel."

"No thanks, I'm going to get started on my plan. I'll tell you if I get anywhere."

"You're a great brother. Don't beat yourself up over what happened with Carol. Like you said, you didn't mean to hurt her."

"Me and my big mouth, I don't know why I don't learn."

Tim gave him a playful grin. "Don't worry, you'll always have Peggy to help you, no matter what's going on."

Forty-Four

IN THE DIMLY lit grayness of his bedroom, Arel drifted in and out of sleep. Was it night or day? He couldn't tell anymore. Past and present blended together too. Was his father haunting him for real or was he just remembering his childhood? He didn't know. His screaming fits were down to zero. He didn't have the energy to indulge in them now. Fevers ravaged his body. His lungs were like heavy bellows he barely had the strength to work.

I'm finally going to do it. I'm really going to die.

The trick was not to care about anything. Up until recently, he'd lived on and on because a small part of him refused to give up. That part clutched at the lie that there was something in life besides his pain.

What a stubborn fool I've been, but no more.

He welcomed the darkness, his downward slide into oblivion. He longed to plunge so deep into its depths that everything would cease to be. Sleep was a perfect vehicle. Sometimes, he was able to drift into a dreamless state and remain there for hours.

And I need to get some sleep now. I need some relief from this splitting headache.

How did his body still have enough vitality to hurt this much? Why didn't he just pass out permanently? The answer didn't matter. Nothing mattered. He started to turn over when a spark of light caught his eye. He stared back through a haze of pain. There was an area of brightness across from the bed, and it was getting bigger.

If that's you Abrigail, forget it. I don't believe in your kind anymore.

If it was Abrigail, she didn't listen to his protest. A wavy outline began to appear in the light. After a moment, a form came into focus.

"I'm not an angel," a voice announced.

He froze and tried to swallow. He knew that voice. It had flesh and blood roots.

Oh my god, it's the old woman from the hospital.

The sound of soft laughter shattered the stillness of the room. "When you came to see me, I didn't feel like I was so old. You helped me to forget about age."

His heavy lids opened wide. With effort, he managed to sit up and stare at the shadowy form. "It can't be you. You're dead."

More unrestrained laughter filled the space as the form solidified in front of him. Standing tall and straight, Mrs. Hayes looked back with radiant blue eyes. She had a youthful face, not the lined and wrinkled one he remembered.

"I look pretty good for being in my grave, don't I?"

Her lighthearted remark made him grab for his pounding temples. "This isn't happening," he said in as steady a voice as he could manage. He couldn't allow a new bout of madness to start up. Maybe he was weak, but his will was stronger and more determined than ever. As he got closer to his goal of exiting the land of the living, he wasn't going to let himself falter.

Mrs. Hayes stepped closer. "My dear, please, don't be like that."

"Go away!"

"But I've come to visit."

"You don't exist!"

"But I do," she whispered insistently. "I guess you're right about the ghost part, but I'm not your imagination, I promise you. Just listen for a moment, please."

"No!" He croaked out the word in a hoarse shout of desperation, realizing that she frightened him. He shut his eyes, struggling for air, wondering why he was trembling more than ever.

Of course, I'm afraid. A part of me wants to pull me back into the world. Some insane portion of my mind is using more tricks to confuse me.

The glowing form moved closer. "Now just stop that! I'm not a projection of your mind." If the words were stern, Mrs. Hayes' smile was compassionate. "It's not easy to appear like this, and I don't want to waste any of our precious time together on nonsense."

"Our time? What time are you talking about? You gave me five minutes in the hospital, and then you were gone. Now I'm supposed to believe that you're here again. If you really were a sweet old lady, you'd never have been so cruel."

"You're wrong. I did care, and I care about you now."

"If you cared, you would have stuck around, at least for a little while!"

"I wish I had, for your sake, but you were so helpful when you came to see me. Your presence, the things that you said, made my fears melt away, and my soul slipped out of my ailing body so easily."

"What?" His blood pressure soared so fast he was instantly dizzy. "Are you saying that you died because I was nice to you?" A swirling mass of new anger intensified his headache, turning it into a blinding migraine. He had to take a moment to calm himself. When he recovered a little, he couldn't stop himself from expressing his outrage. "How dare you! I'm rotting here, ready for the grave myself, but it's nice to know that you benefited from my visit."

"I never wanted to hurt you. I'm sorry."

"And that's supposed to mean something? What good does your apology do? I have no one, nothing!"

"That's not true. No matter what you think, you're mistaken about things. First of all, Michael is real. And secondly, your grandmother still loves you."

"More lies."

She gave him an imploring look. "I know it's hard to believe, but maybe this will help to convince you of the truth." She turned and went to his dresser. "It's a present from your grandmother."

Seething with indignation, he started to get out of bed, grabbing hold of the nightstand, forcing himself into a standing position. He teetered on unsteady feet. "What are you talking about now?"

She pointed to an object sitting on the bureau. "Isn't it lovely?"

He blinked back, trying to make out what she was showing him.

"Your grandmother knew you needed it," she said as her image began to blur.

"I don't believe you!"

"Please try." Her form was quickly dissolving as she spoke. "She loves you, Arel, you have to know that."

Her voice echoed, hung in the air as the room returned to a shadowy darkness. As the last of the light disappeared, he looked towards the space where she had stood by the dresser. The room was empty again. He was empty.

"What the hell?" He was about to turn away when he noticed a shiny glimmer on the dresser. Something was catching a few rays from the night light. With a hasty gasp, he pushed off from the bed and staggered towards the chest of drawers. He traversed the ten feet in a stumbling gait as the fever escalated and made his legs feel like rubber. When he saw what beckoned him forward, he froze.

"My angel, it's back." He was instantly overwhelmed by a dizzying sea of questions. He grabbed for the dresser. Could it be true? Did his grandmother really want him to know she was thinking about him, even now, after all these years?

"You're still my boy." He heard his grandmother's voice. He smelled her wonderful lavender scent. The fragrance filled the room. It conjured up a feeling of softness and belonging to someone who would love him, a person who would protect him from living nightmares.

"Grandmother?" His heart sped up, but not in a steady way. It was jumping around every few beats, unable to find a rhythm that synced with life. His mind felt the same way, jumping from present to past. For a moment, he was a child again, a child with wishes and hopes for something better. He picked up the glass angel and pressed its smooth surface against his cheek, trying to cool the inner fires of fear and distrust. "Grandmother, do you hear me? Please, answer me!"

He slumped against the dresser as he waited and listened. But the only sounds he heard were his heartbeats. The vessel in his chest thumped out an erratic message of weariness, reminding him of how old he felt. He wasn't a boy anymore. He couldn't be tricked with words or a shiny piece of glass.

Still, he remembered his fit of anger, and how he'd destroyed the angel figurine. He remembered seeing it explode into a thousand pieces when it hit the fireplace. Now, its exact replica was in his hand, whole and perfect. How could that be? It was an impossible puzzle. He didn't have the energy to explore a mystery. Instead, he pulled himself up, placing the angel back on the dresser. "It doesn't matter. Nothing matters."

Forty-Five

SITTING ON HER living room couch, Carol grabbed the remote and switched off the television. She moaned as she put an empty bowl on the coffee table. "Oh lord, I can't believe I ate all that popcorn," She had to remember not to make so much now that Kevin was gone. She let out a heavy sigh that had nothing to do with overeating. It wasn't only Kevin that she'd lost. Arel had vanished too. And Peggy was caught up in her own world.

Carol's life scenario was repeating itself. Somehow, when she got too involved with people, she always ended up miserable. Sure, things started out great, but that's not how they ended.

She'd been such a happy child, skipping on the beach with her mom and dad, thinking she was the luckiest little girl in the world. Fast forward ten years. She was in her room with her hands over her ears, trying to shut out the shouting matches between her parents, crying herself to sleep when the word, divorce, got past her efforts not to listen.

After that, she was abandoned in the backwaters of their lives. Her parents' bitterness and crumbling marriage took center stage. They looked at her and mouthed some 'I love you' sentiments. They told her things would be okay, but the truth was that they forgot about her.

So I ran away.

She wanted to punish them for what they'd done to her life. They destroyed everything.

Still, that was a dumb move.

She sat staring into her past, acknowledging her failings, but giving herself credit for rebuilding her life after her bad decisions. Little by little, she learned to be on her own. Then she had the bright idea that she wanted more. First there was Arel, who turned out to be a friend, which was fine. But, then there was the whole mess with Peggy getting weirded out over him. Then there was Kevin's reaction.

Kevin, I thought you might be the one, but now, you've ruined everything.

They had enjoyed being together. They didn't have to do anything special to have a great time. There was chitchat and interesting discussions, snuggling and sharing. When Kevin laughed, the sound filled the room just like his physical presence. She missed his solid body next to hers. Now, she had to move on.

Give yourself a break. Get busy. Start rebuilding.

She stood up, grabbed the popcorn bowl and hesitated. Rebuilding didn't mean that she had to give up on her desires, did it? Sure, her old life was safer, but she didn't want to go backwards. She wanted more than the same old routine. Before her breakup with Kevin, she'd actually paged through a bride magazine at the drug store checkout counter.

She walked to the kitchen and practically threw the plastic bowl into the sink. A new wave of self-pity hit and so did the tears. Before she could find a new box of tissues, her cell phone rang. It was Kevin's ring tone.

"What now, more excuses?" She paused, wiping her nose with a napkin and taking a deep breath. When she answered the phone, Kevin's voice was the one she remembered from their dating days. He sounded nice. She was lulled into a momentary daze of desire. It was interrupted by what he was telling her. She pressed the phone closer. "You did what? You located Arel? Really?"

The call was over quickly, the conversation brief. Afterwards, she felt a little better. Maybe it was because she could put her rebuilding plans on hold and concentrate on seeing Arel again. Maybe it was because she still had dreams that Kevin might somehow redeem himself. She took a deep breath and let it out quickly. "No, stop it, don't go getting carried away. You already fooled yourself once, don't do it again."

Forty-Six

MICHAEL STOOD KNOCKING at Arel's bedroom door. "I have to talk to you. It's very important." He'd had to honor Arel's delusions and his seclusion. With Arel's decision to abandon the world and the angelic realm, Michael hadn't been privy to what was happening in the closed chambers. Arel had become extremely proficient in shielding himself.

Answer the door, Arel. You're going to want to hear what I'm trying to tell you.

For nearly a week and a half, Michael had waited patiently. Now he stood firm. "Arel, please! I don't want to alarm you, but Kevin and Tim are tracking you down. I think they might be coming here to see you very soon."

Again there was silence, followed by the sound of movement, of something being banged about, Arel bumping clumsily into furniture. Finally, the door lock was turned back.

Arel peered out of the crack. "You're not real, so how am I supposed to believe you?" His tone was wheezy, overlaid with panic.

"I'm as real as that glass angel on your dresser."

Arel's face remained shrouded in the darkness of the room. "I don't understand what happened, how it got there."

"We don't have time to talk about it now. You're going to have visitors soon."

The door opened wide enough to expose Arel as he clung to the doorjamb. His face was almost healed, but all the light was gone from his eyes. He tried to run a bony hand through his hair, but it was a mass of impossible tangles. After a moment, his hand slid down to his overgrown beard. "My mind isn't working very well," he mumbled. Rubbing at the unruly stubble, he teetered back and forth.

"Arel, what have you done to yourself, to your body?"

Michael studied the person who stood in front of him. Arel was more of a shadow than a solid man. His life force was edging towards empty. Searching deeper, into Arel's heart, Michael felt his own pull back. He needed a moment to maintain his calm, to believe that the vessel he was viewing wasn't damaged beyond repair.

Arel didn't seem to understand Michael's concern. Legs and body trembling, he reached out a hand, touching Michael's arm. "Are you sure that you're real?"

"Of course I'm real, and I'm telling you that Kevin found a way to get your license plate from the security system at the hospital parking garage. He was able to find out where you live. Peggy is desperate to see you again."

"Are you sure?" Arel's brows came together, as if he was trying to understand, but he couldn't quite put the information all together.

"They couldn't reach you any other way. But they're coming here to see you."

Arel blinked back. Finally something seemed to click in his brain. His eyes caught and steadied. "How long? How much time do I have?"

"A couple of hours, maybe."

A sudden fit of temper replaced Arel's passive expression. "They have no right to do that!"

"They simply wanted to find you, to talk to you."

Arel ignored him, turning and making his way back into his room. "I won't let them . . . they can't do this. I'm leaving." After only a few steps, he began to falter.

Michael followed and reached out to take Arel's arm. "Why are you so afraid of them?"

"They have no boundaries, only their own agendas! They've already violated my privacy. Who knows what they want from me." Pulling away from Michael, Arel used the bed railing for support as he stumbled over to the closet.

"Running again isn't going to help. How many lifetimes do you need in order to stop and realize that you have other choices?"

"As many as it takes to be left alone."

"It doesn't have to be that way. Let me help you."

Arel's hand tightened on the shirt he was holding. Turning towards Michael, his eyes were accusing. "You can't. Even if you are real, your offers are worthless."

"Why would you say that?"

"Why didn't you help me when I called out for you, when I begged you to be there for me in the hospital?

"You called out, yes, but then you decided that I couldn't help. You shut me out again."

"I was scared out of my wits. What do you expect?"

"You can't have it both ways. You can't make decisions for yourself, and then blame me for the consequences. You say that you want me to help, but what does that mean?"

"It means keeping everyone away from me! I want to be left alone!"

"And I'm here to help you embrace life, to find happiness and joy again."

"That's it then, isn't it? We have nothing to say to each other."

"If you keep running, you're going to run yourself into the grave."

"That's my business, not yours!"

"No matter how you feel about yourself, it's not right to destroy your life."

"I don't give a damn about what you think!"

Michael walked over to the nightstand and picked up the car keys. His simple action was like water on a grease fire. Arel's bony frame straightened instantly.

"Give me those!" Arel made a staggering lunge at Michael. Falling short of his mark, he landed on the floor. Spread out like an awkward fledging, he managed to raise his head enough to glare at Michael. His face was a mask of bitterness. "You're like the rest of them, trying to take what little freedom I have. I hate you all!"

"I see." Michael looked down with a mixture of compassion and frustration. "If that's how you feel, why am I here?"

"I never asked you to come in the first place."

"I remember a child calling out to the angels for help, but perhaps I shouldn't have come." Michael turned and put the keys back on the nightstand. "I won't bother you anymore," he said as he walked briskly to the door.

"Where are you going?"

"If you want to die, I can't stop you."

"You bastard! I trusted you!"

Arel's loud, shrieking sob pierced the air with so much sorrow that Michael paused and looked back with tears in his own eyes. "And I have always loved you more than if you were my child or brother. I have always wanted to protect you more than you could know. But your trust in something outside of yourself has been conditional for many lifetimes, and I've always had to honor those conditions. Just like now, you give me no choice. Goodbye."

"Stop!" Arel's rage melted into a submissive look of despair. "What am I going to do? I don't have the energy to get up."

Michael hesitated. "Isn't this the way it was when you were a boy, when your father beat you? But he's not responsible for you laying here now. You're not that boy anymore. And I'm not your enemy, even if you think that I am."

Arel looked up, trying to get his breath. "Every time I want to believe that something good exists, I'm proven wrong. I'm tired of trying."

"It's not about finding goodness. You have to believe in who you are, that you have the power to create a better life for yourself."

"I don't know how! But that doesn't matter now. Peggy and the others will be here soon. My god, what am I going to do?" He paused and stared at Michael again. "You said that you want to protect me. Stay and keep them away, please."

"Is that what you really want?"

"Yes!"

Michael came over and held out his hand. "Agree to see them for a few minutes, and then I'll see that they leave after that."

"You won't let Peggy get her hands on me?"

Michael shook his head. "No, I won't."

* * *

As the late afternoon sun lost itself behind a neighbor's tree, Arel laid back on a garden lounger. He was wearing his dark glasses, recovering from the stress of simply getting ready for his visitors. He'd had to cling to the shower walls, letting the soothing hot water revive him a little. Shaving was too big a task. He'd merely trimmed his beard in a few places. He was too weak to manage his wild hair by himself. With Michael's help, he'd tamed it back into a short, pony tail. He dressed in baggy sweats instead of his usual crisp shirt and slacks. By hiding the worst of his emaciated body, he hoped to appear fitter. Of course, that was a ludicrous desire. He looked as frail as a brittle bird, and he felt worse.

Michael tried to use his healing powers to help with Arel's body issues, but his physical body was in an extreme state. It was going to take time to work with it, especially with all of Arel's trust issues. On the plus side, he'd begun to see Michael as a friend again. When asked, Michael stuck around.

As Arel's advisor, Michael was very encouraging about what they could say to their visitors. "We'll simply tell them that you've been ill."

"Right, that's plausible. People get sick all the time."

Michael's eyes had been so kind when he nodded. "Of course they do."

Arel tried to calm his nervous tremors. "Promise that you won't let any of them close, Michael. I've never felt so edgy."

"You've indulged in a lot of prolonged paranoia recently. It's taken a toll."

"I feel like I'm in one of those Hitchcock films and something scary could jump out at any minute." He looked up at the tree branches overhead. "The garden is safe, isn't it? The birds aren't crazy, right?"

Michael let out a laugh as he glanced up. "I'll stand guard against the birds and beasts too."

When the doorbell rang and Michael went to answer it, Arel realized that he felt a little better being in the garden. His surroundings were lush and vibrant. Michael's energy was in every flower, tree and even the grass. There were no Hitchcock birds around, only the sweet sound of a wren singing a song to its mate.

"I can do this. Just a few minutes of sitting here, letting Michael do the talking, and they'll be gone." Arel held on to the thought as he closed his eyes.

Forty-Seven

WHEN THE DOORBELL rang, Michael answered it promptly and observed the four people who stared back at him. Arel was right in some respects. They did look like they had an agenda. "Hello, can I help you?"

There was a general shuffling of feet, but Carol stepped forward. "Yes, thank you. We know this might be an intrusion, but I wanted to know if a person by the name of Arel lives here."

"Yes, that's right."

A general sigh of relief went through the group.

"That's wonderful," she said, glancing around at her companions. "My name is Carol, and these are my friends, Peggy, Tim, and Kevin. We would like to know if we can see Arel."

"Yes, of course," Michael said with a welcoming gesture. "Come this way. Arel is in the garden."

* * *

"Arel! Hello!" The sound of Peggy's voice rang out in the garden like a call to arms. Arel jerked up reflexively, gripping the thin cover he had over him. "Bloody hell!" He'd calmed himself enough to actually relax for at least thirty seconds. Now his startled gaze swept the garden path, following the carefully laid stones that led up to the house. He had a moment of relief when he saw Carol. She was walking down the path, slightly ahead of the others, but Peggy was behind her.

Where's Michael? My god, where is he?

A moment of panic set in as his eyes zigzagged across the garden. Then he heard Michael's voice in his head.

Don't worry, I'm here. I'll join you momentarily.

Michael was following the stream of visitors. His smile was reassuring. On the other hand, Carol's smile was anxious as she hurried towards him. She stopped a few feet away from where Arel was lying on the lounge.

"Hi, Arel," she said quickly. "Oh goodness!" Her voice elevated into a higher tone of disbelief as she stared at him.

Arel hesitated, reminding himself to keep up the ruse. He wasn't supposed to know that she was coming. "Carol, what are you doing here?"

Before she could answer, Michael speedily moved in close to the side of Arel's lounger. "Maybe you can give Arel a little room."

The group seemed oblivious to his request as they formed a semi-circle in front of Arel.

"Holy smoke!" Kevin gasped. His wide, questioning eyes did a double take. "What happened to you?"

"Arel's been under the weather," Michael said. "And he needs a bit of space. Why don't you all sit down over there?" He pointed to some lawn chairs that were at least eight feet away.

Ignoring the suggestion, everyone continued to stare at Arel.

"Oh Tim," Peggy cried out, clinging to her fiancé, "I told you he was in trouble."

Tim looked like he was alarmed himself. Instead of saying anything, he tightened his hold on Peggy's arm.

Arel narrowed his eyes. His faulty vision was playing a game called, "Now you see them, now you don't." Being in terrible physical shape was another bad move. Even if he tried to run away, he'd probably only get a couple of feet before he dropped like a rock. "I'm fine." He wheezed out the words.

Carol stood statue-like, blinking at him as her eyes misted over. "I'm sorry that you're so sick."

Arel had been shocked too when he saw himself in the mirror earlier. His color was nonexistent, so white he'd give chalk a run for the money. And he shook, trembled like a person did when they'd fallen through ice. But the temperature in the garden was pleasant, even warm. With large, black circles under his eyes and a scarecrow body, he could probably get an acting job in the Theatre of the Macabre.

Carol seemed to have a similar opinion. She looked at him like he belonged in a morgue.

When he picked up on her thoughts, they were questions. Where has his flesh gone? Can a person live without flesh?

Kevin directed his attention to Carol and spoke up. "Arel's friend asked us to sit down."

Arel noted that the muscular man's voice had a gentle quality, but Carol frowned back at Kevin, as if his presence offended her.

When the group finally took the hint and found seats, Michael went around to each and introduced himself. Arel enjoyed the fact that Michael appeared to be very capable of interacting with Tim and Kevin. He made shaking hands look like an easy task.

Tim stared openly at the tall, blond man who was Arel's exact opposite. "Glad to meet you, Michael."

Kevin also seemed curious. He studied Michael and then Arel. After a moment, he pulled Michael close and spoke in a hushed tone. "So he's just sick? He looks like somebody beat the hell out of him."

Arel's sensitive ears picked up the remark, but he interrupted Michael as he was about to answer. "By the way, how did you guys find me?" He let the question slip out so naturally and so unexpectedly that it took the group by surprise.

Tim and Kevin shot each other guilty glances, while Carol blinked again. Peggy stared straight ahead as if she'd been caught stealing candy.

Kevin spoke up. "Finding you was a pain in the ass if you want the truth, and also expensive. Bribing people isn't cheap. But I'm sorry for barging in. We didn't know you were sick."

"Yes, we are sorry, but we didn't know what else to do," Tim added. "Kevin and I were both worried about Peggy. She's been very concerned about you. It was affecting her health."

Peggy shrugged. "I just wanted to know that you're okay."

Arel was relieved to see that Peggy wasn't as bold as she'd been in the hospital. "Please don't concern yourself. Michael is here, and he's taking care of me."

Peggy's eyes flickered back and forth from Arel to Michael. "Arel, I hope that you don't get offended, but I have to know . . . is Michael your . . . partner?"

Arel's colorless cheeks finally managed to turn a bright shade of red. "He's a friend." He glanced up at Michael. "A very, good friend."

Michael's eyes widened as the group shifted their attention in his direction.

"Oh, lord, I'm sorry," Peggy cried. "I just wanted to let you know that if you did have someone, they would always be welcome in our homes."

Kevin and Tim were both borderline crimson, with faces that clearly indicated a need to disappear, but instead they started nodding at Peggy's explanation.

Carol had been sitting quietly. Now her brows arched as a look of mortification set in. "I'm so sorry that we've intruded, Arel. We had no business barging in like this." She frowned disapprovingly at her friends. "Please accept our apologies." She stood up and motioned to the others. "Come on, guys, we're leaving. We've troubled Arel enough."

Kevin and Tim were instantly on their feet.

"Yes, sorry if we bothered you," Kevin offered.

Peggy was getting up too, but it was easy to see that her neck injury was causing her to move more slowly. Michael immediately came to her aid.

"Thank you, Michael," Peggy gasped in a pained whisper. "I hope you'll forgive me." Her eyes began to well up. "I've really been so worried about Arel. I wanted to help him if he needed anything. Now I've embarrassed everyone. I've made a fool of myself." She began to cry. A moment later, she was sobbing.

The sound of Peggy's raw, plaintive outburst hit Arel like a massive wave. It wasn't just that he was taking on her pain. This time the sounds of her misery ripped through his psyche. He was instantly sick with grief. Whatever kept him anchored to the world was destroyed by the impact.

I need to take care of her.

The words were meaningless as they echoed through his conscious mind. They came from some unknown depths. Yet, he felt compelled to comfort her. Even his fear of Peggy was sacrificed to some greater duty he had to her. He pushed himself forward on the lounger and tried to reach out to her. But when his eyes met hers, everything began to spin. Darkness closed in, and he began to fall off the lounger.

Michael tried to catch him, but it was too late. As his body hit the ground, Arel's mind kept going. It fell through time. He wasn't in the garden anymore. He was standing in the doorway of a thatched hovel, not as himself, but as a boy of about sixteen. A girl stood in front of him, at a crude table, dishing porridge into bowls. When she looked at him, her eyes brightened.

"Brother, you're home," she said.

They were magic words that opened up the life they shared as siblings. He wasn't just her brother. He took care of her, protected her when their father was in a rage and tried to beat her. He offered himself instead. But he wouldn't have it any other way. He loved her.

"My sister—"

The words were on his tongue as Arel came back to himself in the garden. It was like waking up from a dream, a good dream. Hours before, he'd been convinced that he wanted to die. And the thought of seeing Peggy was terrifying. Now, he felt so different about everything.

Michael helped Arel back onto the lounger, but he didn't acknowledge Arel's vision. Instead, he hastily ushered their visitors out. "Please everyone, if you could leave, Arel needs to rest. He's really not up for company."

Forty-Eight

AS THEY DROVE back home, Peggy sat next to Tim in the back seat of Kevin's car. Cradled in Tim's arms, she'd finally calmed down. "I can't believe I started crying like that."

Kevin gripped the steering wheel and glanced back at her. "Geez, Peg, it's understandable. You were right about Arel. I never saw anyone that bad off who wasn't in a hospital or a funeral home."

"Kevin, please!" Peggy cried out.

"It's okay. Take it easy," Tim said as he pulled her a little closer.

Peggy dabbed at her nose. "I hope that I haven't made it worse. I seem to be constantly upsetting him."

Tim gave her a consoling smile. "At least Arel knows that you're concerned about his welfare."

Peggy directed her attention to Carol and sniffled. "Carol, you knew Arel first. I'm sorry that I've been a buttinsky and such an embarrassment to you. It's just that I have these strong feelings about him, and I want to help." She started crying again. "Sorry everyone, I feel so sad every time I think of him."

"Your heart is in the right place," Carol said as she looked back from the front passenger seat. "I think we overstepped our boundaries just dropping in, but your instincts were amazingly accurate about Arel's condition."

Kevin flashed a smile as he slowed for a stop light. "Michael gave me their phone number as we were leaving the garden. We can call and check on Arel, how about that?"

Peggy smiled weakly. "Thank you for everything, Kevin. You've really been a great brother, trying to help me and all."

Carol stared at the road, but when the traffic light turned green, she sighed reluctantly. "Peggy's right, Kevin. You did try to help out with a tough situation."

"Thanks," Kevin grunted back.

Peggy sighed too. It was clear that her brother and Carol were still a long ways from being comfortable with each other. For once, considering her current track record for making things worse, she held her tongue, but the situation was another reason for feeling sad about the events she'd set in motion.

Forty-Nine

AFTER SHOWING THEIR visitors out, Michael returned to the garden and found Arel staring at the twilight sky. "Are you alright?"

"Yes, how about Peggy?" Arel asked.

Michael pulled up a chair and sat down. "She's still somewhat upset, but everyone was relieved to see you again."

"I know who they are." Arel's voice went quiet, and his eyes had light seeping in again. "They were my family and friends in another life."

"They're still your friends."

"Yes, perhaps. But I think that whatever we once shared was very grim. I think that's why Peggy frightened me when we met."

"Don't dwell on any of that. It's the present that's important."

Michael knew that Arel's condition was extremely fragile. Arel needed friends. He needed to have contact with other people, but he wasn't strong enough to tap into past events that were indeed grim.

Arel frowned. "But you wanted me to meet them. Now I have. Shouldn't I search for our deeper connection?"

"There's time for all of that later. They came here because they want to know the person that you are now."

"They wanted to visit a wreck? Did you see their faces, how they stared at me?"

"They looked very concerned."

Arel let out a huff of mirthful protest. "Peggy and the others saw what happens to a human being who thinks he can handle angel blood." He glanced at Michael. "As they say, 'Pride goeth before the fall.'"

"I'm sorry that it's been so hard for you."

"It's weird, you would think I could relate to your kind since I have your blood. But seeing Carol and the others, I realize that I'm still very much connected to the human side of life."

Michael studied Arel's eyes. When they caught the light from the setting sun, they were dark, golden orbs staring out with desire. He could also feel Arel's loneliness, his need for affection from other humans.

"There wasn't always such a great distance between the world of man and angels."

"What happened?"

"People began to think that they were alone. Eventually, they couldn't see us anymore. We became the stuff of stories, nothing more. People became units of isolation and fear. Our realm never went that route. We continued to know and feel the connection to everything and everyone."

"If that's the definition of humanity, I fit right in. But I am experiencing more of the 'everything' part. In the hospital, I knew all about Mrs. Hayes. Out of the blue, her life was there in front of me. And just now, I remembered a part of a past life of my own."

"Our realms are coming together."

Arel flashed a hopeful glance in Michael's direction. "Am I becoming an angel too?"

"No, not exactly."

"Then what?"

Michael's gaze faltered for an instant, but he remained silent.

"You don't know, do you?"

"No."

"Then I am a science project."

"I wouldn't put it that way."

"Maybe you would if you were me, if you had to hide in the dark, never knowing what hell was coming at you next."

Michael could feel Arel's somewhat optimistic disposition giving way to a heavier mood. "Do you want to know something? If I were you, who knows? I might not be as strong as you are."

"Really?"

"When we were in the alley, and you wanted my blood, I had my doubts about it all, remember?"

"Yes, and I'm sure you've regretted your decision ever since."

"No, that's not what I'm trying to say. I understood that even someone like you, who is as courageous as any that I've known, was going to be up against a tremendous battle. I'm sure it's been extremely difficult. You've felt so cut off and powerless as all the harsh facets of life and draining emotional storms pounded you."

Arel smiled sheepishly. "So I haven't just been a baby about it all?"

"No, indeed, I didn't want you to have to go through this, my dear friend. And yet, I knew that you wanted to be free again."

Michael's words seemed to make Arel's good humor go up another notch. He actually grinned. "You know something, I feel like the worst is behind me. I feel like I'm on a new page. A few hours ago, I was so scared of meeting Peggy and the others again. Now I see how ridiculous I was. Maybe I'm doing better than I realized."

"I'm very happy to hear that."

Arel sat up straighter. "It's time to start living again. I can be like you. I can embrace life like you said." He swung his feet over the side of the chair.

Michael held up a hand. "Yes, but maybe you need to do it gradually. Your body's compromised at the moment. You'll have to be careful for a while."

Arel waved him off. "This isn't the first time that I've abused myself. I may not be all vampire anymore, but I'm better than that. I've got your angel blood flowing through my veins. Why should I be careful?"

Michael moved uneasily into a more upright position and sighed. "I didn't know that this would happen. I'm sorry."

Arel gave him a playful frown. "What now? I'm sitting here feeling like things are finally making sense. I want to enjoy life. I want to enjoy this place." He gestured at the garden. As the sun was setting, everything was bathed in a sparkling, golden glow. "You know, I've never appreciated what you've done. This piece of ground was nothing but weedy grass when I moved here. But now, I'm practically sitting in paradise, and you're telling me that you're sorry. Sorry for what?" He let his voice drop into a conciliatory tone. "I'm the one who's sorry that I've been so difficult these past months. Do you forgive me, Michael?"

"There's nothing to forgive. You've done your best. That's all that's expected."

"Good," Arel said as he grasped the arms of the lounger. "Now give me a little tour of your handiwork. It's time to start smelling the roses as the saying goes."

Arel started to push himself up, but he only got halfway there. Clutching his chest, he froze. "Dammit—" His protest was cut short as he teetered back and forth.

Michael moved quickly to Arel's side, took his arm and helped him to sit back down as he started gasping.

"Don't try to move."

"Do I have a choice?" Arel croaked out.

"I think you'll be better in a bit."

After a few minutes, Arel began to breathe easier. His hand was still gripping Michael's, but his eyes became hard and questioning. "Tell me what's going on."

"Your body's changed."

"Changed? My chest feels like an elephant is sitting on it." His ashen face contorted with confusion as he let go of Michael. "Your blood should have an opposite effect. The sun can't hurt me. I haven't had any desire to eat. I think I'm moving up to super-being status, don't you?"

Michael pulled his lawn chair closer to Arel. "You've been very . . . unhappy lately. You've punished your body unmercifully. Now, there's concern that this 'exchange' might not succeed."

Arel's brows went from surprise to a narrow glare of understanding. "Let's not sugar coat it. You're saying that I'm dying, correct? After all the crap I've been through? I've hated myself forever. Now I get a chance to find some real happiness with old friends, and you tell me the 'exchange' has an unexpected glitch?"

"Getting upset is exactly what you don't want to do. If you can learn to relax and enjoy what you've been given, I think we can get your condition turned around."

"You're using the 'we' word again, and the truth is that I'm the one who's clearly got a problem." Arel raised his voice as he tried to sit up again, but he was rendered immobile a second time.

Michael watched helplessly as another bout of acute pain seized Arel's heart. When the pain eased again, Arel's eyes were suddenly innocent, pleading, and also clearly tuned into his body.

Arel gasped out a few words. "Oh hell, I'm a goner."

Fifty

ABRIGAIL SAT ON Arel's king size bed, leaned back on pillows that were stacked against the beautifully carved, ornate headboard. Arel had his head on a small, soft cushion in her lap. When he looked up at her, his golden eyes were admiring as she gently stroked his brow.

"Do you know why you're the most perfect angel?" he asked.

She smiled. "Why is that?"

"You're perfect because you're quiet and nurturing. You take care of people in the most loving ways without ever asking anything of them. Whereas other angels that I know come barging into one's life with all these plans about how they're going to change your life. Of course they forget to tell the person that there's a possible penalty attached, nothing much, just that they might end up dead."

As Arel spoke, his innocent gaze, like that of a fawn in the forest, moved sideways to target Michael. The angel sat in a chair close by. It was enough to make Michael glance up only briefly before he went back to his book.

Arel sighed heavily. "Now I'm on the edge of a cliff. It'll only take a little nudge, and I'll go over. And that will be the end of me. Goodbye, no more science project," he said as he glanced over at Michael again. "The guinea pig will be gone forever."

Michael sighed too as he stood up. "Excuse me. I have some chores in the garden. I'll be back in a little while."

"Michael?" Arel held out his hand, his eyes suddenly sad and pitiful. "You won't be gone too long, will you? It's comforting to have you close."

Michael paused. "If you want, I can have Abrigail take care of the garden duties."

Arel pulled his hand back as he let his gaze drift up to Abrigail's face. "No, that's alright. The garden needs you too. Go ahead. I'll be fine, I guess."

* * *

Later, Abrigail came out of the house and glanced around the garden, looking for Michael. He was in the far corner, changing the water in the birdbath. Studying his face, she saw the hard set of his brow as he busied himself.

"I thought I'd get some air," she said as she waved to him and continued on down the path to a stone bench. It was located in the rose section. She inhaled deeply as she sat down. "The air is so fresh and fragrant. Your roses are absolutely magnificent."

"Thank you," Michael replied as he finished his task and started retrieving the hose. "How's our boy?"

"He finally fell asleep."

Michael's frown deepened. "I hope he rests for more than five minutes. His mind is still very busy."

"Yes, and he's enjoying playing the victim. After you left, he asked if I'd read to him. He wants to hear 'War and Peace.' He said that it would help him to forget his own problems, but he kept looking up at me with those sweet, defenseless eyes. I must confess I couldn't help but give in to him. He's terribly charming you know."

Michael smiled. "At least he wants company now."

"Oh yes, what did he tell me? If he only has a few days left, he wants to enjoy as much happiness as possible. But there's something that I don't understand. Why does he always seem more content when he talks about dying? Did you notice that his energy soars when he tells us how little time he has left?"

"Yes, I noticed."

"He said that God owes him."

"What?"

"I think his exact words were 'This is one hell of a screw-up. God owes me big time.'"

Michael paused. "It *is* quite a problem."

"Well, you and I both know that people, like sheep, can sometimes stray very far afield. They can find themselves battling alone, drifting further and further from safety. But thankfully for Arel, you've always been a perfect shepherd."

"Tell that to Arel."

"You let him get away with a lot, Michael. Is his self-pity a good thing?"

"It's a distraction. It's giving his body a respite from his emotional turmoil. He's shelved the memories for now, and his guilt has definitely been pushed to the side."

"Yes, that's true." She got up to inspect a large, white rose a few feet away. "But you indulge him, my friend. You know that you do."

"He has to blame someone, and I don't want him turning his energies back on himself."

"He is looking better. Soon, he'll be strong enough for visitors."

Michael dusted off his hands. "Carol and the others will rally round him. I'm sure of that."

Abrigail gave him an anxious look. "Oh heavens, I hope he's not too hard on them. He keeps us both busy with his demands. Those poor souls might be in for quite a difficult time."

Michael's face took on a wilted look, like one of his roses that wasn't getting enough water. "He is going through a very self-indulgent phase, but perhaps they'll bring out his best."

Abrigail sighed, hoping that Michael was right. A noise pulled her attention back to the house. Arel was standing at the door, leaned against its surface. He was tapping on the glass with his dark hair mussed and eyes wide and beseeching. His voice was muted as he cried out to her.

"Abrigail, I was calling for you, but you didn't answer. I can't sleep."

Abrigail stood up quickly and glanced at Michael. "Oh my, he managed to climb the stairs."

Arel tapped the glass again. "Are you coming back in soon?"

"I'll be right there, dearest," Abrigail called back. As she moved towards the house, she gave Michael a parting look. It expressed her doubts about Arel's future interaction with his friends. "They'll bring out his best, or perhaps he'll test their loyalty. Either way, I think he'll enjoy himself."

Fifty-One

TIM EXITED THE expressway, knowing that if it were up to him, they wouldn't be going to visit Arel. Still, Peggy's happiness was what counted. Giving her a sideways glance, he noted her dark eyes actively focused on the road as if she were ticking off the miles to her objective. She was on a mission of mercy, and his job was to support her, but he was worried about what it would do to her if she failed.

I hope that you're not kidding yourself, Peg. With the shape this guy's in, I think you'll need a miracle to get him back on track.

"We're probably going to be late," Peggy said, cutting into Tim's thoughts with her curt tone. But when she looked over at him, her eyes were anxious.

He gave her a reassuring smile. "I think we'll be fine."

"That call from Michael sounded nice, but his tone was serious," Kevin commented from the back seat.

Carol sat across from Kevin. "The important thing is that Arel wants to see us. He even insisted on us visiting."

"I hope he doesn't fall over and die on us," Kevin grumbled. "That would be a mess."

Peggy gasped. "Kevin Bailey, don't you dare talk like that!"

Tim's eyes shifted to the rear view mirror. He shot Kevin an 'Are you crazy?' look.

You're a great guy, old buddy, but you do have a way of saying the exact wrong thing.

Kevin's face reddened. "Sorry, Peggy, I'm sure that Arel will be fine."

Peggy ignored his apology. "I want to know more about what's going on. I'll have to take Michael aside and ask him about Arel's condition."

"You better prepare yourself just in case," Kevin insisted.

Tim saw Peggy bite her lip and grab for her tissue. He reached out with his free hand and gave hers a squeeze. "I don't think we should think in those terms for now." He gave Kevin another glaring frown. "Let's simply pay Arel a visit and see what happens."

Kevin seemed to get the point and turned his face to the window, crossing his arms.

Tim understood the look on Kevin's face. Peggy's brother really did want to spare Peggy too, just like Tim. Unfortunately, he didn't know how to express his feelings in a way that had an ounce of diplomacy, not with Peggy. Theirs had always been a challenging relationship.

"Could you put on some tunes, Tim?" Carol asked. Her face was strained too. "I don't think I can stand hearing any more about what might happen to Arel."

Peggy grabbed for the radio dial before Tim had a chance to respond. "Good idea," she said with a forced smile. "I found a great eighties station the other day."

John Lennon's voice, singing *Stand by Me,* filled the car's small interior. Its occupants were all immediately caught up in the lyrics.

When the night has come

And the land is dark

And the moon is the only light we see

No I won't be afraid, no I won't be afraid

After thirty seconds, both Carol and Peggy were crying softly.

Kevin grimaced with emotion as he averted his eyes. "For crap's sake, Peg, turn it off!"

Tim was surprised when the song affected him too. They brought up feelings he wasn't prepared for and didn't want to address. The dark, foreboding lyrics stirred something that felt dreamlike with a nightmare overlay. As the miles slipped by and the group got closer to their destination, he had one of his rare hunches.

We're in way over our heads.

He was sure of it.

***

When Michael opened the door to welcome in the group, their energy hit him like a somber, funeral dirge. Arel was doing better, but he needed optimism, not more misery. Instead of letting the unhappy group in, he closed the door behind him and quickly joined them outside.

"Is everyone alright?" he asked.

Peggy spoke up immediately. "We need to talk."

"What can I do for you?"

"What's wrong with Arel? And don't beat around the bush. Give us the facts." Peggy's voice was adamant, but her eyes were on the verge of tears.

"Peggy's right," Carol said. "Anyone can tell he's in bad shape."

Michael looked at Kevin and Tim, who stood behind the women like two hulking guardians, but their faces couldn't hide their own fears.

"Out with it, Mike," Kevin said with impatience.

Michael moved closer to them, gesturing to gather round. "Arel has a heart condition, a pretty serious one. But with all of you cheering him up, I think that he'll feel better."

"Oh heavens," Peggy lamented. "He's got a bad heart, and I'm dragging him down to the hospital."

"No, don't feel bad," Michael soothed. "He needed to get out a bit. Staying home all the time depresses him."

"Take it easy, Peg," Kevin chimed in. "If the worst happened, a hospital is the perfect place for a heart attack."

Peggy gave him an 'I hate you look' that was cut short by Carol's teary confession.

"I made him come to a diner!" she cried.

"You couldn't know," Michael said quickly. "And if you hadn't asked him to come, he would have never become acquainted with all of you."

Kevin gave Tim a thoughtful look and a nudge. "He really went downhill after that second trip to the hospital, didn't he? I feel bad about making him come back."

Watching the group pull out all the guilt stops, Michael felt like he was juggling four Arel-type dolls. They were all emotionally charged with self-inflicted pain, and they were dropping out of his hands, left and right. "Please, everybody, can I have your attention?" he asked. "Arel is waiting for you, so please leave all your anxious feelings out here. Come in and have a nice dinner."

The words were barely out of his mouth when Carol's face brightened.

"Arel!" she cried out.

Michael turned back towards the door. It was being held open by the original Arel doll. Staring out at the group, he looked like he'd been dropped too, but he had a gracious expression on his face. Arel's appearance meant that he was actually being sociable.

"What's everybody doing out here?" he asked, playing the happy invalid with a smile that Michael didn't recognize. "Come on in."

Smiling back, the group went into formation. Like dutiful school children, they ignored Michael as they filed past him into the house.

Michael brought up the rear. If angels had nerves, he knew *his* would definitely be getting threadbare. Arel by himself was a challenge. It would be interesting to see what four more, similarly wired individuals would add to the mix.

Fifty-Two

SEEING THE AMICABLE group again felt almost dreamlike to Arel. He had never formed a bond with anyone except William. Now four people filed past him, all giving him the most generous smiles and well wishes, as if he were their long lost comrade. Could it be that easy to have people around him that cared? It was an exhilarating thought that was allowed now that he had so little time left.

"Go into the living room, please," he said as he gestured for them to precede him.

I hope to God that I look better than the last time.

Fresh and sharp in a Forzieri, button-down shirt accented by gold and blue enameled Faberge cufflinks, he certainly felt better about himself. He was definitely more carefully groomed. He still had facial hair, but it had been trimmed back to a small goatee and mustache.

What the hell, don't worry too much. You're only going to see them a couple of times before you leave the world.

Still, he wanted to seem worthy of their affection and tried to stroll into the room, but his stroll was more of a shuffle that old people did when they were exhausted. Luckily Michael went ahead and began to seat everyone.

"You look very handsome," Carol remarked as she hesitated, waiting for him to catch up.

He smiled at her, taking in her beauty from a friend's point of view. "Thank you. Now please sit down there on the loveseat next to Kevin." He needed to make sure that she knew that it was alright with him if she'd patched things up with the tall, imposing, young man.

Carol's frown made it obvious that she hadn't done anything of the sort.

Kevin confirmed it. "I better take the chair over here."

Arel could only stare at the two young people mutely. Their clearly hostile relationship struck him as very sad. Since he'd become a candidate for the grim reaper, his jealousies had vanished. He wanted to see a smile on Carol's face when she looked at Kevin. He didn't want her to be alone anymore. He knew how hard that was. He paused by a chair, leaning a hand on it as he felt a bout of weakness coming on. It was accompanied by a face lined with disappointment as he thought about Carol spending her days raising cats and playing solitaire.

Carol noted his reaction with obvious concern. "But it's fine if Kevin wants to sit next to me," she said with a flourish of forced enthusiasm.

Kevin's face sunk into confusion, and he glanced at Peggy for directions. His sister frowned back and did a quick nod towards the seat that Arel had offered. Kevin moved towards it with gritted teeth. "Right, I'd love to sit next to such a lovely gal."

Tim, seated on the sofa next to Peggy, seemed to understand that a diversion was needed, and fast. "Something smells good," he said in a robust voice.

Arel did find Tim's comment satisfying, and his spirits began to lift again as he made his way to one of the recliners. He'd been very preoccupied with making the visit a successful one. "I kind of exaggerated when I said Michael is a great cook. He's actually still learning his way around the kitchen. I am too. Thankfully the internet is great for finding recipes. We're having a simple meal, crab cakes, fish, baked potatoes, and a salad."

Michael cleared his throat and laughed. "I barely boil water. Arel made the dinner, and I helped."

Arel gave Michael a glaring censure, and then he looked at Carol. "I guess I'm still not totally reformed, with lying that is. I also have another confession. I'm on a very different diet, and I don't eat what I cook. So please don't feel awkward when you sit down to your meal and I abstain."

"We didn't want you to overdo it," Carol replied. "And please, your fibs were always good intentioned ones. So let's not hear any more about that."

"Aren't you supposed to be taking it easy?" Kevin asked.

"Yes, Arel, you have to promise to rest from now on," Peggy said forcefully.

Arel smiled contentedly at their combined concern. "Dinner was hardly any work at all. It's good for me." In fact, Michael had been the perfect assistant, following Arel's many directions for all the items prepared. "Come on, everyone, I wanted to get together so that we could have some fun."

When the group failed to rally, Arel glanced over at Michael again. "But I can see that Michael has been spreading rumors about my health, hasn't he?"

The group started shaking their heads and denying it, but Tim cleared his throat and spoke up in a more forceful tone. "We just want to make sure that you're okay, simple as that."

Arel paused, noting a dramatic shift between his last meeting with the group in the garden and the present gathering. It was a little like knowing things about Mrs. Hayes. In the case of the group, he didn't have all the details of their lives. Instead, he sensed the qualities that each of his guests embodied on a very pure level. Tim was the man who could be trusted to say and do whatever, with a forthright honesty. Next to him, Peggy was the pixie princess. She was the face of driving concern and commitment. Across from them, Carol and Kevin were like the two innocents. No matter what their ages, there was something young and still forming about both of them. And like children, their hearts were open and giving.

Together, the group formed a body of support that was there for him if he wanted it. Did he dare to let them into his life? He took a couple of deep breaths, as if he were contemplating a high dive, a plunge into waters that could be deadly or warm and inviting.

But what if I'm just making another mistake?

Before he had a chance to answer himself, he was speaking aloud. "If you still want me, I'd like to be part of this family."

Peggy responded at once. "That's wonderful news."

Her voice was filled with happiness, but beneath her sentiments, Arel felt her sense of apprehension, as if she were adopting a crippled child who wasn't long for the world. Kevin's internal response was even louder – *Hope he doesn't die on us now that we've taken him in.* Carol's eyes conveyed her message, 'My poor Arel, I feel so helpless. What can I do to make it better for you?' Only Tim's thoughts were shielded and unreadable.

* * *

Nobody felt sorry for Arel by the end of the evening. At his suggestion, they all joined in a game of poker after dinner. For Carol, it was a totally new experience, but expertise didn't seem to make a difference. By the time the last hand was played, almost all of the chips were in Arel's pile.

"Where did you learn to play cards like that?" Tim asked as he fingered his two lone chips. "We need to take you to Vegas."

Arel's eyes sparked with a playfulness that had been hidden away for a long time. "Sorry, but I have to have a few secrets."

He was in his element, and he knew it. Many a night, when he and William were university students, he'd played until the sunrise, often taking the final pot as his opponents sulked away. But playing poker was never about the money. It was about proficiency and natural talent. Cheating had never interested him. And on this night, he had taken great care not to access private information from his fellow players. He didn't have to.

Kevin threw his remaining chip into Arel's pile. "You finished us off good, you scoundrel."

"I'll be happy to give you a few tips," Arel offered.

Kevin stretched his long arms upwards and did a couple of neck rolls. "I might have to take you up on that."

Carol gazed at Arel with pride, as if he was still the gem that she'd found and now shared with the others.

Peggy seemed happy too. Halfway through the game, as Arel hauled in another stack of chips, her distress had melted away. "After this, I think I'm going to do less worrying about you and more about my poor Tim's wallet."

Tim pushed back from the table and stood up. "On that cheerful note, I think it's time to call it quits."

As the group prepared to leave, Arel remained seated.

"I'm going to let Michael see you out," he announced. "We'll get together again soon."

Michael heard his cue and got up from a chair in the next room where he'd been reading. He'd passed on the poker game. Now, looking at the group, he seemed pleased with his choice.

"Good night, sweetie," Carol said giving Arel a light kiss on the cheek. "Thank you for a wonderful dinner. Everything was delicious."

Arel had heard the same thing a number of times earlier, but he felt warm inside each time the praise was repeated.

Peggy leaned over and gave him a gentle hug. "Have sweet dreams. Maybe one of these days we can talk," she whispered.

Her words reminded him of what they shared. For a moment, a memory tried to surface, but he pushed it back at once. What good would it do now that he was going to die?

As Peggy started to pull away, he held on to her for a moment, "Start giving yourself a break, that's an order."

"Yes, sir," she said obediently as he let go of her. "And promise that you'll do the same."

He nodded in agreement and was glad to see her smiling as she started out of the room. His chest swelled with a bit of pride. His first dinner party had been a success.

When Michael returned from seeing their guests on their way, Arel realized he'd had another first. "I actually had a wonderful evening with friends."

Michael smiled back. "Yes, I can see that."

"It has me thinking. I've decided that I don't want to sleep downstairs tonight. I'm going to use one of the bedrooms up here."

"Why don't you take the master?" Michael suggested. "I use the middle bedroom anyway."

"Good idea. I'll be able to see your gardens from the window."

Michael's smile broadened. "By the way, I wanted to say that you were a perfect host tonight. Everyone left here in much better spirits then when they arrived."

"Thank goodness. Being privy to their thoughts was a little dismaying, but I think I changed their minds about me."

As he recalled pleasantries from the visit, he started to get up. "Oh, hell, not again—" For the first time in a couple of days, his heart grabbed, throwing him back into his chair with a sharp pain. When the pain eased, he gave Michael an imploring look, remembering the angel's earlier warning about taking it very slow. "And do me a favor, don't tell me that you told me so."

"I wouldn't dare," Michael said in the same dutiful tone that Peggy had used.

Fifty-Three

STANDING IN THEIR bedroom, Peggy watched Tim as he threw his car keys on the dresser and headed over to the closet to get undressed. "Did you have a good time tonight?" she asked, sitting down on the side of the bed. "I know you weren't crazy about the idea of seeing Arel again."

"It was nice."

"But?"

With his hand on the closet door, Tim paused. "No, I mean it. The dinner was great, and Arel can be kind of fun for a card shark."

Peggy held her hand out and gestured him over. "Yes, but I can tell that something is bothering you."

Tim walked to the bed and sat down next to her. "I don't know, Peg, there's something about him that gets to me. He's different."

"Arel just needs people that care."

Tim took her hand in his. "Maybe you're right. But he's not my first priority, you are. I don't want you to get really upset over him again. I've been worried about you. So has Kevin."

"Tonight really helped. I feel a little better after seeing him smile. He seemed almost smug after the poker game."

"Hey, if you feel better because he took me to the cleaners, that's fine with me. I'll do whatever it takes to make you happy again."

"I'm sorry if I've made it hard for you and Kevin." She paused. "Of course, now I feel bad about Carol and Kevin. It's my fault that they're not together anymore. They were doing so great before I had the accident."

"Kevin got himself into this. You have to let him be responsible." Tim leaned in and kissed her cheek, then her neck.

She snuggled back, leaning against him. "I guess you're right. But you never do that sort of stupid stuff. How did I get so lucky to get you?"

Tim put his arms around her and held her tight. "Are you kidding? I got the prettiest girl in the world."

Breathing in Tim's cologne and enjoying his embrace, Peggy shut her eyes and sighed. "Do you realize what a horrible crush I had on you when we were kids?"

"No, I guess not."

"You were my prince charming, so handsome and solid."

"But it was Kevin that did most of the fighting for you. I was there more as a referee when you two went at each other."

"But aren't you proud of me? I think I won most of those fights with the bullies by just standing up to them."

"Yes, I remember being quite impressed with how you, this scrawny, loud mouthed little kid, could take charge."

She hit his shoulder lightheartedly. "I think you need to learn to describe my aptitude for greatness with more style."

"You were and still are amazing," he said as he began kissing her again. "Don't ever change who you are, Peggy Leggy."

Fifty-Four

KEVIN WALKED UP to Carol's apartment door, started to ring the bell, and hesitated. He had apologized and explained himself to Carol, and she'd been stubborn and unforgiving.

So why am I doing this to myself.

He knew why. Carol had asked him to come over, and being a nice guy, he'd agreed. Why couldn't he be like a lot of the men he knew at the office? They played it cool. They didn't let their emotions sway them, and women flocked to them anyway.

Dammit, I can't be like that.

He paused. He was fooling himself, letting himself off the hook too easily by praising his virtues. In truth, he was worse than the guys at the office. He'd wounded Carol, the gentlest of people. It wasn't intentional, but he'd hurt her deeply.

I can't expect her to recover with a few words of apology.

He forced his finger to the bell and pushed. After a few minutes, he was about to ring it a second time when the door opened a few inches.

"Hi Kevin," Carol said. She studied him for several moments before she gave him a polite smile.

He shifted uncomfortably as he waited for her to invite him in. When the door finally swung open, Carol positioned herself behind it.

"I'm glad you could make it," she said quickly.

Carol's voice sounded off, like she didn't know if she wanted to talk to him or not. Kevin knew that he didn't want to talk to her. Whether it was guilt or anger, either way he wanted to forget the mess he'd made. As a kid, he used to run off to the woods when he'd made mistakes.

Oh hell, Peggy's right. I'm like a child. I still want to run away.

Yet, as he followed Carol into the living room, he wasn't seeing her with a child's eyes. A grown man's gaze swept over her, noting that her lime green, silky shirt and pants accentuated all the right curves. In spite of his mental protests, he felt his body responding, remembering. It hadn't been that long since he'd held Carol's soft, yielding body in his arms. She'd been so sweet when he met her, his image of the perfect woman. And he'd spoiled everything with his big mouth. He had to accept that.

Be accountable, Kevin. Be a man.

* * *

Carol heard the door bell and approached the entrance with a firm intention. She'd be businesslike with Kevin and keep her feelings out of the way. Arel had suggested a friendly reconciliation. As a favor to him, she was following his advice. Of course, there was also Peggy to consider. Peggy felt she'd been partly responsible for the mess they were in, and Carol needed to sort things out for her friend's benefit too. She needed to put the whole, wretched affair to rest.

However, when she opened the door and saw Kevin, her thoughts were put on hold. Time reversed itself as she gazed up at him, mesmerized by his clear, forthright eyes and his handsome presence. It was like the first time that they met, when her judgment was untainted by pain.

He was a really good guy. Have I been too hard on him?

The moment passed. "Come in," she said politely, but she avoided any further eye contact. Still, she couldn't keep her heart from aching as she shut the door and moved quickly to the living room. She wanted what had been taken from her, wished all the unhappiness could disappear. But reality set in as they took their seats. She sat on the sofa and Kevin chose the chair furthest away from her. There was a chill in the air that separated them.

Kevin glanced over with hands tightly clasped. "You wanted to see me?"

She hunched her shoulders, trying to comfort herself as she prepared to tell him why they were meeting. "After being at Arel's the other night, I feel like we need some kind of closure. Peggy is my best friend and your sister. I guess I'd like us to be able to feel somewhat comfortable around each other again."

Kevin's eyes retreated. He stared down, studying the rug. Finally, he glanced up at her with a narrow, focused gaze. "Look, I was wrong, totally wrong. I know I apologized before, but this time I want you to know how sorry I am that I hurt you. I was a jerk. That said, I'll do whatever you want. If it's closure, I'm all for it." His tone was quick and deliberate, but also sincere.

At first, Carol could only nod back at him. She hadn't expected him to be so conciliatory. In their past conversations, he'd hung onto his reservations, reasons to excuse his behavior, but now he seemed stripped of them all.

"Apology accepted," she said.

Kevin nodded back with a gaze that was honest and direct, but it didn't have that open wanting, that connection that had been between them. He seemed ready for the closure that she had suggested.

He offered a quick smile. "From now on, when we're around each other, maybe we can behave like friends."

The term 'friends' made Carol's heart sink. It was her turn to look away. She didn't want a friend. She wanted a person who loved her and someone she could love in return. Kevin had been that person for a short time. Why couldn't he be that person again?

I can't trust a guy that turned on me. Or can I? Arel thinks that I should.

She recalled an earlier phone conversation with Arel. He had advised her in his quiet, understanding voice. "He's young, Carol. And I know that you're young too, but it takes longer for men to mature."

Carol had objected, but Arel wouldn't have it. He became a wise sage who seemed to see more in Kevin than she could see. "Try not to be too hard on him," he said. "He truly didn't want to hurt you. He doesn't know *how* to hold in his feelings. And you know that Peggy has never helped him in that department."

Carol had laughed, but she was also mystified at Arel's keen observation after knowing Peggy for such a short length of time. "Peggy just makes her brother shut up."

Arel agreed. "That's right, but Kevin doesn't need people pointing out his shortcomings. He's had that all his life with Peggy."

"I guess I acted the same way with him," she said, falling under Arel's ability to soothe her, to help her put her anger away long enough to get a different point of view.

While she was pondering his advice, Arel continued. "But you're understanding and very forgiving. I know that from personal experience. Promise me that you'll give Kevin another chance too."

She'd given in to Arel. She couldn't refuse him. She couldn't add to the pain that he was already in. But maybe, just maybe, she also wanted him to be right. But it wasn't as simple as Arel made it sound. Even if she wanted to give Kevin another chance, she didn't know how. And when she glanced over at him, it was clear that he wanted to leave. His eyes were furtive, like those of a kid outside the principal's office, waiting for his dismissal. But there was something else in the way he looked.

Arel is right. Kevin seems lost.

The more she studied Kevin, the more she could feel that on some level, he was as helpless as she felt at times. Sure he was a smart, tech guy, but he had never learned how to handle a crisis that involved someone whom he loved. He had no one to show him how. Peggy always told him what to do.

For an instant, she thought she saw Arel looking at her, like he had at his home, like he was depending on her. "Help Kevin, for me."

It seemed like an impossible task. That's when all of her frustration and fear hit home. It came on as fast as a summer storm. In the past, she had shed tears off and on. They were showers of loneliness and anger. Now, a new, treacherous storm of despairing emotions hit. "Life is so sad," she cried out. "Arel is dying. You'll probably be clueless for the rest of your life. And I'm going to end up alone, an old maid! It's all so horrible."

As soon as she started sobbing, Kevin jumped up and grabbed a tissue off the end table. "Please don't cry. I might be clueless forever, but you could never end up alone. You're too beautiful and sweet." He crossed the four feet of distance between them and handed her the tissue.

Carol could feel his desperate desire to comfort her. It made her feel even sadder. She reached out for him, like she reached out for Charlie bear. "Can you sit down next to me?"

Kevin obeyed immediately and took a seat.

She sniffed and leaned back against him. In return, Kevin put his arms around her and began to gently rock her. Neither of them spoke, but Carol felt safe in Kevin's embrace again.

***

Grace and Fred sat on Carol's apartment balcony. Both were soaking up the rays of the moon as it streamed down, bathing everything in its silvery radiance. Grace had her wings spread out behind her. She enjoyed the idea of having the adornments even if her natural angelic body was more formless. After so many eons of humans expecting angels to have wings, she felt quite at home with the idea. Fred hadn't been as interested in the concept, but he was trying it out as he sat next to her.

He smiled. "You're right, wings can be quite interesting. When the moon's energy connects with them, it's very relaxing."

"I have to say that I'm already completely serene. The happiness coming from my Carol is so wonderful. She really missed Kevin, even if she was hurt by his actions."

Fred nodded. "Thankfully, he had the courage to come and face Carol again, to make up for his blunders."

Grace's glow dimmed a little. "I hope her memories of a supposedly perfect world don't create more problems. She adored her parents and the security of having them together and happy. When they went their separate ways, she was devastated. She's been afraid of taking chances ever since."

"Kevin will try his best, I'm sure."

"I know, and I'm not blaming him. It's Carol. She's still learning how to be responsible for her happiness when things go wrong. She takes everything very personally." Grace hesitated. "I don't know what to say, Frederick, Kevin might not be the one for her. He's got a lot of growing to do too."

Fred gave her a sideways glance and smiled teasingly. "Kevin's not perfect, but at least he's not a vampire."

Grace's wings stiffened immediately. "Indeed he isn't, and I'm eternally grateful."

"Speaking of former vampires, have you heard how Michael's fellow is doing?"

"From what I've gathered, Arel has become extremely demanding. I didn't get specifics, just the idea that he's generally pushy about his many whims. And if he doesn't get his way, he uses his trump card."

"What trump card?"

"Abrigail quoted him as saying, 'Give the guinea pig a break. I wouldn't have bitten one of God's legions if I'd known it was going to kill me.'"

"And how does Michael respond?"

"He knows that Arel should be more accountable for his condition. Still, he finds it hard to deny him anything. It was Michael's idea to try and assist in the way that he did. Now, Arel's not doing well."

"But Arel was miserable before all this started."

"Of course he was, but that's what happens when you're working with a soul that's been a . . . a . . . you know . . . a vampire."

Fred paused and stared at Grace.

She stared back. "What is it? What are you looking at?"

"Your wings, they're different."

She smiled. "Yes, I've been thinking that if Carol ever gets a glimpse of me, she might be impressed with larger wings. She'll see that I'm always there trying to protect her."

"Or she might think that you're a giant bat." Fred grinned broadly. "I think you have to work on the feather part."

Grace glanced behind her. "Oh my, every time I think about that time when Arel showed up in Carol's bedroom, I have a tendency to go into a more outwardly impressive form." She paused. "But really, Frederick, those are not bat wings. With a bit of tweaking and color, they can be perfectly beautiful and dragon-like."

"Well, from what you've told me, you don't have to worry about Arel at this point, except to pray that he pulls through."

"Heavens, you know that I wish him the best. But unfortunately wishes aren't enough. From the way Abrigail described his heart condition, he's in real trouble. Neither Abrigail or Michael seem able to help at this point."

"Michael will find a way," Fred said in a confident tone. "Now there's an angel who does have big wings. He'll get his sheep back to the fold."

"Abrigail doesn't call Arel a sheep. After what she's experienced working with him, she's changed the metaphor. Michael is trying to bring back a lion who's pretending to be a sheep."

Fifty-Five

MICHAEL CAME THROUGH the kitchen door carrying an armful of fresh cut roses. He glanced at Arel who was perched on a stool next to the table. He'd taken up the art of flower arranging and was filling a large, crystalline vase with an assortment of Michael's offerings. The man was still rail-thin and his eyes were lacking and unhappy again. When Michael smiled, he tried to put extra energy behind his well wishes. "Are these the kind of flowers that you wanted?"

Arel barely looked up from his task. "Yes, they're fine, thank you. Just put them with the others."

Michael did as he was told and stepped back. "Your arrangements have added a lot of color and beauty to all the rooms."

Arel's brows furrowed at the comment. "It's a rather pathetic hobby, but I don't have the energy to do much else." He retrieved a large, yellow rose from the group. "Just think, this flower could be the last thing I see if my heart suddenly goes."

"I thought you said you felt a little better today."

"Perhaps, but what does it matter, a day more or less. Anyway, I have bigger problems." Arel paused and gave Michael the full brunt of his wide, golden, listless gaze. "I don't think I'm going to heaven after all."

Michael prepared himself. It was going to be one of Arel's *'no heaven for me'* days. The ailing human often switched from expecting paradise when he died to claiming that he'd probably be reincarnated almost immediately into some hellish, new life. Michael moved a little closer. "This topic isn't helping you."

"Help? I'm beyond help. I have to face facts. Even if God does owe me, I'm still not worthy of any reward. I'll get recycled very quickly once I pass over. I'll come back as some ignorant slob." Arel paused, letting out a hopeless sigh. "I won't be able to see you, Michael. Angels don't exist for most people, and I'll be one of them. I'll be alone again, totally alone."

Michael reached out for Arel's shoulder. "You have to stop dwelling on such negative thoughts. It negates all the strides that you're making towards a recovery."

Arel's hands dropped to his sides. "Once I die and you're gone, all hope will be gone."

"Arel, you have power to create something better for yourself right now. So put your energy into living *this* life. Besides, you know that I'll never desert you."

"If I can't see you the next time around, what difference will it make?" Arel heaved out a heavy breath. "As for this life, I've tried to be responsible. I've tried to prepare myself. Do you know that I've gone through all the steps in the grieving process? They were supposed to bring some peace, but I still feel doomed."

Michael hesitated. He had to put a stop to Arel's dialogue before it became a full blown dive into despair. Of course the problem was that Arel's victim mentality came from a deeply wounded past. When Arel insisted on being right about his misery, it could be tricky trying to dissuade him.

"We need to have . . . um . . . another one of those talks," Michael said firmly.

* * *

As soon as Michael made the announcement that they needed to talk, Arel felt his heart flutter. He reached out a hand and held on to the edge of the table edge to steady himself. "What? The last time we talked, I found out that I'm going to die. What could you possibly want to tell me now?"

Michael avoided Arel's abysmal eyes and took his arm instead. "Let's go into the living room where you can be comfortable."

Arel balked. "Me? Comfortable? Is that your angelic humor?"

The truth was that his heart felt like it had engine knock, a bad case of engine knock. There were also the bouts of crushing pain and the constant weakness. He did have his good days, but this one was definitely headed in the wrong direction.

"Come along," Michael said with an encouraging smile. "I want you to sit down in the living room and listen to me before you bring on another attack."

Arel realized that he didn't have the strength to resist. "Oh god, what now?" he moaned. Feeling weaker than ever, he held on to Michael, using him as a crutch as he slowly made his way to the living room sofa. When he sat down, he clung to the sofa arm. "You have my complete attention, but before you start, do you understand that I'm barely holding on?"

"This has nothing to do with making you feel worse. It has to do with a part of you that we don't discuss very often. This is about your soul."

Arel clasped the sofa arm more aggressively, his bony fingers digging into the white linen upholstery. "My soul is going to die too? I didn't think that was possible."

"Did I say that your soul was going to die?"

"No, not yet." Arel started taking deep, wheezy breaths. "I guess I was jumping ahead."

"Please, Arel, don't do that," Michael said more forcefully.

Arel blinked back, barely taking in any air. "Why are you using that harsh tone with me? You don't use that tone unless it's really serious."

Michael sighed. "I'm just trying to make a point."

"What point? You never mentioned that my soul could die! What a damnable complication!"

"Arel, your soul is not going to die."

Arel leaned forward, holding his chest. His heart was racing so fast, he didn't know if his chest wall could restrain the vessel. "What *is* going to happen to my soul? Did your blood do something to it that can't be reversed?"

"Arel, just listen—"

"You're the one that started the soul thing, Michael, don't get mad at me."

"I don't get mad, you know that."

"And vampires don't bite angels and come down with a terminal case of death." Arel's body began to sway precariously. "I don't feel well. I think I need to lie down."

Michael paused for a long moment. "You don't want to have this conversation. Is that what's happening?"

"Maybe."

"I had something very positive to tell you, but you're not going to let me, are you?"

Arel hugged himself nervously. "Just give me time to adjust. You keep springing things on me. I'm just a weak, human being. I can't keep up."

Michael stood up. "Fine, we'll talk later."

Arel remained in his seat as Michael walked out of the room. Michael was right. Angels didn't get mad, but sometimes they did *know* things that humans weren't always privy to, especially when it came to a person's soulful nature. He decided he was better off in the dark.

* * *

Michael opened the kitchen door and stepped out into the back yard. He was still going over his conversation with Arel. When he saw Abrigail waiting for him in the rose garden, he waved. He walked over and joined her on the stone bench.

"How did our shepherd and lion do?" she asked.

Michael gave her a look of bewilderment. "The shepherd barely said two words, and the lion was running for cover."

Abrigail gave him a sideways smile. "He was a cowardly lion?"

Michael gazed upwards, studying the white, fluffy clouds overhead. "Not cowardly, but he's still got all of his defenses ready in case he needs them."

"And he wasn't willing to learn more about his soul self?"

"No, not yet."

"What are you going to do now?"

"Arel doesn't want my advice, but hopefully, when the group comes over tonight, he'll let them help him."

Fifty-Six

AREL SAT AT the dining room table dealing out cards, trying to distract himself from his earlier talk with Michael. But in spite of being surrounded by his new friends, he was finding it difficult. "Anybody want to play for pennies instead of chips," he asked, hoping for a change of pace. Winning all the time was getting boring.

Peggy snatched up each card that was dealt. "Maybe next week."

"Maybe next year," Carol giggled, letting her cards alone until Arel was finished dealing them out.

"How about you two?" Arel asked, looking at Tim, then Kevin.

"Forget it," Tim said in a brusque tone.

Peggy stopped and studied Arel. She zeroed in on his trembling hands and anxious face. "Sweetie, you look a little worried. Is there something we should know?"

Arel put the deck aside and placed a finger to his lips, giving everyone the 'Be quiet' sign. Glancing around, he waved them closer. "I need to talk to you," he whispered in an almost inaudible tone.

As all four at the table leaned in, Kevin frowned. "What's up?" he asked in a normal voice.

"Shh!" Arel scolded.

"What is it?" Carol whispered.

Arel pushed himself out of his chair a few inches and scanned the living room for Michael's presence. "Good, he's gone," he said with a gasp of relief. For a moment he hesitated, trying to catch his breath. When he had enough oxygen, he continued. "Have any of you ever heard of 'soul death'?"

"Soul death?" Tim exclaimed loudly.

Arel gave him a fierce glance. "Keep your voice down, please!"

The group exchanged puzzled looks. As the phrase, "soul death," was mumbled back and forth, everyone started shaking their heads. Everyone was saying 'No' at the same time.

Carol reached out to Arel. "Do you know something about soul death?"

Arel shrugged. "Not too much, but I was having a conversation with Michael earlier and—" He paused, not knowing how to go on.

"And he told you about it?" Peggy gasped. "That's absurd. There's no such thing."

Arel did an eye check to make sure the living room was still unoccupied and returned his gaze to the group. Their faces were all anxious and completely focused on him. "Please, everyone, we have to discuss this as quietly as possible," he ordered in a hushed tone.

"Why? What are you whispering about?" Michael asked as he came out of the kitchen.

Arel jumped and grabbed for his heart. "Bloody hell, Michael! Where did you come from? I thought you were in your room. How did you get here without my seeing you?"

"I walked down the hall and around."

Peggy looked up at Michael. "Have you been telling Arel that there's such a thing as soul death?"

"Of course not," Michael replied.

Kevin spoke up. "Well Arel said you did. So what's going on?"

Arel held up a hand. "Everybody, please, don't blame Michael. I think that he's as confused about it as any of us."

Michael moved closer to the table. "I'm making an announcement. There is no such thing. A soul cannot die."

Everyone nodded in agreement, and then they looked at Arel.

"Sweetheart," Peggy said putting her hand on Arel's. "Does this have something to do with how you feel about your condition?"

Arel looked at Peggy's hand on his and realized that he found it comforting now. "I guess it does," he said as the full impact of losing everything, including Michael and his new family, hit him. What little color he had in his face drained away. "I'm afraid that Michael was right when he told you about the possibility that I might—"

When Arel paused, Tim gave Peggy a quick glance. Usually the most reserved, he reached out and took hold of Arel's arm. He spoke in a tone that was very direct. "Listen to me, Arel. We haven't known each other for very long, but if you need some extra support, I have a lot of leave saved up at work, I'll be happy to spend some time helping you get through this."

Tim's gesture and his firm grip of support sent a wave of solidarity through Arel. He even got a flash of their lost ties. He had a vision of their connection in another life. Tim was running towards Arel, trying to help him. Arel knew that they'd not only been friends, but they were best friends.

"I know this sounds pathetic, but I don't want to die," he whispered.

Tim tightened his hold on Arel's arm. "If I have anything to do with it, you're going to get better."

Arel glanced over at the strong, muscular man. Tim's eyes were the same loyal, devoted ones that he remembered. And he knew that he cared about Tim as much as any real brother.

"Thank you," he gasped as he began to look at each one of the group. "I've gotten myself into a pretty bad situation. Thank you for being here for me."

* * *

Later that night, Michael reflected on the interaction between Arel and his friends. As Arel explained his plight and everyone responded with offers to help, Arel did the unexpected. He threw open emotional doors that he usually kept hidden away. He'd invited people into areas of his life that had been off limits for many lifetimes. It was a surprising turn of events.

Fifty-Seven

THE AFTERNOON SUN was beating down on the dining room side of Arel's house. Tim tugged at his collar as he sat at the table, but he didn't blame his heated condition on the temperature of the room. "Why do I feel like I'm swimming in shark infested waters every time I play poker with you?" he asked, staring at Arel and letting out a snort of weariness.

Arel answered with a shrug. "Show me your cards, and I'll tell you why you're going to lose again."

"I'm not showing you my cards! And you don't know for sure that I'm going to lose."

Arel gave him a smile of satisfaction. "Oh, but I do." He spread out his own cards on the table.

"What? No way. How the hell did you get four aces?"

"I told you that I'm lucky, but I also know how to play my cards. You and Kevin should listen when I try to give you pointers."

"Yeah, sure. I *have* listened, and your damn pointers don't work."

Arel sat back in his chair. "Sorry, the only explanation I can come up with is that you two are pretty hopeless when it comes to poker."

Tim glared back and threw his cards down on the table. Arel's voice had an irksome 'I know that I'm great' tone to it, and his eyes glowed more brightly than those of the kid who'd just robbed the candy store. "You can be very irritating, Arel. How does Michael stand your attitude?"

Michael was sitting close by in the living room, reading a gardening magazine. "You're finding out what a charmer he is, aren't you?"

Tim let out a sigh of disgust. "He's a charmer alright. I let him talk me into playing for my spare change, and now I have no money in my wallet. If Arel keeps this up, he won't be the only one who doesn't eat regular meals. I won't have money for groceries."

Arel pushed his chair back and stood up. "I wouldn't want you to go hungry. It's getting late, and you didn't have lunch. I'll fix you a sandwich. Maybe it'll improve your mood."

"Maybe you better let me do that," Tim said hastily. Arel was perpetually threatening to fall prey to a bout of weakness at the slightest exertion.

"Nonsense, you've done enough. The windows never looked so good," Arel said as he went to the kitchen. He paused in the doorway. "But I did see a rather large smudge that you missed on one of them in my bedroom."

Tim stifled a protest as he stood up. "I'll get it after my sandwich, okay?" Walking into the living room, he went over to Michael and leaned in. "Between you and me, Arel is a piece of work. I'm here on a mission of mercy and when I leave, I feel like I've been sucked dry."

Michael stared at him for a moment, looking rather amused. "He gets a little spirited."

"I could kiss a coral snake and fare better," Tim groaned as he made his way to the sofa. He took a seat with a thud of exhaustion. "I hope that he's feeling stronger soon. I didn't realize that cheering a person up could be so draining."

"Be assured that he's never been happier," Michael said with a broad smile. "You and the 'gang' as Arel refers to your group, are doing a great job."

"I believe that he thinks the poker massacre I just endured was my reward for washing the windows and cleaning the garage."

"I've tried to offer my services, but he says you do a much better job with everything. I didn't realize how inadequate he thought I was until all of you started helping out."

"That's comforting," Tim grumbled. He laid his head back, using the moment to relax. He was just closing his eyes when the front door flew open.

"Hi everybody!" Peggy came into the foyer looking her happy self.

Tim got to his feet again and welcomed her in to join them. "Thank god, you're back."

Peggy gave him a sweet smile. "Hi honey, did you have a good day?"

Tim returned a blank stare. "What do you think?"

"Oh my, was Arel a little restless again? What did you do?"

Tim looked at his hand and started counting off his fingers. "We had to play Arel's favorite computer game, but we stopped when he got bored with beating me. Then he wanted to get some prep work done for dinner tonight, but as soon as we got started in the kitchen he felt tired and had to go lay down. I ended up peeling about six pounds of potatoes and washing a crap load of salad stuff. Excuse my French, Peggy, Michael. Somewhere along the line, I washed some windows. When I was finished, I went in to check on him. He was having trouble sleeping so I read him two chapters of *War and Peace*. After that, he took a ten minute nap and woke up wanting to play poker. And now my wallet is light thirty bucks."

"Wow," exclaimed Peggy. "Sounds like the poor baby had a full afternoon."

Tim started towards the foyer stairs. "I know that I'm ready for bed. Tell the little darling that I'm downstairs taking a nap."

"Sweetie, you're taking a lot of naps over here, are you okay?"

"Yeah, sure, I'll be back up in a little while."

* * *

Michael watched as the young man disappeared down the stairs. Both Tim and Kevin seemed to be using the lower quarters as an "Arel free zone" where they could escape for short periods. He hoped that Tim got a good nap in. There was a dinner party planned for that night. Tim was first on Arel's list of helpers.

Peggy walked over to where Michael was sitting and frowned. "Tim's been so tired lately."

"He's a very caring person. He's doing a great job, and—" Michael paused when Arel came into the living room carrying a sandwich.

"Great to see you, Peggy," Arel said with a smile. "I heard you and Michael talking about someone doing a great job. Were you discussing me again?" Before Peggy could answer, Arel glanced around the room. "Where's Tim? I made him something to eat."

Peggy went over to Arel and hugged him carefully, as if he might break if she squeezed too tight. "Hello, sweetheart. Tim's taking a nap downstairs. But that was so thoughtful of you to make him something. You're such an angel."

Arel beamed back at her. "Why don't you eat it? Are you hungry?"

Peggy nodded. "Yes, hungry and tired from shopping. It's a good thing we postponed our wedding for a month. With my accident and everything, it would have been too much. By the way I picked up your shirts from the cleaners, but the drugstore was out of that special brand of toothpaste that you use."

"Thank you so much. You're so considerate and helpful," Arel said with a sigh. "But I really wish you hadn't postponed your wedding. I feel like I'm a big part of why you had to push back the date."

Peggy gave him a dismissive wave. "Don't be silly. It's worked out better this way."

Arel's face was still contrite as he held out the sandwich. "At least eat this. You need your strength," he insisted.

Peggy took the sandwich and started for the dining room. As she was about to sit down, Arel held up a hand.

"Allow me, my lady," he said as he pulled out her chair.

Peggy's eyes sparkled brightly. "Thank you, sweetie. You're such a gentleman."

After Peggy sat down, Arel tried to help push the chair back in and gasped. "Ow, ow, ow." He made short, plaintive sounds as he grabbed his chest.

Peggy was off the chair instantly. "You and Tim overdid it, didn't you?" she cried out. "I have to talk to him."

Michael hurried over too. "What can I do?"

Arel ignored him and turned to Peggy for help. "Don't worry, it'll pass, but maybe I should sit in the living room."

Peggy responded at once. "Of course, lean on me."

"Thank you," Arel gasped as he grabbed Peggy's arm and let her help him over to a recliner. "And please promise me that you won't say anything to Tim. We were just having fun, really."

Michael watched as Arel's second victim of the day was called into service. He tried to intervene. "Peggy, I'll stay with Arel while you eat your lunch."

Peggy barely looked up at him. Instead, she hovered anxiously over Arel, pushing back his hair and cooing at him as if he was her child. "That's okay, Michael, I'm fine."

Arel still had a hand on his chest as he looked up at her. "Michael's right. Go eat, please," he said breathlessly.

"Yes, you need to take care of yourself," Michael suggested. Of course, being an angel, he could feel Peggy's energy of rising concern. Saving her from the fragile beast in the recliner wasn't going to happen.

Peggy smiled back at him sweetly. "Arel's health is more important than my lunch."

Arel frowned and shook his head. "No, Peggy, you need to take care of yourself too. Besides, I put lots of love in that sandwich. You can't let it go to waste."

Peggy blushed and then kissed Arel's cheek again. "You are the sweetest baby, aren't you?" She looked at Michael. "Would you be a dear and bring over my sandwich? I'll sit on the footstool and eat it here, close to Arel."

Michael watched the interaction between the twosome. Arel's eyes were dreamily focused on Peggy as she fanned him with a section of newspaper. As he started to retrieve the sandwich, Peggy called out to him.

"And please, Michael, turn down the air conditioner," she said. "Arel looks like he's getting too warm."

As Michael left them to carry out his duties, he was quite amazed. Arel was not only an impeccable poker player, but his people management skills were faultless.

* * *

By evening, Arel felt stronger. He insisted on going ahead with the scheduled, dinner party. He felt even better when Carol and Kevin arrived. They were holding hands, with Kevin looking very cheerful as he clung to Carol like found treasure. The feeling seemed to be mutual. Carol's face was radiant whenever she glanced up at him.

Arel had never seen her glow like that before, but he knew that look. Justina had once gazed at him in that way. Now he was overjoyed that the couple could share that same feeling of bliss. In a small way, he'd helped to bring it about, but he'd never dared to hope that they could fall so deeply in love after their rocky break-up.

"It's good to see you both," he said with a smile.

Carol let go of Kevin and rushed over to where he was sitting on the sofa. "You've been wonderful. Your advice has been so helpful," she whispered as she hugged him. "Thank you."

Kevin caught up a moment later. "How's it going, old buddy?"

Arel released Carol back into Kevin's arms and smiled. "I'm fine, but Peggy and Tim chased me out of the kitchen. They insisted that I stay here until they tell me otherwise."

"Good man," Kevin said. "If you listen to them, you'll be back on your feet very soon."

As Kevin was speaking, Peggy and Tim came out of the kitchen. Peggy went over to Carol and hugged her while Tim stuck out a hand to Kevin.

"It's good to see you two," Tim said as he shook hands with Kevin. "Arel's planned out quite a dinner."

As Kevin pumped Tim's hand, his eyes narrowed. "My god, Tim, you look like you've been working in hell's kitchen."

Kevin's announcement made everyone stare at Tim. His shirt sleeves were rolled up to his elbows, his brow was sweaty, and he wore an apron that bore the spatters and stains of a four course dinner menu.

Arel shrugged out a sigh. "He insists on being my right hand man, don't you, Tim?"

"Yes, I have that honor," Tim grunted back. "But I imagine that Kevin would love to use more of his vacation time to help out too."

Kevin put an arm around Carol. "I'd love to, but I'm kind of busy right now."

Carol blushed, but the added color in her cheeks was accompanied by her leaning into Kevin's embrace.

For a change, Peggy was quiet. She hugged Tim as she looked at Carol and Kevin. Her dark, brown eyes were shiny with happy tears.

Ailing or not, Arel's heart swelled with an unaccustomed joy. He'd never known that the idea of friendship could create an atmosphere that was so warm and inviting, a sparkling pool where the water was just the right temperature to renew body and soul. Later, after dinner, things became even more festive. Sitting at the head of the table, he got another surprise.

Carol stood up and raised her glass in his direction, making everyone look his way. "I think I speak for all of us when I say that these last few weeks have been so special. So here's to all of us, Arel's devotees, and to Arel for being in our lives."

Everyone joined in touching glasses. Tim looked more like a sacrificial victim as his eyes came in line with Arel's, but he managed a genuine smile when Arel beamed his thanks back to them.

"You're my reason for living," Arel said. He wasn't trying to sound melodramatic. The words he spoke came out without any thought. Finally and unexpectedly, he was an object of love and concern. Michael and Abrigail loved him too, but he figured they had to love him. But these friends were human, and they wanted his best in spite of all his faults. "With your support, I think I'm going to beat this heart problem," he said as he gazed back at the group gathered around him.

"I told you that you would," Tim said teasingly, "even if it does involve making us your slaves."

Catching the glint of camaraderie in Tim's eyes, Arel laughed. "So this is what it's like to have a family. I never expected it to feel this way. It's better than anything I imagined."

Fifty-Eight

THE WEEKS SLIPPED by faster than Arel could keep up with them. His friends were always dropping by and helping out. Now, as he watched Peggy load the dishwasher, he was concerned. "I've been thinking. Your wedding is around the corner. You have a thousand details to take care of, and you're trying to do most of them by yourself. I can see why you're exhausted."

Peggy straightened up from her task and gave him her full attention. "Don't worry about me, I'm fine. What's important is your health."

Arel handed her a cloth to dry her hands. "I'm feeling better, and I have a lot of time. So I've decided that I'm going to help you with the wedding."

Peggy's eyes went wide with alarm. "No, please sweetie, you can't. If anything happened to you, Tim and I would never forgive ourselves."

"I totally agree," Tim said emphatically as he walked into the kitchen. "We're just getting you stabilized."

Arel smiled. "Your real gift was to help me to make a decision. I think you made me see how to embrace the road to health. Without your example of what it means to give with loving hearts, I don't think I'd have a reason to do it."

Tim smiled back. "That's high praise. Thanks."

"You're welcome, but my point is that it's not what I *do* that counts. If I make up my mind to stay alive, then I will."

Tim scowled. "I wish you'd told me that last weekend, when you had me repainting your bedroom."

"You really have a dry sense of humor, don't you?" Arel laughed. The happy gesture added a bit of color to his cheeks. They didn't look nearly as gaunt as before.

"My goodness, look at you," Peggy said as she reached out and put her hand on the side of Arel's face.

Arel's old habit of pulling back almost resurrected itself, but he managed to stand his ground. "What? What is it?"

"You have dimples!"

"I do? Oh yes, I do."

Peggy smiled. "You've been so thin, they weren't noticeable."

"We're getting off the subject of your wedding," Arel objected. "I've made a list of the things that you talked about, the things that still need to be done before your big day."

Tim returned a look of surprise. "You've been listening enough to make a list?"

"Of course he's been listening," Peggy said as she continued smiling at Arel. "He's extremely sensitive to other people's needs."

Tim let out a sigh. "Sorry, I guess I've been too busy to notice, but—"

"So here's what I intend to do," Arel said, cutting in to Tim's observation. "I'll take care of any remaining details concerning the flowers and the catering. I'll also get things coordinated with the band. You'll have to bring me up to speed on anything else that you need."

Peggy started to object, but Arel put a hand up. "Now don't start worrying. Most of what I've got on my list can be coordinated by phone. I'll be able to shift your duties to broader shoulders. Tim and Kevin can easily take over the chores that you've been trying to attend to, Peggy."

Tim frowned. "In other words, you'll be in charge of giving out the orders?"

Arel nodded to Peggy. "See that? Tim understands my part perfectly." With a wistful look of satisfaction, he turned to Tim. "You know me pretty well. My plans don't sound like they'll harm my health, do they?"

Tim's mouth opened slightly, then closed tight as he sucked in a breath.

Peggy looked up at Tim for reassurance. "Then you don't think that Arel will overexert himself?"

"No, I think he'll be fine," Tim muttered.

"Great! Then it's settled," Arel said. "I'll talk to Kevin tonight and get the ball rolling."

Peggy smiled back at him with relief. "You're the most thoughtful person in the world. How can we ever thank you?"

Arel took her hand in his and squeezed it. "If it weren't for you, I would probably be pushing up daisies right now. I owe it to you to make sure that you're relaxed when you're standing at the altar."

Fifty-Nine

KEVIN LOOKED AROUND the dimly lit tavern and then at Tim. "How long has it been since we've had the time to come here?"

Tim leaned forward and groaned. "My head is spinning too fast to answer that. I can't decide if Arel's a blessing or a curse with this wedding planning. I feel guilty taking a few minutes out to sit here and relax."

Kevin snorted. "I feel like I live in Arel's kitchen. My hands are always in dishwater."

"Yeah, now that I'm on wedding duty, I've been released from kitchen cleanup. But I can give you a tip on hand creams. Peggy's got one that really works if the chapping gets too bad."

"Hand cream? Will you listen to yourself?" Kevin hesitated as he tightened the grip on his beer. "Hell, you're right, I'll need some. I've never washed so many pots. On dinner nights, Arel uses every one he owns."

"For a guy that never seems to eat, he sure likes to cook. On the plus side, I do enjoy his meals."

"Yeah, I do too, but I wish he made something simple once in a while. The pans are usually piled to the ceiling."

"But maybe we shouldn't complain too much, Kev. There is a good part to all of this. Peggy's happy."

"So she's okay with Arel taking over the wedding details?"

Tim let out a huff. "It's like he gave her the moon. She has time for bubble baths now. She even goes to the spa. Arel gave her some gift certificates."

Kevin sipped his beer. "Well I know who's doing all the work? It's you and me, old buddy."

"Yeah, but I'm glad that we're helping Peggy."

"So am I, but Arel is getting all the credit. Not exactly fair when he calls me for three minutes, and my butt is running errands for two hours."

"I guess there's a lot to get done with the wedding coming up in a couple of days."

Kevin smiled and gave Tim a sideways glance. "Are you happy?"

"Yes, I'm a very lucky man."

Kevin stared at his beer without comment.

Tim frowned back. "Are you okay?"

"I was just thinking about Peg's accident, how she kind of lost it. She's not as tough as I thought. But knowing that you're going to be there for her is . . . well—"

Tim gave Kevin's back a sound thumping. "I'll always be there, I promise."

"Good."

"Changing the subject, what about you and Carol?"

"We're doing great, but I've discovered that it's not just my charm that got things patched up. I think that Arel is running a personal counseling service on the side. I gather that he's always advising Carol. Funny thing is, I have this feeling that he's helping."

Tim shook his head and laughed. "I don't want to think about it."

Sixty

SITTING AT THE quaint, outdoor café table, under the canopy of a wispy leafed tree, Peggy wore the kind of smile that only came from a moment of total contentment. "Thank goodness for the spa. I feel renewed."

Carol sat across from Peggy, smiling too. "You needed that time away from your busy life a lot more than I did, but it was very sweet of Arel to give me a gift certificate too."

Peggy noted the way Carol's face brightened when she talked about Arel. "He's been a big help, hasn't he?"

Carol caressed her tea cup sheepishly. "I'm sorry, Peggy, but I didn't think there was any hope for Kevin and me after, you know. Anyway with Arel's help and advice, we were able to get over our problems."

Peggy dangled her red sandal off her newly massaged foot. "Kevin looks happier than I've ever seen him. So do you."

"I guess I am."

"Is there something wrong again?" Peggy heard the slight change in Carol's tone and sat up more attentively. "Are you sure you're happy with Kevin?"

"It's not that there's anything wrong, but I don't want to fool myself. My mom and dad looked happy until their awful divorce."

"Kevin isn't perfect, but I know that he loves you and that he'll do his best."

Carol shrugged. "I know Kevin is great. When I hear myself, I wonder if I'm looking for a problem. Still, how can I trust that things will work out in the long run?"

"Maybe you can't. We want somebody to make us happy, but I don't think it works that way."

"Half the time I'm as happy as can be, and the other half I'm confused."

"People are easily hurt. It's normal to shy away from pain after they've had a bad experience."

"Very good observation, Peggy Bailey."

Peggy laughed. "You're not the only one who's talking to Dr. Arel."

Carol returned a puzzled look. "What? You too? I don't get it. How can he be so wise and yet so—"

"Clueless about himself? I don't have an answer to that one."

Carol sipped her tea. "He is making progress." She laughed. "You're right about his dimples."

"Someday, he might even be ready for a relationship."

"I don't know, Peg, relationships are challenging."

"Sorry, I don't mean to go pushing things again. I'm just happy that you and Kevin are okay."

Carol reached over and patted her hand. "You've been a wonderful friend through it all. Thank you for seeing my side when Kevin and I had our setback."

"You'll always be my friend, no matter what happens with you and Kevin." As Peggy was speaking, a sudden breeze caught the tree limbs that shaded the table. As the branches lifted, the table was exposed to the bright sky overhead. When she looked up, the sun's brilliant rays seemed to reach out and warm her heart. She felt a shiver of joy fill her chest. She glanced back at Carol and sighed. "Sometimes I think we worry too much. Maybe we should pay more attention to beautiful days and simply being alive."

Carol looked up too. "Yes, life can be beautiful. I have to remember how to see some of that beauty when I get scared."

Peggy giggled happily. "Or you can call Arel."

* * *

High above the patio of the outdoor café, Glory and Grace were observing Carol and Peggy. They were also enjoying an almost perfect day. Glory let her heavenly form spread out into a field of glittering light that blended perfectly with the rays of the sun. "Being in the open air is so extraordinary."

Grace sighed wistfully. "I wish that Carol could get out more often. The fresh air and nature would do wonders for her."

"Peggy too, but at least she's over most of her worries."

"Unfortunately, that's not true in Carol's case. As you know, she has a tendency to project things that aren't the best for her happiness."

"I've gathered that Arel's been helpful."

Grace let out another sigh. "I must admit how pleased I am with his counseling efforts. He can be very persuasive when Carol needs a little push in the right direction."

"He's more than persuasive with the men. He's quite the . . . how would I put it?"

"The despot?" Grace suggested with a bit of mirth. "Frederick and Tim's angel, Kell, say the same thing. However, now that we're privy to the bigger picture of what's going on, I suppose it's natural. Arel was their first in command lifetimes ago. Besides, everyone is so independent nowadays. Maybe a little discipline and service is good all around."

"I've heard that Arel is enjoying himself immensely."

"Michael says it's helpful for him to be involved. The happier and more self-confident he gets, the more he allows his body to heal."

"He's not in danger of dying anymore, is he?"

"I don't know about that." Grace hesitated. "Abrigail says that his power is growing in spite of his ill health. Bodies are fragile. Too much energy, too soon, is dangerous."

Before Glory could comment, their attention was drawn downwards. A gust of wind shifted the tree limbs and opened a window for them to see that Carol and Peggy were looking upwards.

"Look at those beautiful faces!" Grace said with delight. Her radiant, angelic waves of love joined the sunlight that washed over the women below. "I hope that they let life flow a little more easily in these next weeks."

Sixty-One

UNDER A VELVET black, night sky, Arel lay on the garden lounger. He ignored the galaxy of stars overhead as he contemplated other matters. Peggy and Tim were getting married the following day. He'd never gone to a wedding before. Even as a child, he'd been left at home. He wished he didn't have to go to this one. It was a damning thought. He was being a selfish bastard, wanting things to remain just as they were. But he had to face the truth.

Peggy and Tim's beautiful day of celebration marked the end of a very short, exceptional time in his life, one that was filled with sweet memories. They weren't big event memories, but everyday occurrences that felt like magical moments. He'd always remember Carol's wide eyed delight with his mastery of card tricks. When he came up with her correct card, a red king of hearts, in a rather complex deception, her clearly amazed reaction delighted him. It was so easy to make her laugh, to make her proud of him with a simple parlor trick.

Then there was Peggy and her loud outburst of laughter when he allowed her to gel down his unruly hair. He ended up looking like a mobster, and he laughed at himself too. Moments like that made him forget about how serious life normally felt.

Tim regularly shook a fist at him and threatened to go on strike, but he always wore a mischievous smile when he played the rebellious slave. Kevin liked to entertain him by juggling grapefruit or even worse, glass jars of olives. He obviously had no idea how stressful the uptight, adult Arel found his circus act. Of course, Arel's lighter, child side loved it.

Now, being well enough to manage without them, he had to release his new friends. He had to let them get back to their own lives. After Peggy and Tim got married, they'd want kids, their own family. Soon, hopefully, Carol and Kevin would do the same. None of them needed a third wheel around, a sickly one at that.

As for him, he knew he should get a life too. But he wasn't like his friends. He was still a wreck. He was one step above invalid status physically. And emotionally?

My god, I can't imagine being like them. They're excited about life. But I don't feel that way. Life still scares the hell out of me.

Take away his friends, and he didn't know how to navigate the waters of solitude without constantly running into those fears that still told him how incapable he was of facing the world at large.

And why should the world want me in it? Look how I've treated the people who tried to help me!

Since his friends had offered to help him, he'd taken advantage of their sweet and generous natures, even basked in their volunteer servitude. Of course, it was easy with people like Peggy and Carol fussing over him. And Tim, that solid rock who performed so many menial chores, was an example of devotion to a cause. Tim loved Peggy completely and knew she cared about Arel. So Tim made it his business to care about Arel too. Tim was a real man, inside and out. Kevin was Kevin. He couldn't quite find himself, but he still tried his best and would do whatever to help a friend.

It's so easy to love them. They truly are like my family.

He shut his eyes, trying to keep his feeling of loss and grief from weakening his resolve. If he loved his friends, he wouldn't abuse their kindness anymore. That meant severing his ties with them.

Sixty-Two

ON THE DAY of the wedding, the weather was perfect. The temperature, which had been hitting the high 90s, dropped down to the 80s. The humidity was low. Chicago was showing off. When Arel and Michael arrived early at the church, the interior was pleasantly cool and inviting.

"Michael, check all the flowers. Make sure they've been put where they belong. Here's my placement chart. Make sure you don't miss any."

As Michael moved down the aisle to do as he was told, Arel pulled out his list and began going over it again. He couldn't believe how nervous he was. He'd hardly slept, and when he did, he had nightmares. He kept dreaming that Mrs. Hayes was reaching out to him and when he reached back, his mother's face was glaring at him, laughing at him. "You're such a disappointment, such a burden to your father and me."

Every time he woke up from the dreams, he was trembling, realizing that his mother was probably right. He was a burden to his old family and to his new one, but not for long.

He did have one small way of giving back before he let his friends go. As he stood in the church, he would try to make sure that everything was perfect for Peggy and Tim's wedding. "And see that the ribbons on the pews are attached properly!" he called to Michael. "And I don't think the floor runner is as straight as it should be."

Michael turned and smiled at him. "Can we talk for a moment?" he asked as he walked over to where Arel was standing.

Arel checked his watch. "Now? We don't have time—"

"But maybe you could take a few minutes out. If you like, there's a garden behind the church. Enjoy the setting there. And I'll take care of anything that needs attention here."

"But—"

Michael's face was totally serene, but his eyes held the slightest look of exasperation. "Don't worry. I've attended a few weddings. I know what needs to be done."

Michael's simple explanation seemed to clarify everything that Arel had been thinking about the night before. "Yes, you're right. I'm making a fool out of myself with all my demands."

"No, that's not what I'm saying."

Arel swallowed the lump forming in his throat as he studied Michael's face. He'd already accepted the fact that he'd been taking advantage of everyone. Now, looking at Michael, the truth cut deeper. "Just spit it out, Michael. I'm a tiresome, obsessive, tyrannical fool. That's how you see me. That's how I look to all of you, isn't it?"

"You've had your moments, when you might have been a little demanding—"

"A little demanding? I listen to myself, and even I'm amazed at how stupid I sound." He let out a loud, scoffing laugh that echoed throughout the still chapel. "I've become a laughing stock, yelling at people while I arrange flowers. God help me, I never thought I'd end up like this! I was better off hunting rats in an alley! At least I had the strength to function. Now I can't lift a heavy pot off the stove. I'm totally pathetic."

"It takes time," Michael said, putting his hand on his shoulder.

He shrugged it off. As the time neared for him to let go of the group he'd come to love, his misery rekindled old anger. After losing Mrs. Hayes, he should have learned that attachment always led to heartache. "Leave me alone! Get out of my life once and for all. I don't want family. I don't want you!"

"Please calm down. It's Peggy and Tim's wedding day. You don't want to spoil that, do you?"

He gritted his teeth. The lump in his throat had turned to bile, a vile fluid that made him sick to his stomach. "No, dammit, of course I don't." Taking a few gasping breaths he started backing away again. "You take care of everything. I need some air." As he turned and walked slowly up the aisle, holding on to the backs of pews, Michael called out.

"Arel?"

"What?"

"One look at your face and they'll see that you're upset. Come back, and we'll try to work this out."

Arel stopped and glanced back. He gave Michael a charming smile that made his face go bright. A moment later, he let it fade away. "Poker face, remember? They'll never know."

* * *

Pausing, gathering his strength, Arel gave the wrought iron, garden gate a hard shove, making it swing back so fast that it hit the iron fencing with a clang. His jaw tightened as he walked towards the beautifully kept church gardens in front of him.

Look at this place. Michael's clone must take care of it.

Sunshine flooded a winding, brick path that meandered through vibrant, colorful flower beds. Towering maples and old oak trees dotted the edges like stately overlords. The chirping of birds added a chorus of sweet, lively song. Was he supposed to be inspired by his surroundings, calmed down by a bunch of marigolds and trees?

As he stepped foot on the path, he clenched his fists. He'd meant what he'd said to Michael. He was finished with everyone. He'd move out of state, buy a place where people couldn't find him. He'd bar Michael from his life and become a hermit again.

I'm so much better off by myself.

His argument for solitude was met by the facts. He hadn't fared well on his own. He was sick and dying when Michael came along.

He brought his gaze back to the idyllic setting. Everything around him knew how to live and to love its life. The flowers, the lush green grass, the squirrel scampering up a tree, all seemed to have the gift that he was missing. He was the only one that was lacking, barred from the joy of being alive.

It was the same way when he'd been with the group. They made each day seem so easy. Sure they had their problems, but underneath, they had a buoyancy that he didn't have. The happiness that they shared with him was something that was a part of them. For him, it was always on the outside, something he couldn't manufacture on his own. Then the truth hit him. He suddenly understood the difference between himself and his friends, including Michael.

To know love on a permanent basis, one has to have a vessel that's capable of holding love, and mine can't do that. Love spills out of my heart faster than it can be replenished.

He knew that Michael was right when he said that human and angel were both fueled by love. There was a reservoir of the stuff that flowed out of them, but not in his case. When he listened to his heart beating, it had a hollow sound.

Michael's blood might have driven out the curse, but I was broken before the curse. I'll always be broken, until the day I die.

He raised his eyes to the clear, blue canopy of sky. "If there is a god up there, he's cruel and pitiless. To give me life when I'm destined to only know loss is beyond cruel, it's evil!"

His eyes burned, not with light, but with a dark resentment. A rising fury stirred in his gut. He sensed its explosive power, one that he'd never experienced before.

"Why should the damn birds be happy when I'm so wretched?"

Looking up again, he even loathed the sun.

"Where's my light?" he screamed. "Why is my soul kept in darkness?"

The solar orb seemed to answer by withdrawing from him, needing to hide itself from his scathing, venomous eyes. In its place, a black, threatening cloud drifted over the garden. Its ominous presence was as hostile as the spitefulness that poured out of him. He was shadowed in a deep, dreary gloominess that he remembered from childhood. He sneered back. "Is that what you want?" he bellowed at the heavens. "Do you want me shrouded in darkness forever? So be it!"

He opened himself to a well of hopelessness. He embraced it with a desire so ferocious that he felt his body shutter violently.

Life isn't fair! It's a never ending torment! It's hell in all its glory!

The proof was in the heavy burden of sorrow and anguish that came up from the depths of his soul. It filled him with its virulent power. A great mass of black rage joined in and began to swirl inside. He tried to keep the tears away, but they came anyway. They turned into racking sobs of grief and loss.

Mrs. Hayes, Carol, Peggy, Tim and Kevin all rose up in a circle around him, laughing at him like his mother. In the end, they hadn't served him. They'd been there to show him how gullible he was to think that he mattered. In truth, he was a pathetic loser.

He raged at himself and all that was around him. He dropped to the ground and straddled the grass on his hands and knees, heaving and gasping as an incredible energy expanded inside of him. He thought he was going to be sick. But instead, a great blast of desolation spewed out from him.

Sixty-Three

THE CHURCH WAS filled with music and joyful smiles as Peggy walked down the aisle. When Arel saw her glance his way, he made himself smile too. He was a blackened shell inside, but he had to hide his true feelings from her. He couldn't let her call his bluff. He had to slip out of her life before she had a chance to know what happened.

And you won't find me this time. None of you will find me again.

After the ceremony and the compulsory photo session, Arel knew he had one last stop to make. He had to go to the reception. After his earlier outburst, his mind felt empty. He was physically exhausted as he walked to his car. It didn't matter. He was determined to keep up his ruse. He'd maintain his normal behavior until Peggy and Tim were safely on route to their honeymoon.

Michael intercepted him in the parking lot and grabbed hold of his arm. "Come with me," the angel demanded as he steered Arel in the opposite direction.

Arel scowled back nervously. Michael's voice had never sounded so harsh. Something was very wrong. "Where are we going?"

"You'll see."

"No! We're finished!"

"Not yet."

Arel resisted, but only momentarily. Michael's hold on his arm was tight. He had no choice but to follow the angel towards the church garden that he'd visited earlier. His body was beyond tired, but his senses went on alert as they proceeded. He could feel everything changing. The air got heavier and so did the energy around him. The feeling was so intense and dense that it sapped his ability to move forward. Michael was practically dragging him along by the time they reached their destination. As they rounded a corner close to the garden entrance, a cold chill went through him, warning him that he needed to brace himself for what was coming. When they arrived at the garden gate, his breath caught. Michael released his arm, but he had to grab hold of the iron balusters to stay upright. Open-mouthed, he gazed at the landscape. "My god, what happened?"

A war zone lay in front of him. The flowers were gone. The trees had become stark, ghostly creatures, reaching out with barren limbs. There were no birds, no small creatures, no life at all.

"You're wrong. There is life," Michael insisted.

"Where?" Arel looked closer and pulled back in disgust. The once green gardens had been cannibalized by malignant vines and weeds. Their greedy, thistly forms had choked out the beauty and left the area looking desolate and hellish. His first thought was that he was looking at a scene from a fairy tale. In the fable, a wicked witch had waved her wand and cursed the area.

Michael opened the gate and gestured for him to enter. "It wasn't a witch's wand."

Arel shook his head. "I don't want to go in there."

Michael took his arm again and pulled him forward. "I'm sorry, but you have to."

A sharp, biting wind greeted them as they passed through the gate. Arel trembled as the gust knifed through his body. "Why is it so cold? I don't understand what's going on."

Michael let go of him and sighed. "Arel, you did this."

Arel laughed, knowing the angel was completely mad to make such a statement. "That's ridiculous. I can barely go up and down the stairs. You know that."

Michael stared back with a mixture of conviction and compassion. "Here's what I know. Your power has been growing, but up until now, that power has been directed towards your body. You've been taking something beautiful, a design of the Creator, and destroying it. Your friends helped to slow down the process, helped you to start valuing yourself, and your body got better. Now, in your present, negative state, that power is not only being turned on yourself, but expanded."

Arel shrugged. "What has that got to do with this mess?"

"This morning, you destroyed this garden."

"No!" Arel's protest was almost shouted. He wouldn't believe such a horrible lie. Yet, as his gaze traveled over the dark, thorny plants and the bleak trees, something in his chest stirred. In his heart, he knew that the plot of ground was a perfect expression of how he'd felt earlier. The ugliness around him was like the ugliness inside of him. The idea came as a terrible blow. He had to grab for Michael's arm as he began to remember what had happened before the wedding ceremony.

Arel stared up at the angel. "Oh god, Michael, it was me! It was like I hated everything. Then I kind of lost it. After that, I couldn't stop what happened."

Michael's eyes softened into pools of blue light. "Arel, when you saw yourself in the mirror this morning, didn't you notice you were looking so much better? You were getting your health back. Didn't that give you hope? Why did you throw it all away?"

Arel swallowed hard. "What do you mean?" As he asked the question, the answer was already forming in his mind. Michael was talking about what he'd done to his body. When he'd lost hope in the garden that morning, when his feelings rose up out of him and he showered the landscape with his rage, the energy sapped his physical vessel of its newly won strength. What he had regained was lost.

"Dear friend, you've done more than that to your body. You've added to the damage."

Arel paid no attention to Michael's grave expression. He let out a bitter laugh. "So what? What does it matter?"

He turned back to the desolate garden again, despising what he saw. His soul craved beauty. That's why he collected art and surrounded himself with things that would take his mind off of what was abhorrent. Now ugliness was all around him. He walked over to one of the most misshapen and twisted of the tall weeds. Its form repulsed him. It was a reminder of all the horrors he'd been privy to in his life. In a rush of fresh anger, he grabbed hold of the spiny, outer stem, pulling at the tough plant, cursing it. But it resisted him. Its roots were already deep and unyielding.

"Stop it, please!" Michael ordered. "You're not strong enough."

"Leave me alone!" Arel shouted back as he pulled at the horrid thing with more fervor. The thorns dug deep into his tender hands, but he paid no attention to the pain. Finally, unable to loose it, he dropped to his knees and began to dig in the muddy soil, clawing at the dirt, needing to uproot the miserable plant. Michael tried to pull him back, but it was too late. "Dammit, not now!" he gasped as his heart seized. "I've got to fix this mess."

A second devastating attack took hold of him. He'd never experienced anything as crushing before. He knew at once that he'd pushed his body too far. In a panic, he clung to the plant as he looked up.

"Michael—" He wheezed out the one word. It was all that he could manage. His breath, where had it gone? Where was the oxygen that he needed? His mouth was gaping, hoping to take in the invisible substance, but like the thorny weed, it resisted him. "So tired," he finally gasped in a barely audible tone.

The atmosphere around him, his body, everything was so heavy. An enormous weight pressed down on him, and he was helpless to resist it. His mind was exhausted too. He'd tried so hard, but he couldn't measure up. A silent plea went out from him.

I try to be what you want, Michael. Why do I keep failing?

The thought was lost as the pressure squeezed more of the life out of him.

Michael fell to his knees next to him. "My dear friend, I never asked anything of you, except to be yourself, to love who you are."

Arel stared back with eyes that were dark, golden pools of confusion. "Love myself? What is there to love?"

As he asked the question, another attack of pain hit, slamming him so hard, he fell forward like a stone. Michael caught him, pulling him close, cradling him in his arms. "I'm here."

Arel felt his heart grab harder. "Don't leave me," he begged.

Michael's soft eyes became resolute and determined. "Never! I'll never leave you."

Barely able to hold on to the world that he'd hated and fought, Arel tried to hold on to Michael's face. Using all his strength to touch Michael's cheek with his muddy hand, he could only keep it there for a brief moment. "Please . . . forgive me."

"There's nothing to forgive."

Michael's words were spoken in the kindest way, but Arel's heart wasn't as understanding as the angel. He heard its cry, its accusation.

I've gone too long without love, not the love of friends, but without your love.

Like a child thrown in the closet and forgotten, the vessel hadn't been tended to or nourished. It had been created to carry blood and joy. But in its neglected state, it had been forced to carry all the emotional burdens that Arel had thrown its way. Guilt, remorse, self-loathing, and rage were his heart's daily fare, along with a myriad of other dark matters. Now the worn out vehicle inside of him couldn't go on.

"I think . . . I'm . . . dying," Arel gasped.

"Hold on to me," Michael said. His eyes were intense and pure, like crystal blue windows of love and gentleness. There was also a fierce strength in their gaze. Michael was fighting for him, pitting his own beautiful energy against the force that was carrying Arel away from his cradling arms.

It was enough to give Arel the breath he needed to speak. "These horrible feelings come over me. I don't know how to stop them."

"You're not alone."

"Why can't I feel that?" he asked in between heaving breaths. His lungs were becoming useless. So was his heart as it went into a spasm of pain. He did everything he could not to cry out. If he was dying, he was determined to do it with dignity. But he was frightened.

He tried to grab hold of Michael's shirt, but he couldn't sustain the effort, and his hand fell back. "It's getting so dark . . . I'm going to lose you, aren't I?"

Michael reached over and carefully took the bleeding, frail offering, holding it in his own strong hand. "How can you lose me? Our bond can never be severed."

He pulled Arel to his breast, embracing his failing body carefully, as if it were a precious rose in his garden, a rose that had been trampled by ignorance and brutality. "You're wanted, my beloved one," he said as he rocked the man he'd tried so hard to care for.

The gentle motion and Michael's soothing words broke through all the pain, and for a moment Arel was able to smile back at him.

Michael smiled too. "Nothing, no power in heaven or on earth will take me away from you as long as you want me with you," he promised. "But you have to let me help. Don't try to do it all yourself. It's too much to do alone. You were never meant to do it alone."

For a moment, Arel felt the darkness lift. A piece of the sun came through. Then he realized that the light was coming from Michael. He was looking at the angel's face for the last time. "Thank you for staying with me to the end," he said in short gasps. "Just like you told me."

He could feel Michael trying his best to reach him on a deeper level. The angel was pounding on the walls of fear that separated them, but even more powerful was the feeling of Arel's own spirit. It was trying to break away from the curse that had been his life, from the battered body that wanted to rest.

In a final gesture of caring, Michael pushed back a thick, dark lock of Arel's hair and leaned closer. "Don't give up," he whispered as if he could see Arel's soul ready to take flight. "Trust me."

Arel blinked back a little of the darkness as it was closing in. "Friends?"

"Always, for all eternity."

He tried to smile again, but the pain was too great. "I trust you," he said with his last breath. Then his hand went limp again, falling away from Michael's grasp.

"Find the truth," Michael said as he once again held Arel's frail body close to his own.

Sixty-Four

AS IT GREW in volume and intensity, the roaring in Arel's ears blotted out everything else. It was the sound of his soul freeing itself. The roar became a great wind, blowing through his body and mind. Its power shook him at his roots. He tried to hold on, but it was no use. He lost his grip on life itself. After that he was at the wind's mercy. It carried him away from all that he knew. It carried him away from Michael and the body that lay beside the angel. As it carried him, his awareness was laid bare, open to the winds of time. He was pulled into the currents of history.

When the wind had completed its task, he began to fall from a great height. He fell towards the scene spread out below. A silent scream of dread and terror filled him as he was returned to a terrible night he knew he shouldn't remember. Fire and pain were waiting for him.

When he stopped falling, he became aware of a dual perception. He was a young man named Aelred who faced impending doom. He was also the soul who was revisiting a time that had changed everything.

* * *

The bleak village square was ablaze with torches and excitement. The night was cold, and Col was hungry. His stomach rarely had enough to keep it from twisting inside him, a constant reminder that he couldn't provide for his family. The winter before, he'd lost his son to want and disease. He'd tried desperately to find food, but there had been a scourge on the land, and it was as barren and as empty as his stomach. But tonight he wasn't only hungry for food. He was hungry for retribution. He held his torch high, and his usually dull eyes blazed as bright as the fire he held aloft.

Col knew that the woman tied at the stake was responsible for his miseries. "You killed my son, witch! And tonight we're going to burn you for your sins!"

He ran back and forth around the pyre, between the condemned woman and her brother. He spat at them, feeling rage as he remembered all the times the young man and his sister had looked at him with eyes that were too brilliant, with eyes that pitied him, like they were better. But it was the brother and sister who were the different ones. The brother visited with the crazy, old man in the village. The sister gathered herbs and made potions that could be used to cast evil incantations.

But it was Col's turn now. He held the torch close to the young man's face, letting its heat singe his skin, causing the young man to cry out. Col laughed in triumph. "Cursed devil, you're going to pay for your sins! You and your sister are going to burn!"

Aelred looked at him with blistered skin, breath heavy with pain. His pale, blue eyes were pleading with him. "Please no . . . ."

Aelred's pleas made Col's eyes burn brighter. He danced in front of the man who thought he was better. He waved his torch like a staff of victory. "You're the devil! And we're sending you back to hell!"

When the order was given, Col would be one of the first to light the kindling. He would set the fire joyously, with the zeal of the righteous. He would make sure to look at each of these evil ones, catch the terror in their eyes as the flames caught and the fires rose. When the smell of burning flesh and their screams filled his senses, he would feel some atonement for the son that had been taken from him.

* * *

Aelred's body was bound to a stake. The ropes were tight, cutting into his flesh. His body was already racked with the pain of his tormenters beating him, flogging him with their whips until his blood ran free in the dirt around him. His handsome, young body, so full of promise was spoiled by their defilement. They had taken God's perfect child and turned him into something broken and limp.

But they hadn't wanted to only break Aelred's body. Their purpose ran deeper. They wanted to break his mind. And they were good at what they did. As they applied their torturous instruments of pain to open his body, they knew that his mind would also open. They could drive their wills deep into his psyche. They could use their vicious assaults to batter at his steadfastness. They would inflict their sinister intentions on him when he couldn't defend himself. They could tell him what they were doing to his sister, Elvina. But the best way they could break his mind, was to let him hear her screams. Aelred hardly recognized her screams. They were like those of a mutilated animal as she too was torn apart by her attackers.

Aelred had always been able to protect his sister from the blows of their harsh father, but bound and bloody, under the curse of his own captors, he was powerless. In his despair, he did the only thing he could. He confessed to them, admitted his guilt where there was no guilt. For he would go to any limits, betray any truth, to stop her agony. But they laughed at his meager bargaining.

"Tell it to God, when you stand in judgment," they jeered at him as they continued to inflict the most grievous pain on his persecuted body.

After the men were finished with him, Aelred was dragged through the town square. Limp and helpless, he was tied to a knotty post that was surrounded by dried wood and bundles of sticks. He tried to hold on to consciousness. He tried to reclaim the faith that had been torn from him. He tried to believe that God was real, but all that he saw were the faces of those who wanted him dead.

These vessels of hate had already stoned his friend, Oswyn, before his eyes. His friend's transgression was his desire to protect those he loved. As he raced towards Aelred and his sister, he was struck down by rock and stone. Now the crowd was thirsty for more pain. They banished their torches with the enthusiasm of executioners who took great pleasure in hurting those they deemed sinful.

Elvina, his younger sister, was only inches away from him now. But he couldn't touch her. His hands were too tightly bound. When he tried to call out to her, the only sound she made was a pitiful whimpering interrupted by new cries of torment as the crowd punished her further.

Before the pain of the fire that would take them, before he heard his own screams, Aelred heard the breaking of his heart. His sweet, gentle sister, whose only crime was tending to the sick, would soon light up the night with her burning body. She was the latest victim of the murderers who called themselves men of the cloth. They had beat her, mutilated her body, and defiled her. Now they would kill her.

Aelred shut his eyes trying to close out the pain. He desperately fought to gather back the remnants of his mind. He could only find pieces of what he knew as himself. With his last bit of trust, he offered those tiny shreds of hope to God. He pleaded to the Creator, not for his life, but for the life of his sister. He begged that she might be spared.

His prayers were met by the roar of the crowd as they surged forward, eager to add their torches to the fuel of the pyre. When the darkness became bright with flame, and he was burning, Aelred knew that God had abandoned both of them.

* * *

Michael hadn't been in human form in that life. But his angelic presence had tried to reach Aelred from the moment that he'd awoken that morning. The young man, preoccupied with all that he had to do, had been too busy to notice Michael's repeated urgings. As he lived another life among those who'd lost their way to ignorance, Aelred too was being tainted with the lie of fear. Now, it was almost impossible for the angel to be heard.

If he had been able to converse with him, Michael would have tried to help Aelred understand the truth about what was to come. He was caught up in a drama of historical proportions. Mankind had slipped far from the love and joy that the Divine had intended. Now, there was a mass consciousness of fear and destruction. Life became a dark, frightening series of conflicts, people divided into opposing factions that grew more and more brutal as their beliefs became more and more unforgiving.

On this day, the nightmare swallowed up Aelred. While he worked in the fields, his sister was arrested, tortured, and asked who her conspirators were. In a moment of agony, she called out to her comforter, the one who always helped her. She called out her brother's name.

Later that day, they found Aelred toiling in the fields, but they didn't have to drag him in. When Aelred found out that Elvina had been arrested, he screamed and kept screaming. His pain wanted to pierce Michael's heart with its pitiful intensity. The ones who captured him could hardly hold him back. All that he could think about was saving his sister. But they beat him until he couldn't fight back any more. The gruesome details that followed were unspeakable.

When Michael saw Aelred tied to a stake, when he heard the man's prayers, he tried to intervene. He tried to draw off the fear so that Aelred's soul could slip easily from his body and be returned safely to its true home in the Divine's embrace. At the same time, he saw Elvina's angel trying to reach her.

Multitudes of angels, legions of holy helpers, were gathered at the scene. All were trying their best to get through to the mass of humans that were taking part in the horrendous drama. But the wall of bitterness and rage and hatred was thick and heavy, forming a barrier that no angel could cross. They were messengers of the Divine and powerful, but the humans were using their free will in a way that thwarted all their efforts. People were mired deep in beliefs that had no room for miracles.

Normally, Aelred had been able to see beyond the emotions that ruled the masses, but now, even he was falling into a pit of darkness. He was exchanging the truth for the lie that anger and hatred were more powerful than Divine love and compassion.

* * *

As the flames consumed his body, as Aelred screamed in agony, he lost all hope. But something he'd never known took its place. He felt a great, violent fury take hold. He felt rage. It was fed by his sister's screams and the hideous faces of the mob that burned them.

Rage consumed him. It destroyed his identity as surely as the fire destroyed his flesh. Finally, it released his soul from that which bound him to the earth.

When his spirit flew up into the darkness, it was burning. Nothing was allowed to touch it. It fled from men who hated it, from a god that was powerless to protect that which he loved. The rage was so great that it blocked out the stars and the heavens. It kept burning in him until there was nothing left. The rage that consumed him left nothing but smoldering hatred. Hate existed where once there had been a man. Where once there was a soul of God, radiant and unlimited, now there was a soul of man. For the men had been good at what they did.

And when the earth called him back to his next life, and the next, as he went from one body to the next, he found no joy in life. He simply knew failure. He didn't know how to fight the ignorance and the darkness that swarmed over the earth. Eventually, he claimed the failure as his own. He turned all the hate on himself. His hate was so great that it blinded him to everything but his pain.

But God had not abandoned His beloved child. God had called the man's soul from the flames, called His Beloved back to him. For God knew that humanity's ignorance and fear cannot destroy the soul that knows itself, knows that it is God's child. But Aelred's soul had forgotten who it was. It flew past God's outstretched hand, distancing itself from the pain and the flames, distancing itself from the ignorance of what called itself human.

Lifetime after lifetime, it existed in the darkness, eluding Michael, the great angel who tried so hard to bring it home. The soul saw only itself, alone and isolated from creation. Its only comfort was its freedom. It never wanted to be tied to a stake again. It never wanted to be at another's mercy again.

* * *

Time shifted once more. Arel knew himself as a formless soul, suspended in an in-between world. He had seen the fullness of what had driven him from the love that he craved. Now there was a great pause, a space where nothing seemed to exist. Yet, in that endless expanse, a sound called out to him. An exquisite note in the song of creation rose up from below. It was so sweet, so filled with love that he was unable to resist its invitation. He had to investigate. As soon as he entertained the thought, he was transported back to the church garden, to the place where he left his body. He soared high above the place, like a wild bird. He was torn between the freedom he valued above all else and an alluring sound that called to him. Several times he started to fly out of the world. Then, as he began to penetrate the heavens, the sound would reach out from below and draw him downward.

Like a bird, his soul circled the garden, letting itself come closer with each pass until it saw a man, still and lifeless, laying on the ground. Next to the man, an angel was kneeling. The soul recognized this beautiful expression of love. It was Michael.

Still, Arel's soul had been wild and untamed for so long. Dare it come closer? The question was quickly joined by words that had been uttered earlier in the garden when Arel had been dying.

"I trust you," he'd said to Michael.

As it pondered those words and the sincerity behind them, the soul was surprised. It hadn't expected the hand of the Creator to be so quick. The Almighty's grasp, lightening fast and so careful, caught the flighty spirit and held it carefully to His breast, close to the infinite expanse of pure joy.

In that moment, nothing existed but the bliss of homecoming. In a pause outside of time and space, golden currents of comfort and calm filled the fluttering pulse of the soul. Gentle stillness settled over it, and it knew eternity.

Let me stay here forever. Let me be a part of Your Heart for eternity.

Perhaps an eternity elapsed after that, or perhaps, only a few moments passed. In either case, when time started up again, so did the sound that called from below. It was a song that filled the soul with a new longing. The beautiful melody carried the call of creation. It was at the core of every rock, plant and animal. It was the sound of the birds as they sang, of the brooks as they carried their waters with joy. It was the sound that stars made when their laughter splashed down from the heavens, blessing the earth below.

Arel's soul realized that it knew the song very well. It realized that the song was the energy from which its own lifetimes had sprung. It was the song that called him to the earth again, to descend once more into matter.

Sixty-Five

AREL'S BODY LAY dead, but someone was giving it a gift of life. Breath entered his lungs as gently as the sun's light dawning. It made him aware of his need. He wanted more of the precious thing called oxygen. His lungs wanted to expand again.

Arel inhaled deeply and was rewarded with the exquisite bouquet of roses. The delicate scent made him want to take another breath and another. As he did, he heard the breeze blowing through the trees. He heard a voice calling.

"Arel, wake up."

He didn't know how to open his eyes, but they had a mind of their own. Like inquisitive children, they wanted to peek at the world, to know where the sound was coming from. His heavy eyelids gave them their wish. They lifted, like tiny stage curtains, letting his two golden orbs feast on the face of an angel.

Arel had never seen Michael smile so broadly. But he only caught a glimpse of his happiness, for the angel was gathering him up at once. Putting a hand under Arel's body, cradling his head with the other hand, he raised his limp form against himself. His head lay beneath Michael's chin and his body was held tight against his breast.

As he rested in Michael's embrace, he knew only joy. He took breath after breath and felt a tremendous heat radiating from the angel. Its energy flowed into his body, filling every cell with a comforting sense of wellness. He went from cold and stiff to warm and feeling.

As Arel's icy chill was banished, he became aware of Michael's heart. It was unspoiled and pure. Its steady beat seemed to broadcast that purity. Arel still couldn't move, but inside, he was smiling. He knew about Michael's tricks. The angel was showing Arel's heart what to do. And Arel's heart was a fast study after its trip to the other side. It responded joyfully, eager to learn from this master. With gratitude, it synced itself to the rhythm of the angel's mighty vessel that knew only love.

Once started, Arel's heart did what it was designed to do. With strong, steady beats, blood started to flow from the center of his being, branching out to nourish and nurture every cell with the precious, red liquid.

As he was gently laid back on the ground, Arel reached out to Michael's eyes and held on. When he was able to manage movement again, he smiled. He tried to speak and coughed. With effort, he raised a finger and beckoned Michael close to him. Finally he was able to whisper. "You don't have any more surprises waiting for me, do you?"

Michael's laughter was so filled with joy that for a moment he couldn't contain himself. Beautiful, crystalline tears sparkled in his eyes. "Welcome back, my friend," he cried out.

* * *

When Arel was able to sit up, he looked around at the garden. A surge of relief made his smile broaden into a grin. Everything was beautiful again. Cool, green islands of lawn caressed flower beds that were crowded with colorful blooms. The buzz of the attending honey bees added a quiet hum to the scene.

"Thank you for never giving up on me," he said softly. "And thank you for cleaning up my mess."

Michael shook his head. "I didn't have anything to do with the garden. As you came back, your soul's love was so powerful that you blessed everything with new life."

Arel blinked back with surprise. "Really? That wasn't hard." Then he remembered that he'd been dead only minutes before. "On second thought, maybe it was tougher than I think."

He blinked his eyes and enjoyed the ease of movement as he looked around. "It truly is a magnificent garden." In front of him, the sun played hop scotch on the shiny surface of a small, nearby pond. A wren sat singing on a limb above them.

Michael sighed. "That was a close one."

Arel's brows narrowed with concern. "Are you saying that I almost didn't find my way back?"

"I think you know the details better than I do. I think you also understand things in a way that should help you from now on."

Arel paused and reflected on what he'd seen. "There were so many angels gathered in that dark square where we were burned. I realize that they tried to help us, but it was like we were so removed from feeling their presence. The fear and darkness blotted out all the light. Even the Divine seemed like a lost cause."

Michael smiled and laid his hand over Arel's forehead, letting it rest there. "There's more. Let me show you a little of what you missed."

Arel knew that he wasn't afraid anymore. He shut his eyes, giving himself over to Michael's energy and to life. In his stillness, he felt his heart beating. It was strong again. He took deep breaths of the garden air and rejoiced in the fragrance of the earth. He listened to a sound that went beyond human hearing and gave thanks for the heavens that were singing to him.

As he relaxed into a state of total peace, a great panorama, a great window opened in his mind. It was bright with a blinding light, and he was standing in the middle of it. There was fire all around him, and yet as he stood in its midst, he remained unharmed.

A crowd of jeering, angry people were staring at the bright flames and the persons burning, but he didn't see the mob's ugliness or feel the pain of burning flesh. He saw the multitude as they really were. They were lost, ignorant people who were afraid from the moment that they woke each morning until they went to bed, hungry and cold. Their pain was so great that they'd gone numb to all that was good and beautiful. All that they knew was a constant fight for survival.

As Arel let their faces slip away, he realized that he wasn't alone. He was a part of the angelic presence, adding his own light to the scene. He was offering his forgiveness, along with his love and understanding. For a brief time, he felt like he was in two worlds. The past and the present were both there for him to experience. He opened his eyes and looked at Michael through his tears. "I slipped so far from the light too. I'm so grateful that you've been here to help me find my way back."

Michael smiled. "You trusted me."

Arel was about to comment further when the vision begin to fade. It felt like a dream, and he was losing touch with what he'd understood. "What's happening?" he asked in a panic. "Why am I forgetting what I just saw?"

Michael gazed back knowingly. "You don't have enough energy to hold on to it. After all, this is only the beginning of your new journey. Today you're taking your first step. Someday, you'll remember it all again."

"First step? That's all I've taken? I died! That should be worth more than a first step!"

Michael laughed and let out a contented sigh. "Your soul has come back from the darkness. That's a huge accomplishment. Be proud of yourself, you've taken a leap towards enlightenment."

"Tell me that I don't have to die again to get more enlightened."

"I truly hope not."

"You hope not?"

"Stop worrying," Michael said with a playful smile. "If you can simply trust and let the process work, everything will be fine."

"If you say so." Arel knew he should be more illuminated after the miracles worked that day, but he began running the phrase, 'I hope not' thru his mind.

Michael stood up and reached down to him. "Did you forget? We have a reception to go to."

The thought brought Arel back to the moment. "Oh hell, I did forget." Standing up, he looked at his muddy clothes and his hands, all bloodied from the weed pulling fiasco. He held them up for inspection. "Why didn't my hands get healed?"

"Just a memento, in case you think what happened here was only a dream."

* * *

Crystal chandeliers and golden-cherub, lighting fixtures decorated the ballroom. The elegant accents set the mood for the reception. When Arel and Michael arrived and noted their surroundings, they couldn't help smiling. They were ready to celebrate Peggy and Tim's wedding and Arel's return to the land of the living.

Peggy was the first to see them. Her happy face became even brighter as she grabbed Tim's hand and ran over to greet them. "Where have you two been? Did you get lost?"

Arel gave Michael a brief look of relief. "Yes, you might say that, but forget about us." He smiled at the newlyweds. "Congratulations again to both of you."

"Thank you," Tim said. He gave Arel a quick inspection as he extended his hand. "What happened to your tux?"

Arel glanced down at his dark blue, pinstripe suit, then took Tim's hand and shook it enthusiastically. "Sorry, but I had to change."

"And you're all scratched up!" Peggy said with a frown. Reaching out, she snatched up his free hand and stared at the numerous red marks and half dozen band aids. "How did you hurt yourself?"

Arel laughed. "Talk to Michael. He had a gardening emergency."

"Gardening emergency?" Peggy gave Michael her motherly look of disapproval.

"Long story, long, long story," Michael said as they all walked into the ballroom.

Sixty-Six

CAROL STOOD IN the living room, looking at Kevin. He was lying on the sofa. When he stretched out, he took up most of the couch. "You look comfy," she said with a smile.

Kevin roused himself and sat up. "I had a stressful day at the office, but now I'm here with you. That's all that matters." He sounded tired, but his tone changed as he studied her. "Come here," he ordered playfully.

Carol smiled back as she sat down. She snuggled close to Kevin, enjoying his arms around her. "Do you know that you sometimes remind me of a life-size Charlie?"

"Your old stuffed bear? I don't consider myself vain, but I thought I looked better than that."

"Don't let this go to your head, but you're extremely handsome."

"That's nice to know, but I'm also hungry," he teased. He began nibbling at her neck with quick, little bites.

Carol raised her shoulder defensively. "Stop it! You know that tickles."

Kevin pulled her closer. "I can't help it, I can't get enough of you."

"You better stop it. I know where you're ticklish too!"

Kevin pulled back. "Fine, let's call a truce."

Carol sighed contentedly. "I never thought I could be so happy. These past couple of months have been amazing."

"That goes double for me. Why didn't I find you sooner?"

"I don't know about the whys in life, but I do know that Arel would be pleased if he saw us."

Kevin ran his finger over the places he'd nibbled. "Who would have guessed that he's a matchmaker at heart?"

"Thank goodness he's doing so much better."

"I know. One minute he's as frail as a baby mouse, and now he's asked me to help him with an exercise program."

"Do you believe him when he says that he experienced a miracle healing?"

"What else could have happened? He's not the same man. The last time I dropped in to see him, he was blasting out tunes on his CD player, burning incense, and trying to lift ten pound weights." He paused. "The key word in that sentence is 'trying.' He's still got a very long way to go as far as being in shape."

"He's always been very sweet. That hasn't changed," Carol insisted.

"Yeah, but it's kind of nice that we don't have to be his servants anymore."

Carol took a deep breath and studied Kevin's eyes. They were a little intense, but they also had a pleading quality about them. Arel had explained that, at times, Kevin didn't know how to express his feelings. Maybe this was one of those times. "Was Arel really that bad?"

Kevin shrugged off the question. "Hell, if I'd been in his shoes, I might have been worse."

Carol had defended Arel, but she wasn't blind. She knew that he had been *very* demanding with Kevin. But Kevin never refused to do what was asked of him. "It's nice that you feel that way."

Kevin's eyes brightened.

She took his hand and held it close. It made two of hers, but she squeezed it firmly. "You're very sweet too,"

Looking pleased, Kevin kissed her cheek again. "Can we sit here and be this happy forever?"

* * *

Fred and Grace sat together on Carol's small, apartment patio. Both were enjoying the evening and the night sky. Fred noted that Grace looked especially happy. She was smiling serenely as she fluffed out her wings behind her. He was trying out a sparser pair of wings himself. He could feel the moon's silvery rays bouncing off his feathery energy like iridescent rain drops. When they splattered on the floor, it became a palette of vivid, dancing sparkles.

He glanced at Grace and grinned. "It's nice to see that you're back to your usual self. No more bat wings."

Grace's eyes widened for a moment, but she ignored his remark. "I'm thinking about Carol and Kevin. They seem so in love."

"Yes, that's true."

The two angels didn't like to pry, but they had peeked in on the young couple while they were enjoying a movie.

Grace continued. "My heart is literally leaping for joy. I've waited so long for Carol to find someone to adore her."

Fred sighed, but didn't respond.

Grace looked over with a frown. "You're very quiet about it all."

"I'm sure that they can have an amazing relationship that lasts their whole life if they choose to. But you know that they've charted out some events—"

"I know," Grace interrupted, letting her wings sag.

"Are you okay?"

"I'm sorry. I've been observing humans for so long that at times I almost let myself indulge in some of their moods."

"I didn't mean to upset you. And on the bright side, Michael seems very calm about it all."

"Of course he's calm. His attitude is exemplary."

"Don't be hard on yourself, even Michael has his moments."

"So true." Grace brought her gaze in line with Fred's. "You heard about the garden scene, didn't you?"

"Grace, you haven't been listening to those rumors."

"No, my information comes straight from Abrigail."

Fred fluttered his wispy wings and closed them like he was snapping an umbrella shut. Tiny sparks of light flew in all directions as he came to attention. "That's different. What did she tell you?"

"If Michael hadn't used all his devotion, his vigilance, and his speed, there wouldn't be a certain former vampire with us today."

Fred glowed with admiration. "Thus his name, *Who is like God?*"

"Amen," Grace whispered. "He's given all of us a great gift. What would happen to Carol, Kevin, Peggy and Tim without Arel being there to help them?"

"Very true."

"There is a small concern."

"What is it?"

"As you know, the events coming up will be physically exhausting for Arel. He's working with his body, but have you seen his arms? I hope that he can get them in shape quickly."

Fred *had* seen Arel's arms. They were about one half the size of Kevin's. "He'll be in my thoughts and prayers."

"Amen," Grace intoned again. "I wish him the best."

Sixty-Seven

IN THE EARLY morning sunlight, Arel's face was flushed and glowering. "This pace is too much," he protested as he dragged himself along the side street at a very slow jog. In the weeks following his amazing escape from death's door, he'd been truly happy, swept up by revelation and rebirth. Now, he felt swept up by a much more down to earth regimen.

"Stop complaining," Kevin insisted.

Arel glanced up at the tall man who was jogging next to him. "You have an attitude, and I don't like it."

"You wanted to get in shape, didn't you?"

Arel's pace slowed to a crawl. "I can't do it. My body is ready to drop."

"Keep it moving!" Kevin yelled out for the umpteenth time. "You have to break through the pain barrier."

Arel's legs were so rubbery that he knew they couldn't go through a thick sheet of paper much less a pain barrier. "That's it," he gasped as he let momentum deposit him against a tree. "I've had it."

Kevin was still jogging in place beside him. "Look, you said you got a clean bill of health from your doctor, right?"

Arel glared back. "Yes, what's your point? You want to prove him wrong?"

Kevin laughed. "You've been running for two blocks. I know you have more in you than that."

"How would you know what I have? Do you have x-ray vision? Look at me. Have some pity."

Kevin shrugged him off. "You're not the first person I've coached, and I've coached people in worse shape than you."

Arel dropped down to the curb and spread out his legs in front of him. He found it hard to believe that his limbs looked okay. They felt like they belonged to a month old baby. "Are those people you coached still among the living?" he gasped.

Kevin grabbed Arel's arm and pulled him back into a standing position. "They're fine and so are you. If you can't jog, we'll walk."

Arel groaned back, but he tried to be compliant as he limped along. In spite of being a hard task master, Kevin's heart was in the right place. After all, Arel had asked for the young man's help. Now he needed to distract himself. Happily, he remembered a favorite subject that he wanted to discuss. "How are you and Carol doing?"

Kevin stopped short and stared back. His broad smile was an answer in itself. "We're really happy. At least I know I am."

"Great, so elaborate a bit. Are you finding it easier to listen and respond in a way that makes Carol comfortable?"

"It's getting easier all the time. Like you said, women need to express their feelings, so I let her talk. I'm using the '*I'm here to support you, not to try to fix your problems*' technique. It's working."

Arel didn't tell Kevin his secret, but he'd been reading everything he could find on relationships. Now one of his students was acknowledging that his advice was valid. Yet he was ever vigilant. It was part of his nature. He stared at Kevin with furrowed brows. "Don't get over confident. Women are very sensitive."

As they went on chatting, and Kevin rambled on, Arel realized his legs were getting a rest. He'd have to remember to keep this ace in the hole available whenever Kevin tried to kill him in the future.

The young man looked at Arel as if he'd read his mind. "Why are we standing here? You need to keep moving. And from now on, there will be no discussions. I promised to help you, and I'm going to keep that promise. Let's start jogging."

Arel glared back as he walked lamely forward like a skinny dog following its master. "What did I do to deserve such a dedicated guy like you?"

Kevin smiled. "I guess you're just lucky. You'd have to pay a trainer a lot to get this kind of personal treatment."

"How much would I have to pay to have someone put me down? You've got a suffering animal here."

Kevin didn't stop, but he did grab Arel's shoulders and gave them an encouraging squeeze. "Man up, Arel. By the third week, I guarantee, you're going to see some real muscle on those legs."

Sixty-Eight

THE DIM INTERIOR of the pub was filled with lively conversations as Tim and Kevin sat on adjoining stools at the bar.

"Sorry, I haven't had time for a beer lately," Tim apologized. "Ever since we got back from the honeymoon, we've been house hunting. It's taking almost all of our spare time. We've looked at a lot of neighborhoods, but we've come up empty." He took a sip of his beer and sighed. "I really needed that game of racquetball today, even though you beat me."

Kevin laughed, "I think I got lucky. We both know that you usually shut me down. As for the house hunting, I'll trade you. I'll look for a house, and you can take over coaching Arel."

"No way, I can't imagine that sort of punishment."

"Let me fill you in. The first week, he complained constantly. The second week, he complained even more. The third week, things changed, we hardly had a civil word between us. We sort of grunted at each other. Finally, the fourth week, a miracle happened. I realized that Arel's actually adding muscle. His legs are starting to look pretty good. His arms are getting a lot stronger too."

"You're a tough guy, Kevin. Most people would have folded by now. Of course, I've seen you when you set your mind to something."

"Yeah, I was this close to giving up on him." Kevin's two fingers captured a half inch of air. "But you know Arel, he can be the world's biggest pain in the ass, and still, somehow, he sucks you in. I knew I was his only chance of doing what he needed to do."

Tim slapped Kevin's back. "Be proud of yourself. You walked through the fires of Arel and survived."

Kevin laughed too. "Yeah, well next time you get to do the walking."

"Sorry, too busy."

"Are you enjoying married life?"

Tim's red face was all that Kevin needed. "Never mind," he laughed as he drained the last of his beer.

"How about you and Carol?"

"We couldn't be better."

Tim hesitated. "So you and Carol are . . . uh . . . really together?"

Kevin's face, the opposite of Arel's poker face, flushed darker than Tim's.

Tim gave him a good-humored smile, and then he sobered. "Carol has a good man. I'm happy for you both."

Sixty-Nine

SITTING AT HER kitchen table, having a cup of tea, Peggy studied the real estate section of the morning paper. "Nothing again," she sighed as she tossed the paper aside. She raised her face heavenward. "We need some help. I know there's something out there for us, so give us a shove in the right direction. Thank you."

She didn't know why, but she had a bad case of nesting fever. She looked up again. "And I almost forgot, thanks for helping Arel get in shape now that he has his health back."

Everything in her life was perfect except for the house hunt. She tried to get her focus off of the dozens of homes that paraded through her mind. It was easy when she thought of Tim. She looked at her hand and smiled. The gold, wedding band on her finger was simple, with no engraving work or extra diamonds. It was exactly what she'd wanted. It expressed their simple, steadfast kind of love. She'd been blessed with the best guy in the world.

When Tim took her into his arms, she felt pressure, a great swell pushing at the boundaries of her heart. Sometimes, she loved him so much, she felt like she needed more room in the vessel. Just the thought of his body wrapped around hers could give her goose bumps.

"Stop it, girlie!" She grabbed the paper again. Now she had to get her mind off of Tim. Why did her body seem to want him all the time lately? "I'm becoming a sex addict," she groaned.

She started searching the ads again, running her finger down the columns. She paused halfway down the third column. There was a newly listed house on the market, one that she'd missed on her first time through the ads. "Oh my goodness, this might be the one!"

Seventy

AREL INVITED CAROL into the foyer and gestured to the living room. "This is an unexpected pleasure. It's so nice to see you."

Carol returned a weak smile as she walked over to the sofa and sat down. She remained very quiet as she studied a tissue in her hand.

Arel took a seat too, wondering why he felt suddenly nervous. "Is everything okay?" he asked. The question slipped out so automatically, he didn't have a chance to censure himself.

Carol shrugged and settled back into a corner of the couch. "I wanted to see you, but I hope that it's not a bad time."

Arel offered an enthusiastic smile. "Of course not. You're always welcome."

Carol glanced back at him. After a long moment, her eyes recovered a bit of their usual sparkle. "I know you've been working out. It shows. You look great."

"Thank you." Arel was pleased that Carol had noticed the change in his body. He certainly saw a big difference when he looked at himself in the mirror. His slender build had taken on a wiry, athletic look. His eyes were brighter, and his cheekbones weren't hollowed out any more. He even had a tan. "It's been a long time since I felt this good."

"You must have really worked hard."

"Well, I guess I have to give Kevin most of the credit. He's quite the—" He paused, needing to be careful about how to word his feelings. "Kevin is the kind of coach that doesn't give up on raw rookies."

Carol giggled softly. "He was happy to help."

Arel knew Kevin's take on coaching him wasn't much of a secret among the group. He gave Carol a knowing, embarrassed glance. "I'm sure that he was." He quickly changed the subject. "But there's more exciting news than my workouts. I hear that you and Kevin moved in together."

Carol blushed. "Too fast?"

"Oh no, I wasn't thinking that. When you're with someone you love, why wait? Share every minute that you can."

"I didn't want it to seem impulsive."

"I'm glad that the two of you are happy. That's all that counts."

Carol bit her lip. "It was going perfectly until—"

Arel leaned forward. "Was?"

Carol's gaze dropped to her lap. As she tore at the tissue she was holding, she began to take little gasping breaths.

Arel got up and went over to the sofa. He sat down next to her and reached out for her hand. "It can't be that bad, can it? Tell me what's going on. Why are you upset?" As soon as he asked the question, he knew he'd made a mistake.

Shrugging again, Carol burst into tears.

Arel reacted just as fast. He put his arm around her shoulder and gently hugged her. "It's going to be okay, I promise."

Carol fell into his embrace and sobbed so hard that her body shook.

Arel tried to comfort her. "I'm here, I'm here." The words were repeated with genuine concern, but he doubted that Carol heard him over the sound of her sobs.

"I'm sorry," she sniffled when she was able to calm down. "I guess I've been holding that in."

Arel nodded reassuringly, but remained quiet. He'd learned that simply listening was his best bet.

After a couple of heavy sighs, Carol sat up straighter and pulled back. With a forthright gaze, she brought her eyes in line with his. "I'm pregnant!"

Carol blurted out the news so unexpectedly that Arel jumped. "What?" The word was a loud whisper, a raspy sound of awe.

Carol clarified her news. "I'm going to have a baby."

Arel was instantly lightheaded as if he'd never heard of such an event before. He tried to give voice to words he hadn't spoken in his entire long lifetime. "Baby . . . you're going to have a baby?"

Carol looked concerned. "You're not feeling sick, are you? You've gone kind of pale."

Arel finally rallied and found the words to express his feelings. "I'm thrilled! This is the most wonderful thing I can imagine."

"Really? That's a relief, for a moment—"

Arel jumped to his feet. He'd gone zombie for an instant, not knowing how to integrate Carol's momentous news. Now, his mind and body reacted together. A ripple of joy surged through him. The thought of a new life reinforced his own recent rebirth, his appreciation of how beautiful life could be. Taking Carol's hands in his, he pulled her into a standing position. "Let me look at you. What a miracle!" He pulled her into his arms and hugged her so enthusiastically that she made a small, squeaky sound.

He let her go at once. "I'm sorry. I guess I forget that I'm stronger now. Are you okay? I didn't hurt you . . . the baby?"

She smiled back at him through her tears. "No, I'm just surprised that you're happy."

"Why wouldn't I be happy? A baby!" As he was celebrating, he paused long enough to look at Carol again. She didn't seem to be as excited as he was. "You don't want . . . it?"

Carol started to sniffle again. "Of course I want it. It's just that I don't know if Kevin will. I haven't told him yet. We've never discussed children seriously. It was a general, someday in the future, sort of thing. We didn't know we had to think about it. We thought we were careful."

Arel straightened. "Now listen to me. I know Kevin. And I know that he'll want this child."

Carol's eyes sparked a little. "Really, do you think so?"

Arel took her hand and gave it a gentle squeeze. When he spoke, he made sure that his tone was soft, but stern in a fatherly way. "Please, tell him the good news tonight."

Seventy-One

KEVIN COULDN'T MOVE. He sat on the sofa stiff as stone. When he looked at Carol, at the mother of his child, he suddenly knew how Arel felt when he was ready to faint. "Are you positive?" he managed to gasp out the words with what little breath he had left in his lungs.

"We're going to be parents," Carol said more forcefully. She was suddenly in charge of their lives, telling him things that he couldn't change no matter how scared he was.

A voice in his head began yelling out orders. It was a triage voice, one that yelled at a soldier who'd just been wounded in battle. "Stay calm! Stay calm!" The phrase kept repeating, but another message was overriding the directive. "This can't be happening!" When he tried to look up at Carol again, his eyes dropped to the floor instead.

"Say something," Carol urged. "Are you happy?"

He tried to think, but his brain stalled. "Just surprised," he managed. The words came out in a rush as he stared vacantly into his future.

Carol frowned back. "Yes, me too."

He knew he needed to say more. He even tried opening his mouth, but nothing came out.

Carol backed up, putting her arms around herself. "You don't want it. You don't want our child." Her voice had a breathless quality, like she'd fallen off a swing and couldn't get any air. "I can't believe this. I thought you wanted me, that you wanted a life with me."

He was finally able to look up at her. He hated what he saw. Carol's eyes were filled with disappointment. He'd failed her completely, but he didn't have a clue about what to say. "I'm sorry," he finally whispered.

"I'm sorry too, sorry that I ever gave you another chance!" Carol half sobbed out the words as she turned and ran from the room. A moment later, the bathroom door slammed. A miserable sound followed that brought Kevin out of his immobile state. Carol was crying, but her uncontrolled weeping frightened him even more. "What the hell do I do now?"

He needed help. His best friend, Tim, was the first to come to mind. But if he called Tim, Peggy would also get involved. As low as he was feeling, he didn't think he could take advice from his sister. There was only one other person he could turn to.

Seventy-Two

AREL DROVE TO Kevin's apartment with a tight grip on the steering wheel. Memories from childhood were surfacing. His father had been a raging maniac with eyes that were glassy pools of washed out blueness, swimming in hate. The message his father had beat into him was repetitive. Arel should never have been born.

His father's hatred reached up to the heavens. He despised a god who took his cherished and beautiful, firstborn son. His hatred reined on earth as well. Its black presence filled up the place Arel called home, where he hid in closets, trying to escape the physical pain of a beating and the emotional anguish of knowing that he wasn't wanted.

In a strange twist of fate, Arel's friend, Kevin, seemed to have deep reservations about having a child too. Arel didn't understand his father or Kevin. How could a parent not want their own child?

A few hours earlier, after Carol's visit, Arel was in a state of jubilation. He had dreams of holding a rosy cheeked baby, of taking a sweet, adorable toddler to the park in a stroller. At Christmas, he'd dress up like Santa and put presents for the little one under the Christmas tree. He'd set up a college fund. Then he got Kevin's call. Kevin's voice was anything but jubilant. The young man's speech was halting and desperate. Arel reacted at once, promising to put things right.

Now, he didn't know how to keep that promise. Instead, he pressed down on the Mustang's gas petal, speeding through the dark streets with desperation too.

How can you not want this baby, Kevin? It's so wrong!

If only he could reach Kevin quickly, if he could somehow patch up some deficit in the young man's character, things would work out. At least that was his fondest wish. When he arrived at the apartment complex and stood in front of Kevin's door, he rapped on the structure with his neediness still in place. Whatever he told Kevin, he was determined to change Kevin's mind, to get him back on the right track. He began to rehearse what he'd say to the young man. "This is a wonderful blessing. Can't you see that, Kevin?" As he practiced the words, he heard someone call out to him.

"Arel!"

He jumped back, wide eyed and suddenly frightened. For a moment he thought he'd heard his father's voice. He was clutching at his chest when Kevin stepped outside the apartment.

"Arel, are you okay?" Kevin asked.

Arel blinked back. When he realized that his mind was playing tricks on him, he nodded. "I'm fine," he lied. He stood up straighter and even tried to smile. "I came as quickly as I could."

Kevin shut the door behind him. "I appreciate it," he said as he motioned to Arel. "There's an open area close by. Let's talk there."

Arel hurried to keep up with Kevin. "What's going on? On the phone—"

"I screwed up. That's what is going on."

"I don't understand the problem. When I talked to Carol this afternoon—"

Kevin jerked to a stop and spun around. "You talked to her? Carol told you about the baby before she told me?"

"Yes, and I was thrilled. I told her that you'd be thrilled too."

Kevin clenched his fists. "You had no right to tell her that!"

"Why? I thought you'd be happy, I—"

"You thought wrong!" Kevin's breath heaved in and out as he scowled back. "This is a real mess!"

Arel paused long enough to note Kevin's rigid posture. He saw the anger in the young man's eyes. It was clear that Kevin wanted no part of his own child. The idea hit Arel's gut so powerfully that he was instantly sick and furious at the same time. "So that's how it is. You bastard! How can you call an innocent child a mess? How can you want to wish it out of existence? How can you hate a baby?"

The color drained from Kevin's face as he stepped back. "What are you talking about? I don't hate any baby! I love children. Is that how you see me? Do you think of me as some heartless monster?"

"The things you just said . . . I don't know—"

"That's right! You don't know!" Kevin yelled as he made his way over to a bench. He sat down heavily, clasping his hands and rocking himself.

It was enough to bring Arel back to his senses. He'd projected his own fears on Kevin, but Kevin was nothing like his father. Yet, he'd been so ready to judge Kevin without even knowing the facts. "I'm sorry, maybe I got the wrong idea."

"Yeah, you did. I love Carol. I want to be there for her and this child, but—"

Arel sat down too. "But what? Talk to me. Tell me why you're so upset."

"I'm just learning how to love Carol and how to be there for her. The idea of being responsible for a helpless baby scares the hell out of me. Ask Peggy, I act like a kid myself half the time."

"I know that feeling, but can't you try to give this thing a chance? You might surprise yourself. People grow and change. Look at me. When we met, I was self-destructive and ready for the grave. But you and the others helped me to see things differently."

"You don't understand, Arel. You only have yourself to worry about. This is about a baby, a helpless infant who needs a good dad. I'm not cut out to be that person."

Arel took a couple of deep breaths, trying to understand how he was supposed to help. His earlier plans for Carol's baby came to mind. "How about this? Talk to Carol and tell her that you'll be there for her. If you still feel this way when the baby is born, I'll help out. I can't be the baby's father, but I can make sure it's safe and has what it needs. To the best of my ability, I'll love it like my own. I give you my word."

Kevin slowly raised his head and looked at Arel. "You mean that, don't you?"

Arel nodded. "Of course I do."

As Kevin paused and pondered his offer, Arel's mind skipped ahead in time. He'd make sure that Kevin's child had everything he was capable of providing.

Kevin finally sat up and ran a shaky hand through his short hair. "That really helps. I mean, I want to be responsible, but if I screw up, knowing that you'll be there—"

"I will, I promise." Arel reached out and patted Kevin's shoulder. "You're not alone, remember that."

Kevin studied him for a long moment, and then pushed Arel's hand aside. "Thank you." He leaned in and clasped Arel in a powerful bear hug.

* * *

Arel walked back to the car in a daze. His head was spinning. Did he actually offer to raise a child? He leaned against the Mustang's hood to steady himself. Suddenly the future he'd envisioned changed drastically. He wasn't holding a rosy cheeked baby. He was holding an economy sized case of diapers, wondering what to do with them. He was in a principal's office trying to explain why his child refused to interact with other children, why his child was so shy and backward. His answer was lame. "I guess Junior has been watching me."

His shoulders slumped under the burdens he saw in his future. He'd been so quick to judge, to make Kevin out to be the bad guy. Now he knew how the young man felt. But he meant what he said.

I will be there for Carol and her baby.

Just having that thought bolstered his ego enough to have a second thought. He had eight months to figure things out. Maybe he'd come up with a solution. His grimace eased a little.

I've got eight months to get Kevin in shape to be the father of his child.

The thought didn't last long. He was making excuses. He couldn't expect Kevin to do something he wasn't prepared to do himself. He had to get used to the idea of fatherhood. He'd buy diapers and learn what to do with them. He'd take Junior to the park twice a day to play with other children.

Feeling a little better, he thought about Kevin and their interaction. When he'd first arrived, he'd made a few blunders, He'd accused his friend of being a bastard, but he'd quickly made amends. They had finished up on a good note. When Kevin returned to the apartment, he seemed much more secure and stable.

I guess I did alright.

He got into the car and started to put his seatbelt on. He was just starting to relax when the next thought hit. He didn't have eight months. His job as a parent had already started.

Kevin needs a fatherly role model. That's why he called me. And Carol came to me too. I already have kids, grown up kids.

He groaned as he snapped the seatbelt into place and put the key in the ignition. He had to be the adult from now on.

It's not just me anymore. People are depending on my being there for them.

His body went weak at the thought, but only for a moment. As he searched for a solution, he smiled. "Michael! He's always saying that he'll be there for me. Now's his chance to be there for me and whoever else I'm parenting. And dammit, he can learn to diaper a baby too."

Seventy-Three

AFTER TEN MINUTES of listening to Kevin outside the bedroom door, begging for forgiveness, Carol threw her soggy tissue in the trash. She got up and slowly turned back the lock on the door. When she opened it and saw Kevin, she scowled. "You were horrible," she said, crossing her arms.

Kevin put a hand on the door jamb and leaned in. "Please, Carol, I'm so dumb when it comes to stuff like this. Please forgive me."

Carol's first impulse was to yell at him for making her feel so miserable and alone. She hesitated long enough to look at Kevin's face. She'd never seem him look so scared. Even when Peggy had her accident, Kevin had remained strong in his anger and determination to be there for his sister. Now his eyes were more like those of a frightened child. She looked away and grabbed another tissue from the box on the vanity. "I don't understand why you acted like you did."

"Help me to know what to do," Kevin pleaded. "Tell me how to be a good father."

"Is that what you think, that you won't be a good dad?"

"I'm always screwing up. Like now, look how I made you feel. I don't want to keep doing that, especially with our baby."

She paused. Kevin was looking to her for answers. It made her swallow back a little of her anger. "You're not the only one with doubts. I might be a terrible mom."

Kevin straightened up at once and shook his head. "No you won't. That's one thing I know for sure."

"Really, you think I'll be a good mother?"

"Of course, you're always sweet and thoughtful. You're not a fumbling dunce like me."

"Kevin, don't say things like that."

"That's how I feel when I do stupid things, like how I acted when you told me about our baby."

"That's right, it's our baby." She stepped out into the hall and pulled him closer. "And I wanted so much for you to be happy about it."

"If it's like you, it'll be a perfect baby. I just don't want to ruin it."

"So you do want our child?"

"Of course. That's not the point—"

"It is for me. We'll figure out the rest as we go along, okay?"

Kevin nodded. "I love you, and I want to do whatever I'm supposed to do."

"You will, sweetie. I know you will," she whispered.

Seventy-Four

MICHAEL WALKED INTO the living room carrying a two tier, crystal platter and placed it on the coffee table in front of Carol and Kevin. "Some hors d'oeuvres for our festive occasion."

Carol's eyes lit up with delight as she examined the carefully presented appetizers. "You said that Arel made these? They're almost too beautiful to eat,"

"Let's not go that far," Kevin laughed. He leaned over the assortment with an appraising eye and pointed to one. "What have we got here, Michael?"

"Arel told me, but I have to admit, I wasn't paying close attention."

"I can't believe you weren't listening," Arel teased as he came out of the kitchen. He joined the group wearing a spotless, white apron over his shirt and slacks. He began pointing out his masterpieces. "We have artichoke and goat cheese bruschetta, filo tomato tarts, and smoked salmon and cheese crostini. There are various cheeses mixed in."

"They all sound good to me," Kevin said as he reached for one of the tarts. He popped the small sampling in his mouth and smiled just as the doorbell rang.

Carol stood up immediately and hurried towards the foyer. "That has to be Peggy and Tim."

Before Carol reached the door, Peggy was already letting herself in. She called out in an excited voice. "Thought I'd give everyone a heads up with the bell," she explained as Tim followed her into the house.

"We've been waiting for you," Carol said as she greeted them.

Peggy grabbed Tim's hand and followed Carol into the living room. "We've been house hunting all day."

Kevin gave her a brief glance before he picked up another appetizer. "Did you have any luck?"

Peggy's face lit up. "Yes, Tim and I found a house."

"Congratulations!" Everyone shouted out the word at the same time.

Carol was the first to give Peggy a hug. "We're so excited for you. Where is it? Did you finally find a neighborhood you like?"

Tim looked at Peggy and hesitated. "We both decided that we love the neighborhood and the house. But there is one possible consideration, the next door neighbor."

Kevin stopped eyeing the food and looked up. "Did you hear something bad? Are they unfriendly?" he asked with concern. "I remember growing up with a crabby, old lady next door. What a nightmare. You might want to reconsider buying a house with a miserable neighbor."

"Oh, but the house is perfect, and it's in our price range," Peggy moaned.

"Kevin's right," Arel added. "I'd be very careful. You might have to put up with an annoyance for years."

"Actually, I hope the guy stays around for a long time," Tim smiled.

Arel crossed his arms. "Why would you deliberately move next door to a problem?"

Peggy laughed mischievously. "We didn't say he was a problem, did we, Tim?"

"Alright," Kevin said, checking out Tim's shifty eyes. "What's going on?"

"Shall I tell them?" Peggy asked, looking up at Tim.

Tim hugged her back. "Sure."

Peggy's gaze targeted each one in the group. "We bought the house next door to Arel!"

"Yep," Tim said sternly. "He's going to have to keep his music turned down."

Arel's jaw sagged as his hands dropped to his sides. "What are you saying? Are we . . . are we going to be neighbors?"

"You bet," Tim smiled.

Arel walked slowly over to the sofa.

"Are you alright, sweetie?" Peggy asked. "We're not overwhelming you, are we?"

Arel blinked a couple of times. Finally, a broad grin spread across his face. "I can't believe it. I just never dared to think that you'd want to live that close."

"Of course, we want to be close," Tim said. "If you need me to paint the outside of your house or add an extension to your back bedroom, I won't have to go far to crawl into bed at night."

Arel blushed. "I guess I have been a little overbearing."

"Excuse me," Kevin interrupted as he stood up. "I know you'd love to continue figuring out Tim's work schedule, but we have an announcement too."

Peggy blushed and looked at Kevin, then Carol. "Oh, my goodness, I'm so sorry. This little gathering is all about your special announcement. We shouldn't have blurted out everything like that. I was just so excited."

Carol smiled. "It's fine, but like Kevin said—"

"Are you two getting married?" Peggy asked excitedly.

Kevin looked at Carol, "Well yes, but—"

"Great going!" Tim said as he went over and patted Kevin on the shoulder.

"We'll be sisters," Peggy gasped as she grabbed Carol's hands.

"There's more." Kevin raised his voice trying to get the floor again.

"We're having a baby," Carol said quietly.

Peggy and Tim were stopped in their celebratory tracks. "What?" they said in unison.

"Oh my heavens, congratulations!" Peggy's eyes softened as her gaze settled on Carol. "A baby," she cooed. "How far along are you?"

"Not very far, only about six weeks."

Tim's eyes went to Carol and then lingered on Kevin. "I'm really happy for you both."

* * *

After Arel's four course dinner, Tim moaned out an excuse, saying he needed some air. Kevin followed his lead. The two men went outside on the back patio where the night air was cool. It was a sure sign that fall had arrived. Tim sat down on one of the cushioned chairs and eyed Kevin. His friend showed signs of anxiety several times during the evening. It was time for Tim to find out why. But first, he'd begin the conversation with a neutral comment. He looked up and smiled. "We'll need jackets soon."

Kevin rubbed his hands nervously. "I can't believe how fast time goes. Before you know it, winter will be here."

"And the baby's due in the spring, right?"

"Right." Kevin glanced at Tim. "All of this was kind of sudden and unexpected."

"*Good* unexpected or *bad* unexpected?" Tim asked, taking on the older brother role. Kevin was skittish enough about marriage, but he'd bypassed that institution and went right for the biggest responsibility, a child.

Kevin shrugged. "Just unexpected."

"How's Carol doing, really?"

"I think she's a little scared. But she's being a trooper about it."

"You're going to make a great dad, Kevin."

"I wish I could believe that. And sometimes, I can stop worrying a little."

Tim laughed. "Like when you were polishing off those canapés?"

"Yeah, I feel like a kid myself half the time."

"I thought that was Arel's role."

"Actually, Arel seems thrilled about the baby. I've prayed to feel like he does."

"Give it time. You will. It's all new."

Kevin gave Tim another hard look. "What about you? How would you feel if Peggy . . . you know, if she—"

"Gets pregnant? I don't know if anyone feels totally ready. Raising a child is a big step, but I'd be fine with it. Peggy and I both want kids, and to tell the truth, we're not doing much to prevent something from happening."

Kevin took in a deep breath of the chilled air. "We really thought we had our bases covered."

"Sometimes, the unplanned stuff works out great."

"Maybe you're right. But I don't know anything about babies. I don't even know how to pick one up."

"Kevin! Tim!" Peggy called out. She stood at the kitchen door, holding it open. "Come inside, quick!"

The two men exchanged glances and ran for the house.

Peggy gestured them in. "We have to get Carol to the emergency ward. She thinks that she might be losing the baby."

Seventy-Five

AS SOON AS Arel felt he could get away from the hospital waiting room, he grabbed Michael's arm. Once they found a place where they could talk, Arel blurted out his concerns. "What's going on, Michael?"

Michael sighed. "What do you want me to tell you?"

"Is the baby going to be okay? What about Carol?"

"Sometimes, you have to wait and see."

"No!" Arel shouted out the word and glanced around to make sure they were alone. "You know about these things, just like you've been to a million weddings."

Michael crossed his arms. "Sometimes a soul who's planning on another lifetime in the physical, waivers and changes its mind."

"Why? Carol and Kevin would be great parents."

"How can you know what's best for them, or what would be best for the soul involved?"

"Michael, I know I'm no expert on most things, but if Carol and Kevin lose this baby, they may not get over it. They're on shaky ground already."

"That's their choice, their life."

"Of course it is. But I also know a little about Kevin's makeup, and I know a lot about guilt. This time you have to trust me. It could eat him up if they lose this child. He needs to know he's a good man."

"There are other ways to learn that."

"Michael, please!"

"What would you suggest?"

Arel leaned in closer. "Talk to the child's soul! Tell it to give these guys a chance."

"You don't have any idea about what you're asking."

"So it's hopeless?"

"I didn't say that."

"What are you saying?"

"I'm simply telling you that I don't have the answers."

"But I need answers!" Arel's voice was a shouted whisper. He was discussing Carol and Kevin, but he knew that his needs were there too. He'd promised to act as the baby's father if Kevin couldn't handle the role. Now, he almost felt like this was his child too. Finally, he pulled back. "I'm doing it again, aren't I? I'm thinking of myself at a time when I should be there for Carol and Kevin."

"They could use your support no matter what happens. And Kevin's having a very hard time."

"What do I say to him?"

"Trust yourself. You'll know."

"You've been telling me that forever."

Michael gave him an encouraging smile. "Then maybe it's time that you took my advice."

* * *

When Arel got back to the waiting room, it was quiet. In one corner, a middle-aged man had his head laid back against the wall and was sleeping. A couple of chairs away, a white haired, matronly type was reading. On the other side of the room, Peggy and Tim sat in adjoining chairs. They held hands as they chatted. Kevin sat a few seats away from them. He was leaned over and wore the disappointed look of a player who'd been benched. He barely looked up when Arel came over to him. "Can we talk?" Arel asked, motioning to the hall.

Kevin's eyes remained distant, but after a moment, he nodded. Like Michael, he allowed himself to be guided away from the group. When they got to a private area and stopped, Kevin's brows were still creased with worry. "What is it?" he asked.

"I want to apologize again for the way I acted that night you called me. Some things that I said . . . I was way out of line. Again, I'm sorry."

Kevin lowered his gaze. "No, I was the one who—"

"You were doing your best."

"I was thinking about myself instead of what's important."

"You're human, Kevin. You have feelings that need to be expressed. When you found out Carol was pregnant, it triggered all your self-doubt, that's all. Those were normal feelings. People who truly care sometimes get upset while they're trying to gauge their abilities."

"I didn't feel caring, just scared."

"But how do you feel now?"

"I'm worried as hell about Carol and the baby!"

"Exactly, underneath your doubts, you love Carol and the child that she's carrying."

"*Was* carrying!" Kevin snapped.

"You don't know that."

"I do love Carol, and I want to be a good father. Now I've lost my chance to prove it." Kevin huffed out the words. His eyes were wide, like those of a bull in the ring who doesn't know how to get at his tormentors.

"No matter what happens tonight, you do have a chance. Carol feels alone. She needs you. She wants you."

"I wish I could believe you."

Arel let out a gasp of frustration. "I'll admit it's not easy. Hell, you know me, Kevin. I've been the ultimate case of self-doubt. But you and the rest of the group refused to give up on me. You were there so many times, putting up with my crap."

"We were concerned about you."

"But why? Talk about a self-indulgent jerk, I was the worst."

Kevin let out a snort of aggravation. "Don't talk about yourself like that. When it counted, you didn't hesitate. Dammit, Arel, you're willing to raise my child."

"That's right, I am," Arel whispered, surprised at himself. He was filled with a brief moment of pride. "That's the point. I didn't know I had that in me either. It took a long, long time to find out that I do. Michael says that facing ourselves takes tremendous courage."

Kevin's eyes drifted over to Arel's face. "But this is different. I dropped the ball . . . big time."

Arel's smile faded into a determined grimace. "I've dropped a hundred balls. But don't do what I did. I nearly destroyed myself before I had any faith in who I am."

"I hope you never feel that bad again. You were really hurting, but Michael is right. You've got guts."

"The same thing goes for you."

"Please," Kevin sneered.

Arel's eyes flared. He wanted to argue, to insist that Kevin listen to what he was being told. That's when he realized how hard Michael's job was. Kevin was being just a stubborn as he'd been. For a moment, they stood staring at each other with nothing left to say. The moment was interrupted by Tim. He was walking down the hall towards them.

"Hey, you two," Tim called out. "I've been looking for you. Great news! Carol hasn't lost the baby!"

Kevin reacted instantly, practically tossing Arel aside as he moved forward. "Can I see her?" he asked as he began racing down the hall.

Arel breathed a sigh of relief. He was being given another chance in the fix-it business.

<h1 style="text-align:center">Seventy-Six</h1>

KEVIN SAT NEXT to Carol in their queen size bed. Happily, Carol didn't have to stay very long in the hospital, but she had orders to take it very easy. Now, as Kevin held her hand, he was focused on their visitor. Arel was pacing back and forth in front of them. He was excited about a plan he had just presented.

"I think this will work, don't you?" Arel insisted as he paused to check out their reaction.

Kevin stared back, slightly mesmerized by Arel's sales pitch. "You want us to move in with you until the baby is out of danger."

Arel's eyes flashed with enthusiasm. "It'll be the perfect arrangement. I can take care of Carol while you're working. When you get home, I'll have dinner waiting. Hell, I could learn to iron your shirts."

"Arel, my shirts are wash-and-wear."

"Whatever, you can call it payback for all that you did for me."

Kevin looked at his hands. Were they still chapped after his stint in Arel's kitchen? Next he turned to Carol, wanting her input. "He does have a point."

Carol shrugged back. "We can't impose on Arel," she said hesitantly. Her voice was tired, and her eyes were still overcast with fear after her trip to the hospital.

Arel crossed his arms. "I won't take 'no' for an answer."

Carol bit her lip. "It sounds very nice, but—" She glanced at Kevin again.

Kevin squeezed her hand. "Honey, we both know Arel has more willpower than either of us. Maybe we should think about it."

Arel smiled triumphantly. "And you'll have your privacy. I'm moving back to my quarters downstairs."

"So let me get this straight," Kevin said in a firm tone. "You're going to cook and clean and do everything. We just sit back and relax."

Arel shrugged this time. "How hard could it be? I have lots of energy. I'm up to jogging almost three miles a day."

Carol's face finally brightened. "Maybe we could try it for a little while."

Kevin climbed out of bed and extended his hand to Arel. "You drive a hard bargain, but I guess we're up for it." As he stood waiting to shake hands, Arel looked hesitant. "Is there a problem?"

"No, of course not," Arel said stepping forward.

As Kevin sealed the deal with a hearty shake, the tightness in his muscles relaxed a little. "This is quite a surprise."

Kevin really did appreciate the generous offer, but Arel suddenly looked a bit taken aback when Kevin released him. The smaller man's brows were narrowed, and he worked his hand as if he needed to check for breakage.

"Sorry, I keep forgetting," Kevin said, feeling instant remorse.

Carol's concern was directed at Arel too. "Sweetie, are you sure that you're up to this?"

Arel glanced up at once. "No problem. Just relax and let me take care of everything."

Seventy-Seven

AREL DEPOSITED THE two, weighty suitcases in the foyer and tried to straighten his bent frame as quickly as possible. After he gave himself a short moment to recover, he turned to his house guests. "Welcome to your new home away from home, my friends. Just go straight on back to the master bedroom where you'll be staying."

"Thank you," Carol said as she and Kevin trooped past him. "But are you sure that you want to give us your bedroom?"

"She's right, Arel," Kevin said. "We could use the spare bedroom."

"Absolutely not. Everything is ready for you two. I even did a little redecorating to make things special." Arel had bought new drapes, new bedding, and new accessories for the bath.

"Oh, that's so sweet of you," Carol called back as she walked down the hall.

Arel waited until Carol and Kevin were out of view before he took a deep breath and picked up the suitcases again. They belonged to Carol, but they were surprisingly heavy. Judging from the weight, he was sure that they contained iron ingots, not fluffy women's apparel. The laborious chore of toting them the last twenty feet to the bedroom was a reminder that he'd clearly neglected his arm strength. When he deposited the cases next to the bedroom closet, he let out a quiet sigh of relief.

"My goodness, Arel," Carol said fretfully. "I think you got the cases with all my books, my old laptop and all my toiletries. I usually buy the extra large sizes of shampoo and conditioner. It's so much cheaper that way."

"Smart thinking," Arel wheezed. "I'll have to remember that when I'm shopping."

"Carol is a whiz at saving money," Kevin added.

"Thanks, sweetie." Carol's eyes brightened as she glanced around the room. "Everything is gorgeous."

Arel smiled back with pride. The room was a very comfortable place for anyone who needed serenity. Three sets of paned windows took up most of the exterior wall. Their wide expanse welcomed in the afternoon's soft rays of sunlight, making the room warm and inviting. French vanilla walls and creamy white, linen curtains contrasted beautifully with the furniture's dark, rich woods. The sleigh bed stood out as the focal point. It was elegantly dressed in a snowy white comforter with gold trim. A half dozen high loft pillows completed the look. Arel had also put two long stemmed, red roses on a central pillow. The accent added the only vibrant color in the room.

As Carol tried out the bed, Kevin inspected the master bath and reported his findings. "Wow, Arel, I never paid any attention to this part of the house. The bathroom is really something," he said. "I like the gold fixtures, very fancy. And the garden tub and separate shower are great, especially with the floor-to-ceiling tile."

"Good, I'm glad you like it." Arel remembered when he'd first redone the bathrooms in the house. He'd been very pleased with the imported Rosa aurora marble tile from Portugal. "Now, I'll let you two get settled. If you want anything I'll be in the kitchen, working on dinner."

"Is Michael going to help you or do you want one of us to pitch in?" Carol asked.

Arel started for the hall. "Michael's been called away. It's just the three of us." What he didn't explain is that he'd asked Michael to stay out of the picture. He wanted to prove himself. He didn't know about babies, but how hard could it be to take care of two, young adults?

Kevin called after him as Arel started to leave. "Are you sure you don't need a hand in the kitchen? After I'm finished unpacking, I'll be happy to—"

"Rule number one, no helping," Arel called from the hall. "You two are here to rest and enjoy some time together." He paused with a contented smile and went back to the bedroom and peeked in. "And if you need me at night for any reason, there's an intercom by the bed. Just give me a buzz."

Seventy-Eight

WHEN THE ALARM went off early the next morning, Arel was totally prepared and eager to begin his caretaking duties. He was armed with a detailed schedule to keep him on track. For starters, he had moved his normal waking time back three hours.

So this is what service is all about.

He did a few stretches, letting the idea sink in. As he did, he understood what motivated Michael. No wonder the angel always looks strong and resilient. Being there for people that he cared about put a spring in his step.

As he dressed, he went over his new routine. He'd take his three mile jog, come home and fix breakfast for Kevin, and get the young man off to work by seven. Next, he'd take a shower and spend some time relaxing on his computer. Refreshed, he'd be ready to fix breakfast for Carol when she woke up.

"And I'll have accomplished all of that before I normally get out of bed." It was a happy thought that buoyed his spirit even higher. He'd wasted so much time in his life. Now, all that was changing.

By five thirty, he was out the door, breathing deep, and running down the street. Fortunately, his three mile trek was getting easier every day. He even got back home before the scheduled time. He was able to work on Kevin's breakfast at a leisurely pace. It wasn't until seven o'clock, that he felt the first sting of frustration. He was on schedule, but Kevin wasn't.

He let out a sigh of impatience as he went to check on his guest. "Where is he? He's supposed to leave by now."

He gave the master bedroom door a couple of light raps, trying not to wake Carol. He waited for an answer and finally knocked again.

"Is that you, Arel?" Carol called back.

"Yes, I was just checking—"

"Come in, please."

He hesitated for a brief moment, wondering why Carol's voice sounded so anxious. "Is everything okay?" he asked as he opened the door. He did a quick survey of the room's occupants. "Kevin, what's wrong? Why do you have a pillow over your face?"

Kevin let out a loud, muffled moan. "Just shoot me. It's the kindest thing you can do."

Arel quickly walked over to Kevin's bedside. "What's going on? Are you sick?"

Carol was sitting up in bed, wearing flannel pajamas that featured little rosebuds and hearts. When Kevin didn't respond to Arel's questions, she offered some answers. "Kevin has a stomach bug and an awful headache. He was fine when we went to sleep, but this morning he feels terrible."

As Carol was giving Arel an explanation, Kevin tossed off the pillow and jerkily managed to sit up. Groaning again, he got to his feet and pushed Arel aside. "Watch out!"

Arel observed Kevin's mad dash to the bathroom with blinky, questioning eyes. He hadn't been down with a cold or flu in a very long time. Sure, he'd had the heart problem, but that was different. As he sucked in a compassionate breath, he heard horrible, retching sounds coming from the bathroom. The miserable noises made him appreciate how lucky he'd been. He glanced at Carol for directions. "What should I do?"

Carol threw back her cover. "I'll go check on him."

"No, no, no! You need to rest!" he ordered. As he gestured for Carol to stay put, he hurried towards the sound of Kevin getting sick again. "Leave this to me. I'll take care of everything."

He felt quite confident until he saw Kevin. The poor man was draped over the toilet, gripping it with white knuckles as he continued to vomit. Arel's first impulse was to gag too, but he swallowed hard instead. That was the moment when he realized that all his plans and scheduling were a farce. But even the 'plans of mice and men' moment was forgotten when Kevin finally got to his feet.

"I don't think I've ever felt this bad," Kevin gasped. As he swayed to and fro with dizziness, his eyes met Arel's for just an instant. The next moment, Kevin was in motion again. "Oh geez," he cried out as he turned back to the toilet. In a violent gush he vomited again, but this time he missed his mark. When he came up for air, he groaned out an apology to Arel. "I'm really sorry, old buddy. I made a mess of your floor."

Arel steadied a hand against the cool, marble tile. He knew his face was probably as pale as Kevin's as he contemplated the chore in front of him. "Don't worry about it," he managed. "I'll clean it up."

As he went to get a mop and bucket, Carol was getting out of bed.

"I'm a little nauseous myself," she said as she held a hand to her stomach.

Arel felt a twinge of panic as he rushed over to her. "Do you think you have this bug too?"

"No, it's morning sickness. Can you get me some crackers? They might help soothe my stomach."

Kevin let out another groan as he put himself back to bed. "Can you bring me something like Gatorade? I'm sure my electrolytes will be low if I keep throwing up like this. And maybe something to help my stomach."

Arel nodded to each of them as a new schedule began to take shape. He'd get Carol her crackers, clean up the bathroom, and then run to the store for Kevin's supplies. It was an excellent plan for starters. He didn't anticipate what his actual agenda would entail. As the day proceeded, numerous other duties were added to his list. Since Carol couldn't abide the fancy rosemary crackers that he had on hand, he had to make a second trip to the store for plain saltines. Afterwards there was the eventual breakfast for Carol, then snacks. In between, he was trying to take care of Kevin who had turned into a small nightmare. He drank the Gatorade too quickly and just as quickly he'd thrown it up. Unfortunately, he was dizzy and missed the commode a second time.

As the hours dragged by, Arel was amazed and horrified by how much could be packed into a morning. By noon, he'd run out of paper towels and his previous ideas about caregiving. Why had he sent Michael away? Why had he been so full of himself to think he could take care of Carol and Kevin alone? Still, he was resolved and determined to demonstrate his abilities, no matter what. It became a matter of pride.

* * *

It was evening time, and Abrigail, Michael, Grace and Fred were still in their invisible, observation mode. They were all fascinated by the ongoing saga that they had named, *Arel's Adventures with the Houseguests*. The drama was getting louder and more intense as patient and caregiver continued a day long battle of wills.

"I'm not going to say it again, eat some of this consommé," Arel insisted as he hovered over Kevin with a spoon. "You've had enough of that damn Gatorade."

"I just need some rest. I'm not hungry," Kevin argued. "Go away."

Arel's voice went up in volume every time Kevin refused his efforts. "Do it for Carol. She needs you to get well!"

Fred shook his head as he watched the interaction between the two men. "Arel is wasting his time. When Kevin doesn't want to eat something, nobody can change his mind."

"That's too bad," Abrigail replied, "It took Arel a long time to make that soup. I couldn't believe how many steps there were in the recipe."

"I'm sure that Arel couldn't believe it either," Michael added.

Grace agreed. "I think Kevin needs to try a spoonful for Arel's sake. The poor soul can't take too much more without losing all his patience."

Fred laughed good-humoredly. "Patience? That virtue was gone around noon from what I could observe. Arel is running on raw willpower."

"The last ten hours have been pretty intense," Abrigail said. Her remark was punctuated by a shout of exasperation from Arel.

"Fine! Have it your way!" he yelled as he slammed the bowl of broth down on the night stand. "I'm going to bed."

Abrigail smiled broadly at Michael. "I think he's going to reevaluate his idea of service being fortifying, don't you think?"

There was a glimmer of mischief in Michael's eyes. "Yes, I'm sure he will."

The angelic group watched as Arel pushed his fatigued body towards the door. His face was gray and grim, looking as if he was coming off of a battlefield instead of nursing duty. Pausing, he glanced back at the intercom on the night table and practically sneered when he delivered his last message to Kevin. "If there's an emergency, buzz me."

Grace looked at Michael. "Maybe you should make an appearance, my friend."

Michael shrugged helplessly. "So far, Arel is adamant. He wants to do this on his own."

"You have to admire him," Fred said. "When he makes up his mind, he's amazing."

"Amazing or not, I hope he doesn't snap," Abrigail said as she watched Arel leave the room. "His day isn't over yet."

* * *

Arel covered his mouth and yawned. With effort, he put one foot in front of the other as he made his way through the living room.

Sleep, oh how I long for you, to lose myself in sweet slumber.

"Going to bed?" a small, feminine voice called out.

The sound startled him, making him glance around uneasily. He'd forgotten about Carol. Now she sat curled up like a small, contented cat on the sofa, reading a book. He tried to smile, but those muscles didn't seem to be working anymore. "Are you okay? Can I get you something?"

"You've already done too much," she said, stretching out her tiny feet.

She was wearing pink slippers. Normally, Arel would have found them quite adorable, but one slipper had a dark smear of jelly on it. He made a mental note to put it in the next day's laundry.

He let out a sigh as he looked back at Carol. "Don't worry about me. The important thing is that you've had several naps today and look rested. That's so important."

Carol stretched out the messy slipper again, pointing a toe in his direction. "Thank you for insisting on taking care of Kevin by yourself. He sounds like he can be a little difficult. But I feel wonderful."

"Excellent," Arel managed. He felt like he was caught up in an exhausted daze and was about to continue off to bed when Carol put her book aside and stood up. "What are you doing?" he asked.

"I know I just ate a couple of hours ago, but I'm starving again," Carol said as she walked past him. "Are there any leftovers?"

As Arel watched her heading for the kitchen, all thoughts of rest slipped away like the last drops of water on a dying man's parched lips. "What about an omelet?" he asked, trying to keep his voice steady. "I could fix one for you while you read a little more."

Carol paused and turned towards him. "Yum, I love your cooking and that does sound good, but only if it's not too much trouble."

"Trouble? It's no trouble." He was amazed with himself. He was able to lie so effectively, even when he felt ready to keel over.

Carol's smile broadened as she walked over to him and kissed him on the cheek. "You're such a jewel."

For a moment he felt like it was the Judas kiss, but he quickly stopped himself from going down that road. He might never come back. He pointed to the sofa instead. "Now go sit down, and I'll get that omelet started."

"Arel?"

"Yes, my dear?" He turned back to look at her, noting that she was a picture of calm and serenity. Da Vinci could have used Carol as a model for a Madonna. "What is it?"

Carol gave him an adoring look. "You know, I've never seen anybody more thoughtful when the chips are down. Where do you get all your patience and energy? You'll have to share your secret with me."

* * *

"Where do I get all my patience and energy?" Arel repeated the question as he fell into bed two hours later. He pulled the covers up to his ears and lay still and unmoving, listening to the quiet.

Solitude, you are a companion I've scorned when I didn't know any better.

He knew better now. How innocent he'd been when he started off that morning. He hadn't thought that Kevin would be a challenge. And he imagined dear Carol, that gentle lamb, would be so easy to please. When he reviewed his actual day, he wondered how Kevin could get sick so many times. How could he miss the toilet, not once, but twice? Carol was a lamb alright, one that required constant tending. Crackers and a light breakfast were only the beginning of her need for sustenance. She had to have food every two hours because she had low blood sugar. She got bored easily, needed only short naps, and enjoyed 'keeping him company' when he desperately needed a moment to himself.

But it's over . . . finally . . . and I did it.

He shut his eyes, letting the vomiting, the moaning, and the demands all drift away from him. Still, he renewed a vow to remain steadfast.

This is just a temporary situation. After a good night's sleep, I'll be fine. And I will help those two as long as need be.

He tried to be strong, but he couldn't help himself. He let out a final sigh of self-pity as he was drifting off. Unfortunately, his slide into nothingness was interrupted a moment later by the loud buzz of the intercom.

"Oh no!" His loud moan was as pitiful as Kevin's had been earlier. Gripping the blanket edge, he clung to it as he listened to the voice coming through. It was Carol's voice, sounding upset again.

"Arel, can you come up and help? Kevin's had a relapse. He's sick again."

Seventy-Nine

SITTING IN A linen-covered, bedroom chair, Tim stretched out his legs and smiled at Carol and Kevin. "You two look like you've been on vacation for the past week."

Kevin pulled Carol close as he grinned back from the bed. "It started out pretty rough, but thankfully the bug I had only lasted a couple of days."

"Arel took such great care of him," Carol added.

Kevin's grin broadened. "Hotel Arel is a five star gem."

"You're right," Peggy said as she came out of the bathroom. "The place is spotless. I've never seen such an immaculate bath."

"I told you that you had to check it out," Kevin said. "Every morning, I drop my clothes in the hamper and get a shower. When I get back home from work, the place is perfect and my clothes are clean and back in the drawer. It's like having maid service."

"That's great, but we're not all so fortunate," Tim said, crossing his arms with a frown.

Peggy sat down in a chair next to him and let out a disgruntled sigh. "Now I'll have to go home and work on our place. But I don't think I'll ever get our bathroom to sparkle like this one."

"You do a great job," Tim insisted.

Peggy gave him an appreciative shrug. "Thank you, but you're always helping me, so it's easy."

Carol squeezed Kevin's hand. "Kevin does the same thing when we're at our place."

"But there's only one Arel," Kevin said almost reverently. "I have to take back a lot of stuff I said about his demanding personality. Helping him out was worth it."

"I wonder if we'll get a turn," Peggy asked with an impish smile.

Tim chuckled. "We'll be living next door soon. Maybe he can drop by in his spare time."

Peggy giggled too as she glanced around the room. "By the way, why are we meeting in here? Or should I ask, what is Arel up to now."

Carol leaned forward. "We're going to learn to meditate. It's supposed to be good for both us and the baby."

It was Kevin's turn to laugh. "According to Arel, if we do it in here, the room will have more serenity vibes."

"After the rocky start with that stomach flu, you probably need some good vibes," Peggy teased. "Arel said you vomited about ten times."

Carol and Kevin looked at each other, and Carol blushed. "I'm afraid we almost did Arel in that first day."

Kevin shuddered. "I'm grateful that he was around. Damn, I've never had a bug that brutal."

"You still look at bit tired around the eyes," Peggy said.

Arel walked into the bedroom and looked at his guests. "Tired? Who's tired?"

"I would think that you are, you poor baby," Carol replied.

Arel shot her a playful frown as he put a white, pillar candle on the dresser. "Me? I'm fine."

"So we're going to meditate?" Peggy asked.

"We will if you and Tim are game," Arel replied.

Tim shrugged. "I don't know anything about it, but I'll try anything once."

"I guess I'm way ahead of you," Peggy said. "They had a class at the spa. I tried it and liked it. It was relaxing."

"Do you meditate, Arel?" Carol asked.

Arel shook his head as he lit the candle. "No, but when I have time—" He paused and covered his mouth, yawning. "Excuse me. As I was saying, I've been doing some research on the net and found a lot of information that says it's beneficial." He yawned again. "Goodness, it's not that late, I don't know why I'm so sleepy. Anyway, meditation helps in any stressful situation, and it's good for pregnant women."

Carol smiled back. "I'll be happy to learn more about it, especially if it helps me to be a better mother-to-be."

Arel stared at her with dreamy, adoring eyes. "You're going to be so wonderful as a mom. And when I think about the baby, I can't tell you how excited I am for you and Kevin."

Peggy stared at Arel. "I don't think I've ever seen you look like this before, sweetie. Pregnant women are the ones who usually glow, but when you mentioned the baby, I swear you lit up."

Arel shrugged. "I don't know why, but I've never been more thrilled about anything. This child, this new life, is so extraordinary."

"Then we better get to the meditating part," Tim said. "Show us what to do."

Arel looked at Peggy as he took a seat in a wing chair by the dresser. "Since Peggy's done this before, maybe she could get us started."

Peggy's eyes brightened. "I'd love to. But I only learned a simple technique."

Arel gripped the arms of the chair and adjusted his posture. "That'll be fine, but I do know the first step. You close your eyes to start." He shut his eyes as if to demonstrate. "And you let go, relax . . . ." His tone was quiet and slow. "Just relax," he repeated as he took a deep breath. As he exhaled, his shoulders slumped. "Relax."

As the group waited, Arel's head fell to his chest.

Peggy studied him for a moment and spoke up. "Arel, honey? Are you asleep?"

Everyone smiled at each other. The answer was obvious.

Peggy stood up. "Let's not wake him. We can go into the living room," she whispered as she made her way to the door.

Carol, Kevin, and Tim all agreed and followed her out of the room.

"What have you two done to Arel?" Peggy asked when they reconvened in the living room. "He looks like he's on Prozac."

Kevin held up his hands defensively. "Hey, don't blame us, right Carol? We try to help, but Arel insists on doing everything himself."

Carol nodded. "All I did was explain that I need to snack every couple of hours because I get these sugar lows. It was never a big deal for me. I just eat some crackers or a bit of candy. But Arel says that everything I put in my body is important."

"Yeah, she's got a good thing going," Kevin added. "Arel's always fixing her great snacks like strawberries and special organic fruit shakes."

Tim looked at Peggy with raised eyebrows. "And we bought the house next door. We should have moved in here."

Peggy winked back. "We'll have to ask him if Hotel Arel is taking in new guests."

"I don't think so," Kevin teased. "We're thinking that the second empty bedroom would make a nice nursery."

Tim slapped him on the back. "Good plan. You could give Arel the two o'clock feedings."

Carol gave both men a playful frown. "You two are bad, but I have to admit, it's tempting. Just kidding, of course."

"Hello, everyone." A familiar voice rang out. It was calm and steady, but it had the power to make the group look towards the foyer with expectant faces.

Peggy rushed over to greet their unexpected drop-in. "Michael! Thank goodness you're home."

"Why? Is there something wrong?" Michael asked as the group came over.

Carol spoke up. "No, but Arel is absolutely worn. I think he could use some help."

"He fell asleep in the master bedroom," Peggy said.

"I see." Michael gave the foursome a sweeping smile. "Tell you what, I'll get Arel to his quarters and into bed, and why don't all of you take in a movie."

"We're supposed to be meditating," Carol said guiltily.

Michael's smile broadened. "But you can meditate tomorrow. How about that? Perhaps you need to have some fun tonight."

The group exchanged glances.

"Sounds like a plan," Tim said.

Kevin's face lit up. "Yeah, and there's a new thriller out." He stopped himself and looked at Carol. "Or we could go see a comedy."

Carol laughed when she saw his smile slip away. "I love thrillers. Let's go."

Eighty

AFTER MICHAEL ROUSED Arel from his slumber and directed him down to his own bedroom, he lay in bed, thankful that Michael had returned. On the whole, he enjoyed his role as a caretaker. People depended on him. He was needed, and that was great, but every night he was more tired than he cared to admit. Still, as he enjoyed his chance to relax, the house seemed too quiet. With everyone out for the evening, he missed hearing Carol's laughter and the sound of Kevin's heavy footsteps as he walked through the upper level of the house.

The guy loves those late night snacks.

As he thought about Kevin's insatiable appetite, he began to go over meal planning for the next day. He was tempted to write down a few more items on his shopping list, but the thought of his alarm going off at five thirty made him pull up the covers instead. He needed his sleep, but it was hard to quiet his mind once he started thinking about all the duties that came with his live-in house guests.

Maybe I should give meditation another try. It worked for me earlier.

He closed his eyes and began to recall the steps that led to a tranquil mind. "Relax . . . just breathe and let go . . . as you let it all go . . . tune into the stillness." He'd just about managed to clear his mind when an image of Carol popped in.

Carol, the beautiful mother-to-be! She looked so young and pretty sitting next to Kevin tonight.

He smiled contentedly. As the days passed, Carol's confidence was coming back. Her fears were being replaced by a sense of wellbeing. She was happy again, knowing her unborn child was safe.

"How foolish of her," he sighed.

The words he'd uttered came out of nowhere. He tried not to panic as he reasoned with himself. He was probably still shaky about

Carol's baby. Like he told Peggy, he'd never been so excited about anything before. Now, his subconscious fears were coming up.

He tried to let go and relax again, but the ache in the pit of his stomach wouldn't go away. What if he was sensing real danger? He'd begun to accept his steadily increasing intuitive abilities. Facts appeared out of the blue. Now, a certainty, a deep, inner awareness took hold. Carol's happiness was ill founded. He knew it.

That can only mean one thing. Michael said that souls sometimes change their minds about incarnating.

Immediate grief flooded in. The baby they were all so excited about wasn't going to make it. The thought was followed by a rush of anger and resentment. They were the same feelings that he'd had in the hospital waiting room.

Why would a soul do such a thing? Why would it make a decision that caused so much misery?

Gritting his jaw, fighting the temptation to let his feelings go crazy, he knew he had to stop himself if he wanted answers.

Remember, you have the power to access information.

He'd done it with Mrs. Hayes. Why couldn't he find out more about the soul that was backing out?

I have Michael's blood. It's time to start using it.

That meant that he had to think like Michael, which meant getting into the meditative mode again.

Yes, that's probably why I had the premonition in the first place.

He started emptying out his thoughts a second time, but in the background he made his intention clear. He'd find the soul that was supposed to incarnate as Carol's baby. He'd reason with it and explain why it was wrong to do what it was doing.

Relax . . . first relax.

After only a minute, he felt his nerves calming. He did let go. He fell asleep.

* * *

Arel stood in darkness and damp, breathing in the smell of rot and decay. As his eyes adjusted to the dim lighting and he could examine his surroundings, he knew he needed to wake up. The bowels of some ancient dungeon was the last place he wanted to be. Even if he was only dreaming, everything felt solid and real. The stone walls, embedded with chains and rusty wrist irons, were sinister reminders of man's bleak history of torture and cruelty.

"Oh hell, what have I gotten myself into?" he whispered as he remembered a life when he'd been tortured unmercifully. But he didn't have time to think about that life for very long. A sound brought him back to the grim dreamscape where he stood. Or maybe he wasn't dreaming. What if he'd slipped into another past life? He heard the sound again. Dream or not, he wasn't alone. He jerked around, scanning the shadows. "Who's there?" he called out. "Show yourself!"

"Go away! Leave me alone!"

Arel pulled back, struck by the plaintive voice of the person who answered him. Whoever was in the cell with him was clearly terrified. As soon as he had the thought, he remembered why he was there. He'd fallen asleep with an intention to find a soul, the soul of Carol's unborn child. "Listen, whoever you are, I just want to see you, okay?"

Silence followed, forcing him to make the next move. He took a few steps forward and stopped under the meager light of a lamp that hung from the ceiling. "Please, it's alright. I won't hurt you."

"Arel?" His name was called out in a timid, barely audible tone. "I can't believe it. What are you doing here?"

Arel squinted at the corner across from him. "Do I know you?"

"It's Faine."

"Faine?" He repeated the name, letting it linger on his lips, but he couldn't put a face to the name. "I'm sorry, but I don't remember you."

There was a groan of frustration and disappointment. "We were friends, long ago."

The statement carried a terrible sadness that filled Arel's mind, but he still couldn't remember a person named Faine.

His fellow occupant let out a small huff of disappointment. "You've forgotten our ties. I disappeared from the physical world so many lifetimes ago. But it doesn't matter. You're here for another reason."

Arel nodded. "Yes, I'm looking for someone."

"You're looking for me."

Arel grimaced. For some reason, when he thought about Carol's baby, he'd pictured heavenly clouds and a chubby cherub just waiting to make its entrance into an earthly life. "I don't understand. You're the soul who—"

"I can't go through with it. I tried to incarnate again. I thought that if I could be part of the family that adopted you, I'd be able to try another life. But my fear has been growing with every passing moment. I keep remembering what your world is like. I can't do it. I can't go back there, I can't."

"But Carol and Kevin would be wonderful parents. They'd love you." He paused, seeing himself standing next to Carol as she cradled a tiny newborn in her arms. "I'd love you," he said softly.

There was a long pause of silence, then a whimpering moan. "I know, that's why I thought I could do it." A trembling hand reached out from the darkness. The slender, bony fingers were so crooked and twisted that it was hard to tell if they belonged to someone young or old. It was clear that they'd been broken and never set. They were grim testaments to some horrible experience. Finally, a man stepped into the open, exposing the rest of his thin, battered body.

"My god, I do know you," Arel whispered. But the friend he remembered didn't have a scarred, mangled face. His version of Faine was one that was youthful and handsome. His eyes were passionate and as blue as the morning glories that grew on the back fence in summer.

Shivering and bent, this Faine gazed back with foggy, dim eyes, eyes glazed over with dread. "My soul was lost many lifetimes before yours fell into darkness."

"What happened to you?" Arel blurted out the question, but he knew at once that it was a mistake. His search for answers went too far. It probed too deep into unholy caverns of despair where people died slowly at the hands of heartless humans. It laid open the places where the screams of the innocent, Faine's screams, went unheard, until now.

Arel tried to shut out the vision of a blameless boy who was being tortured for being who he was, a bright, loving soul who didn't know how to hide his light.

"When they were done with me, there was no light left," Faine said in a cowering voice.

Arel moved towards the shadows where Faine stood. He reached out in a gesture of goodwill, hoping to close the gap that had separated them for so long. "I'm so sorry that I forgot you."

"Stay away from me!"

"What's wrong?"

"Stay back!"

Arel hesitated. He'd had an aversion to human contact too. "I understand, but you don't need to be afraid of me."

"I can't let anyone touch me again!"

"It's alright, I promise. And I promise that if you return to the world as Carol's child, I'll always be there for you. I'll protect you no matter what."

"No, go away! My decision is final!"

"Please, Faine, I know all about fear, but you have to face it sooner or later or you'll always be its prisoner."

Faine threw himself against the wall. "I told you to stay away!"

Arel moved closer. "I can't just leave you like this."

Faine wasn't listening. He covered his head with his misshapen hands as if he was trying to ward off the blows of an attacker. "No! I don't want to be hurt anymore." His body shook violently as his protests became pleas for mercy. "Please, no more!"

As the man's pitiful cries filled the fetid air, details of their friendship were resurrected. Arel remembered how they'd laughed together, how Faine's smile was so happy, so open. "Faine, we were like brothers. As a brother, I would never hurt you," he said as he reached out and took hold of Faine's shoulders.

"No! Please!"

Faine's horrified screams ripped through Arel's body like a searing wave of misery. His gut twisted with pain, but he had to help the man who'd once been his friend. He held on tighter, pulling Faine into a compassionate embrace. "You've been wasting away here forever. This might be my only chance to help you."

His actions only made Faine fight harder, like a wounded animal that was being taken from its safe, dark shelter. His inconsolable shrieks became those of the brutalized. They became the screams that Arel remembered when his sister was tied to the stake and was burning. He had to do something.

I couldn't help my sister, but I will help this man!

A trigger instantly went off in his gut. A powerful force was activated, taking on its own life, its own intention to champion those victims who couldn't defend themselves. It became a swirling "fix-it" vortex, targeting Faine's agony, the memories stored in his meager flesh, in his broken bones. It sought out the anger and rage that kept him bound, unable to go beyond what people had done to him. It became an unstoppable engine, trying to consume it all.

As soon as the compelling force was put in motion, Arel regretted it. He'd made a mistake. Whatever he'd initiated was too powerful. He knew that he couldn't control it.

What am I doing? What's going on with me?

He remembered the church garden and how Michael warned him about his capabilities, how careful he had to be when his emotions got away from him.

But I only want to help!

It seemed like a reasonable excuse until he had a moment of acute clarity.

Michael never forced himself on me. But I'm forcing myself on this poor soul. He's terrified of me!

Arel instantly became just as terrified of himself and his power. Faine's every misery was being sucked into his gut, and he couldn't do anything about it. He began to relive Faine's memories, to know the horrors he'd endured. As Arel's own terror escalated, he cried out. "I'm so sorry!"

Faine's wretchedness continued to flood him, fueling a furnace in his gut. He was burning up with an inner fire that would soon consume him too. He had to do something fast. He finally remembered something important.

Shields! I have to drop my shields. I have to let Michael in.

Eighty-One

MICHAEL RUSHED TO Arel's aid as soon as he realized that there was something wrong. He would have acted sooner, but Arel had made sure that didn't happen. Knowing Michael's wishes were not in alignment with his own, Arel had acted in secret, barricading himself behind walls of deceit that kept Michael from finding him. Now those walls had been dissolved. Arel's needy cries were loud and clear.

Michael stood over Arel's bed, shaking him, trying to bring him back from the dream state, trying to break his connection to Faine. "Come back now!" Michael called out.

Finally, Arel let out a soft moan, the first response he'd made since Michael found him. He was burning up with fever. His body wouldn't last much longer if he didn't return to his normal reality. Michael slapped Arel's cheeks repeatedly, trying to get another response. "Arel, wake up!"

His efforts finally bore results. Arel's golden eyes opened wide. He stared at Michael as if he were some horrible demon and started screaming hysterically. "Don't touch me!"

Before Michael could calm Arel down, the man became a frenzied creature, fighting for his life. Kicking, lashing out, he landed a hard punch on Michael's jaw. But Arel's outburst only lasted a few moments. When his strength gave out, he lay gasping, his fight turning into whimpering pleas for mercy.

Michael understood what was happening. Arel was overwhelmed with Faine's energy. He'd taken on too much of Faine's pain. Michael had to do something to stop the process and the fever. He had to get Arel into the shower as quickly as possible. Luckily the energy from the dream dimension was still in a contained state. The unlucky part was that it was still a very real danger. Arel had managed to bridge the gap between two dimensions, to deluge his physical body with Faine's negativity. To make matters worse, his own vestiges of paranoia and his tendency to see himself as the victim were being revived, fueled by Faine's similar energies.

"Arel, look at me!" Michael demanded as he tried to hold Arel upright in the shower. "Look at me now! We don't have much time."

Michael's warning was based on what he observed. Arel's destructive energy, the energy that destroyed the garden, was turned inward. Now, raw, muddied fear was threatening to destroy Arel's body. It wouldn't be long before the volatile nature of the energy reached a lethal stage.

Michael turned on the cold tap full force, allowing a blast of icy water to hit Arel directly in the face. Arel moaned again, then breathed in some of the liquid and started coughing. As he sputtered reflexively, he began to regain a small measure of himself. His eyes came in line with Michael's. After a moment, they sparked with recognition.

"Michael . . . my head . . . I think it's going to explode."

"It's not just your head that's in danger."

The seething mass that Arel harbored was still expanding. Physical bodies weren't made to handle that kind of energy. It was capable of igniting and incinerating flesh if it escalated further. Every second counted.

Arel lifted his gaze. "So hot—"

"Let go of Faine's energy! Let go of it now!" Michael ordered.

Arel's eyes flared bright with guilt and sorrow. "I tried to help him," he groaned. "I didn't want to abandon him to that god forsaken place."

"I know, but you have to focus. You have to take control of what's going on inside of you."

"I don't know how!"

"You're still trying to be Faine's savior. But your power isn't there for you to play God. You're doing more damage than good. Try to understand that! Tell that part of yourself to let go."

Arel swayed, blinking back with beseeching eyes. "I never wanted to hurt him. But he's in so much pain."

Michael pulled Arel tight to his breast, trying to sooth away some of Arel's heartache, trying to draw off the waves of heat radiating from his body. "I know, my dear friend, but you're killing yourself, and it won't help Faine. There are some things a person has to do for himself. Faine has to believe in himself again. You can't do that for him."

Arel seemed to finally understand, and he began to weep. As he began to release Faine's energy, great racking sobs of grief poured out of him. "Will he be alright? Will you help him?"

"I promise that if he allows it, he'll get our help, our love, our support. It's been there for him all along."

Arel stared up with repentant eyes. "I've screwed up everything, haven't I? I should never have interfered, but—"

"You wanted to help Carol and Kevin."

"I thought I knew best until I met that poor soul. If I could go back, maybe apologize again—"

"No!" Michael held up his hand.

Arel looked away. "I'm sorry. That must sound so ridiculous."

Michael took hold of Arel's arm and helped him out of the shower. "You need to rest, to let go of everything that you've taken on. You'll feel better."

"I don't deserve to feel better," Arel snapped back, but the effort of getting angry was too much for him, and he faltered.

Michael steadied him. "So you want to go on suffering? Do you think that's going to help?"

"I guess that's what I've done forever, isn't it? I've been stuck like Faine, only in my case, I've suffered with guilt."

"Not forever. You turned things around, and your world got better, and you wanted to keep it that way."

"That's right, I did. That's how I got into this mess. I wanted things to work out with the baby. Now, I've failed miserably on all counts."

* * *

After Michael helped him back to bed, Arel couldn't sleep. He kept going over what had happened. While he was in the shower, clinging to Michael, he'd felt like all his progress was going down the drain. When was he going to learn not to be so irresponsible? He'd traumatized Faine, nearly killed himself, and he didn't help Carol's baby. They were the acts of a maniac or an idiot. Either way, he couldn't forgive himself. He could still hear Faine screaming, begging

Arel to leave him alone. The man's pleas were so helpless, so filled with dread. And Arel was responsible for the man's utter wretchedness. There was no way he could simply forgive himself. That well-worn rut of guilt that he knew so well was pulling him in again. He needed punishment, some way to atone for his actions.

He glanced over at Michael. His devoted helper was sitting in a chair in the corner, keeping watch. Michael didn't believe in the merits of guilt. But that was because he never did anything wrong. He didn't know what Arel knew, that guilt could sometimes be a comfort.

Hell and damnation, I can't help it. I have to hate myself a little!

He threw up his shields, did several rounds of cursing himself out, and let his shields drop again.

Michael put down his book. "Are you having a hard time sleeping?"

He gave the angel an irritated scowl. "Don't you realize that repentance is good for the soul?" He pounded his chest. "I need to—"

Michael finished his thought. "You need to curse yourself out some more?"

"How do you know I'm doing that?"

"Shields or no, your patterns are predictable."

"I can't help it."

"Could I offer a few thoughts?"

Arel pushed himself up into a sitting position. His fever was almost gone, and his strength was slowly coming back. "Yes, I suppose, as long as it doesn't give me even fewer options in backsliding."

"Do you still want Faine to incarnate?"

"Are you kidding? I keep seeing him fighting me with those feeble, crippled hands. He makes me realize that I wasn't as bad off as I thought." He glanced up at Michael. "I should have listened to you. Each soul has a right to choose its path."

"So you're saying that you're giving up judgment?"

"Absolutely."

"Including judging yourself?"

"I have to feel remorse after what I did to Faine. I don't know how long it'll be before he recovers from my bumbling intervention."

"I'm not saying that you shouldn't learn from your mistakes. But afterwards, it's better to move on."

"I'm not going to win an argument with you, am I?"

"I'm not here to argue, you know that."

Arel paused and looked at his knuckles. They were bruised and painful. "I wonder how this happened."

Michael rubbed his jaw. "If you insist on finding more things to lament about, I would appreciate an apology for that punch you gave me."

Arel's face was just returning to its normal color. Now it flushed with embarrassment. "I hit you?"

"You didn't mean to, but you did land a good one when you thought I was the enemy."

Arel stiffened. "How do you do it? How do you take everything so calmly, never letting anything upset you? What are angels anyway, God's robots?"

Michael stared back for a long moment. "No, we're not."

Michael's tone was soft, but there was a sadness there, almost like Faine's sadness at being forgotten. If Arel needed another reason for remorse, he had one now.

Oh hell, I'm being insensitive with Michael again.

Michael retrieved his book from the side table and stood up. "If you'll excuse me—"

Arel jerked upright and held his head, struggling to focus as the room spun around. "Michael, wait. I'm sorry. I shouldn't say things like that to you."

Michael didn't look at him. Instead, he continued walking towards the door. The angel wasn't letting go of Arel's indiscretion as easily as usual.

Oh hell, I've gone too far this time.

Arel threw off his cover, stood up, and held on to the nightstand. "Michael, please. What do you want from me?"

Michael stopped and turned. His blue eyes were darker than usual and very direct. "I almost lost you tonight. Do you think that doesn't concern me?"

Arel took a deep breath and let himself remember Michael's quick intervention on his behalf. Michael's face was so concerned when he tried to come to Arel's aid. The angel wasn't robotic. He was the exact opposite. No friend, no brother, no parent could have been more caring or protective when Arel needed someone. It was always like that when he was in trouble. "Forgive me," he said as he made his way over to where Michael was standing. "Even if you don't believe in judgment, forgive me for everything, please."

He needed to be penitent. He'd grovel if he had to. Groveling like repentance was also good for the soul. He was sure of it. "I'm sorry that I've ignored your feelings. You've been so much more than a friend. Hell, you're like the father I always wanted. You have to believe that." He put his hand to Michael's bruised jaw. "And I'm sorry about acting like a maniac."

Michael finally brightened. "Apology accepted."

Arel nodded and let his hand drop to his side. "From now on, I'll be careful, and I'll do my best to make better decisions."

"That would be wise."

"I'm turning over a new leaf, no more missions on my own. And I'll also do my best to help Carol and Kevin with whatever happens."

Michael's eyes returned to their beautiful, sky-blue color. "I have good news. Another soul is taking Faine's place. Carol's child is safe."

Eighty-Two

THE BIG DAY finally arrived. Peggy and Tim were moving into their new home. In a few hours, they'd be Arel's official neighbors. He was anxious to help, to be a part of the move. It was a new experience for him, but he was sure he was up to it. After all his jogging and working out, his body was in great shape. He'd never felt so strong and fit. Michael had volunteered to help out too. They both stood in Peggy's kitchen awaiting orders. When he saw a number of cartons sitting in the corner, he wanted to get started. "Peggy, do you want us to take this stuff out to the truck?" he asked.

Peggy was busy removing an assortment of items from the deep interior of a hall closet. She backed out and stared in Arel's direction. "That would be great. But remember, they're pretty heavy. Some boxes have china, iron skillets, that type of thing."

Arel bent down to lift a moderately sized box. "No problem. We'll have them out in a jiffy," he said as he eased the box off of the floor.

"Not with your back, Arel!" Peggy shrieked.

Her piercing screech made Arel jump backwards and lose his balance. It was like the hospital cafeteria all over again. This time Michael was behind him and reached out in time to stop his fall.

Peggy shook her head. "This is why I worry. You aren't being careful enough."

Clutching at the box, Arel gave her a weak smile as he steadied his nerves. "I'll be careful. I promise."

Peggy gave him a stern look and went back to her closet chores.

Arel set his box on the table and mopped his forehead. "She's got a good set of lungs," he whispered to Michael.

"Yes, indeed." Michael looked impressed too. Following Peggy's advice, he began to lift a large box using the correct method, the "Peggy" method.

Arel grinned. For a change, Michael looked ill at ease. "I know you've probably attended countless weddings, but how many times have you been part of a moving team?"

Michael took a moment to balance the box he'd chosen to lift. "I've never done anything quite like this, but it's actually rather rewarding. I enjoy using my body this way."

Arel nodded, noting that Michael's box was a lot bigger than his. "You're right. I think I'll take a bigger box too. Here goes," he said as he bent at the knees to try his hand at a more impressive challenge.

Michael nodded. "I think we're both getting the hang of it."

Arel grunted out his agreement. "This is what you call man's work." It wasn't easy, but he was able to wrestle the box off the floor. "Glad I stuck it out with Kevin's workouts."

"Arel! Not that one!" Peggy yelled as she rushed towards the kitchen. "That's a two person box!"

For the second time, her voice, six feet closer, hit with such force that Arel's equilibrium was blasted out of existence. Next, it was dominoes. He fell into Michael, and Michael lost his grip on the box in his hands. Both of them fell backwards.

"Holy hell!" Arel screamed as he went down.

Peggy ran over with alarm. "Oh my lord! Look at you two! Are either of you hurt?"

Arel glanced over at Michael. The angel stared back mutely, but it was Michael's red face that told him everything. "No, we're fine, just a little embarrassed."

Peggy's frown deepened as Kevin and Tim came running into the kitchen.

"We heard you scream, Peg, what happened?" Kevin asked.

Tim nearly bumped into Kevin. "Yeah, what's going on?"

Both men's attention went to the floor. Arel and Michael were sprawled out flat on the tile.

Peggy pursed her lips. "I'm going to have to watch these two every minute of this move. That's what's going on. They don't know how to take care of themselves."

"We'll be more careful," Michael offered in a guarded tone, gathering in his dignity. He was surrounded by kitchen ware and assorted kitchen compliments from the broken box that he'd dropped.

Tim pushed away a toaster and a skillet to get to the stricken twosome. "Need a hand up?" he asked Michael.

Arel let out a gasp. "I'm a little surprised at how many rules there are for moving a box."

Peggy tapped her foot with annoyance. "I hope I don't have to watch you this closely on the other end, when we're unloading."

After Michael was back on his feet, Tim gave Arel a hand up too.

"Thanks, Tim," Arel said quietly, not voicing his thoughts about the 'other end' of the move.

Once Peggy went back to attacking the closet again, Arel noted that Michael looked surprised, even a little taken back. Smiling, he clasped Michael's shoulder. "Are you sure you're okay?"

Michael continued to stare in Peggy's direction. "Maybe this is a novel experience in more than one way. I think she has the most powerful voice I've ever observed in such a small person."

Kevin overheard the remark and leaned in to whisper. "She's something, isn't she? Tim and I heard that scream of hers all the way out in the truck."

Arel wouldn't have been surprised if they'd heard Peggy in space. But he was happy in spite of Peggy's lungs. Soon his friends would be living next door to him.

Eighty-Three

PEGGY SAT ON the couch in the living room of her new home. Tim sat next to her, holding her hand. Her guests, Carol, Kevin, and Arel, were seated around the room. She smiled at each of them. "We wanted to thank you guys for all your help getting us moved and settled."

"You two did all the settling in," Carol corrected as she looked around. "You even have your pictures up. How did you do so much in only a week?"

Kevin nodded. "Yeah, Peg, you had so much squirreled away. When Tim showed me the storage unit, I thought we'd have to get a bigger truck."

Tim laughed. "Don't look at the garage. I've posted avalanche warnings out there."

"Talk about an avalanche, Michael took quite a tumble from what I heard," Kevin said. "I gather that he tried to pile stuff a little too high. He's lucky he didn't get his brain splattered when that wall of boxes tipped over on him."

"Happily he's fine," Arel said as he held back a smirk. He'd never seen his friend passed out before. But even an incarnate angel has to be careful with his physical body.

Peggy's face turned a bright red. "I think that was my fault. I startled him, and he tipped over a stack of boxes, but he was trying to do too much."

Arel's smile broadened. "I tell him that all the time, but he's the type that doesn't know how to pace himself."

"Please convey my apologies again," she said.

"Peg, you were only trying to help," Tim said quickly.

She glanced at her friends again. "I worry because I care about all of you. I'm so lucky to have such a wonderful husband and family.

Now we have a home of our own and—" She paused and looked up at Tim.

Tim put his arm around her. "And there's more. Shall I tell them, sweetie?"

Peggy clutched at a tissue in her hand and nodded back with a smile.

"Carol, Kevin, you're not the only ones in the baby business. Peggy is expecting too."

* * *

All of the group's angels, including Michael, were in attendance when Tim made the announcement. They couldn't be seen by the humans, but that didn't lessen the joy that they felt. Peggy's angel, Glory, was absolutely beaming. Without her armor, she looked like a much softer angel, but her glow was so powerful that it made Grace laugh.

"Dearest, if you get any brighter, I might have to put on sunshades."

Tim's angel, Kell, the least verbal of the angels present, was unusually radiant too. As waves of elation passed back and forth between Tim and Peggy, his heavenly energies flowed out to them, blessing them with his well wishes.

Fred and Grace looked divinely contented. A new soul had happily agreed to come in as Kevin and Carol's child. Now, after Tim and Peggy's announcement, a second baby was on the way. They knew that the two souls involved were close and would enjoy growing up together.

Grace almost cooed with delight. "My sweet Carol is already thrilled to have Peggy as the sister she never had. Now they can share the journey of motherhood."

"And Kevin won't feel so alone either," Fred sighed. "He's always looked up to Tim. After this, their brotherly ties will be even stronger."

Michael paused at the mention of strong ties. He thought about Faine. Fortunately, after Arel's visit, Faine calmed down enough to reflect on Arel's true intention. Arel wanted Faine to know that someone cared about him. It would take time, but hopefully Faine would soon let go of the past and allow himself to be helped.

Eighty-Four

PEGGY STARED AT herself in the wide, mirrored closet door. "After all these years of thinking about a family, being pregnant doesn't seem quite real."

Tim came out of the bathroom and crossed his arms. "How about those bouts of morning sickness? I bet that's real enough."

She rubbed her hand over her silky nightgown and the slight curvature beneath. "I don't have a bad case like some poor gals. For me, a few soda crackers and weak tea do the trick." She furrowed her brows and gave herself a stern, reprimanding look. "I only wish I could eat something that would make my shortcomings go away."

Tim walked over and looked at the mirror too. Putting his arms around her, he pulled her close. "What shortcomings? You're an amazing, beautiful, and perfect woman."

"But will I be a good mother?"

"You're going to be a great mom."

"I wish I could be sure of that. Maybe I don't know how to nurture. When I try to help Kevin out, I always seem to aggravate him."

Tim laughed. "Kevin isn't a child, and you're not his mom."

"I know, but what if I do and say the wrong things with our baby?"

He bent down and nuzzled her cheek. "You won't. I'm sure of it."

She turned around and put her arms around his neck. Tim seemed incapable of finding fault with her. When she was with him, she always felt better about herself. "I just want our baby to feel loved. I want to do all the right things that a mother should do."

Tim answered her with a kiss on the top of her head. "You will."

"You're positive?"

"Yes, I am."

Gazing up at Tim's strong, confident face, she let her shoulders relax and even smiled back at him. "I hope you know how much I love you."

"And I love you."

She inhaled a hint of shaving lotion that lingered on Tim's neck. She took a deeper breath and let herself get lost in his scent and his words of comfort.

"Everything is okay," he whispered.

"I hope Kevin knows that I care about him. I hope he feels that I'm only hard on him because I want the best for him."

"He just needs time. He'll come around."

"I don't know about that. He puts on a good show, but I think he's very afraid of becoming a father, especially now that he and Carol are getting ready to move back to their apartment."

"Kevin is smart. He'll figure it out."

"You're both almost the same age. Why are you so secure about it all? If only Kevin were more like you."

Tim pushed back a lock of her thick, red hair and nibbled an ear. "Maybe you're too concerned about him."

"I can't help it. He can be such a mess."

"You have to stop thinking about it. Anyway, that's what Arel would tell you. You know how insistent he is about mothers being happy."

She let out a sigh. "Yes, I know."

Tim's eyes were bright and mischievous. "Maybe we should go back to bed for a while."

She smiled, getting caught up in the playful look he gave her. It short circuited her concern over Kevin. "Maybe we should."

She felt a wonderful shudder of anticipation as she watched Tim climb into bed and gesture her over. She quickly put her worries on the back burner, but she also made a promise to herself. Tomorrow morning, she'd ask Arel about her feelings and see what he thought.

Eighty-Five

AREL HAD A problem, and he needed to pass his burden on to broader shoulders. Michael's seemed like the obvious choice. "Good, you're here," he said as Michael joined him in the downstairs living area.

Michael walked over and gave him a look of surprise. "Why the scowl? You looked fine earlier."

"That was before Peggy's daily visit. You know that she's been coming over the past couple of weeks. She has a cup of tea before she goes to work."

"You two seem to get along very well. She always leaves with a smile after your chats."

"Yes, I'm sure she does. After she's deposited her load of woe on me, she's free to go her merry way."

"What's this load of woe you're talking about?"

"Each morning she's been going over her life, trying to see if she'll be a fit mother. She feels bad about being unkind to Kevin when they were kids. It seems that she was bossy and demanding. She's afraid of being like that with her child. Anyway, every day it's a new litany of sins from her past. She's made me some kind of father confessor."

"What do you tell her?"

"I tell her what she wants to hear, that she's not really like that. That's when the argument starts."

"What argument?"

"She makes me the devil's advocate. I have to convince her that she's wonderful." He gave Michael a questioning grimace. "Don't you pay attention to what I'm going through?"

"I'm not here to invade your privacy. I'm here as your friend, one who will help out if you're in trouble."

Arel sat up straighter. "That's the point. I am in trouble." His golden glare was directed at his own father confessor. "I love Peggy dearly, but my nerves are shot."

"Maybe you need to tell her how you feel."

"Are you insane?"

Michael's eyes took on a puzzled look as if he had to contemplate the question. "No, I don't believe so."

"Obviously you don't know anything about women when it comes to this kind of thing. You can't ever tell a pregnant woman that she's a pain in the ass."

"Well, I didn't know that you were going to put it like that."

Arel stood up, pushed Michael aside, and began pacing. "In her condition, Peggy is a sensitive creature that's doing the best she can to navigate between happiness and crap. It's fallen to me to captain her unsteady vessel to safe shores."

"And you're doing a wonderful job."

"That's what you think." He walked back to where Michael was standing. "The captain's boat is sinking. Who's going to get the captain to safety? You've got to intervene in this situation. Just adjust her hormones a little."

"I'm sure that's not necessary. Nature knows what it's doing. Peggy's moods will even out in time."

"That's great. I figured that you'd have an excuse."

"I'm sorry."

"I'm desperate," Arel groaned, bowing his head, going back into the role of a penitent. "If you can't do anything about Peggy, you have to help me."

"Tell me what I can do?"

Arel's eyes came alive with his petition. "Give me the patience of a saint. Surely if you can bring me back from the dead, you can help in the patience department."

Michael smiled broadly. "Arel, let me tell you about the patience of a saint. You're up at 5:30, and you're going nonstop until you fall into bed exhausted every night. No matter how irritated you are, you try never to be hurtful. You're always there for all four of these young people, with everything from a meal to an encouraging word. You've put your own interests on hold to help them out. You're already an example of patience. I couldn't add anything more if I tried. Be proud of yourself."

Arel paused as Michael's praise sank in. "Thanks, Michael. I think."

"It's going to get easier soon. Aren't Carol and Kevin moving back to their apartment this weekend?"

"Yes, Carol seems to be out of the woods. They can start living a normal life again."

"So you can relax a little more."

"I'm really going to miss them. Isn't that crazy? Life will be easier, but—" He didn't know how to finish the sentence. One minute, he was complaining about Peggy, and the next, he felt a forlorn sense of regret about Carol and Kevin not needing him anymore.

Michael came over and put a hand on his shoulder. "You've got empty nest syndrome."

He jerked his head up. "Empty what?"

"It's common. Parents feel sad when their children leave home. You're not Carol or Kevin's parent, but you essentially took on that role. Thus the name, empty nest."

"Well, I don't want some accursed syndrome. The name alone is offensive. I'm not some nesting chicken who's had its eggs ripped off."

Michael almost grinned, but sobered immediately. "I'm glad you feel that way. Being sad isn't something I recommend."

Arel scowled down at the rug. He didn't want to admit it, but he did feel sad. "Oh hell, just tell me what I can do about it."

"Focus your energy in another direction. Let me show you."

Arel felt his gut tighten, a sure sign that Michael was up to something. "I think I'm too tired."

"This won't require any of your energy."

"On second thought, I'm fine."

"Close your eyes. I can help."

"Geez, Michael, please don't send me to the dark ages again. I've had enough of that for a while."

"I promise, now let everything go."

"Easy for you to say, you don't have Peggy, Carol and Kevin running around in your brain."

"Exactly, so let's help you put them where they belong."

Arel shut his eyes tight and frowned. "And where's that?"

"You'll see, but you have to remove your focus from your thoughts."

"Like that's easy." He took stock of his mind. After a busy day, a myriad of details were still processing. Plus, there was a list of items for the next day wanting his attention. "I don't think that I know how."

"Pull your concentration downward, into your heart, the actual physical vessel," Michael said soothingly.

"I'm trying, but—"

"Stay with it. If you need to, put your hand on your chest. Get in touch with your center."

Arel let out a great, weary sigh, knowing he was in a bind. If he didn't follow Michael's suggestion, he'd probably be plagued by a restless night and wake up the next day feeling like hell. He obediently put his hand over his heart, tuning into the pump that moved his blood steadily in and out. "What's next?"

"What do you feel?"

"Nothing, except for the steady beating."

"Are you sure that there's nothing else? Let your vision expand. See your friends in a space with you. Make it a special place, with the sun shining down. There are no agendas, nothing to think about. See yourself going somewhere that's serene."

"I like the idea of summer and the seaside." Arel's brow smoothed out as visions of sparkling, white sands and palm trees filled his mind. He'd never experienced vacation envy before. Now, getting away for a while seemed like exactly what he needed.

"And you can have a vacation of sorts, right now," Michael continued. "Tell me what you'd see if you were actually on that beach."

Arel smiled dreamily. "There's an ocean breeze. Carol and Kevin are in lounge chairs, and so am I. Tim and Peggy are there too, but Peggy is so quiet. She's sipping lemonade." He paused. "I see you, Michael! You're wearing shades and cut offs, and you're walking along the water."

"Sounds great."

Arel sighed again, but this time it was a happy, blissful sound. "What a wonderful place."

"And remember, it's there for you whenever you want, for however long you want."

Arel heard the sound of seagulls. Palm fronds waved softly overhead. "All my worries are gone when I'm here. It's strange, but I don't feel bad about Carol and Kevin leaving."

Michael grinned. "Perhaps I've cured your empty nest syndrome. When you visit places with your heart, you're reminded that you're never alone."

Eighty-Six

"NO, STOP, DON'T!" Kevin woke up shouting. His heart pounded as he tried to sit up. He couldn't manage it. His legs wouldn't move. He knew he had to do something, but he was helpless. Finally he opened his eyes and realized he was in a modern, living room, not some dismal, thatched hovel.

Oh god, I was having that nightmare again! It's the old man in the dream who's paralyzed, not me.

He blinked several times, trying to wake himself up completely. If he didn't put distance between himself and the nightmare, he'd never escape the blanket of despair that accompanied the dream.

Carol rushed into the room. "Kevin, are you okay? What's wrong?"

Kevin's heart was still racing as he tried to move his legs again. The numbness was going away. "I'm fine," he said in a hoarse whisper, relieved that he was telling Carol the truth, at least about his legs. He sat up as quickly as he could, gripping the sofa arm. "I woke you, didn't I? Sorry about that."

She sat down next to him. "No, I woke up a few minutes ago. Your side of the bed was cold." She smiled sweetly. "I missed you."

He rubbed his face, still fighting the remnants of the nightmare, still trying to break the spell of hopelessness that had grabbed hold. "I couldn't sleep. I came out here to watch a little TV. I must have dozed off."

"Kevin, talk to me. Tell me what's going on? Since we moved back to our own place, you don't want to go to bed with me. And when you do, it's only for a little while. Is there something wrong between us?"

Carol sounded so unhappy. He wanted to take care of her. He wanted to be there for her, but what could he do? It wasn't just that he was having nightmares. Even when he was awake, he felt like the old man from the dream was haunting him. If he couldn't help himself, how could he help Carol? "What do you want me to say? I can't sleep."

"I feel like you're pushing me away."

"I don't want anything to happen to you or the baby, that's all."

"The doctor said that I'm fine, that the baby is out of danger."

"That's good. So let's go back to bed." He tried to be positive, but he couldn't keep his voice from sounding miserable. The nightmare kept flashing in and out.

Carol stood up too. "Never mind. It's clear that you feel like I'm a burden, a big problem that you don't want to deal with."

"No, that's not true. I love you."

Carol bit her lip as tears welled up and streaked down her cheeks. "Why don't I feel like it?"

"Don't cry. I really do want to be with you. Let's go back to bed, please. Let me hold you."

"You say it like you mean it, but when I look in your eyes, you seem so far away." She put her hands on his chest. "What's happening to you, to us?"

"Nothing." Carol's touch was so gentle. How could he tell her that everything was falling apart inside of him? "I'm trying. You have to believe that."

* * *

Carol lay in bed, wondering what Kevin wasn't telling her. Since they'd left Arel's house, he'd been acting so weird, so nervous and jumpy. Now he was holding her, just like he promised. But Kevin's body felt tense. Earlier, when they were talking, his grey-blue eyes were awash in stormy seas. She wondered if their fragile boat of love would survive the tempest she could feel building inside of him. As she listened to him breathing, she sighed. "Kevin?"

"Yeah?"

"I'm here for you too. You know that, don't you?"

Kevin pulled her closer. "Of course I do. Now please, sweetie, get some rest."

"Only if you promise to do the same."

"I promise to try," he answered in a despairing tone. "That's the best I can do."

***

Sitting in their usual spots on the patio, Fred and Grace talked about their favorite subject, how humans handled life and what angels could do to help.

"People are curious," Fred mused. "Kevin is so prone to doubting himself. I can't seem to get through to him. He even shuts me out in the dream state when I try to advise him."

Grace gave him a gentle smile. "Kevin's problems go way back many lifetimes. He was part of Arel's group. He didn't burn at the stake, but the part he played has left a mountain of guilt."

"Guilt, that's a tough one. Kevin's charted out quite a situation to confront it."

"Yes, he has. However, he does have a special ally. Arel has become quite the take-charge individual. Perhaps he'll do something daring to help Kevin out."

"Perhaps." Fred looked up at the stars, but he didn't share certain information that he was privy to. He didn't think the episode concerning Faine was something that Grace would appreciate.

Grace glanced over at him. "Frederick, is there anything that I should know?"

"Of course not. We both agree that Arel has been a true guiding light for both Carol and Kevin."

Grace sighed. "Just so he's permanently over the vampire thing."

"Yes, of course." Fred pondered the meaning of the word, vampire. He wondered if Arel's ability to suction out and consume Faine's negative energy counted.

Eighty-Seven

TIM CAME AWAKE with a start. He was sure that he'd heard Peggy cry out in her sleep. He blinked at the darkness and waited for a sign that he was right. A moment later, Peggy started to mumble again and shifted restlessly from side to side.

Tim sat up and shook her shoulder. "Honey, what's the matter?"

Peggy let out a sleepy moan. "What?"

Tim switched on the table lamp by the bed. "Honey, you must have had a bad dream. Are you alright?"

Peggy squinted back. "I guess I was dreaming, but it wasn't a regular dream. It felt more like when I was worried about Arel."

"Are you worried about him again?"

"No, this time it's about Kevin. Something's wrong."

Tim looked at the clock. "It's three in the morning. What do you want to do? Should I call him? Do you want me to go over there?"

Peggy shut her eyes and moaned again. "I don't know. Maybe it was nothing. I don't want to keep being an interfering sister."

"Kevin's going to be alright. You have to believe that. Look at Arel. You were worried about him. Now he's fine."

"I guess you're right. I keep forgetting that Kevin is a grown man."

Tim reached over and turned off the light. "No more dreams, and in the morning, I'll call and check on him."

* * *

Arel's first thought was that the intercom was buzzing. "I'm coming," he stammered, more asleep than awake. He started to push himself out of bed. He was getting used to obeying the buzzer without thinking. When he realized the phone was ringing instead, he eyed the caller ID and the clock. Why were Peggy and Tim calling so early? Was something wrong?

"Hello?" His hand trembled slightly when he answered the phone.

Tim's voice was calm, but his message was an unwelcome one. Arel frowned as he asked a couple of questions. "What did you say? Kevin's in the hospital?" As Tim responded, Arel was already out of bed and walking to his closet. "You're going to see him? I'll be dressed in five minutes. I'll meet you outside."

After signing off with Tim, Arel grabbed for a shirt without thinking. His mind was busy digesting what he had to do.

Damn, another trip to the hospital. What's with these people?

He was about to put on his shirt and stopped himself. How could he think such a thing? How could he refer to his family as "these people"? It was old programming. In truth, he wanted to help. As he continued to dress, he brought his mind back to the facts. Tim said that Kevin was out jogging and got hit by a car. His injuries weren't life threatening.

Arel took a couple of breaths and felt a little better. Kevin was tough. He'd be alright. Or would he? Arel remembered his nightmares. Kevin was always in the middle of them, looking like a lost soul. Were the dreams trying to tell him something?

He snatched a pair of slacks off a hanger, not giving much thought to what he was putting on. He barely ran a brush through his hair. It was getting easier to disregard his appearance after taking care of houseguests at all hours.

Hang in there, Kevin. If I can come to grips with life, so can you.

Still, he had his doubts. He'd been there for Kevin the entire time the young couple had stayed with him, and it didn't prevent Kevin from doing something foolish once he was on his own again.

On some level, this wasn't just an accident. You did this to yourself, Kevin. I know it.

Eighty-Eight

AREL FOLLOWED PEGGY and Tim into the hospital lobby with a confident step. He'd overcome his hospital fears. He was sure of it. He was sure of it until he inhaled a little too deeply and nearly gagged. There was no evidence of antiseptics or other noticeable hospital smells, but his overly sensitive nose wasn't appeased. It issued a warning. 'You know this place, and it's always proven to be hazardous in one way or another.'

No, that's not true. I was here with Carol, and that episode turned out fine.

While he was having the argument with himself, Peggy came over.

"Are you alright?" she asked.

Arel realized that he was still lingering close to the entrance doors, probably looking nervous. Now Peggy was staring at him with anxious eyes. He didn't need to add to her worries. She was already upset enough over Kevin. "I'm fine. I just need a moment. Maybe you and Tim should go ahead to Kevin's room? I'll meet you there."

Peggy reached out and tried to smooth back his hair with her hands. It was thicker than ever now that he was healthy again. She let out a fussy sigh. "You don't look quite yourself. But lord knows what I look like. I was too worried to care when I got dressed."

"You're fine," Tim said as he joined them. He took Peggy's hand and gently pulled her towards a wide corridor. "We'll see you soon," he said glancing back at Arel.

As they disappeared around a corner, Arel was glad that Tim was there for Peggy, but perhaps he'd been too hasty in sending them ahead. Now he was on his own.

Just move along. Stop stalling and breathe. Hospital air is not going to kill you.

He stepped into the main thoroughfare, glancing furtively to the right and left, eyeing the numerous staff members. They moved up and down the hallway in crisp, white coats that made him leery and fretful. He didn't like what the nurses and aides wore either. Their colorful scrub tops, sporting kittens and other happy themes seemed like false advertising. Who were they fooling? They worked in a hospital. That meant sick people were lying in beds, probably in pain. What good was their bright clothing going to do?

He had to stop halfway down the hall. He was getting caught up in his negativity again. In fact, he was hardly breathing. Run-away fears and oxygen deprivation were making him lightheaded. He sucked in a couple of breaths of air and felt worse. Maybe he didn't need to breathe.

Forget about yourself. You're here for Kevin.

The young man could be caring and helpful. He could also be an obstinate, "dig in your heels" kind of guy. From what Arel gathered after a recent conversation, Carol had a similar take on the man she loved. She painted a very sad picture. Kevin was unhappy most of the time, and he wouldn't tell her what was wrong. As a result, Carol was going downhill too.

Oh god, what if they both go under? I'll have to be both mother and father to their baby! I'll have to raise it myself!

That thought was enough to get him breathing, but not normally. He knew what was coming next. Before he started into full-scale hyperventilating, he managed to find some privacy down one of the empty halls. The cure was a paper bag and a shift in his thinking. Neither was available. He kept imagining a bleak future. What if he made a terrible parent? What if the baby ended up hating him?

Oh hell, I think I'm going to faint.

He grabbed for a drab, hospital-green wall to steady himself as he felt the first signs of blacking out.

"Arel, calm down! You're not alone. I'm here."

He heard Michael's voice in his mind. He also felt the angel's energy soothing his body. Within a couple of minutes, he was able to slow his breath. It was enough to help him get a measure of clarity back. "Michael, please, tell me how to help Kevin. If you don't, I might end up a single parent."

He could feel Michael's light-hearted response. Was Michael laughing at him?

"I'm not laughing at you, Arel," Michael announced. "But you have to have some faith in Carol and Kevin. They're both very capable, even if they don't always act like it. They're still finding their way."

"I wish they'd find it faster."

"I know, but in the meantime, I have something to share with you. It's something that might help you keep your mind on other things."

"What do you mean?"

"When you go back to the corridor, look at the people closely."

"I already looked at them."

"Look again, and I think you'll see more than you did before."

"Great, what now?"

This time Michael did laugh. "You'll see."

"I'm glad you find this amusing," Arel replied. When he felt well enough to trek back to the main hallway, he resisted Michael's suggestion. He didn't want to check out people. However, after his incident with Faine, he'd promised Michael that he'd listen to his advice. So he didn't have any choice but to take a closer look at the passersby. Strangely enough, he liked what he saw. Every person who walked by him looked like someone out of an animated, Disney film. Everyone was engulfed in layered cocoons of color. "Bloody hell, am I seeing people's auras?"

Michael laughed again. "When you had that moment of panic, you opened up for a fraction of a second. I used the opportunity to activate that aspect of your perception. It's normal from my point of view. It can be helpful when used as a tool. You can get a peek at what's going on with people's moods and emotions."

Arel snorted. "I'm in a hospital, so you gave me a diagnostic tool?" He did another sweep of the people around him. "You're right, this is fascinating."

"Seeing auras might make it easier for you to manage your interaction with the energy fields around you."

"You mean that I can see what I'm doing."

"Precisely."

Eighty-Nine

CAROL STOOD BY the hospital bed with her arms crossed. It was hard to ignore Kevin's more glaring injuries. The entire right side of his face was raw and exposed from sliding on road gravel. His hands had suffered a similar fate. She was afraid to touch him for fear of hurting him.

"I'm fine," Kevin insisted. "The doc says I have some bruised ribs and a bump on my head. I guess I was out for a while so I'm here for observation. I'll be released very soon."

"You don't look fine."

"It was a dumb accident."

"Why weren't you paying attention?"

Kevin grunted out a heaving breath of frustration. "I don't know, okay?"

There was a long pause. Accident or not, Carol knew that Kevin was still emotionally detached. When Peggy had called her brother a clam, it was an accurate description.

"So you contacted Peggy and Tim?" Kevin asked.

"Yes, and Arel's coming too."

Kevin's face went flush. "This is so embarrassing. Do you know how many road safety lectures I gave him, not that he didn't need them. He was worse than a four year old. He was so busy complaining that he didn't have the sense to watch out for traffic."

Carol smiled, trying to lighten the mood. "You did a wonderful job helping him. He still gets out and runs at the crack of dawn every day."

"Yeah, I guess I did okay."

Carol put a hand on the hospital bed. "Do you have to be this way, Kevin?"

"What? What am I doing?"

"You have such a defeatist attitude."

"That's ridiculous. I'm fine."

She hesitated, inching her hand closer to Kevin's. "Please sweetie, for the last time, tell me what's bothering you. I know there's more to all of this than carelessness."

"Can't you see I'm hurting," Kevin groaned. "Why do you have to keep grilling me?"

His question hung in the air like a sinking boat on a sea of mutual doubt. Pulling back her hand, Carol frowned. The worst was happening. They were both losing touch with each other, crashing into an emotional dead end.

"Hi, Carol, we're here!"

Peggy and Tim stood in the doorway. Peggy's cheerful greeting was enough to interrupt Carol's downward spiral. She smiled back. "Hi guys, come in."

Carol's first happy thought of the day was that Peggy could help Kevin. From what she knew, they had always been there for each other. Now, she'd have an ally, someone who would help Kevin to open up and talk. The thought was dashed almost immediately. As soon as Peggy stopped next to the hospital bed, she scowled at her brother.

"Oh, look at you, Kevin! You're a mess," she cried out in a disappointed tone. "Why do you do this to yourself? You've had so many accidents over the years."

Kevin's brows hardened into a straight line of defense. "Dammit Peggy, do you have to lecture me as soon as you get here?"

Peggy stepped back, but her face remained stern and uncompromising. "I'm sorry. I just hate to see you like this."

Tim came over to the bed, placing himself between the twosome. He reached out to give Kevin's shoulder a friendly thump. "The last time you looked this mauled up was when you had that playground accident. Didn't you fly off a merry-go-round and land on your face?"

"I think we can forget that one," Kevin said irritably. "I was six."

Ninety

AS AREL MADE his way to Kevin's room, he noticed that he wasn't the only one who was being observant. People were checking him out too. Heads turned in his direction as he passed. People's energy fields sparked with brighter colors. It took a little while to understand the reason, but a polished chrome surface and his reflection explained what was going on.

Oh hell, look at my hair. And I didn't shave.

No wonder Peggy tried to make him more presentable. His dark mane was wilder than ever. A five o'clock shadow surrounded his beard and added to his untamed look. When he examined his eyes, they'd never looked more intense. After Michael's helpful boost, they blazed with an eerie, golden glow. All in all, some would say that he exhibited an air of danger, but a couple of passing nurses seemed to approve of what they saw. They each gave him a generous smile. With embarrassment, he smiled back. When he did, one of them giggled and the other girl said something about how cute he was.

I'm cute? That's a new one.

Still, he did feel rather special. When he looked in their direction, more women lit up and grinned back. He was also getting comfortable with seeing auras, noting that when people were happy, they were brighter and rather beautiful to observe.

By the time he reached Kevin's room, he felt better about his hospital visit. He was even smiling to himself when Kevin saw him at the door and gave him a small wave.

Tim noticed him too. "There he is. Come in, Arel. Join the party."

A party? Arel's spirit spiked a little more. When he walked into the room, he was sure his own aura was glowing. He'd never seen so many people smile at him when he was out in public. Maybe a hospital wasn't so bad after all. "Hi everyone!" he sang out enthusiastically. The group responded with greetings, but after about thirty seconds he knew that Tim had lied. The mood was definitely not festive.

No party going on here.

He glanced around at the unhappy faces that surrounded Kevin's bed. It wasn't easy, but he tried to ignore them and turned to Kevin instead. For a moment, he stalled, trying to find the right words for the young man. "You're a little banged up, but you look like you're in good spirits, Kevin." It was an open faced lie, but what else could he do? Kevin looked like hell, like he'd been dragged through the streets by an irate mob. An aura scan was more damning. Kevin's color scheme was the worst he'd seen that morning.

No, not true, there was that guy they were wheeling around on the stretcher.

Muddied red, muddied pink, muddied green. Every bit of energy around Kevin was corrupted and heavy. Masses of dark gray areas covered his solar plexus and chest, making a light bulb moment go off in Arel's brain.

All this time, Michael has talked about shields. The thick, gray areas are what he's talking about.

He could also feel the misery behind the aura horror show. It reminded him of when Kevin was violently sick and throwing up. He hadn't seen his aura then, but he'd sensed its dark, ugly qualities.

I can't go there! I don't want to think about cleaning up that mess again.

He suddenly wished that one of the giggly nurses had asked him to coffee. He wouldn't drink it, but he could sit across from her and admire her sparkling, rainbow colors and sweet demeanor.

"Arel, are you alright?" Carol asked. "You look kind of dazed."

"What?" He glanced at Carol, hoping for a little sparkle. He had to look away after only a brief inspection. Generous amounts of dark, clearly unhappy blues and greys surrounded the young woman. Her aura was bleak enough to inspire a dozen melancholy songs of woe. Carol was almost as dismal as Kevin.

When his scan traveled to Peggy, he knew he'd hit the jackpot of volatile activity. Dark, red energy mixed with heavy browns swirled like a small funnel cloud around the petite woman's body. Tim was the only person in the room who was stable and fairly clear.

Pulling back from the group, he wished Michael was around. He'd give the angel a full report on his new diagnostic ability. The report would be brief and to the point. "Dammit, Michael, this so-called tool sucks!"

"Arel, are you still with us?" Peggy snapped her fingers, trying to get his attention.

He came up with the first lie he could think of. "Sorry, I was wondering if I left the stove on at home."

Peggy ignored his concern. "Arel, can you explain to me why my brother is sitting here looking like meat from the butcher's? He was your coach. What did he teach you about cars?"

Kevin protested at once, raising his voice. "Aw, don't drag Arel into this!"

Peggy put her hands on her hips in a fast, impatient jerk. "Somebody needs to get through to you! You can't act like a kid forever!"

Kevin's damaged face got even redder. "You never let up for a minute, do you? Maybe I wouldn't be like this if you'd butt out of my life."

Peggy looked just as incensed. "I have to keep an eye on you! You can't even cross the street safely!"

"You think you know everything, Peg, but you don't! So leave me alone!" Kevin yelled.

Peggy added more fury, more smoldering flames to her fired aura. "I'd love to do just that! Do you think I like having to babysit you?"

As the shouting continued, Carol and Tim tried to intervene, but neither could get a word in. Arel pulled back, cringing at how caustic brother and sister were with each other. He literally saw the sparks fly between the two of them. It might have been an interesting display if it weren't so loud and abusive. Peggy had always been sweet with him, but her voice was shrill and bullying when she spoke to Kevin. And the young man was fighting back as if he faced a hostile enemy instead of his sibling. As their energy flared out in greater volume, it filled the room with its darkness, and left Arel with a feeling of doom.

"Stop it!" He came alive with his own wrathful shout, one that came from a deep down fear that his small, secure world was coming apart. "What's wrong with the two of you? Why do you want to destroy everything that I love about this family? Is this what siblings do, hurt each other?"

The group froze. Their eyes became those of innocents as they stared at him.

Arel felt their confusion, and he had one more thought.

If only I could fix them all.

It was the only thought that was needed to set off his gut. It did a replay of the Faine intervention. Again, the internal switch was flipped, the vortex was activated and ready for action.

"What the—" After his talk with Michael, he'd told himself that he wouldn't let himself interfere, but obviously his decision had been overridden by his emotional angst.

Oh hell, I'm out of control again!

His observation was barely acknowledged when he began drawing everyone's energies towards him. Great waves of fiery reds, stagnant blues, and a kaleidoscope of murky colors were being pulled inward. In a panic, he tried to stop the deluge of energy, but he couldn't hold back what was coming his way. All that was discordant, all that was blistering and revolting in his loved ones' energy fields was headed towards his gut. The barrage created a loathsome nausea as Kevin's anger, loneliness and confusion mixed with Peggy's worries and need to control. Carol's helplessness and resentment were additional appalling ingredients.

Oh god, what have I done this time?

He shut his eyes, knowing that he was doomed. He wouldn't go up in flames. He'd probably explode like a balloon stretched to the max and beyond. He'd be done in by his friends and their depressing energies.

Family, I should have known it would kill me in the end!

As he prepared himself for the worst, everything stopped. A circuit breaker shut down his power. The circuit breaker was Michael. In his magnificent and powerful angelic form, he stepped in front of Arel and put a stop to the energy exchange.

* * *

Michael never saw anyone siphon off energy at the rate that Arel had demonstrated. When the man decided that his family's happiness was at stake, his power jumped to a new level. Michael and the other angels present had acted at once. As soon as Arel turned himself into a human vacuum, they all went into protection mode. Their charges were saved from being sucked dry, but the group didn't escape totally unscathed. They all looked pale and drained after only a few moments with Arel. Happily, Michael was quickly able to give him instructions on how to return their energy.

"What happened?" Glory asked afterwards. The situation had been rectified, but she remained in front of Peggy in her full, armored attire.

"He went kind of crazy, didn't he?" Fred commented as he relaxed the shields he had around Kevin.

Kell stood close to Tim, looking more understanding. "I think Arel was actually trying to help. On the plus side, no one is fighting anymore."

Michael nodded in agreement. "Arel's become very powerful, and he hasn't quite learned how to control it."

"Do you regret giving him your gift?" Glory asked.

"No, he gets confused, but all and all, he's doing very well."

Grace let out a little huff of disapproval. "I'm sorry, Michael, but Arel almost had my Carol's life-force for breakfast. I thought that you said his vampire days were over."

Michael gave her an apologetic smile, but little else. What could he say? He still wasn't sure about where Arel's transformation was headed, only that Arel's heart was in the right place. In the meantime, Arel still had to deal with his fears and weaknesses.

Ninety-One

ON THE RIDE home from the hospital, everyone in the car had remained silent. Hardly a word had been uttered. Tim finally spoke up as he pulled the car into Arel's driveway. "Here we are, Arel."

Arel opened the door to get out and hesitated. "Again, I'm sorry about my outburst earlier—"

"And I told you that there's no need," Peggy said quickly. "My behavior was horrible. You were right, Kevin is really hurting, and I hurt him even more."

Arel climbed out and looked back at her. "I don't know if this is an appropriate time, but could I talk to you about something?"

Peggy returned a look of confusion and surprise. "Now?"

"Yes, if it wouldn't be too inconvenient."

She glanced at Tim. "I'll be home in a bit."

Tim nodded. "I'll get some brunch started."

* * *

Arel sat down in a recliner in the living room. Peggy sat across from him on the sofa. Thankfully, his normal perception was back. His interaction with Peggy was going to be strictly friend to friend. Still, he didn't like the way she was fidgeting nervously. "I didn't mean to spring this meeting on you."

Peggy frowned. "I don't know why I feel so anxious. It seems silly. We talk all the time in the mornings."

"I know what you mean." Arel looked down at his hand as he ran it back and forth over the arm of the chair. "In fact, I think I know how you feel when you have those visions about the past."

Peggy's eyes flared. "Those were awful times. I wish I could forget them."

"Maybe that's why we never really discussed them."

"Maybe we don't need to."

Arel's hand stilled. "That's true, but I think you'll agree that the past is still affecting our lives. And recently, more information has come to light about why that is." He didn't tell her where he got the information. He'd been privy to a lot of personal data when he gobbled up everyone's energy at the hospital.

Peggy's nervousness was immediately tempered by her curiosity. "What are you trying to tell me?"

"This part isn't so much about you and me, so I don't know if it's my business to talk about it."

"If there's something that you think I need to know, tell me."

"In that life together, we were tortured and burned."

Peggy looked down. It was her turn to focus her attention on upholstery fabric. She started picking at the nap on the sofa cushion. "I haven't let myself think about it very much."

"And I hate bringing it up. I can't bear to remember how you suffered."

She cut in. "It's the same for me. When I remember details—" She paused. "What they did to you, I know that it was all my fault."

Arel quickly got out of the chair and came over. He sat down next to her. "No, no, it wasn't. We talked about this before. You didn't do anything wrong. No one could fight what they did to us. After that life, we were both left with scars. I think our fears carried over."

"Our fear of the people who hurt us? Is that what you mean?"

"Yes, we feared the men who had the power to torture, who had the power over life and death."

"What difference does that make now?"

Arel put his hand on Peggy's, hoping that he could explain the insight that he'd had on the way home from the hospital. "You've always fought against the bullies, haven't you?"

She shrugged. "Yes, but I wasn't alone. I had help. Kevin was there."

"He took care of you."

"I never gave him much credit for it. I guess I expected it from him." She looked down again. "As I've told you, I was pretty tough on him. I guess I still am."

"Think about it, he was the one man that you could order around. When you were around Kevin, you could be in charge. You had the power. You were in control."

* * *

Tears, shame, and guilt half blinded Peggy as she stumbled across Arel's front lawn. Maybe she'd known this day of reckoning was coming. Hadn't she felt guilty about Kevin for a long time? But that didn't stop her from badgering him at the hospital, telling him what he was doing wrong. She'd used the excuse that it was for his own good, but was it? Was Arel right? Did she need to be the powerful woman who could dominate a man?

When she got to her front porch, she stopped and swiped at her face. She didn't want Tim to see her upset. He'd insist on comforting her.

That's my MO, isn't it? I boss Kevin around. I tell him to be responsible, but look at me. I have to have Tim there when I'm the needy one.

Was she really tough? Or was she simply able to push her brother around, to use his brawn when hers failed? She couldn't face the answer or the chill, gusting wind that whipped her hair around in a wild frenzy. The weather was getting colder by the day. She shivered as she quickly let herself in to the house. She shut the front door quietly behind her.

I told Kevin to grow up, now I better do the same!

The sound of Tim unloading the dishwasher made her want to cry again. She didn't feel grown up. She wanted to be the four-year-old, running into daddy's arms. She wanted to forget about people being hurt, but Kevin's raw-faced image came to mind.

"Honey, is that you?" Tim called to her. A moment later, he came out to the hall to greet her. His welcoming smile quickly turned into a frown. "What's wrong?"

She shrugged back hopelessly.

"Was it Arel? Did he say something to upset you? I know that he was a little harsh at the hospital—"

"No, it's not him," she said, speaking in a repentant, miserable voice. "It's me. I'm a terrible person!"

Tim's eyes narrowed. "It's not true. You're sweet—"

"I'm a first class tyrant! You've seen me around Kevin! I'm horrible."

"Peg, that's ridiculous." Tim came over and tried to reach out, but she pulled away.

"I know what I know! There's nothing more to be said."

Tim paused, squared his jaw, and started for the door. "I'm going to see Arel and find out what the hell he said to make you feel like this."

"No!" She backed up, putting herself between Tim and the exit. "I'm doing what I always do. I'm shooting off my mouth and making you think you need to protect me. But the only thing that sweet man next door did was show me the truth."

A hard knock on the door made them both pause.

"Can I come in?" Arel called out from the other side. "Please!"

Peggy turned and undid the lock. As soon as she opened the door, Arel came forward. He tried to reach out to her, but Tim intervened and pulled her towards him.

"What's going on?" Tim asked, raising his voice. "Peggy is upset as hell, and I want to know what you said to her."

"Stop shouting at him!" Peggy pulled away from Tim's embrace. "I told you that he didn't do anything."

Tim's brows froze in confusion. "So why are you acting like this?"

Arel started to answer for her. "I was trying to explain some things to Peggy—"

Peggy cut in. "We were discussing the time, the lifetime, when we were burned . . . burned at the stake." She paused. "You remember, Tim. I told you about it."

"Yes, but what does that have to do with you being a terrible person?"

"Is that what you still think, Peggy?" Arel asked. "It's the last thing that I wanted for you. I was just trying to explain how that lifetime has affected this one, how it's affected all of us. But you ran out before I could finish."

Peggy looked down. "What he means is that ever since that life, after what I experienced, I've been scared of powerful men."

Tim came over and stood close to her. "Go on."

When she refused to answer, Arel put his hand on Peggy's arm. "It's natural to want to control a situation after we've lost control."

Peggy bit her lip. "But I took all my need, my desire to be some kind of little dictator, out on Kevin. I guess I knew that I could. That's not right."

"No, it's not," Tim said, "but from what I've just heard, you didn't do it consciously."

Arel moved closer to her. "Tim's right. What you did came from a deep down fear. You weren't even aware of it, were you?"

"Of course not! I love Kevin. I do!" Peggy cried out.

"Of course you do," Arel said quickly. "Besides, there's more to it. You left before I had a chance to discuss Kevin's part in all of this, his lack of responsibility."

Peggy flashed sad but hopeful eyes in his direction. "What do you mean?"

"I think that it works like this. We all play roles for each other in each life. In this one, Kevin never really stopped you from doing what you do, even as an adult, did he? Deep down, I don't believe that he wanted to stop you."

"He's tried," Peggy protested. "But I'm too much of a bully to let him."

"No, I don't believe that's it," Tim said. "Kevin can stand up for himself if he really wants to."

"It's true," Arel agreed. "He let you stay in that role. Now he's backing away from a new responsibility, being a husband and father."

"But why would he do that? And why did he let me hurt him? What part did he have in our past life together?"

Arel gestured to the living room. "Let's go sit down, and we can talk about what I know."

Ninety-Two

CAROL'S FINGERS TREMBLED as she buttoned up her flannel pajamas. She looked over at the corner chair. "My world is coming apart, Charlie Bear. I'm going to be one of those moms who have to raise their baby alone."

She paused listening to the sound of the television in the living room. Kevin had come home from the hospital that afternoon, but he went straight to the couch and had remained there for the last six hours. She snatched up the bear, took him back to her bed, and climbed in. "Kevin hardly talks to me anymore. He's made it plain that he doesn't want to be with me."

She looked over at the shopping bag in the corner. A yellow teddy bear peeked out over the rim. Arel had purchased an early baby gift and hadn't been able to resist giving it to Carol right away. She'd loved it when she first saw it, now it made her sad. She swiped at her eyes, then dug down into the nearly empty tissue box and snagged a tissue.

"Kevin should be that excited," she sniffled. "But the truth is that he doesn't really want to be a father. Peggy was right. He refuses to grow up." She blew her nose and threw the tissue into the overflowing trash can. "So I'll have to be the strong one." She turned out the light and slid down under the covers. She held Charlie in a hug and stared out at the darkness. "I know what it feels like to be forgotten by parents who get too involved in their own problems. I refuse to let that happen to our child."

* * *

Arel groaned as Michael shook him awake. "Go away. Too tired." After his episode at the hospital the day before and his talk with

Peggy and Tim afterwards, he'd gone to bed early, hoping to recharge his batteries. He'd slept for ten hours straight. He would have slept longer if it weren't for Michael urging him to open his eyes. "What? What's the problem?" he asked, trying to pull the cover over his head.

Michael shook him again. "Carol is waiting for you upstairs."

"Carol is here?" He threw back the cover and stared hard at the angel, trying to understand his message. As his mind started working again, he frowned. "What about Kevin?"

"Carol said that he's home from the hospital, but that's all she said."

Arel grunted out a protest as he forced himself out of bed. "Maybe Carol's like Peggy. She probably just needs someone to talk to." He stretched, did a couple of neck rolls and went to the closet to retrieve some clothes. He was still trying to button up his shirt as he started for the bedroom door. He paused and glanced back at his bed. "Maybe after Carol's gone, I'll climb back in for a nap."

Michael held up a hand and gestured for him to wait. "I better fill you in on everything. Carol has a suitcase with her."

"A suitcase?"

"I think she's left Kevin."

"Oh hell, not now. The poor guy's in trouble, Michael, and you said that my job was to believe in him, but he doesn't believe in himself. Now, if Carol's left him, I don't know what to say to either of them."

"Sometimes the best thing you can do is listen."

Arel grimaced. "Don't you know that this is a crisis? What other suggestions do you have?"

"Don't try to take on both of their problems at the same time. Work with Carol now, and then you can talk to Kevin."

"Is that the best you can come up with? What about a miracle?"

"I believe in them, don't you?"

Arel paused in front of his dresser mirror and took a long look at himself. "Yes, I guess I do. I'm still here. I haven't incinerated myself yet or blown myself up."

Michael smiled. "Maybe when you go upstairs, you can do a little angel work."

"Angel work? No way. I'm swearing off all my idealistic ideas. After yesterday's fiasco at the hospital and nearly sending Peggy into a state of guilt-ridden despair, I'm going to keep my mouth shut, period."

* * *

Arel sat in his chair, eyes forward, observing Carol's strange attitude. He'd changed his mind. He decided that he did want to help, but Carol wasn't letting him. She sat stoically at the kitchen table, not asking for anything. Instead, she quietly sipped her morning tea. Wearing a linen dress instead of her usual slacks and t-shirt, she held up her chin. When she spoke, her tone was crisp and curt. He felt like they were having a business meeting instead of a friend-to-friend chat.

"Can I get you anything else? I could make you breakfast," he suggested.

"No, thanks. I stopped and had something on the way over. And again, I want to say 'Thank you' for letting me stay here for a few days. It's only until Kevin can move back into a place of his own. After that, I'm going to arrange to work from home." She paused for a moment and folded her napkin neatly before she looked up again. "I have to act like an adult now that I'm having a baby. There's no more time to behave childishly."

"It sounds like you've thought a lot about what you want to do."

The set of Carol's mouth tightened. "What a person wants and what is required are two separate things."

"What about you and Kevin?"

Carol sucked in her breath, then shrugged as if she'd been asked about the weather. "I can't worry about him." She put her hand on her stomach. "If I have my say, this baby is not going to be saddled with a couple of emotional cripples."

"You know that I'll do whatever I can to help, but maybe you're dismissing Kevin too quickly. He needs—"

"Arel, please, you're the person I thought about when I was making the decision to change my life. You didn't stay a casualty of your situation. My goodness, look at you. You're strong and capable of doing whatever you want to do."

"I had lots of support."

Carol's eyes were locked into a grim determination. "Whatever, the point is you're doing fine. And you did a great job at the hospital too. You put an end to the battle that Peggy and Kevin had going. Unfortunately, Kevin won't even fight with me." Carol smiled and frowned at the same time. "But I won't worry about that anymore."

Arel sat back, almost afraid to disturb the unusual air of containment that surrounded Carol, but he was her friend. If she needed to express herself more openly, he wanted to be there for her. "Tell me, where did this new Carol come from? You always struck me as a little more fragile."

The question made Carol pull back slightly, but otherwise, she seemed unmovable. She gave him another frowning smile. "That's easy. I'm tired of crying, and I'm tired of putting myself through the emotional wringer. It doesn't help."

He pressed on bravely. "I hear you, but expressing your feelings can take the pressure off. I know that you want the best for your child, but are you forgetting about yourself, about needing a loving partner?"

"Kevin has taken that choice off of the table." As Carol spoke, a tear slipped down her cheek. She quickly batted it away. "So, if that's the way it is, I have to forget my needs and desires and concentrate on being a parent."

"I see." He'd come upstairs prepared to hold Carol's hand, to dry her tears, but he wasn't prepared to hear that she'd given up on a loving relationship. He leaned forward. "I know you can do whatever you set out to do, but maybe, just maybe, you can have everything that you want. And if you let me, I'm going to do everything in my power to help you to achieve that goal. All that you have to do is agree to let me try."

Carol pushed her cup and saucer away. Then she got up from her chair and brushed down her dress. Bending over, she kissed his cheek. "You're the most loyal friend I'll ever have. I'll keep an open mind because I believe in you too, but let me warn you now, I think Kevin is a lost cause."

As Carol let him go, Arel could tell that she was fighting to stay strong and succeeding. He hoped he could be just as strong. "I'm determined to prove you wrong."

"I'm happy that one of us can dream," Carol said as she started out of the room. "Now if you'll excuse me, I need to make some calls."

Watching her leave, Arel frowned too.

She wants Kevin. I know she does. And I know he wants her.

But desire didn't guarantee anything. If it did, he would have married Justina and lived out a long and happy life with the woman he loved. Now, he might have to accept that another love story was going to end tragically.

No, I can't and won't accept that without at least trying to change the situation.

Ninety-Three

KEVIN WOKE UP, touched his swollen face, and pulled back with a wince. He started to get up and pain shot through his bruised ribs. He had to stop halfway up and grit his teeth. If he'd been alone, he'd let out a yell of pain, but he didn't want to let Carol hear him.

She's already completely turned off when she looks at me. And can I blame her? I'm screwed up.

Peggy was right. He'd run out into traffic like a child. What was wrong with him? As he limped his way to the bathroom, he stopped. The bedroom door was open. When he investigated further, he noted that there were a number of empty hangers dangling in the closet, all on Carol's side.

"What the hell?" Making his way through the apartment, he started to get a queasy feeling. "Carol, where are you?"

He went back to the bedroom, scanning it carefully, still trying to deny the obvious. That's when he realized that it wasn't just clothes that were missing. "Charlie's gone." The old, stuffed bear that always sat on the chair close to Carol's side of the bed was also missing. Kevin's stomach flip-flopped. He was sick.

I've driven her away with all my crap!

His first thought was to find her. His second thought was to sit down and think about what to say when he accomplished that goal. He drew a blank. But he had to get her back. Carol and the baby were the most important things in his life.

The next thought made him even queasier. He'd have to call Arel, again. Before he could find his cell phone, it rang. It was Arel's ringtone. Arel was calling him.

* * *

As Arel drove to Kevin's apartment, he went over his list. No preaching. No judgment. No fixing. The last item was the most important. He wasn't going to interfere with other people's lives ever again. He'd simply be Kevin's friend.

He repeated his intention a couple of times as he walked up to Kevin's unit. Straightening his shoulders, he knocked on the door and waited. He knocked again. Another long wait. "Come on, Kevin, where are you?"

When the door finally cracked open, Kevin hung unto its edge. He looked out with an unwelcoming expression of pain. "Hi Arel, glad you're here."

Arel noted the distaste in Kevin's tone. It could have been used on a funeral director after someone died. He'd been hoping to project a better image than that. "Glad to be here," he said, trying to muster some enthusiasm. That enthusiasm waned very quickly. After using his new "aura vision" to scan Kevin, he knew the young man was in trouble. His energy field was even duller and more muddied than before. The guy was a walking orb of gloom and doom.

Arel made a decision. He'd forget about auras during the visit. They were too distracting. That left the physical side of things. In Kevin's case it wasn't pretty either. The man's face was like raw meat that oozed. Instead of fixating on it, Arel reached out and tapped Kevin's arm gingerly. "Are you going to invite me in?"

"Yeah, sure. Come in," Kevin said as he turned and led the way to the living room. Each step seemed labored, with Kevin adopting a hunched over posture as he held his side. Arel followed him, remembering the hospital. He'd seen people with walkers who moved faster than Kevin. "Do you need something for the pain?" he asked with concern.

"No, not right now," Kevin said as he slowly seated himself on the sofa. "So, I haven't asked, but how are you?"

Arel took a seat across from the couch. "I'm just fine, thanks."

Kevin's eyes went from cloudy to resentful. "Well, I'm not fine. I'm in deep shit. Carol's left me, and it's all my fault. I've messed up everything." He clenched a damaged fist and winced. "Dammit, it makes me so mad?"

Arel sighed penitently. The glass breaking rampage he'd gone on after Mrs. Hayes' death was still a cause for regret. He sat up straighter, trying to forget his own shortcomings, searching for something he could offer Kevin that might help. Michael's words of wisdom came to mind. "I know how that is, but getting angry isn't going to get Carol back." Next, he threw in his own observation. "But let's face facts, there's a lot going on here besides your problem with Carol. A car hit you."

"I wasn't paying attention. You should know all about that. How many times did you forget about traffic when I was getting you back in shape?"

"Yes, you're right." Their training workouts were still fresh in Arel's mind. He'd been the intimidated rookie, struggling to put one foot in front of the other. All the while Kevin growled out orders with all the compassion of a well-trained Rottweiler.

I didn't pay attention for a reason. The only way that I had the strength to keep going was to indulge in some fantasies.

He'd conjured up countless ways to make Kevin disappear, to transport him to the other side of the planet. Even now, the daydreams could be sweet when he thought about Kevin's coaching methods. But his present visit wasn't about Arel's difficulties. He took a deep breath, pushing back the memories. "I was simply preoccupied. I wasn't out to hurt myself."

"And you think that I was?"

"I don't believe in accidents, but here you are, in all this pain. So tell me what happened."

Kevin glared at him. "Let it go! I need your help, not reminders of my mistakes." His tone was sharp and reprimanding.

"I'm trying to help."

"Well, it's not working!"

"I'm doing my best!" As soon as Arel realized he was raising his voice too, he tried to correct the situation. He had to remain calm and let Kevin vent. "Sorry, I didn't mean to shout," he said as he offered Kevin his most understanding smile. "I'm not saying that you did anything wrong."

"But you're thinking it, aren't you? You think I'm a jerk, that I've been horrible to Carol."

Arel stiffened, holding back his feelings. He wouldn't say what was obvious.

Of course you're a jerk! Carol is alone and afraid too, but she's putting aside her feelings, trying to be mature. She's taking responsibility!

The thoughts fired off in Arel's brain, making him ashamed of himself. Who was he to judge? He'd been a jerk countless times. Yet Michael was always kind and understanding. "All of us make mistakes, Kevin, but there are reasons why we act like we do."

Kevin let out a loud moan. "Forget that crap, just help me get Carol back. Tell me what I need to do to show her that I care."

"First you have to understand why you're acting this way."

"Dammit! I need some advice!"

The Rottweiler's bark was back, but Arel was determined to stay in control. "No, you need to stop hiding from what's bothering you."

Kevin targeted him with a sullen, defiant face, refusing to answer.

"Please, Kevin, don't be like this. I'm trying to be your friend. Don't shut me out." Again, he found himself in Michael's position, having to deal with someone who was stubborn and unyielding. He glanced heavenward.

And I hate it!

His fingers went from rubbing the chair fabric to drumming out a staccato beat of frustration. Kevin was leaving him no choice. He already knew all the answers to the questions he was asking. He'd seen Kevin's problems clear as day when he sucked in his energy at the hospital. Still, he knew what Michael did in similar situations. He didn't push. He let Arel figure things out.

But this isn't just about Kevin, I have to think about Carol too.

It was time for a little directive counseling. "Tell me about the dream."

Kevin's gaze had been directed at the floor. Now he glared up at Arel. "What?"

"You've been having a bad dream. Tell me about it."

"How could you know about that?"

A flush of embarrassment warmed Arel's face and he stared back mutely. What could he say to the young man?

Sorry, Kevin, I violated your privacy when I sucked up all your energy yesterday.

Kevin gave him a threatening scowl. "I asked you a question."

"I can't explain it. I guess I'm a little like Peggy. Sometimes, I know things."

"Yeah, well you and Peggy can both stop interfering in stuff that's none of your business."

"I'm asking you these things because I care."

"I said 'No,' and that's final!"

Arel took a deep, slow breath and stood up, going over to where Kevin was sitting. He gave himself explicit instructions before he continued.

Steady, man. Kevin is hurting. You know all about that. He just needs your patience, your wisdom.

"Listen Kevin, that dream is tearing you up inside. You have to find out why."

"Like hell I do."

Arel put his hands together in a gesture of good will. "Please, my friend, work with me."

"Back off, Arel!"

"Fine," Arel whispered through clenched teeth. He retreated, feeling his fragile nerves being tested to their limits. He knew it was the consommé thing all over again. Kevin was being totally uncooperative just like when he was sick with the stomach bug. Now Arel's stomach was in a knot of aggravation. He knew he should leave quietly, that he wasn't going to make Kevin budge. He even turned towards the exit. Then Carol's face appeared. She was trying very hard to be strong and to shoulder the responsibility of a child by herself. It seemed so unfair that Arel stopped in his tracks, glared back at Kevin, and let his feelings have their way. They came out in a seething order. "Just open up Kevin! Try the damn soup!"

Kevin's eyes widened in surprise. "What the hell are you talking about?"

Arel blinked a couple of times when he realized what he'd said. "Uh . . . sorry, I meant . . . just tell me what's eating you. I know the dream is disturbing. Let's—"

"Soup! Dreams! You're nuts, Arel. I should have never asked for your help!"

Arel was about to yell something back when he felt a flare go off in his gut. It was a warning. At this point, he wasn't just upset with Kevin. If he didn't stop himself, he'd make another terrible mistake. He couldn't let that happen. "Fine, do whatever you want. It's obvious that you don't need what I have to offer."

Kevin's eyes darkened. "So that's it? You're giving up? Did I give up on you? Do you know how tough it was to keep listening to you whine every morning when I coached you? But I hung in there, didn't I?"

Arel knew Kevin was right about staying the course, but he didn't know if he could trust himself or control his emotions. He'd give it one more try. "Fine, I'll stay," he said as he walked over to the sofa and sat down again.

"Don't hurt yourself," Kevin said caustically. "If it's such a big deal to help out a friend, just get the hell out, now!"

Arel never thought something could snap in his brain so fast. But Kevin managed to push him too far. He wouldn't let his gut get out of control, but he sure as hell could let the young man know he wasn't helping himself. Jumping up from his seat, he went over to Kevin and grabbed the front of his shirt. "Dammit, Kevin, if you want Carol back, you'll tell me about the damn dream! Otherwise, you can sit here forever feeling sorry for yourself! It's your choice. Start talking or I'm out of here!"

Kevin pulled back, clearly impressed by Arel's volume and directness. "Crap almighty, Arel! It's not a big deal. Not a big deal at all. It was just a dream about an old man, a dirty old man, a disgusting old man." He heaved out a sigh of loathing. "There, are you satisfied?"

Arel held on to Kevin's shirt. "Go on. Tell me more."

Kevin stared back almost helplessly. He was clearly intimidated by the fiery stance Arel was taking. He removed Arel's hand and pushed himself into a standing position. "You're not going to let it go, are you?"

Arel could feel himself calming down. After he let off a little steam he felt more relaxed. But he was serious about what he'd said to Kevin. "No, I'm not letting anything go," he said in a quiet whisper.

Kevin let out another groan. "The dream is always the same. There's an old man in it. He's all screwed up. His legs are covered in sores and useless. The place where he lives is dark and depressing as hell."

Listening to Kevin's description, Arel closed his eyes. He saw the old man very clearly. He saw the squalid dwelling in detail, from the thatched roof to the dirt floor. But he wasn't just seeing Kevin's nightmare. Kevin was describing a place and a person that Arel remembered too. As more details flooded in, he looked at Kevin. "You're wrong about the old man. He was a good person."

Kevin fired back an angry scowl. "What the hell do you mean? It was my dream. How would you know about the guy?"

Arel maintained a steady gaze as he stared at Kevin. "The old man was always trying to help us."

"What do you mean by 'us,' Arel? I think you've gone around the bend."

Arel smiled and shut his eyes again. He let himself connect with a vivid scene that appeared in his mind's eye. "I'm just telling you how it really was. The world outside of the old man's hut was harsh and cruel, but the old man's home was a refuge. And when he looked at me, he could make me forget everything for a little while. I felt safe."

"Safe? Are you kidding? Just the thought of the old bastard scares the hell out of me. Besides, it was just a dream, a nightmare."

Arel felt himself drifting. "I wouldn't be too sure about that."

Kevin held his ribs as he walked back to where Arel was standing. "You're scaring me, Arel. Wake up or open your eyes or something."

"It's too late," Arel sighed. Reality was shifting. Energy was stirring as he connected deeply with an old man's kindness and a feeling that he was a young boy again. He was a boy in a long ago lifetime. He was a boy who was seeking wisdom at the feet of his beloved teacher. As he allowed the vision to take hold of him, he didn't feel confused anymore. He didn't need to fight Kevin or himself. He could simply enjoy a complete moment of peace.

Kevin reacted by taking hold of his shoulders and shaking him. "Arel, please, look at me!"

Arel took a deep breath, feeling at ease, no longer burdened by a duty to help. Compassion replaced control when he thought of Kevin. "Are you sure that's what you want?"

"Yes, dammit!" Kevin cried out.

His sharp demand was enough to do the rest. Again something inside of Arel took charge. But it wasn't something to be feared. Arel knew the power he was tapped into. He'd felt it in Michael. When his lids slid open and he gazed at Kevin, he experienced a feeling of complete and utter serenity.

Kevin let go of him at once. "Holy crap!"

***

Kevin couldn't stop staring at Arel's eyes. They were golden, illuminated spheres that held him captive, immobilizing him. He was the moth drawn to their bright mystery, to their seductive whisperings.

Never moving, Arel spoke to him in the softest voice. "If you let their energy consume you, it'll burn away the fear. It'll help you to face the nightmare you've been trying to escape."

Kevin swayed unsteadily. He was incapable of fighting the beguiling message. His legs began to buckle. He began to fall, but Arel was gripping his arms. Arel's steady gaze seemed to grow in strength. It contained a golden fire, a fire that consumed the person who Kevin thought himself to be. His world began to spin faster and faster. He couldn't hold on to anything. When the spinning stopped, he was back in the old man's hovel. He was dreaming again, but he wasn't just observing this time. He was in the old man's body. His limbs were weak and withered. He was bent with age and years of toil and hardship. When he tried to move his legs, they didn't have the strength to respond. A feeling of profound uselessness came over him.

"Are you alright?"

The question came from a young man sitting across from him. As soon as he looked up at the boy, he felt better and smiled.

"Yes, my son. Don't worry about me."

The boy immediately dipped a coarsely woven cloth in a bowl of water laced with herbs. He began to clean the open sores on Kevin's crippled legs. His touch was gentle and soothing. When the boy paused and looked up, he had the most beautiful, clear blue gaze of innocence. When the boy spoke, his voice was filled with need and wonder.

"Teach me, father, please. Tell me about what you know."

Kevin's chest tightened. The old man was childless. The term 'father' was one of respect. His eyes misted over as he reached out and tousled the boy's hair with his bony, gnarled hand. He loved this boy as much as if he were his son. So many young people in the village were coarse and ignorant, adopting the ways and limiting beliefs of their parents and their religion. This boy was different. He was always eager to learn and help others.

"Please," the boy said in a fervent voice. "I want to know how to be a good person."

Kevin felt his heart lighten. He could still teach. He could still try to help those who were bright stars in an otherwise dreary, cruel world. "Very well, but you have to be very careful. The things that I teach aren't the things that are wanted in these times."

"Why? I don't understand."

"My ways are different, and people mistrust what I teach."

The boy reached out to him, putting his hand on the old man's arm. "Thank you for your knowledge and wisdom, father."

Kevin closed his eyes, praying for the young man, praying that he was indeed careful. When he opened his eyes, the dream shifted. The boy was gone. Time moved ahead a number of years, and Kevin was alone in the darkness. He lay on the dirt floor listening, listening and crying out with grief. His heart was breaking, and he was helpless to stop what was happening outside his hut.

* * *

Arel came back to himself slowly. He looked around, but instead of a hut, he was in Kevin's apartment. He sat for a long moment trying to calm his heart. It was beating very fast after what he'd experienced. Kevin lay stretched out on the floor. He was still in some sort of dream or trance state. As Arel returned to normal awareness, Kevin moaned. The sound made Arel even more aware of what they had faced together.

Oh god, no wonder he didn't want to talk about the dream.

When Kevin opened his eyes, they were filled with tears. "So much pain," he whispered in a broken voice.

"Are you okay? You fell, but I thought I caught you. Did you hurt your ribs again?"

"No, it's not my ribs. It's the dream." Kevin paused, swiping at his eyes, taking several, short breaths. "But it wasn't just a dream, was it? What I saw was real, wasn't it?"

Arel extended his hand to Kevin. "That's not for me to say."

Kevin grabbed hold and allowed himself to be helped into a sitting position. Once he got his bearings, he let out a heavy sigh. "When Peggy tried to tell me what she remembered about other lives, I thought she was going off the deep end. Now, I'm starting to think I was the one who was wrong."

Arel stood up and helped Kevin to a standing position. "Whether past lives are true or not, let's think about the good part."

Kevin hobbled to the sofa and carefully took a seat. "What good part?"

Arel sat down too. "I remember that you were my teacher, the father I wished I'd had."

"Stupid bastard would be closer to the truth."

"What are you talking about?"

"If that lifetime was real, and I think you and Peggy believe that it was, then you were both burned at the stake."

Arel hesitated. He'd made peace with the memory, but it still could make his heart pound harder for a few moments. "So what does that have to do with you?"

Kevin's face turned scarlet. "I'm the one who taught you all that crap! I'm the one who filled your mind with ideas about helping others and being the Good Samaritan. You and Peggy listened to me."

"You taught us about love—"

"And they killed you when you practiced it! Peggy was out there gathering herbs. Another of my specialties! They thought she was a witch!"

"Kevin, you loved us."

"I killed you! I couldn't be guiltier if I lit the fires myself."

"Is that what you believe? You're blaming yourself for what happened to us?"

Kevin's face crumpled in despair. "I guess that's why the dream was so horrible, why I didn't want to think about it."

"You can't blame yourself."

"Oh, but I can!" Kevin's tone was grief-stricken, a sound that was as raw as his oozing flesh. "I heard your screams!"

"I forgot about that part. I'm sorry."

"Stop saying you're sorry! I don't know how to deal with this thing, but hearing your apologies isn't helping!"

For long minutes, neither spoke.

Kevin broke the silence with a raspy laugh. "And I thought I was just worried about being a father. No wonder I can't trust myself. After what I saw, after what I heard—" He laughed again, but it was hard and scathing. "Carol was right to have left me. I don't deserve her."

Arel stared back, knowing very well how self-blame could eat away at all the joy of life. He began to laugh too, but it was laughter directed at the absurdity of what he was hearing. "Isn't this thing we call 'life' bizarre? I remember you being a teacher whom I loved because he was the kindest man in the village. He practiced what he believed. He tried to make life bearable for me and for my sister. But you only remember him as old and dirty." He stood up and frowned at Kevin. "You only remember a person who couldn't stop the ignorance around him, who was helpless to prevent the people of that time from turning into monsters."

Kevin swiped at his eyes again. He squeezed his fists tight as if it could keep his sorrow from totally consuming him. "I loved you and the girl that Peggy was like my own children. If only they would have burned me instead of you."

"You never intended what happened, but I know that you're right. You would have given your life to spare ours."

Kevin's head fell forward, resting heavy on his chest. "How I wish it could have been that way. The horror of being burned would have been over so much sooner. The rest of my life, I remembered your screams and your suffering."

"I didn't blame you in that life, and I have no judgment now. I only know that you gave us everything you could, out of the loving heart that you had. And you have the same true and loving heart now."

Kevin's gaze was glassy and filled with remorse when he looked up. "I didn't mean to hurt Carol. Really, I didn't."

"I know that too."

"How can I trust myself not to hurt her again? How can I be sure I won't shoot off my big mouth?" He sucked in a breath. "And then there's the baby. How can I know that I won't screw up as a parent?"

Arel put a hand on Kevin's shoulder and shook it gently. "Take it from one who knows, you will make mistakes, and so will Carol. We're all human. It's what we do. But the important thing is that you don't give up."

"How do I live with that? I don't want to keep screwing up!"

"Look, you did your best as that old man. The screwed up part was holding yourself accountable for what happened. Now, with Carol, you're afraid to take a chance again. But the one who created us doesn't give up on us. Our souls don't give up either, do they? We keep coming back. We keep getting more chances to be that person who's loving and forgiving. But before we can be loving, we need to forgive ourselves and get a fresh start."

Kevin grabbed his ribs as he took fast, gasping breaths. "I don't know. It's so damn confusing. I've hurt Carol. I hate that I've done that." His eyes lifted to meet Arel's. "How do I forgive myself knowing that I've hurt the sweetest, gentlest person that I've ever met?"

It was Arel's Achilles heel too.

Oh Justina! If only I hadn't failed you.

Letting out a sigh, he forced himself back to the moment and to Kevin's problem. "I don't have the answer. All that I know is that we have to keep trying. Carol's not asking you to be perfect. She just wants you to stay in the game."

Kevin's face brightened for the first time since they started talking. "The game?"

Arel nodded. "Yes, that's right. The game's not over." Without meaning to, he'd used a term the ex-football player understood. Now Kevin sat contemplating the concept with more openness. As he did, Arel realized they weren't alone. He saw an angel sitting next to the young man. He'd glimpsed Kevin's guardian angel on a couple of occasions, but this angel was different. He had his hand over Kevin's heart. A stream of golden light was filling Kevin's chest. Sensing he'd been discovered, the angel winked at him.

Arel stared back in surprise. This was definitely a more playful sort than Michael. He had a boyish face, with brown, curly hair and blue grey eyes that sparked with a wisdom hidden under his youthful visage.

My name is Gabriel. I'm in your dreams sometimes, but I don't think that you remember.

Arel didn't want to remember. He had enough to think about at the moment. But he was happy to see that Kevin was getting some help. On some level, it was working. When he took a peek at Kevin's aura, it was clearing. The heaviness was being replaced by a colorful, lighter energy.

Kevin allowed himself the smallest smile when he finally looked up. "I guess you're right. When I played football, we all had a common goal, and if one of us couldn't carry the ball, someone else took over. If we got injured or discouraged, the coach reminded us not to quit, but to continue believing in the game, to use our faith to encourage each other. I had to forget about self-doubts in those times, or I'd never been able to be a good player."

"You're right, Kevin. It takes courage just to hang in there."

"Do you think Carol would be okay if I'm on the sidelines sometimes, just there to encourage her when I don't know what to do?"

Arel smiled. "Yes, because you love each other."

"Love? That's not enough. Think about all the people who think they're in love and then get divorced."

"People put definitions on love, but maybe it's more than what we think it is. Maybe it's the game itself." He thought about Michael always being there, never abandoning him. "You wanted advice, well here it is. Hang in there. Don't let the limits that you place on yourself keep you from being with the person that you love."

"Just be there? Is that enough?"

"Why don't you ask Carol?"

Kevin frowned and let out a miserable sigh. "I don't know where she is."

Arel grinned broadly. "I do."

Ninety-Four

PEGGY SAT AT the dining room table and stared wistfully into her china teacup. She studied the dark remains settled at the bottom. Did anyone really find answers in the disjointed pattern of the leaves? She didn't.

And when I look for answers in myself, I'm coming up just as empty.

Tim glanced up from his plate, put his fork down and patted his stomach contentedly. "Great dinner, sweetie. The salmon was perfect."

Tim's glow of appreciation made her smile. "Do you want to finish mine?"

Tim checked out her plate. "You barely touched your meal."

"I don't have much of an appetite. I keep thinking about Kevin."

"I thought we straightened that out when Arel was here. You might have been overly critical at times, but underneath it all, you wanted what was best for him."

"This isn't about me. I'm worried about Kevin's relationship with Carol."

"Kevin's lost his confidence," Tim said matter-of-factly.

Peggy sucked in a ragged breath and crossed her arms tight across her chest.

Tim offered her the kindest of smiles. "Not because of you, Peg. It's what Arel said. Kevin is dealing with some very deep-seated issues."

"I know, but I wish I could help, not like before, but as his friend."

"Stop worrying so much. Look at Arel. He's changed. Kevin can too."

"Do you really think that he can handle this situation?"

"I don't think it's my right to make that judgment, just like I wouldn't want him to judge me."

"I guess that's what I've been doing my whole life. And I don't know how to stop. How can I *not* be afraid that he won't handle something right?"

"Remember, Kevin's a fighter. As a kid, you were always getting yourself in scrapes with the bullies. He was always there, bailing you out."

Peggy's mood shifted as she remembered being a girl who was small for her age, but she had a temper and a big mouth. "Goodness, you're right. Didn't we call him, Kevin the Brave?"

"Yeah, we did. And he had to be brave. That time he came to blows with Tommy Brewster was tough. The kid was bad news, and you told him where to get off."

"I did," she said with a blush of embarrassment. "He was a couple of years older than Kevin. I think I went too far with that one."

"Yeah, he was ready to deck you, girl or no girl. But Kevin pushed you out of the way, and he got decked. Damn it, Tommy was only about twelve, but he could throw a punch."

Peggy shivered. Being an adult, the incident took on a scarier flavor. "I remember Kevin getting up and going for him a second time. I don't know who won the fight, but Kevin made an impression on Tommy. He didn't bother me after that."

"Right, that's my point about Kevin."

She paused and stared at the tea leaves again. "I know I've been hard on him, but I thought of Kevin as one of my knights. His job was to defend me."

Tim laughed. "Was I one of them too?"

Peggy pulled him close and kissed him gently on the cheek. "You're still one of my knights."

"What about Kevin? Is he still part of your legion of helpers?"

"Yes, he is." Peggy thought about seeing her brother sitting in the hospital bed. They had argued fiercely, but she knew that he would fight for her if she needed his help. She narrowed her brows. "Still, I just had a terrible thought."

"What?"

"I think I've been Kevin's role model for what a woman should be like. That's why he went out with that horrid woman, Dahlia."

"You're not a horrid woman," Tim objected.

"Maybe not, but I'm strong-willed. I'm used to getting my way around Kevin."

"How would that explain Carol? She's kind of your opposite."

"That's why Kevin doesn't know what to do. She's not bossing him around. That's why he looks like a lost puppy."

"On the other hand, maybe the puppy wants to grow up."

Peggy noticed how bright Tim's eyes could be when he looked at her. Sometimes they seemed so full of wisdom, a wisdom that helped her understand things about herself and about Kevin. "You're right. Maybe Kevin's ready for a change. I'll have to remember that from now on."

Ninety-Five

CAROL SAT IN the master bedroom waiting for Arel to return home. But why? Why did she care about where he was or when he was going to be back?

Because he said that he wanted to help. Maybe he's gone over to see Kevin.

She sniffled and let out a little despairing cry. "If that's where you are, Arel, you're wasting your time."

Hearing herself, the resentful tone of her voice, she paused. Bitterness and loneliness were at the gates of her heart, ready to slam it shut.

But I can't let that happen. I don't want our baby growing up with a cold, angry mother.

She patted her tummy. "Whatever is between us, Kevin is your daddy. I don't want you to think that he's a bad guy."

She knew deep down that Kevin was a good man, just a mixed-up one. "He's so mixed up that he has no room for me or his child."

She looked up, trying to find a more positive focus and noticed the impressionist painting on the opposite wall. A garden scene presented itself, with soft, pastel colors and a sense of tranquility as its theme. She wished that she could feel soft and tranquil, but she had to be tough. She wouldn't give in to bitterness, but she'd have to forget about her heart's desire. She had to forget about wanting Kevin's love. From now on, she'd have to go it alone. She used a tissue to dab at her eyes when the thought made her cry.

And stop being a cry baby! Kevin's given you no choice. From now on, you have to be the strong one.

Her stern order had the opposite effect. A fresh batch of tears began coursing down her cheeks. As she yanked more tissues from the box, she heard a gentle knock on the door. When she looked up, Michael stood in the doorway.

"May I come in?" he asked.

Smiling back weakly, she gestured him forward, quickly drying her face. Michael could be wonderful, but she didn't want to talk about things that she couldn't change. She pointed to the painting instead. "Is this new? I don't remember seeing it before."

Michael walked over and stared at the artwork. "It's a beautiful piece, isn't it? Arel purchased it recently and thought it would look good in here."

She smiled back. "It reminds me of your garden. Maybe that's why he bought it. I think he'll hate seeing the winter kill everything."

Michael glanced at her with a sparkle in his eyes. "It'll all be back next spring. Everything has its season as they say."

"No, I don't think so," she said in a forceful tone "Some things just die and never come back."

Michael sat down next to her on the bed. "You miss Kevin, don't you?"

She bit her lip hard so that she wouldn't cry anymore. "How can he turn his back on me and on his own child?"

"Is that how you see the situation?"

"How else can I see it?" She glared at him with a green, teary gaze. "He doesn't want either one of us."

"Is that what he said?"

She twisted the tissue. "Not in words."

Michael smiled. "I talked with him on a number of occasions when you two lived here. I didn't get that impression."

"What did he say?"

Michael reached out for her hand and held it in both of his. "I think that he wants you more than anything, but perhaps he doesn't feel like he deserves you."

"What would make him feel that way?"

"That's something that you might ask him."

She let out a sharp laugh. "How? Kevin won't even talk to me."

"Of course I will," a voice called out.

Carol's eyes shot past Michael to the doorway. "Kevin! What are you doing here?"

"I'm looking for you. When I couldn't find you, I called Arel. He said you were here."

She studied him, the way he stood in the doorway, holding his ribs. His face was still raw, but his eyes were brighter than she'd seen them in a long time. She looked away and rubbed her nose with the tissue. "I didn't know what else to do. Like I said to Michael, you clearly have no need of me in your life."

Kevin took a few steps forward. "That couldn't be further from the truth. You're more important than anything. So is our baby."

Carol took the tissue away and blinked back the tears. "Really?"

Forgetting his injuries, Kevin rushed over and knelt down in front of her. "Please, Carol, I know I'm totally dense most of the time, but I love you. I truly do. Please marry me!"

Michael smiled as he stood up and moved towards the door. "Excuse me. I think I'll leave you two to talk in private."

Ninety-Six

AREL SAT ON the couch smiling, listening to the happy laughter that was coming from the master bedroom. When Michael walked into the living room, he gave the angel a wave of triumph.

Michael smiled too. "I take it that you heard Kevin's proposal?"

Arel chuckled. "It wasn't the most romantic way of asking for her hand again, but it was certainly loud and sincere."

"So how did you achieve this miracle?"

Arel's eyes narrowed. "Don't pull that naive act on me. You know just about everything that goes on with all of us."

"Perhaps."

Arel laid back on the sofa and stared dreamily into space. "The truth is that I don't know how I pulled it off, but I'm sure you and your cohorts had a hand in it." He glanced at Michael. "Thank you, I needed all the help I could get. I've never encountered a person as stubborn as Kevin. I'm exhausted after our little tug of war."

"Yes, stubbornness is a rather difficult trait to handle," Michael said with a quiet sigh.

Arel crossed his arms. "I slaved for hours over the stove making Kevin that delicious soup from scratch. Then he refused to even open his mouth."

Michael's brows went up. "How do you know it was delicious? Are you saying that you actually tasted it?"

"Michael, you know that I can't eat."

"Well, that's not technically true—"

"Whatever, but when I've tried eating, food doesn't want to stay down." He glanced at Michael with questioning eyes. "You're not suggesting that I start trying to eat, are you? Do you want to clean up vomit all day?"

Michael backed away a few steps. "Eating is totally optional."

Arel sighed out his agreement. "Besides, you have enough to do without worrying about my sensitive stomach."

"Yes, in fact I better go out and get started on the garden. Carol reminded me that winter is coming."

Arel pushed himself up into a sitting position and gave Michael his most genuine look of sincerity. "I'll help you. It'll be my way of showing my appreciation for everything."

"There is a lot to do."

Arel's sincerity faded into a sigh of resignation. He loved flowers, but gardening wasn't a favorite activity. "I'll go change my clothes."

"Maybe you should stay here."

"Why?"

"You should stick around, just in case Carol or Kevin needs something."

Arel's face brightened. "You're right. With those two, you never know."

"True," Michael said as he continued towards the back of the house.

"And in the meantime, maybe I'll meditate," Arel called after him.

Michael turned and gave him a knowing grin. "Or maybe you should take a nap? Like you said, straightening out lives can be an exhausting business."

"I'm fine," Arel protested. Then he paused, realizing that Michael was teasing him. This wasn't the first time that Arel had escaped garden duty. "And I will help you later, I promise."

"Actually, I'll enjoy a little quiet time," Michael insisted.

He knew Michael was graciously letting him off the hook.

But he's right about my needing a nap.

He laid down again, listening to another outburst of laughter that came from the master bedroom. A moment later, he heard the door being closed. More giggles came through anyhow. Carol's cheerful outbursts were evidence that there was hope for the young couple.

He let out a sigh of contentment. Maybe he was a miracle worker. Didn't he go back to a lifetime where Kevin's soul had been stuck? Didn't he convince the younger man not to give up on himself?

Or maybe I simply reminded Kevin that he's a good man in the here and now.

He let the questions and the day's events slip away. He'd take Michael's suggestion and relax, maybe doze off. He closed his eyes. "No more drama for awhile."

"You can sleep when you're dead, Arel." The voice was forceful and familiar. "And since we are what we are, we don't have to worry about dying, do we?"

Arel's eyes flew open as he jerked upright. He scanned the room. There was no one there, but he was suddenly wide awake. His heart was pounding. Had he heard correctly? Was that William's voice? Where was it coming from?

The voice sounded inside his mind again. "I'm looking for you, old friend. It's time for us to get reacquainted."

The End of Book One

The story continues in book two, AREL'S BLOOD.

The first chapter is included here.

Thank you for taking the time to read *Michael's Blood*, the first book of my series, *The Vampire Reclamation Project*. If you enjoyed it, please consider telling your friends or posting a short review. Word of mouth is an author's best friend and much appreciated. - S. S. Bazinet

AREL'S BLOOD
Chapter One

AREL'S GUT WAS on fire, searing his tissues, consuming his energy. But he was familiar with fever and pain. When he was a child, misery was his constant companion. He'd learned that he couldn't cope with it. He endured it. Now he had to go a step further, he had to ignore it. Carol was in trouble. Her life was on the line, and his mind was issuing orders.

Go back to her bedside! Help her!

But how could he obey those orders? Tim was literally dragging him down the hospital corridor, putting distance between Arel and Carol's room. Arel struggled against the iron grip Tim had on his arm, but he couldn't successfully battle Tim's mass and strength, especially in his weakened condition. At six-foot-three, Tim was four inches taller than Arel. He also had the beefed-up body of a pro ballplayer. Arel came from an English lineage. He bore the slender, genteel frame of an upper-class bloodline. Still, he had to do something to get Tim's attention. He glared up at his captor and barked out a hoarse appeal. "Tim! You have to let me go back to help!"

His croaky-voiced order seemed to backfire. Tim stiffened his jaw and stepped up his forward pace. Arel continued to resist, but spasms of pain were gripping his gut, making his knees want to buckle. The hospital-green walls were closing in on him. The antiseptic smells had a suffocating effect. He couldn't manage enough air. He took short, gasping breaths, trying to get a little oxygen. His pleas came out in breathless spurts. "You're supposed to be my friend! Why won't you listen to me?"

Tim finally gave him a quick, scowling glance as they neared the end of the hallway. That's when Arel noted that Tim was puffing away too. It was a small victory. Maybe Arel was putting up a better fight than he thought. But his triumph was useless, wasn't it? He had no choice but to follow as Tim slammed through a pair of swinging, hospital doors. Luckily, his forced march ended when Tim came to an abrupt stop a few feet beyond the doors.

As Arel tried to catch his breath, he noticed that Tim was scanning the busy waiting area that adjoined the hallway. He saw the person Tim was searching for. A blond-haired man sat in a corner of the room. When Tim waved to him, the man acknowledged the gesture and stood up.

Tim urged the man on in a weary voice. "Michael, get over here fast. Arel is really going nuts."

Arel took the opportunity to jerk free from Tim's grasp, but a bout of dizziness made him brace himself on his knees. "Don't get Michael involved," he huffed. "He doesn't know anything about childbirth."

Tim shot him an imploring look, but he didn't reply.

Michael's face was calm and serene as he walked over to join them. Only his eyes showed any reaction to the situation. They flickered with concern when he looked at Arel.

Tim's face relaxed a little. "Please talk some sense into this guy," he begged.

His request made Arel come to attention. He stumbled forward and grabbed Michael's shirt. "Michael, tell Tim to stay out of this. Carol needs me."

"I don't think so," Tim countered. "Arel's upsetting her. They had to toss him out of the birthing room for her sake and his."

Arel tightened his grip, forcing Michael to look at him. "I was a little nervous, that's all. The bottom line is that I can help."

Tim ignored Arel's comments and continued on with his full disclosure of facts. "Arel fainted twice trying to help."

Arel's face went flush with humiliation, but he couldn't deny the truth. When he was under extreme duress, he passed out. It was one of his body's defense strategies. He shut out the world and all its pain by losing consciousness. How many times had the world gone black when he was really upset? How many times had his friends, Tim and Kevin, intervened when his body was making a quick trip to the floor? As time passed, he was making headway, gaining control over his physical response, but this wasn't one of those times. Still, he looked back at the hospital doors with resolve.

"I don't care how many times I faint. I can't bear the thought that Carol is suffering." Arel's statement was filled with all the passion he could manage. His lungs were heaving in and out like a broken bellows. Why did a hospital always make him feel like he was a mountain climber who couldn't catch his breath? He slowly released Michael's shirt, giving himself time to get more oxygen. "Listen, both of you. Just give me five minutes. I promise to make everything better."

With his hands out in front of him, Arel gave the men a gesture to remain where they were. Tim didn't move, but he squinted back as if he was viewing someone who was headed for a padded cell. Michael maintained a look of concern.

Arel didn't care what they might be thinking. He backed up a couple of steps and turned towards the doors leading to the birthing room.

I won't let Carol down.

His intent was rock solid, but he was having trouble navigating. He couldn't keep his gait steady, and his vision blurred. It didn't matter. He'd force his body to do what he wanted.

I can't let anything happen to her.

The thought spurred him on when he had no reserves left. Before he got very far, Michael snagged his arm.

"Arel, you'll never make it to Carol's room in your condition. You have to calm down or you know what could happen."

Michael, an angel who had taken on physical form, was a couple of inches shorter than Tim. His frame was lighter and less muscular, but he had a definite air of strength and vitality about him. Yet he'd never been anything but Arel's gentle friend and mentor. He had also shared his untainted blood with Arel, offering him a way to escape the curse of being a vampire. Yet the gift could also be a curse when Arel's negative emotions were in play. If Arel lost control, his physical vessel was put at risk.

Michael was very aware of the danger that Arel faced. "Before you can help anyone, take a moment and—"

"How can I take a moment when I know what can happen in childbirth? So many things can go wrong. I've studied the facts for months."

Michael's crystal-blue eyes filled with understanding. "I know what you're saying, but that doesn't mean Carol is in danger."

"You didn't hear her! She's in terrible pain!" Arel's brain was yelling out orders, demanding that he do something before it was too late. He had to find a way to save Carol from some horrible fate. Unfortunately, it was everything he could do to remain upright.

Michael came to his aid, taking hold of him, and leading him in the opposite direction. "You don't want Carol to see you like this, do you? Let's go find a place where you can get yourself together."

It was a reasonable request, especially with the world spinning and Arel's legs feeling like they forgot how to walk. "Okay, but just for a few minutes."

"Yes, yes, for just a few minutes." Michael's voice had the tone used by mothers when their child has lost touch with all that's safe in the world. "But you also have to find a way to relax a little. Your body is overheating."

Arel tugged at his collar. "I know. This place is a death trap. There's no air. And they keep the thermostat at about a thousand degrees." He was rambling on in his croaky voice, not making sense. He could hear himself saying crazy stuff, but his brain had taken a bad turn in the birthing room. "I had a vision, Michael! I saw Carol hemorrhaging. There was so much blood. It was everywhere. In the end, the doctor couldn't save her."

As he related the vivid images, he stopped in the middle of the hallway. Searching out Michael's eyes, he was able to stand up straighter and reinforce his point with more steadfastness in his voice. "That's why I have to go back. I figured out how I can help. Remember when Kevin was in the hospital, and I kind of sucked up all the negative energy in the room? I'll do that now. I'll get rid of whatever might hurt Carol."

"My friend, I think you've had enough negative energy already. That's why you're in this condition, but it's not your job to try to fix everything. Carol wants to do this on her own. Try to respect that."

"After what I saw happening to her?"

Michael let out a knowing sigh. "Your vision resulted from your worries and the negative energy you've taken on. It's clouded your reason. If you keep going like this, you know the consequences."

"I don't care about me! It's Carol who's important!" Blurting out the words, Arel turned and started to stagger down the hall. He barely got three feet when his gut flared again, sending out a shooting pain that crippled him in his tracks. He sunk to the floor, barely able to move.

No, not now!

Arel's gut was a fiery repository for all his fears and nightmares. He'd been fueling those terrors all day, letting a lifetime of misery prove that he couldn't trust that things would work out. Minute after minute, hour after hour, he obsessed about how much danger Carol might be in. He should have been more prudent about the adverse effects he was having on his own wellbeing, but he was in full blown fight mode. Like a soldier, he battled to protect the life of a woman who'd been there for him in his darkest hour.

At the beginning of Arel's transformation, Michael's blood became a powerful purging agent that targeted Arel's psyche. Arel soon learned how much pain he'd hidden from himself. He was overwhelmed by so many agonizing memories surfacing so fast that he nearly despaired. Carol was the first person to befriend him in that challenging time. Michael was around long before Carol, but Michael was an angel, he didn't count.

Yet, in Arel's eyes, Carol was almost as caring. She was kind and sweet and utterly forgiving. Even when he lied and deceived her, her heart was open and always ready to see the best in him. Of course, there were reasons why he needed to deceive Carol in the beginning. He couldn't tell her the truth about himself. In fact, he never told any of his new family the whole truth, that he had been a vampire. He didn't need to. He wasn't a parasite who lived on blood anymore. He wasn't a simple human being either. After Michael's contribution, Arel had some amazing and very potent abilities. Even if he was still unsure about using those gifts, he had to find a way to help Carol, no matter what the cost.

I can do this for her. I have to do this.

He tried to force back the pain as he groveled on the hard tile. He knew it was a hopeless effort when another massive wave of fiery heat made him cry out.

Michael was instantly there to help him. "Arel, please, you have to stop thinking the worst."

When he looked up and caught a glimpse of Michael's face, he knew he needed to heed Michael's advice. Normal people didn't have to worry about killing themselves with an emotional eruption. He did.

"Clear your mind," Michael whispered. "Let everything go, at least for the moment."

"How?" Arel's eyes were imploring, fluid orbs in a wasteland of dry, unbearable heat. Once his gut engaged, once it started heating up, it became its own master. "You know I haven't learned how to control any of this."

With Michael helping him up, Arel got to his feet and staggered to the wall. He fell against it, hugging the cool surface, hoping for some relief from the heat that was overwhelming his body.

Michael tried his best to reverse what was happening. His soothing blue energy could be a powerful, healing balm that counteracted Arel's escalating temperature. But things were moving too fast, and then there was the other problem.

"Arel, you have to let me in. You need to trust me."

Arel blinked back with wide, staring eyes. He'd been determined to handle the situation himself. He'd walled himself off from the angel's earlier efforts. Now, with his smoldering core headed towards a full-blown firestorm, his mind was paralyzed with fear. Trust was a word that made no sense. "I think it's too late," he whispered as he thought about the first time he'd had this problem and how he'd almost incinerated himself.

"Don't give up now," Michael said in a strong, encouraging tone.

Before Arel had a chance to reply, a loud voice called out to them from the other end of the hall.

"Arel, Michael! Great news! It's a boy!" Tim shouted out his announcement as he jogged over to where they stood.

Arel could barely acknowledge Tim's presence or hear what he was saying. He was trying to resign himself to the lethal force he harbored in his core. It threatened to have its way once and for all.

"You're not passing out again, are you?" Tim asked as he grabbed Arel's shoulder. He administered a brisk slap to Arel's flushed cheek. "Arel, pay attention! There's a new baby boy in the world!"

The younger man's stinging blow and eye-to-eye contact were enough to finally interrupt Arel's raging emotions. In the small pause that followed, he blinked back, trying to focus his attention on something besides his misery. "What?"

"It's all over, Arel. Carol had the baby!"

Tim shouted out the message a second time as if he was talking to someone who was hearing impaired. His insistent voice penetrated the buzzing in Arel's ears. Coming back to reality for another brief moment, he mumbled out a couple more syllables. "Baby?"

Tim shook Arel's shoulder again. "Yes, that's right, Carol had a little boy, and they're both doing great."

Arel took several quick breaths. As he did, Tim's message became a drizzle of rain on the hot, glowing coals in his gut. The dread that fed his inner fires was slowly replaced by a sense of surprise and wonder. After a long moment of concentration, he raised his eyes enough to look at Michael. "She did it. She really did it."

Michael smiled. "Yes, she did."

Arel slumped in relief as a sudden joy started to surface. This was his dream come true. His panic had been in vain, just like Michael said. Nothing was going to destroy a member of his family. It was just the opposite. His family was growing. A child was now a part of it.

As Arel's mind shifted, as relief began to dissolve his fears, his body responded. The pain eased as his gut began powering down. His physical vessel could be like that, on the brink of catastrophe one moment and able to reverse its course in the next. "Can I see Carol? Can I see the baby?"

He took a step forward, but his body was still weak and his leg gave way. Fortunately Michael and Tim were old hands at keeping him upright. They were quick to each grab an arm.

Tim gave Michael a teasing look as they walked slowly down the hallway. "Can you imagine what it would be like if Arel was having a baby?"

The question made Michael's steady gaze go wide. His voice was barely a whisper when he responded. "No, I can't imagine that."

AREL'S BLOOD

We hope you enjoyed the first chapter from book two, Arel's Blood.

It's available on Amazon.

Books in the series:
Book One: Michael's Blood
Book Two: Arel's Blood
Book Three: William's Blood
Book Four: Brother's Blood
Book Five: Tainted Blood
Book Six: Forgotten Blood
Book Seven: New Blood